Cotton Candy

and

Tangerines

A Novel

By

MR Chevalier

COTTON CANDY AND TANGERINES   MR CHEVALIER

MR Chevalier

Cotton Candy
and Tangerines

The pursuit of happiness is primary in the heart of every human being on the planet, and one of the basic ingredients for that happiness is being with the ideal partner.

MR Chevalier believes in the continuous search for the perfect soul mate, confident that when that person ultimately arrives in one's life, the earth will tremble, the angels will sing and you will know that person is *the one*.

Hearing from readers is the most rewarding part of life, chocolate for the soul.

COTTON CANDY AND TANGERINES   MR CHEVALIER

Cotton Candy
and Tangerines

MR Chevalier

Cyber Rose Design

FIRST CYBER ROSE DESIGN Paperback EDITION

NOVEMBER 2016

Copyright © 2016 by MR Chevalier

ISBN: 978-0-9981342-0-8

464DB3A3221D3873763AF4C9CCCC1F19A70B82702F4724
EE5C674EE7A9740573

To my soul mate, the extraordinary woman who lovingly has been my strength through the hurricane that is my life.

COTTON CANDY AND TANGERINES   MR CHEVALIER

ACKNOWLEDGMENTS

The author expresses his heartfelt gratitude to WF for his invaluable friendship and support.

Thank you, my friend!

Primal Instinct

Very basic and powerful.

Feelings and emotions that are basic and not the result of thought.

Book One

COTTON CANDY AND TANGERINES   MR CHEVALIER

Kirsten

P ierre walked out of the jet bridge into the main concourse at Lambert Field International airport in St. Louis. He moved briskly pulling his wheelie overnight bag behind him, with his brown leather flight briefcase strapped on top of the device. He'd just brought in the flight from JFK and he was starved. Considering he had a two-hour *'Productivity Break'* in St. Louis, he decided for a quick visit to *Chez Viera's*, the employee cafeteria located in the basement of the main terminal. Of course, that was not its official name, but the crews called it that in deference to one of the short-order cooks working there—Viera— a jovial and friendly two-hundred pounder African-American woman loved by most of the employees of the airlines using the airport because of her kind nature and motherly behavior.

The young aviator walked on the right side of the concourse, trying to proceed in a straight line through the crowds and present an image of professionalism and respectability in his dark navy blue airline pilot uniform and shiny black Bostonian dress shoes. It did not escape his attention that some of the women walking from the opposite direction were checking him out. At thirty-one, dark hair, blessed with good looks and in the uniform of an airline pilot he knew life was good. His Basque ancestry had gifted him with good looks, something he'd really had no control over, but for which he was eternally grateful. He adored women, and anybody could tell you that being attractive to them was a definite advantage.

One more leg to go, one more flight, and then he'd be done for the night. He was flying with a reasonable enough captain, *Marvelous Mark*, they called him. His name was Mark, and so far, he seemed to be a relatively nice guy, so someone must've given him the title of 'Marvelous' and it had stuck. Their remaining one-hour flight to Minneapolis that evening should be a breeze. But by now he was hungry, his stomach reminding him that he hadn't eaten since breakfast. Actually, he was more than just hungry, he was ravenous. They'd not been given crew meals on the flight from New York. That was too many hours without food. No damned way he was going to hold off until they arrived in Minneapolis to get some chow.

Most of the food stands and restaurants in the terminal charged too much for mediocre grub, and besides, ordering an overpriced hot dog at one of those joints and eating it while surrounded by all sorts of passengers was not his idea of fun. Way too many people in the general public felt a desperate need to engage him in conversation because of the uniform. Nah, far better going the extra mile—so to speak—and finding refuge downstairs in the employee cafeteria, which was off limits to passengers. Also, many of the food stands in the terminal sold liquor, and in this day and age it was prudent to steer clear of any such establishments. Too many frustrated passengers out there willing to accuse a random airline pilot of consuming alcohol while in uniform. Pierre had put too much time, effort and money into his career to risk jeopardizing it over something as stupid as that.

The aviator walked through the terminal, occasionally casting a glance at the shiny blue and white Airbus and Boeing airliners visible on the ramp through the concourse windows. Being proud of the fact that he made a living piloting those magnificent machines filled him with enormous satisfaction. He absolutely *loved* his job. How many people could honestly make the same claim?

It was dusk already with daylight fading rapidly. A stunning young brunette dressed in a grey business suit walking in the opposite direction flashed him an intimate, seductive smile. Pierre barely had time to return the smile before she was gone. The terminal was crowded, full of humanity intent on making their flights or just plain finding their baggage so they could get out of the airport.

He was not that much into crowds, breathing a sigh of relief once he entered the privacy of the employees' elevator. The noise level went down significantly, much to his relief.

Silence, he believed, was the most tolerable of all noises. The Otis elevator quietly took him down one level, to the airport employee area. This was an area few passengers ever got to see. The behind-the-scenes area below the airport terminal where airline employees lived and worked out of sight of the traveling public. This was the level where the bags were sorted, where carts were loaded, where the airline mechanics in charge of line maintenance had their break rooms.

The young pilot covered the short distance to the cafeteria, delighted to find it only about half full.

Good. He must be between shifts, otherwise, every single table would be occupied by rampers, mechanics, flight attendants, pilots and customer service agents. The cafeteria faced the ramp immediately below one of the jet bridges, so *Chez Viera's* customers—were they so inclined—could delight themselves eating dinner while observing the delicate ballet being performed outside the windows, where multiple flights were being readied for departure at the same time. Not that any of the dining guests would be too interested, since they all worked in the airline industry and lived it every day.

Pierre picked a table, staking a claim on it by pulling back one of the wooden chairs and placing his wheelies with his flight bag and suitcase right next to it. That time of day, he probably wouldn't have to share a table with anyone, since the place was only half full.

Walking to the food display counter, he grabbed a plastic tray and some silverware from one end, waiting for the server to notice him. All sorts of delicious-looking dishes stared back at him from behind the glass. The aroma of a variety of hot foods delighted his sense of smell. The place reminded him of Luby's cafeterias, in Texas, which he loved.

"Are you married?"

The unexpected question startled him so much he just about jumped out of his uniform. Turning left to see who had spoken he faced a *stunning* young blonde with enchanting clear blue eyes, wearing the uniform of his airline. The young woman was standing about a foot from him. She'd just placed her tray next to his on the metal rails.

"*Married?* No, why?" He was totally taken back by the captivating smile one foot away. *Wow, she was really good-looking. A real doll. And those big, baby blue eyes!*

"Nothing. Just—*that* would've been a terrible waste, that's all."

Pierre couldn't help but laugh, sizing her up. She was maybe four inches shorter than his five-foot-ten frame, petite and beautifully built, or at least from what he was able to discern of her figure in the uniform of an airline flight attendant.

He had absolutely no idea who she was. He'd never seen her before. Pierre desperately tried to think of something witty or clever to say.

"How about you, are *you* married?" He was sorry he said it even before it was completely out of his mouth. Real blah, Academy Award performance for the dumbest line of all ages, but he couldn't think of anything else to reply.

"Do I look married to you?" she shot back, with a suggestive, teasing smile.

"What can I get you?" The female server asked from the other side of the display, interrupting their conversation.

The blonde with the captivating smile ordered a bowl of cottage cheese with a half peach in syrup.

"A cheeseburger will do for me," Pierre replied, still checking out the very attractive girl next to him. She was adorable, her hair was the color of golden straw and she smelled of some delicious perfume. And *she* had approached *him!*

"Want fries with that?"

"What?"

The female server on the other side of the food display patiently insisted. "Do you want fries with your hamburger?"

"No, thanks. No fries."

The server reached over the counter, handing over the bowl of cottage cheese to the flight attendant. "Here you go, honey."

The blonde angel smiled at him again, depositing the bowl of food on her tray.

"See ya," she offered. She gave Pierre one final, hypnotizing suggestive smile, looking him up and down, then rapidly picked up her tray, walking towards the cashier.

She had a terribly mischievous smile, he mused. Pierre had but a quick chance to check out her petite figure from behind for one more brief moment and then she was gone. He did notice her uniform skirt fit her nicely, not too loose, not too tight. Just perfect, with a real cute little ass. Her curves triggered images of nights of passion in his never-idle imagination.

He really had to get his mind out of the sewer.

Damn. He should've reacted quicker. She had definitely become a 'person of interest' in just a few seconds. Heck, a person of interest? She was hot! He would most definitely consider her a 'dream' in his desirability scale.

Definitely a 'dream.' What a beauty. A real doll.

Pierre was of the opinion all women were beautiful in their own special different ways, and he liked to think of women as peaches, orchids or 'dreams.' His own classification had nothing to do with how pretty a woman was, it had more to do with whether he was attracted to that type and age of female. Peaches, he was not really interested in, orchids he was somewhat interested, and 'dreams' had his full attention.

He compared his logic to a person visiting a restaurant. Was chicken better than steak? Or was salmon better? The answer—naturally—depended on the personal taste and preference of each patron. Not everyone liked the same menu, yet they were all delicious. Something about beauty being in the eyes of the beholder?

This girl however, was definitely a 'dream.'

And he'd just stood there like a perfect idiot.

And now she was gone. And what a flirt! Asking him straight out if he was married. Oh, what a woman. Like a complete fool, he'd just sat there and let her disappear. He momentarily considered chasing after her, quickly concluding it would most likely not be a good idea. He'd just ordered some food, and the server in the kitchen would probably not take too kindly to some random pilot ordering food and then bolting for the elevator without paying. Besides, he certainly couldn't just leave his bags behind, unattended in the dining room while he chased the girl, because his bags could walk away. No, he had to just stand there like an idiot and eat his defeat.

Stand down, boy.

Yep, that's what it was, a defeat. Blonde goddess one, idiot in pilot uniform zero.

"Here's one burger, honey."

Accepting the burger and placing it on his tray he moved over to the cashier, reaching for his wallet. He paid the woman with a ten-dollar bill, collected the change and returned to his table. He'd asked the server for 'no fries,' yet half his plate was nothing but French Fries. Oh, well.

Damn.

That had been an *incredible* brief moment of pure joy, meeting that flight attendant. Gawd, he knew St. Peter was going to give him absolute hell once he reached the Pearly Gates.

"*Why didn't you take advantage of the golden opportunity I sent you to connect with that girl?*" St. Peter would scold.

And just what the hell was he supposed to answer to that one? "Oh, you see, that's 'cause I was busy ordering a hamburger?" St. Peter would then strike him with his sword of fire and send him straight to hell.

And very well deserved, indeed, he thought miserably.

Aww, heck. There would be others, he told himself, not at all convinced. Sure, that was the eternal line losers preferred in the movies. 'There's always tomorrow,' Hollywood was fond of saying. But the truth was he'd blown it, and there would be no tomorrow with the blonde angel. She had stood a foot from him, spellbinding him with her proximity, her scent and her blue eyes. And now she was gone.

PIERRE ATE HIS DINNER, then dumped his paper plate, napkin and most of the fries into the trash bin, disposed of the plastic tray and departed *Chez Viera's*, pulling his wheelies. His day had not been too long, just one leg from JFK to St. Louis, so he was not overly tired. The weather in Minneapolis was forecast clear and chilly, so the flight should not be too much work. He enjoyed flying enormously. The crowded terminal did not bother him quite so much this time around. A full stomach sure made a difference, full tummy, happy heart, they said. Although he still felt a pang of regret after losing the girl.

Pierre confirmed his assigned departure gate from one of the enormous color monitors hanging in the concourse. The gate was a long way off. Better start in that direction. He had an hour before pushback, so there was no reason to fret. He would just head in that direction at a leisure pace.

The image of the smiling girl standing next to him in the cafeteria remained freshly engraved in his mind. He briefly wondered if he were to search for her, how he'd go about doing it. With nine crew bases in the airline, she could be based anywhere. Crap, he didn't even know her name. Maybe crew scheduling could help? Yea, right, all he had to do was ask crew sked to give him the names of flight attendants going through St. Louis tonight. Probably in the thousands. And then again, that would not do him any damned good 'cause he ignored her name. What if he described her, would the crew schedulers be able to assist him then? Nah, the schedulers would just laugh at him and tell him to go pound sand.

Beautiful. When you screw up, you really do it well. You dropped the ball!

The pilot arrived at the assigned gate with plenty of time to spare. Approaching the gate area Pierre noticed four flight attendants sitting around near the service podium. They were seated facing away from him. Those four were probably his crew. Their airplane had most likely not yet arrived from wherever it was coming, and the flight attendants had taken seats waiting their turn to board. He walked to the podium by the gate.

"Evening. Flight's not in yet?"

A middle-aged man in a customer service uniform behind the podium gave him a tired smile. "Nope. It just landed, should be here in a couple of minutes."

"Great. I'm taking 435 to Minneapolis,"

"Good," was all the customer service guy said. He was obviously not impressed.

"What're you doing here?"

Pierre turned to find himself staring into the face of the blonde angel he'd encountered at *Chez Viera's*.

It was as if God had made light again.

Incredible!

He couldn't believe his eyes! He broke into an enormous smile. Too good to be true. She was standing right there, not three feet away, those clear blue eyes penetrating his soul. It was his turn to look her up and down, with desire and admiration.

"What are *you* doing here?" was all he could say back. He could feel the adrenaline shooting into his system at a furious pace.

"I asked first," she said.

"I'm taking the flight to Minneapolis."

Her smile flashed again in all its splendor. "No shit?"

He smiled at her unashamed use of profanity. There was something exciting and sensual about a terribly attractive girl in the very respectful uniform of a flight attendant for his airline using profanity so matter-of-fact.

And political correctness be damned.

"No, I mean, yes!" He was stuttering. "I'm taking 435 to Minnie. Why, what're you doing here?" She was even better looking this second time around. Her face was porcelain-perfect, pale and without a blemish. Her blond hair was thick and golden. Pierre was smitten all over again. He instantly placed her in her early twenties.

"I'm going to Minneapolis with you!"

She had approached to within a foot of Pierre again. He could smell mint in her breath. And that tantalizing perfume scent, the same he had detected in the cafeteria.

"You are?"

"Yes! We're your crew!" She pointed towards the other three flight attendants sitting by the podium. They all seemed to be in their twenties.

"That's great," was all he could think of saying. He was definitely stunned at the turn of events. What luck! Incredible! *Thank you, Saint Peter!* Thank you! No sword of fire for him over this one. He'd been given a second chance! He must not drop the ball this time.

"I'm Kirsten!" she extended her hand, flashing a smile that could light up a room. Her enthusiasm was so attractive. And contagious.

"Pierre," he responded, grasping her hand. "Pierre White." Her hand was small but cool and dry, with a firm handshake.

"I've never seen you around," Kirsten chirped.

"I could say the same thing, Kirsten. How long you been with the company?"

"Four months!" She kept looking back at the other flight attendants sitting nearby.

"Four months? That's probably why you haven't seen me around. You practically just got here."

"Where are you based?" She asked.

She radiated energy, sensuality and was perky as all hell, Pierre observed. And so damned gorgeous. His initial assessment had been quite accurate; she was indeed a 'dream,' but not a *perfect* dream yet. In his mind, other factors were relevant to give any girl that status. For that, he had to get to know her. A *basic* dream was the best anyone could do on first contact with their clothes on.

Pierre had been asked before about his habit of assigning categories to girls. To him, the answer was simple enough. He liked quantifying things in life. He did that with just about everything. Heck, didn't everyone else do that? Book reviews on Amazon, for example, based on a five-star rating. Restaurant reviews on Yelp, based on a five-star rating. How good you did in school? Based on a one-to-four GPA. So, yes, he had his own rules, his own evaluations. They made life easier.

"I'm based here, in St. Louis. How about you? Where are you based?" He was thrilled and absolutely delighted having this stunning girl on his crew. Looking at his watch he confirmed they still had thirty minutes before their scheduled departure.

"You in a hurry to go somewhere else?" She teased.

"No, no. just checking to see how much time we have.   Didn't mean to be rude—I'm based here as well!" Pierre was taken by her enthusiasm. She was so likeable and so straight forward. He couldn't help liking her. He noticed she was standing very close to him, closer than people normally do. Completely inside his own personal space. He loved it.

"Do you end up in Madison tomorrow night?" Kirsten asked.

"Yep, overnight in Madison. Are you guys with us all the way?"

"Yes!" She exclaimed with renewed enthusiasm.

Pierre issued a silent 'Thank you' to St. Peter once again. Kirsten was young, enthusiastic and available.

And on his trip.

He'd checked out her ring finger, no diamond ring and no wedding band. She could still have a boyfriend, but Pierre wasn't afraid of a little competition.

The customer service agent at the gate opened the door anticipating the arriving passengers. A spanking brand new baby blue and white Airbus A321 had just pulled up to the gate.

Kirsten reached for the sleeve of his uniform jacket, gently pulling him with two fingers. "Come, let's go meet your crew."

Pierre liked the gesture of familiarity, smiling as he followed her.

"Ladies, this is Pierre White, our First Officer."

None of the other flight attendants stood, they just waved at him. He noticed all three were in their mid-twenties and appeared a little worn and tired. Pretty normal at the end of a long duty day.

"Nice meeting you all," Pierre said. He right away wondered if Kirsten would want to join him for dinner in Minneapolis. He was already thinking ahead. She was flirting with him, that much was obvious. Her attention was such a pleasant feeling. He was a little gun-shy about asking her out to dinner in front of the rest of the crew. He really didn't want to do the crew thing, going to dinner with a group. He'd be perfectly content taking Kirsten with him just the two of them.

He decided to find the right moment to ask her, out of hearing from the other crewmembers. He had to separate her from the herd if he wanted to get acquainted.

Pierre had to admit he was somewhat rusty in the girl department. Hadn't had a steady girlfriend for three years. A steady girlfriend? Hell, he hadn't even seriously dated. No serious relationships. The past three years he'd concentrated all his efforts on flying and becoming an airline pilot. No distractions allowed.

Because of his powerful sexual drive and his ardent desire to be with girls, those had been the hardest three years of his life. Ignoring women had been almost like ignoring food. One had to eat to stay alive. At his age, he needed women as much as he needed air. Yet, his discipline and determination had carried him through those three years. That had not been easy, but after the fiasco with Nicole, he'd made himself a promise that he would become an airline pilot and not allow anything or anybody to get in the way.

He'd learned the hard way that without money, girls don't stick around, and in order to make money, he had to have a profession. And flying for a living was the profession he'd chosen. Now that he'd been flying as an airline pilot for a little over one year, he could consider dating again. A little drastic perhaps, but that was his nature, all or nothing. He'd not really made a conscious decision to formally date yet, but Kirsten had certainly jump-started him in that direction this evening.

"Hello gang," Mark Wiseman greeted—their captain on the flight, mid-forties, with a pleasant smile and soft voice.

The four flight attendants greeted the pilot, introducing themselves. As the final arriving passengers exited the jet bridge, the crew of six grabbed their bags and descended to the parked Airbus.

At the entrance to the Airbus cabin the flight attendants turned right, scattering themselves, and the pilots turned left. Pierre felt right at home entering the dark flight deck illuminated by the glow of the electronic flight instrument system. The place smelled of leather and hot electronics, and for him the quiet hum of the equipment contributed to making the place into a sanctuary.

His sanctuary.

He removed his bag from the wheelies, strapping his overnight bag below the jumpseat and inserting his brown leather flight bag in a specially built space next to his seat.

"One more leg, then dinner," the captain blurted, climbing into his own seat.

"You didn't get any food here?" Pierre felt a momentary pang of guilt not having asked Marvelous if he would've liked joining him for a burger down at the employees' cafeteria.

"No, I wanted to wait until we got to Minneapolis. Did you grab a bite?"

"Yea, went down to *Viera's* and grabbed a hamburger."

Both pilots began making their 'nests,' snapping their iPads onto special brackets next to their side windows, removing their headsets from their flight bags, connecting them to the airplane and adjusting their electric seats to the exact position needed for flight. Commercial airline pilot seats had to be set very precisely, so as to allow the pilots good visibility over the glare shield during low visibility approaches.

"We have some good-looking gals back there," Mark remarked.

Pierre decided to be nonchalant about it. He knew Mark was referring to the four flight attendants going with them to Minnie. "Yeah."

"Think any of them are fuck bunnies?" Mark asked.

Pierre did not particularly like the crudeness. "I have no idea."

I'm going back there to brief them. See you in a minute," Mark exited the flight deck, leaving Pierre alone in the front office. Marvelous had a reputation as a womanizer, so Pierre thought for a moment about the possibility of Mark hitting on Kirsten. That could happen. Of course, the other three flight attendants were also young and a couple were actually quite attractive, so Mark might pick a different one. However, what were the odds Kirsten would give Mark the time of day when she obviously appeared to like *him*. One of his first captains had taught Pierre that the duty of every First Officer was twofold. When offered a crew meal, the First Officer was expected to say: 'I'll take the chicken tray, captain—you're welcome to the steak.' That was one. The second duty was: 'I'll take the ugly one, you take the pretty one.'

Certainly, that mentality was something new pilots had to keep in mind during their first year while they were on probation. It didn't pay being rude to one's captain during that first year, because some of these old boys could make life very difficult if they felt insulted. And trying to hit on the captain's girl was definitely interpreted as an insult.

But Pierre was not a new hire, so the gloves were off and may the best man win. If Mark tried to hit on Kirsten, he would not play dead. He turned his attention to getting the Airbus ready for the flight to Minneapolis.

AN HOUR AND A half later, Flight 435 pulled up at the gate in Minnie.

"Well," Marvelous said, "That's enough fun for one day. Go ahead and take the rest of the day off."

Everyone was a comedian, Pierre mused. He performed his final duties in the flight deck, double-checking what Mark was doing while reading the Secure Aircraft checklist.

All done. Time to go relax.

Pierre had become rather annoyed with his captain. Marvelous had spent the one-hour flight from St. Louis giving explicit descriptions on what he'd like to do to each of their four flight attendants. His imageries varied from every position in the Kama Sutra to S&M, and Pierre truly had no patience for that crap. Mark was also married, which by the way, didn't seem to bother his sexual banter one bit.

"Time to go!" Marvelous happily chirped. "Lessee if our four sweethearts back there wanna join us for some dinner after we check in."

Pierre glanced at his captain, who was pulling his flight bag out of its niche, strapping it on his wheelies. The last thing Pierre wanted was go out as a group with this guy. His own personal policy was avoiding crew excursions. He hated going out as a crew. Invariably, he would end up spending too much. He overspent because he felt bad the flight attendants didn't make all that much money, so he would buy them dinner.

Too many captains pretended having 'crocodile arms' when the bill came, so they just basically played dumb, paying only for their share of the bill.

Pierre didn't like that game either. His manners were not an affectation; he was genuinely a gentleman.

And also, if there happened to be a particular girl he wanted to meet among the crew, it was just too difficult to accomplish in a group environment. Plus, he was annoyed with Mark, acting as a *Don Juan* totally ignoring the fact that he was married. Pierre certainly didn't consider himself a Bible-banging self-righteous evangelist and he was realistic enough to accept that some men and women played around outside the marriage. However, he'd offered his former girlfriend Nicole unwavering loyalty, and it had taken him nowhere. He had given loyalty and received nothing in return. That only made him desire loyalty from a woman that much more. And conversely, dislike guys like Mark. He'd asked Mark what his plans were for his days off after this trip, and the captain had offered an interesting answer.

"I'm going home to my wife," he'd said. "I'm between mistresses."

Holy shit.

Pierre decided he'd just ignore Marvelous' suggestion to go out together as a crew. He wouldn't commit to anything one way or the other. The flight attendants were already in the jet bridge with all their bags, waiting for them. The very last passenger had already exited the airplane; the cleaning crews were feverishly cleaning up the passenger cabin and now it was just a matter of finding their way to the curb somewhere in the airport where the Marriot hotel van was waiting to pick them up. The flight attendants looked tired. It'd probably been a very long day for them. Pierre had no idea where they had come from before joining them in St. Louis. Kirsten glanced at him, not saying anything. She was probably wiped.

The group walked through the nearly empty terminal, eventually finding the pickup spot for the crews. The Marriott van was already there. Pierre stood by, allowing the women access to the back of the van first. The driver, a young and jovial African-American, received the bags from the flight attendants, loading them into the rear of the van. The vehicle was an extra-long van, with a huge cargo area in the back. Pierre handed his wheelies to the driver then walked to the front passenger door, deciding to ride shotgun. He would've preferred sitting next to Kirsten, but it was dark and he couldn't really see inside the van and had no idea where she was sitting. And since he was the last one in, odds were he wouldn't be able to sit next to her anyway.

The ride to the hotel was silent. The driver drove them into downtown, arriving at the main doors of the four-star hotel. As was customary with airline crews, the crew gathered at the back of the van, receiving their luggage from the driver, tipping him two dollars each. Mark led the march to the front desk.

Pierre noted how Mark didn't have the courtesy of allowing the women to check in first. The captain beat everyone to the front reception counter, finding the crew clipboard already there, with six room keys and a sign-in sheet.

Great manners. Those were the little details Pierre noticed about the men he flew with. That would also probably mean Mark would have terrible table manners.

Kirsten was standing ahead of him, waiting patiently for her turn to sign in and grab her key.

He decided to take advantage of the moment. "Want to go out for a bite?" He whispered close to her ear. Pierre could still smell the faint scent from before. "Don't say anything to the others."

Kirsten didn't bat an eye. "Okay."

He felt a shiver of excitement. Her acceptance had established an instant personal bond between them. Mark hadn't said anything else about all of them going out to dinner together, but even if he did now, Kirsten and him would not be joining them. Pierre took note of Kirsten's room number. He read it straight off the sign-in sheet.

After everyone signed in, the group headed for the elevators. No talking. Fatigue was finally getting the best of them. Reaching their floor, the group spread out, each crewmember looking for their room. Nothing more was said by anyone about going out to eat. Room service was going to be busy tonight.

Pierre found his room, sliding the magnetic card through the reader. The light turned green. Entering the room, he turned on the lights, pulling his wheelies. The door closed behind him. He threw his hat on the desk, removing his coat and pulling off his black tie. He wouldn't dream of tossing his hat on the bed. Definitely bad luck. He was superstitious, although he wouldn't admit that to anyone.

He quickly used the bathroom, then walked to the phone between the beds. He dialed her room number after reading the instructions on the device.

"Kirsten?"

She answered after the first ring. "Hi!"

"Let's meet in front of the elevator in ten minutes."

"Okay."

"Listen, be real quiet exiting your room, don't let your door slam. We don't want company, and if the others hear us leaving our rooms, they're going to come out and join us."

"Okay."

He sure as all hell didn't want Marvelous joining them, and he'd bet even money the captain would show his face in the hallway two seconds after hearing a door slam. The guy was nosey as all Dickens, and if he came out of his room there'd be no getting rid of him. That would definitely be a most unwelcome situation.

Pierre threw his overnight bag on one of the two queen beds, unzipping it. He quickly changed into jeans, a white button-down long sleeve cotton shirt and a brown bomber leather jacket. His white and green Adidas Stan Smith came on next. He returned to the bathroom, reaching for his shaving kit. He washed his face, brushed his teeth with Crest and splashed some Dolce & Gabbana eau de toilette on the sides of his neck. A quick glance and the mirror told him he was ready.

He opened the room door being very careful not to make any noise. Once outside the room, he gently allowed the heavy door to close very slowly, producing nothing more than a barely audible click.

The carpet was thick and plush, so he would walk silently.

The coast was clear. No Mark.

Bite me, Marvelous.

Pierre walked towards the elevator.

Kirsten was already there waiting for him.

His heart soared. He smiled. She looked striking in grey slacks and a white silky blouse. She had a baby blue cashmere sweater casually thrown over her shoulders and gold leather sandals. Good enough to eat.

"Hi!"

"What took you so long?" She asked.

God, he so loved a smart-ass.

"It didn't take me long. It only took me six minutes. I told you ten." He looked into her adorable blue eyes, wondering if she was serious. She sure did a good job sneaking out of her room. He'd heard absolutely nothing. *Good. That also meant Mark had heard absolutely nothing either.*

"I'm just messing with you," she tugged at the sleeve of his leather jacket. He loved the familiarity of her touch, that gesture of hers was adorable.

The elevator arrived, announcing itself with a loud ding.

Soon as the door opened, Pierre placed his hand on the small of her back, gently encouraging her into the elevator. All they needed now was for Marvelous to stick his head out of his room to check out who was using the elevator. Once inside with the doors closed, he reached for her hand.

Kirsten looked up at him, expectation in her eyes. And that veiled smile.

The proximity to her was intoxicating. Pierre could feel the heat radiating from her body. The air in the elevator was saturated with her delicious perfume. Pierre didn't give it another thought, he simply bent down, finding her lips. They were cool and moist and tasted of something cherry. Kirsten kissed him back, reaching up with both arms, wrapping them around his neck. She moved her body against his.

Pierre couldn't believe the delicious sensation. It'd been so long since he'd been up close with a woman like this. Her body made contact with his, generating an instant reaction, he felt himself getting hard. He gently ran his tongue along her lips without entering her mouth. The feel of her arms around his neck was delicious. He was enamored.

The elevator announced its arrival to the ground floor with another loud ding.

Pierre broke the kiss, barely able to breathe from the excitement.

"I never kissed one of our pilots before," Kirsten said, stepping back.

The energy, or whatever it was flowing between him and Kirsten was incredible. They'd both been feeling it all evening, since the first moment they met at the employees' cafeteria in St. Louis, and now they were able to indulge in it.

Her breath smelled warm and sensual. He held her hand, stepping out into the hotel lobby. Kirsten followed him without a word. Pierre had no idea what was nearby, but he figured they'd find someplace to grab a drink and a bite to eat. He'd stayed at the Marriott before, but had never explored downtown Minneapolis, so he decided to just go out in the street and hang a right along the sidewalk.

The night air was not too cold yet, just pleasantly crispy. They walked half a block from the hotel, finding a Mexican restaurant. Pierre led the way in and they entered the establishment. It was bright and cheerful and the hostess led them to a small booth in the back. Pierre smiled thinking of the contrast, a Mexican restaurant in the middle of Viking land, Minnesota.

His life was full of delightful disparities.

Kirsten sat on the bench, inching her way right next to him. He could sense the warmth of her body again, same as in the elevator. He was so damned excited, feeling like he was back in high school again.

Had it really been so long since he'd been with a girl he liked?

The waitress deposited a bowl of chips on their table, and two small containers of salsa.

"The green one's really hot," the waitress cautioned. "Can I get you started with something to drink?"

"What would you like?" Pierre asked.

"Bring me a Margarita, no salt, please."

Pierre was well aware they had to fly early the next morning. "I'll have a Coke, please."

The waitress disappeared.

"A *Coke!?* You're no fun!"

He was expecting that. "We're flying in the morning. I can't drink tonight."

"We've over twelve hours before our flight. I thought you guys only had to watch it eight hours."

"Eight hours bottle to throttle? Yeah, that's the rules, but I like to play it safe. I really don't like those random alcohol checks."

"Oh, yeah, we get those too. The 'pee squad'." Kirsten was referring to the company team in charge of conducting random urine tests on the crews. One never knew when they would be waiting at the next arrival gate, eager to pull crewmembers aside, directing them to the closest rest room in order to provide the company with a fresh urine sample. If drugs or alcohol were detected, the offending crewmember would most likely end up unemployed. And there was no refusing the test. A refusal counted as a test positive, with the same end result.

"Yeah," he smiled at her use of the unofficial name for the drug testers. "Well, I don't want to place my career in the hands of some nitwits who weren't smart enough to land better paying jobs, and who might make a mistake and accuse me of something I didn't do. When they measure the alcohol content in the human body, it is quite possible they could make a mistake, and I don't want to play with close tolerances."

"Chicken!"

"No, it's not fear, it's caution." He decided to change the topic. "I'm glad you joined me."

"You knew I was going to."

"I was hoping you would." He stared into her clear blue eyes fixed on him.

God, she is breathtaking.

Kirsten reached for Pierre's hand under the table. Her hand was cold.

The contact sent wave after wave of delicious pleasure to his groin. A very pleasant sensation, to say the least.

The waitress reappeared, depositing their two drinks on the wooden table. "Do you need a minute to look at the menu?"

"Please," Pierre responded, slightly annoyed at the interruption. He'd had every intention of kissing Kirsten again just then, but the waitress so rudely interrupted, breaking the spell.

"I'm glad you were able to sneak out without Mark tailing you," he offered.

"Yeah, he is a real pain, that one. He hit on me in the van."

"I thought he might do that." *Asshole,* Pierre thought.

She made a face. "I'm so like totally not interested. Guys like him hit on everything that moves. And he is so *old.*"

"I thought we'd be better off sneaking out quietly because I suspected he'd jump at the sound of one of our doors opening. He's the kind of guy who has to know everything everyone else is doing at all times."

"So you think he would've come out of his room if he'd heard our doors opening?"

"I suspect that he would have, yes. And getting rid of him would've been impossible. Guys like him can become a real pest. He's not smart enough to accept that you're not interested in him, but he'd never have the decency of moving aside and letting me have a chance to be alone with you."

"A chance to be alone with me? I like the sound of that."

"Plus Mark is married." It was time to direct the conversation to more pleasant topics. "Where are you from, Kirsten?"

"Fargo," she answered, smiling seductively, "North Dakota."

"As in *Fargo*, the movie?"

"Yep, as in *Fargo*, the movie. And where are *you* from?"

"Los Angeles. The San Fernando Valley, to be more accurate."

Kirsten smiled. "As in *the world capital of porn?*"

Pierre had heard that one before. "And how exactly is it that you would know that?"

"Ha! Everyone knows that. That's where they make all the movies. Every sex flick on the Internet is filmed there."

"Oh? Well, I had nothing to do with any of that stuff. I left there years ago."

Kirsten laughed. "Nothing wrong with porn. My dad owns a tittie bar back in Fargo."

That got his attention.

A tittie bar? Wonders never ceased. Pierre wanted to laugh but kept himself from it. Actually, what surprised him was her nonchalant attitude about it. Just a mundane occupation, being the owner of a strip club? And her calling it a *tittie bar* instead of a strip joint was funnier than hell.

"So that's how you put your money together for your flight training?"

He'd momentarily lost track of where the conversation was going. "Uhm?"

"Being a porn star?" Kirsten smiled mischievously, "that's how you earned your money to become a pilot?"

Pierre stared at her very serious. "No. that's not how I got my money for my flight training."

"Relax, I'm kidding."

"That wasn't really funny because you see, I was actually a male prostitute."

"What—?"

He tried to remember the term ... "A *gigolo,*" he attempted to look as sad and serious as possible, although he was on the brink of exploding in laughter. "Plenty of distinguished older ladies out there willing to finance a man's career. Didn't you know?"

Kirsten appeared confused. Her attentive blue eyes scanned his face rapidly, trying to find some hint that Pierre was kidding. She found none.

"I don't know what to say," she finally admitted.

Pierre broke into a wide smile. *"Gotya!"* He laughed.

Her eyes became slits. "You little shit."

"What? Startled you? You don't think I'm good enough to be a gigolo?"

"No, that's not it. Of course you're good enough. I just didn't see that coming."

"You mean you have no intention of paying me for being out here with you tonight?"

Kirsten bit her lip, appearing thoroughly confused. She glanced around, as if looking for answers.

"I must confess something. I'm an equal opportunity entertainer gigolo. I don't care about age."

"You're full of shit."

Pierre laughed loudly. "Had you going there, eh?"

"You are bad news, Mister." She let out a long breath.

How old are you, Kirsten?"

"Right to the point, eh?"

"It's just a question."

"Weren't you taught it's impolite asking a lady her age?"

"Don't mean anything by it. I'm thirty-one."

She appeared to be studying his face for a moment. "I'm twenty-two."

Whoa. Kirsten was just a tad younger than he'd estimated. Not that it made a heck of a difference to him one way or another.

"Did you decide on some dinner?" The waitress appeared again.

The woman was a curse, Pierre thought, wishing he had telekinesis and could just catapult her through the window. "Sorry, we need a couple of more minutes."

The waitress disappeared again.

"We better look at these," he handed Kirsten one of the two plastic laminated menus. "Hungry?"

"Starved!"

The menu had way too many items on it. Good grief, it was almost like a Chinese restaurant menu. He scanned the first page, rapidly deciding on a *carne asada torta* with avocado, tomato and onions. *Wait!* No onions. He was eagerly hoping kissing Kirsten again was going to be on the menu later that night, and onions would definitely not be a good thing. "What sounds good?"

Kirsten sipped her Margarita, returning the menu to the table. "I think the chicken tacos sound delicious."

The waitress was nowhere in sight. It never failed. First, she won't get lost, then when she should be around she becomes invisible. They could easily starve to death.

"Perfect, I'll order us some food when the waitress returns."

"Do you have a girlfriend?"

Who's being direct now? "No, no girlfriend."

"You're an airline pilot and you're single and you don't have a girlfriend?" Her tone was one of accusatory curiosity.

"That is correct. No special girl in my life." He thought he'd better give her some explanation, since she was obviously thinking he was a little weird. *A little weird?* Definitely pegged on the weird scale, she was right.

"Are you gay?"

That startled him. "Gay?" He laughed out loud. "Heavens, no, not really. Did you forget who kissed you in the elevator?"

"You could be a bicycle."

"A what?"

"A bicycle, AC and DC."

"Oh." He wasn't sure whether he should be pissed or just laugh. That was a new one for him. "No, I'm not that either. Straight as can be. One hundred percent Grade-A all-American heterosexual. I like girls. Period. Why would you ask me that?"

She fidgeted. "No reason. It's just strange that a good-looking guy like you wouldn't have a girlfriend, is all. Usually, when good-looking nice guys don't have girlfriends is because they're gay."

"You can rest assured, milady, I only have interest in one gender, and that's the one you belong to. And in answer to your question, I haven't had a girlfriend for a long time. Intentionally, I must say."

"Intentionally? And why is that?"

"I needed to concentrate on my career. Getting on with the airlines was a tough ride, and I found that I had to dedicate my attention only to flying airplanes."

"And no time for girls?"

"And no time for girls. Relationships can be very time-consuming and draining."

"Other guys seem to find time for both work and play."

Pierre wondered how much he should share with Kirsten. He really didn't want to bore her with long tales of failed past romances. "I was in a relationship that was very intense, and it didn't work. That distracted me terribly from my goal of becoming an airline pilot so I decided to tackle one thing at a time."

"So that's when you decided to become a Franciscan Monk?"

He laughed. "Not exactly, but close."

"How long ago was this intense relationship?"

Now she was taking the conversation where he didn't want to go. "About three years."

"You haven't been in a relationship in three years?"

"Nope."

"So you haven't had sex in three years?"

She was definitely a free speaker. He laughed. "I didn't say that."

"Yeah, you did."

"Not having a girlfriend does not necessarily mean one does not have sex."

"Oh? That's interesting. So you've been having fun with girls who are not your girlfriends?"

"I'll take your order now." The waitress reappeared with her pen poised ready to write on her small notepad.

Thank God.

Pierre ordered their food, ultimately grateful for the arrival of the waitress, drinking some of his Coke from the overflowing glass. Kirsten was not only head-turning but appeared intelligent and quick-witted. He had to admit he was developing a very strong attraction for her. More than strong attraction, he was desperately wishing they would end up in bed together, if not tonight, then soon. Whatever it was that made it work between two people was there, no doubt. Chemistry, or *The Force*, or whatever the hell people called it, it was real, and he was feeling it. And he knew she was feeling it as well. He just wanted to kiss her, touch her, inhale her fragrance, drive her insane with desire.

"Where did you go to school?" Better get on safer ground, he thought, asking her. He didn't have a hope in hell of losing the hard-on, but at least he could prevent it from demanding more of his attention.

"School? I went to high school, in Fargo. Then I started cosmetology school, but it wasn't for me."

"So you decided to become a flight attendant instead?"

Some of the gals he'd flown with the past year had college degrees, some had just some college, and more than half appeared to have only high school. He didn't care one way or another. Far as Pierre was concerned, a woman didn't necessarily have to have a college degree to demonstrate intelligence, or for him to be attracted to her. Heck, the great majority of the college and university degrees out there were a joke anyway. In his opinion, higher education in America had become big business, and the schools didn't really give a rat's ass about the students. It was all a horrible scam.

It seemed Universities and colleges were only interested in making money, and if that could be helped by offering a smorgasbord of useless degrees, so be it. Pierre was very much aware that there were but a couple of dozen useful university degrees out there, although academic catalogs listed hundreds of degrees they offered.

By useful, he meant they could be used to find a good job somewhere, developing it into a career. Higher education was nothing but a fraud and the sting was very well organized; attracting unwary students to the university offering useless degrees, having Uncle Sam provide the student loans to finance the useless degrees, and making a shitload of money in the process. So what if the poor bastards graduated without the ability to hold a job, and loaded with huge amounts of student loan debt.

Bachelor of Arts in the Mating Habits of Bald Frogs. Bachelor in French Poetry. Bachelor in PE. And so on. Pierre truly believed what the schools were doing was downright criminal. Yet nobody seemed to care enough to change it.

"So, where'd you go?" Kirsten's voice brought him back to reality.

"Uh?"

"You seemed to have left Planet Earth for a second or two there, where'd ya go?"

He was that transparent? Crap. "Sorry!" He hated giving the impression that he wasn't interested in her, and that was precisely what he'd done. "I'm sorry, I just got distracted by the waitress."

"In answer to your question, yes, that's when I decided to become a flight attendant. Flying to exciting places sure sounded a lot more fun than sitting in class or doing someone else's hair. So, where did *you* go to school?" She sipped her Margarita again.

"I went to Arizona State University, in Phoenix."

"Party school!"

"Yea, I guess for some. I had to work hard so didn't have too much time to party."

"How come you're not married? Kirsten threw out.

"Married? I guess for the same reason I haven't had a girlfriend. I wanted to concentrate on my career first. Women are expensive."

"What do you mean 'concentrate' on it? The majority of the other pilots your age are already married. They didn't seem to have issues concentrating on their careers and girls at the same time."

"Kirsten. It's just that I wanted this so bad I could taste it, so I dedicated my life to attaining it."

"Why did you feel you had to put all this intensity into it?"

Pierre smiled. She was just being curious, is all. "I had a girlfriend once—as I mentioned—who I cared for very much. I didn't have any direction in my life at the time, so things didn't work out for us. I blamed my lack of direction in life as one of the major causes for our breakup."

"What'd you mean you didn't have any direction?"

"I didn't have a job back then, nor a career. No direction. And obviously, no money. Relationships need money to flourish. I had none. So, she went out looking for other guys. After that happened, I made the decision to dedicate myself entirely to becoming an airline pilot, come hell or high water. No distractions and no girls. Once I finally got here, now I have options. And money."

"I see."

Their food arrived, smoking hot. The waitress held their plates with a kitchen towel. "These plates are really hot, be careful!" She pointed out.

Pierre observed Kirsten attack the chicken tacos. One could tell a great deal about a person from their table manners. She chewed with her mouth closed, dabbing her lips with her white linen hanky before taking a sip of her Margarita. He was pleased with her. Growing up he'd been taught that a woman can make a man or destroy a man just by association. Manners were essential. Not that he would like her any less if she had the table manners of a dock worker, but nice manners sure earned her so many bonus points in his book.

"Do you have brothers and sisters?" he inquired.

"One sister," she responded, after she'd finished chewing. "She's trying to get on with American."

"As a flight attendant?"

"Yes."

"How come she wants to get on with American instead of here with us at Worldwide?"

She stared at Pierre. "I guess there's no reason why you should know this. Worldwide Airlines is asking new hire flight attendants to have at least one additional language. If you're not fluent in two languages, they won't even give you an interview."

"You're kidding."

"Nope. For now, at least, we're not hiring anyone who can't speak a second language."

"That's pure reverse discrimination."

"Tell me about it. We're hiring all sorts of foreigners instead of your average vanilla-flavored all American boys and girls. If that's not reverse discrimination, I don't know what is."

"That's insane."

"Some idiot in Human Resources must've come up with that one." She finished her food first.

Boy, he smiled, she wasn't joking when she said she was famished. He remembered all she'd had at *Viera's* in St. Louis had been some cottage cheese with a half peach.

"You're based in St. Louis, but where do you live?"

"In Creve Cour," she replied.

"Nice. That's one of the prettiest neighborhoods in town."

"I love it. I live with my Aunt Lisa. We share an apartment; she flies for us."

Pierre wondered briefly if her aunt was a flight attendant or a pilot. "She's a flight attendant?"

"Yep. And she's dating one of our pilots. This was delicious," she stated.

"Not bad at all," he agreed.

"Do you live in St. Louis or are you a commuter?" Kirsten asked.

"St. Louis. Been there a little over a year. In St. Charles, on the other side of the river. I've been sharing a small townhouse with two other pilots, but now I'm starting to consider moving out and buying a house." He decided not sharing with her he was considering buying a house in Arizona, in order to live there and commute to St. Louis. He'd had enough of living in Missouri. The weather absolutely sucked. When it wasn't too hot and muggy, it was colder than a walk-in freezer. And the place was full of flying insects. But other than that, he did like the town.

"Buy a house? That's cool. Are you gonna have roommates in this new house of yours?"

Pierre smiled at her question. Maybe the thought had just crossed her mind that she could room with him? Having Kirsten for a roommate? A truly exciting and erotic idea. If she was asking about roommates it could be because the thought had crossed her mind. Then he remembered that he was considering a house in Phoenix, not in Missouri. "No, no roommates. I've had enough of living with other guys."

"Who said anything about guys?"

Pierre smiled at her. "You're right, maybe I should get a big house and invite three or four flight attendants to live with me."

Kirsten didn't smile. "You're not funny."

"Shall we go?"

The super-efficient waitress had deposited the check on their table half way through their meal. Pierre had slipped his Chase Visa card inside the leather holder and the waitress from hell had ran the card and returned the holder before they had a chance to eat half their food.

He noticed Kirsten folding her white linen napkin into a neat square, gently placing it on the table. Little details like that impressed him.

They left the Mexican restaurant walking out into the chilly night holding hands. Kirsten removed the sweater from her shoulders, slipping it on. They walked a block away. Pierre was not really sure what to do next. What he'd like was take Kirsten up to her room and make sweet love to her, but he was realistic enough to know that such an ending was probably not in the cards for tonight.

"Do you have any cash on you?" She asked.

"*What?* Sure." He didn't know why she'd ask that.

"Do you have a twenty?"

Pierre nodded, reaching for his wallet. What was she up to? He held his wallet wide open to her, several bills easily accessible.

Kirsten reached in his wallet, pulling out a twenty. "I'll pay you back in the hotel."

Pierre looked up, discovering the object of her attention. A homeless man was leaning against the building ten feet ahead of them. The unfortunate fellow appeared in very poor shape, unwashed and with a terribly sad look about him. He had a supermarket cart parked next to him, containing his meagre belongings. He appeared in his late thirties, but Pierre couldn't be sure. Very difficult for him to assess the poor guy's age under the layers of dirt. And the poor guy was not dressed warm enough for the chilly air.

Kirsten walked up to him, a friendly smile on her face. "Here," she addressed him, "go get yourself some dinner."

The homeless man appeared quite surprised, accepting the twenty from Kirsten, looking at it, then at her.

"Thank you," was all he said. No smile crossed his face. No visible signs of enthusiasm of gratitude.

Life had been hard for him, Pierre decided.

He was impressed. Kirsten's act of random generosity had touched him deeply. He reached for his wallet.

"Here buddy, go get yourself a warm jacket." He handed the man the remaining cash from his wallet, a hundred bucks or so, if he remembered correctly. He didn't want to top Kirsten, but the poor guy really was in need of a jacket. And Pierre felt quite sad at the reality of what that guy's life must be.

They walked away in silence.

Across the street they approached a bus stop bench covered on three sides with plexiglass walls and sporting a roof.

"Want to sit here for a minute?" he asked her.

"Sure."

The concrete bench was unpleasantly cold. He could feel it through his pants. Pierre removed his leather jacket, placing it over Kirsten's shoulders. The jacket was pleasurably warm from his body heat.

"No! You're gonna freeze!"

"Relax, I'll be fine. Cold doesn't affect me like it affects other people. Really."

"Thank you for dinner. That was perfect." She accepted the jacket when she felt how warm it was.

"No need to thank me, I must admit I greatly enjoyed the company."

Kirsten looked at him, half-puzzled. "Are you always this polite?"

"No, not always. You have that effect on me."

Now what? He couldn't very well keep her there for very long, jacket or not, she was going to freeze her butt. "Why don't we go back to your room and I can give you a nice foot massage?" His smoldering brown eyes locked with hers.

She stared at him inquisitively. "No, I don't think so."

Crap. He cursed himself for asking. Had he misread all the flirting? Unlikely as that sounded, it was always a possibility.

His enthusiasm tanked. Quite naturally, deep down he hadn't really expected Kirsten to jump in the sack with him, but after their long day flying he thought she would've at least been enticed by the idea of a nice massage. He knew he had strong hands and could deliver a very relaxing rub. But she said no. That meant the evening was over. No use hoping. From this moment on, he suspected nothing was going to change and eventually they would each end up going back to their respective rooms for the night.

That being the case, it didn't make any sense sitting there freezing. They could always go back to the Marriott and find some warm place to just sit and talk, but then again the idea of running into one of the other crew members in the lobby dissuaded him. Besides, talking was overrated. He didn't want to talk anymore, he wanted to touch her, kiss her, spoil her, intoxicate himself with her scent, make passionate, wild love to her all night.

"Wanna head back?"

"Sounds good," Kirsten said. She had become less talkative.

They walked back to the Marriott still holding hands. Her hand felt ice cold. The few minutes sitting on the concrete bench had sapped them both. Being courted by a man while freezing one's butt was definitely not conductive to sex. Reaching the lobby of the hotel they caught one of the elevators to their floor. Pierre was saddened by the thought of parting with Kirsten. He really liked her and was enjoying her company tremendously, but the next day they were scheduled for another long duty day, and so perhaps it was better if they just got some rest.

Holy Toledo, their time together had been so brief! The elevator arrived at their floor, its doors silently opening. Pierre briefly wondered if they were going to run into Mark. He planned on walking Kirsten to her room before proceeding to his own, so if Mark showed his face and saw them together he could just drop dead. At this point he was disappointed and sexually frustrated and fresh out of patience.

Arriving at her door, Kirsten removed Pierre's leather jacket from her shoulders, handing it to him, then she inserted her room card into the reader, getting a green light. Pushing the door open, she reached for his hand again, pulling him in the room behind her.

He followed Kirsten, momentarily puzzled by the situation. She didn't let go of his hand, walking straight to the space between the two queen beds. The hotel room was dark, barely lit by a small night light at the bedside and the turquoise display of a digital desktop radio softly playing Lionel Richie's "Say You Say Me."

The room door clicked shut behind them, pulled by the door closer, enveloping them in total privacy. Kirsten had still not released his hand, nor said anything.

Pierre was puzzled and tremendously excited by the situation, his eyes widening, not yet sure what Kirsten was up to. This was utterly unexpected. He had a fluttery, empty feeling in his stomach, rapidly spreading to his groin. Butterflies magically transforming into another magnificent hard-on.

She finally turned, facing him, with eyes that glowed in the dim light. Kirsten placed her hands on his chest, pushing them up until she encircled his neck.

"I am so turned on," she whispered.

"Make love to me."

Pierre about fainted. *Whoa!* His increasing heartbeat echoing in his ears made the situation so unreal. Those were the last words he'd ever expected to hear. The most beautiful words she could possibly have said to him.

Before he had a chance to think about what she said, Pierre felt the soft touch of Kirsten's lips connecting with his, kissing him with a passion which took his breath away. Her lips were ice cold from their walk, but her breath was hot and steamy. Her warm, feminine soft body willingly snuggling against his.

Pierre recovered from the surprise in an instant, pitching his leather jacket on one of the beds, wrapping his muscular arms around her waist, lifting her up just a tad, holding her tight. This time, Kirsten let her soft curious tongue dart inside his mouth, touching his teeth, exploring his lips. The sensation was out of this world. Not having had any contact with a girl for so long, everything seemed amplified one hundred times.

Pierre reciprocated the pleasure, running his tongue along the outside of her lips first, very softly, now darting in and out of her mouth, fencing with her tongue. She smelled absolutely incredible. Some familiar fragrance he didn't quite recognize, but enchanting nonetheless.

Kirsten broke the embrace, her indigo blue eyes locked on his. Her lips slightly parted, shuddering breath coming a little faster. She let her hands drop down to a button on his white cotton shirt, unbuttoning it. Next, she unbuttoned the second one, and then the third. She continued until reaching the last one visible above his jeans. Then she yanked his shirt out of his pants with both hands. Pierre just stood fascinated, his powerful hands softly holding her slender waist.

Kirsten pushed his shirt off his robust shoulders, exposing his bronzed well-toned skin. She ran the palms of her hands down his chest, from the shoulders to his slim waistline, absorbing the beauty of his physique. She pushed Pierre away softly, putting some space between them. Kirsten then removed her baby blue cashmere sweater, pulling it off over her head, flinging it onto the bed. She unbuttoned her white silk shirt. It only had four mother-of-pearl buttons. Her blouse joined the sweater on the bed.

The room had barely enough light for Pierre to admire the beauty of her amazing body, the perfect curves of her shoulders, the fullness of her breasts desperate to escape her cream-colored bra. Kirsten didn't make a sound, reaching behind her back with both hands, unhooking her bra. Pierre was hypnotized, he felt his knees going weak.

Lord, this was really happening. And against all odds. Thank You, St. Peter!

His mind had not yet caught up with the events of the past couple of minutes. He kept his eyes locked on Kirsten's. He was dying to look down at her magnificent breasts, but didn't want to disrupt the magic that was flowing between them. If he broke eye contact to admire her glorious body, that might break the incantation, and if that happened, she might change her mind.

Pierre reached down with his hands, finding the front button on her slacks. Kirsten just let her arms hang at her sides, patiently waiting for his next action, her lustful eyes locked on his. He unbuttoned her slacks, fumbling to locate the zipper, his eyes growing accustomed to the twilight in the room. He unzipped her with one smooth pull. His eager thumbs then found the sides of her slacks, rubbing against the warm satin skin of her waist. Pierre knew he was hard as a rock by now. *Almighty*, he was dying to just rip off their clothes, throw her on the bed and fuck her wild, but forced himself to have some control.

He had to keep in mind that *her* desires and *her* needs had absolute first priority. He had to please her before he ever thought of pleasing himself. Kirsten had made the decision of giving herself to him, and Pierre owed her *big*. He slowly bent down, pulling Kirsten's slacks off over the shape of her curvaceous hips with his thumbs, and then gently lowering them down to her ankles.

His face descended while pulling her slacks down. He caught glimpse of two lovely creamy naked breasts crowned by two aroused rose-colored nipples. He was on his knees by the time her slacks were down around her ankles. His face was level with a pair of white lace bikini panties. They fit around Kirsten's figure as if they had been spray-painted.

He gasped in anticipation.

Pierre reached with his hands, gently grabbing both sides of her panties, pulling them down in one uninterrupted motion to rest on top of her slacks around her ankles. He noticed with growing excitement that her mound was sensually decorated with a minimum amount of neatly trimmed, soft blond hair. Kirsten's delicate hands resting in anticipation on his naked shoulders felt exciting. They were no longer cold.

He stood slowly, reaching for the front of his jeans. Unbuttoning the Levi's and lowering his zipper took but a couple of seconds. Kirsten's enticing blue eyes were still locked on his.

Pierre kicked off his Stan Smith Adidas without untying them, stepping out of his jeans. He saw Kirsten glance down at his hardened cock. He was so ready for her. Time to get on the bed. Pierre bent down, placing his arms around the contour of her lower back and behind her legs, lifting her with ease, depositing her on the queen bed further from the window, her slacks and panties still around her ankles, her gold leather sandals landing on the carpet.

Kirsten stretched with her head towards the foot of the bed.

In spite of the darkness Pierre sucked in a quick breath, in complete awe of her looks. Kirsten was a Modigliani portrait, so perfect and so very *very* erotic, flat on her back with her knees up and slightly apart, waiting for him, her seductive eyes alight with desire. Reaching down he freed her slacks from her ankles, allowing them to fall on the carpet. Her panties went off with the slacks. Now he'd be able to spread her legs unhampered.

Kirsten didn't make a sound; a colorful tropical bird being hypnotized by a King Cobra in the jungles of Borneo.

Pierre positioned himself on the bed, moving and shifting until his face was level with her knees. He used his tongue along the inside of one thigh, gently licking his way up towards the apex of her legs.

Kirsten smelled wonderful. He detected the scent of soap and maybe some perfume, but also behind it all was *her* smell. Her woman smell. The most desirable of all. She smelled of feral and erotic, not unlike a wild animal. He inhaled softly, savoring her fragrance, as his tongue painted its way up her thigh past her hip bones to her navel. She tasted slightly like sea salt, the flavor Pierre remembered on his lips after spending the day skin diving in the Caribbean. He intentionally bypassed her most sensitive area, her most guarded place. There was no doubt in his mind Kirsten was totally turned on and ready for him, but he was going to try his best to drive her senseless with desire and give her an orgasm or two before entering her, if at all possible.

He allowed his slippery tongue to explore her belly button, while simultaneously caressing the back of her knee with the palm of his hand. Kirsten had her hands on his head, holding his coarse dark hair in a strong grip.

The experience was incredible. Pierre still could not believe he was there, in Kirsten's hotel room, nude in bed with her, with his face between her legs and making sweet love. He had so completely given up hope of having any contact with Kirsten tonight, that in a way he was in total astonishment, stupefied, wondering if he may be living in some sort of alternate reality.

He descended once again, licking her firm lower abdomen very slowly, deliberately, starting at her belly button and running his moist tongue down her smooth velvety skin. He could feel her belly getting tight under his tongue, reacting to his touch with mild, soft tremors. Reaching her hairline, he paused. No need to hurry. This was going to happen, so he really should take his time. One of the promises he'd made to himself long before was when he finally found himself making love to a lovely creature again, he would do everything in his power to please her first. Drive her mind into orbit with pleasure. Once her needs were satiated, and she could take no more, then he would allow himself the privilege of losing control of his body.

Kirsten's panting breaths increased his arousal. He moved his hand, slowly reaching upwards along her inner thigh up to the cleft of her legs, gently caressing her passion-moistened lips with his fingers before moving his hand away. Kirsten tensed, exhaling loudly. Pierre ran his tongue along her downy mound very close to her lips, without actually touching them yet.

He did it again, and again.

Kirsten applied more pressure on his head with her hands, attempting to direct his tongue down towards that most special of places, the spot where she really wanted stimulation.

Pierre liked that, but he resisted her wishes. She was *really* turned on now.

Patience was a virtue, and he needed to take his time so when Kirsten's climax finally arrived, it would be triple-delicious.

After several more minutes stimulating her, Kirsten was trembling continuously. He realized she was at the point where more stimulation could be painful, so it was time to ignite her fire.

He used his tongue to paint one long, slow, deliberate brushstroke from the bottom up, right up the middle of her pussy, barely separating her moist lips. She was completely soaked. She trembled, arching her back.

"So wet," he murmured.

"Come here!" she ordered, pulling on his hair.

Oh, no. Not just yet, sweetheart, Pierre smiled.

Kirsten was obviously ready for him to enter her, but that was not going to happen just yet. Instead, he repeated his slow, deliberate brushstroke, gently separating her lips with his tongue again, culminating at the very apex of her sex. He found her clit, already beautifully visible between its folds, from all the stimulation. Pierre ran his tongue back and forth on it, slowly, concentrating on her center of pleasure, painting it with his tongue. Michelangelo, delicately stroking a canvas with a soft squirrel-hair brush.

Kirsten tightened the hold on his hair. She had two hands grabbing Pierre's black head of hair, tugging with a lot of force, trying to pull him up to her. She wanted him inside her, that much he could tell. He reached up with his arm, exploring, finding her breast, ignoring the pain she was causing him pulling his hair. His fingers reached their target, the light pink nipple. Pierre gently held her nipple between two fingers, squeezing it and rolling it, while continuing to lick her button. This would send two separate signals to her brain. Two simultaneous waves of pleasure.

Pierre ran his hand horizontally along her belly, above her hair line. Her abdomen was hard as a board. He smiled. He recognized that as a clear sign that he was pleasing her. His intention was to keep stimulating her as long as necessary while she kept the muscles in her belly as tight as they were now. If he could keep Kirsten aroused like that just a little longer, she would reach an unimaginable orgasm. The light in the room was very dim, but they'd been in that twilight long enough his night vision had finally kicked in. He could clearly see Kirsten on her back with her head to one side, her deliciously sculptured legs spread apart to each side of his head. All while enduring the brutal pain of both her hands grabbing at his hair like an Apache warrior furiously trying to scalp him.

He kept up his rhythm, gently brushing her clit with short, soft strokes of his tongue. Kirsten began moving her pelvis up and down, gently, in response to his stimulation. She was breathing faster, with short gasps.

"Oh, Pierre!" She cried out.

Pierre treasured hearing his name from her lips while he played with her clit. He took this as confirmation that he was indeed pleasing her. Kirsten was moving her pelvis up and down more energetically, up and down and side to side. The muscles in her abdomen as tight as the head of a banjo. Pierre stuck his index finger in his mouth, making sure his warm saliva covered every inch of it. Then he rapidly returned his attention to her prepuce with his tongue. Kirsten didn't miss a beat moving with him. She was drenched, totally wet from the excitement.

Pierre decided it was time to raise her excitement to the next level. He gently searched with his hand, finding the small opening between her cheeks, inserting his left index finger in her ass with one slow, gradual, uninterrupted motion.   Her sphincter felt tight and hot around his finger, and the saliva allowed it to glide inside her without causing any pain from friction.

"*Ahh—mmm!*" Kirsten wooed, in response to the new stimulation. She seemed to approve and enjoy the effect Pierre's latest move was having on her.

Pierre fucked her with his finger, simultaneously keeping up the pleasure he was providing her with his tongue; as he had expected, the entrance of his finger precipitated her climax.

Both her legs shot up around his back, applying strong pressure in a bear grip. Kirsten thrust her crotch hard against his face. Pierre increased the frequency of his licks on her center of pleasure, while moving his finger inside her ass in a circle and in and out, making sure she felt him in there. Kirsten's muscles surrounding his finger inside her ass began pulsating rapidly, uncontrollably, her convulsions of pleasure going on for what seemed an eternity, her lower belly remaining tight as a drum. She rolled and bucked, rubbing her clit against his face, pulling on his hair with renewed vigor.

She shuddered and gave out short sounds of pleasure, taking what seemed forever to come down from her orbit around Planet Pleasure.

Pierre was so turned on. He felt an enormous feeling of satisfaction, suspecting but not entirely sure that he'd just made her come. Of course, everything had happened so fast he could hardly believe what was going on.

Holy fuck. Had he just made Kirsten come?

He was so pitifully out of practice in the art of making love, he barely recognized the manifestation of an orgasm. The pressure from her legs relaxed a little on his back. She was still coming down from the incredible high.

Not so fast, sweetheart.

Her orgasm—if that's what it was—had seemed to last a long time, much to his satisfaction. A minute? Two minutes? He had absolutely no idea, having lost track of time, he just knew it'd been a long one. Pierre slowly removed his finger from her rear, cupping Kirsten's buttocks with both his hands. He then immediately resumed licking her clit.

"No, don't!" Kirsten complained, barely audible. She made a half-hearted attempt at pushing him away with her hands.

Pierre had his powerful biceps wrapped solidly around Kirsten's thighs, holding her in place while he relentlessly kept licking at her center of pleasure.

"No, don't! Please, stop!" She complained, applying further pressure to his hair with both hands, trying desperately to dislodge him from between her legs, rolling her hips from side to side trying to break his embrace.

Pierre ignored her, tightening his grip on her legs. His strength easily overrode her efforts. His rhythmic licking increasing in intensity. He barely felt Kirsten pulling at his hair. He knew she was probably hyper-sensitive to touch just now, but if he continued just a little longer her pain would transform into immense pleasure.

Just as he anticipated, in just a few more moments, Kirsten quit struggling and instead of fighting him she switched to moaning. Now her hands all of a sudden were pulling Pierre towards her open lips, instead of trying to pull him off of her. They'd gone past the point where further stimulation had been painful to this new phase where her body opened itself for pleasure again.

Eagerly so.

You're mine, he smiled, still licking her clit. He had a solid firm grip on her buttocks and her legs. His strong arms had Kirsten nailed in place.

You are going nowhere, sweetheart.

Pierre was going to unlock all the earth-shattering toe-curling orgasms Kirsten had in her— regardless of what she thought were her limits.

"*Aargh, you shit!*" She cried, pumping her hips up and down with a strong rhythm, driving her pelvis into his face, increasing the momentum.

Pierre did not loosen his grip on her buttocks. With two handfuls of her ass, he could feel her cheeks in his hands getting harder as her body tensed in delicious anticipation of another imminent orgasm. *Holy crap*, his tongue was getting a terrific workout with Kirsten. The ligament under his tongue was going to be sore as all hell tomorrow, yet well worth it! He was not about to slow down his stimulation of her clit now that he had her going.

Kirsten moaned louder, shoving her pelvis harder into his face. Pierre backed away from her lips, rapidly licking his index finger again, soaking it in saliva, then he reinserted it in her ass just in time to feel the first pulsations induced by what appeared to be her second orgasm.

This one was more violent. She resumed pulling at his hair with all her strength, forcing his face down against her very well lubricated super-sensitive lips.

"OhGodpleasedontstop!" Kirsten screamed, with uncontained loudness.

This time he was sure she was coming.

Her convulsions and violent spasms lasted for what seemed forever, although Pierre had no way or telling whether she had gone for one minute or ten. And the entire time she was pulling at his hair.

Judas priest, that hurt!

He held her in place with his powerful arms while she bucked and moaned beneath him.

Pierre was up on his elbows, slowly easing off the grip he'd had on her perfect buttock with one hand, slowly removing his index finger from her still very hot rear end for the second time that night.

He slowly pulled himself up, moving his body on top of Kirsten, bringing his face level with hers. Kirsten watched him—dizzy, through a layer of haze in complete sexual stupor. Her eyes unfocused, her golden hair disarrayed against the sheets. Her respiration coming in tiny gasps. Pierre kissed her, gently at first, slowly easing his tongue in her mouth. Her tongue came out to meet him, bashfully, she was still breathing jagged.

Kirsten's hands were still caressing his powerful back, she moved her legs further apart sensing that he was finally going to enter her. She was doing this instinctively and semi-conscious, since her climaxes of the past few minutes had obliterated her.

Pierre put his weight on his elbows, still kissing Kirsten, *time to go inside you, sweetheart,* moving his pelvis up and forward, he felt her hot and very lubricated slippery softness make contact with the tip of his erection.

She felt so hot.

With one continuous gentle, slow motion he felt himself entering her open lips. Her inner walls separated, welcoming the painfully delicious feeling of his invading shaft. Kirsten's entire body stiffened at his sudden presence inside her body. She bit down on his bare shoulder with a vengeance.

All of Pierre's senses were concentrating on the signals generated by his hard-on, so he was oblivious to the pain.

Pierre savored the extraordinary sensation of going inside her, totally beyond words. She was so well lubricated his entire shaft found its way inside Kirsten in an instant without any hesitation. He was so turned on with the difference in body temperatures, the inside of her body was on fire. It was an incredibly erotic sensation. Pierre slowly began going in and out of her, wiggling his hips to induce a rotating motion to their love making. He held off his weight distributing it between his elbows and knees, not wanting to put any weight on her.

Kirsten responded by thrusting her hips up and down gently, meeting him, dancing an erotic ballet with him in perfect sync, her arms around Pierre's neck locked in a hungry passionate embrace.

Pierre slowed the pace, eventually coming to a complete stop, fully inside Kirsten. Her eyes were an inch away from his, mystified. He resumed thrusting in and out of her a few times, followed by another pause. She seemed puzzled, yet aroused by this crazy technique of his, as she proceeded to follow his hips without allowing him to slip out of her at all.

Pierre was fighting his body's desire to push him towards the edge of an orgasm. It'd been so flippin' long since he'd had a girl, his body was not to be trusted. He'd always considered himself a good lover, and in his opinion, the key ingredient of any good lover was keeping control of one's body. He wondered if he should think of something else, distract himself even, so he would not think about making love to Kirsten. That had worked for him in the past. Heck, he could just count sheep, or drive a car, or install pins in hand grenades or something. Dammit! He was *not* gonna cum just yet. His three years of chastity were not going to bite him in the ass.

Then he realized how senseless that was. Here they were, having mind-blowing, wild delicious sex, and he was wasting precious moments thinking asinine thoughts when he should be concentrating on this attractive girl who was fulfilling all his fantasies. She was tight and hot inside, and her tongue was now darting in and out of his mouth. What an incredible moment.

Aw, what the hell.

Pierre resumed pumping in and out of Kirsten with renewed vigor and total abandonment, pounding into her. That was it, he could tell his decision to lose himself inside her was taking him directly towards the light, as they were fond of saying in the movies. The moment had arrived. All of a sudden, and without any additional warning, he felt himself losing control of his body.

That was it! *He was coming.*

His body shook, trembling with energy he didn't know he still had. His cock jamming deep inside her, sending monster waves of inconceivable pleasure through him.

"Ah, Kristen, I'm cummin inside you! Now!"

He abandoned himself to the feeling of immense pleasure overcoming him after losing total control. The feeling of violent pleasure this time began in his balls and expanded to his chest and his legs in ever-increasing pulses.

Kirsten at once sensed what was happening, instantly wrapping her legs around his hips with great force, holding him inside her with such strength totally surprising Pierre. Her arms wrapped around his muscular back pulled him towards her with amazing force, her fingernails digging into his back, sending exquisite reverberating pain to his groin.

The waves of pleasure taking control of his body were incredible, accentuated by the erotic realization far in the recesses of his mind, that he was inside Kirsten, violently shooting his sperm into the depths of her body, joining her fluids with his. He pumped in and out of her faster yet, her legs wrapped around his hips preventing him from going too far out with each stroke.

It was heaven. He had died and gone to heaven. Pierre was overwhelmed by a totally irrational, intense feeling of love and affection for this most striking of all creations. He loved her, he adored her, she was his. He was going to do everything in his power to make her happy.

And then it was over.

Pierre's climax ended just as sudden as it had begun. He found himself on top of Kirsten sucking in several deep breaths to calm his heart, both of them totally drenched in sweat. It was as if some invisible being had doused them with buckets of warm sea water. She was still holding on to him with her arms with enough force to take his breath away. And her strong legs wrapped around him had Pierre locked in an anaconda embrace.

He was deep, deep inside her, and Kirsten was going to keep him there.

She was slippery and wet.

Wow.

He felt ultra-awake, rejuvenated by adrenaline, too excited to think straight.

The way nature had intended it to be between two lovers.

Her face was an inch away. Even in the dim light he could see her smoldering blue eyes, and her eye lashes radiating from her eyes like light rays from the sun, her lips partially open, as if struggling for breath.

She was inconceivable. No doubt in his mind, she was created and designed for love.

And amazingly enough, Pierre had the impression she was still very much aroused after experiencing his orgasm. That was a real turn-on in itself. For the love of God, she'd already experienced two climaxes, yet she seemed ready for more.

Even more extraordinary, Pierre could feel *he* was still hard as a rock. How could that be? That'd never happened to him before. Pierre normally had to wait half hour or so to regain an erection, yet here he was, ready for action, as if he hadn't come. Ludicrous. What was this, magic?

He had no idea how that was possible, undoubtedly, it had something to do with Kirsten, but damned if he knew what. But he wasn't going to waste it.

Pierre pushed himself up on his elbows, forcing Kirsten to ease her strong grip around his neck.

"Let go of me for a sec," he told her, moving back, feeling himself slipping out of her. "Turn around," he commanded, reaching down holding her along her sensuous hipbones, applying pressure so she would roll over.

Kirsten released the grip she had on Pierre's hips with her legs, pushing herself up on one elbow, allowing Pierre to roll her sideways.

Pierre was starting to regain control of his body. He was instantly turned on at the sight of Kirsten turning over on her stomach and her disheveled blond hair cascading across her shoulders. He admired her slim waist and was excited and near delirious at the sight of her well-rounded buttocks presenting themselves to him, invitingly.

Kirsten rested her face on the ornate hotel comforter, her hands reaching back to her clit, her legs spread apart on each side of Pierre, permitting enough space to allow Pierre access to any part of her body he desired.

Pierre quickly reached up, grabbing two pillows. "Here, place this under your head," he ordered, placing one of the two pillows alongside Kirsten's face.

She lifted her head, pulling the pillow under her face one-handed, resting her cheek on it, hugging it.

"Raise your hips," Pierre directed, placing his hands on both sides of Kirsten's hips. She arched up her exquisite ass as he requested. Pierre slipped the second pillow under her pubis, elevating Kirsten's buttocks and the delicious pink area of her lips.

Pierre caught sight of the blue turquoise light out of the corner of his eye. It was the digital clock on a dresser in front of them. It read 1:26 a.m.

He moved back away from Kirsten. The view she presented in the dim light of the hotel room, laying there on her belly, with her ass in the air and her golden hair spread on the pillow, was mind-defying erotic.

A total major league turn-on. There was definitely nothing more beautiful in the world than Kirsten at that moment.

Pierre placed his hands inside her strong thighs, applying gentle pressure to her legs, separating them some more. Kirsten complied with the direction his hands signaled her to go, spreading her legs as much as she could. Pierre went back down on his elbows, looking for her pussy lips, which even in the dim light he could see were moist and pink. Placing his face between her butt cheeks he licked Kirsten with another slow, deliberate, soft, brushstroke, separating her lips with his tongue, from the bottom to the top. He licked the entire length of her opening, allowing his tongue to wander slightly deeper in the center of its path. He promptly felt Kirsten's legs applying pressure against his shoulders, in an attempt to bring her legs together.

She moaned and arched her back.

Pierre repeated the soft brush stroke with his tongue. Kirsten reached back, grabbing her buttocks, separating them gently, providing Pierre with better access. He continued the stimulation of her lips with his tongue and in less than a minute Kirsten was once again gently pumping her hips up and down, rubbing her oversensitive lips against the pillow, transmitting pulses of pleasure to her clit. Pierre directed his attention to her clit. He could not reach it very well with his tongue from this angle, so he stimulated it with his fingers.

"Make love to me again!" Kirsten pleaded.

Pierre inched his way up, kneeling, positioning himself closely behind Kirsten. He glanced down, catching a glimpse of his erect organ aimed at the sexy cleft of her buttocks, less than an inch from her glistening skin. He moved closer just a tad, allowing his erection to come in contact with something hot and moist. He had lined up perfectly on her. Thrusting his hips forward, he felt himself entering Kirsten from behind. His lower abdomen feeling the welcome softness of her two buttocks, confirming that he was deep inside her again.

Kirsten wiggled her hips sideways gently, applying increasing back pressure against Pierre while he pumped in and out of her, filling her with his long and thick shaft. He placed his hands on the sides of her buttocks, below her hipbones, directing her body to move back and forth.

"You're incredible!" She purred. "I can't believe your stamina."

Pierre wedged his knees against Kirsten's lovely legs from behind, forcing her to keep her thighs apart.

He pumped in and out of her, increasing the tempo and getting more aroused each second. No way he was going to make her come like this, though, it wasn't the right angle. But he was going to lose himself very quickly if he kept at it like this. No, as much as he loved what he was doing, he had to give her priority.

He pulled back, slipping out of her, his cock moist and glistening from her juices.

"*What? Don't stop!*" She protested his withdrawal.

"Turn around," Pierre ordered, applying pressure on her hips with his hands.

"*No! Keep going.*"

He secured his hold on her hips with his strong hands, flipping her over. He had at least sixty pounds on her, so he turned her over without much effort. Her buttocks half-landed on the pillow underneath her, elevating her pelvis. Pierre went down on her in an instant—diving on her pussy—this time finding her clit and concentrating all his efforts with his tongue on it. Now he had the perfect angle.

"No! I can't take anymore!"

He ignored her.

Kirsten grabbed two handfuls of hair, fighting to pull him off.

Pierre ignored the pain, concentrating on licking her at an increased pace.

"You shit!" She blurted.

Pierre reached up grabbing Kirsten's wrists, preventing her from pulling much harder on his hair. This time she was really fighting him.

He said nothing. He knew that if he just concentrated on what he was doing, in a few moments Kirsten was going to surrender.

"This is too much for one night!" She complained, her frantic heartbeat confirming her excitement. She was hot and trembling, and totally sweaty slippery.

Pierre continued licking her, intensely yet softly. He felt her hands relaxing the pull on his hair.

Success.

"You are so bad!" She purred approvingly.

He was getting a workout, balancing his weight on his elbows while holding her wrists and at the same time licking her soaked and most delicious sex.

Kirsten finally quit fighting him. He tentatively released his hold on one of her wrists. She gently reached down, caressing his hair.

Time to turn her loose.

Pierre released her wrist, using his right index finger to find her lips. Reaching down he very gently separated the petal-soft folds, slipping his index finger inside Kirsten. The delicious moan and her shudder confirmed he met with her approval. He put pressure on the inside wall of her passage, massaging her G-spot.

Kirsten had reached enough stimulation for one night.

She swiftly tightened her thighs around his neck with great strength, simultaneously pushing her clit against his face with great ferocity.

"Pierre! Oh, Holy fuck!" She finally let loose and entered the threshold of a powerful climax.

For the third time that night.

Pierre felt her clit stiffen, her creamy delicate fluids soaking his face. She began to shake, vibrating and trembling in totally uncontained involuntary ecstasy. Her spontaneous moans pleased him enormously.

It was as if every nerve in her body had electricity flowing through it. Kirsten shuddered, her pulsing nipples feeling the painful pleasure of her out-of-control body. The intensity of her climax taking her breath away. She slammed her pussy against his face, violently convulsing in the grasp of a most delicious orgasm.

Pierre felt immensely happy once Kirsten began to come down, her spasms gradually subsiding and her body unwinding. Her climax did not last as long as her earlier ones, but it appeared much stronger.

Her cast-iron hold on his neck with her thighs had him worried for a second there.

Pilot chocked to death in hotel room. He almost laughed.

He gently moved her thighs aside, crawling up inch by inch, until finally finding himself face to face with her again.

This is now one satisfied magical creature. She's right alongside unicorns and all that is magical.

The entire episode was hard to believe. His brain was having trouble accepting the delightful reality that he was in bed with Kirsten and they had just shared the most delicious intimate experience two people could enjoy together.

Unfucking believable.

He felt himself still hard, but it was time to call it a night. Pierre considered going inside her once more, suspecting Kirsten would probably be just fine allowing him to please himself until he came again, but he didn't want to intrude on her moment of bliss.

He softly kissed her lips, her eyelids, her cheeks. She was hovering on the edge of sleep. Totally exhausted. What an incredible feeling, he mused, holding this gorgeous woman in his arms after having sexually satisfied her beyond his most optimistic expectations.

Oh, crap.

He had to setup an alarm! They had to fly in the morning. What time was it? He raised his head, searching for the turquoise display in the darkness of the room.

2:07 a.m.

For the love of God, they were scheduled for an eight-thirty report down in the lobby—their crew call. He decided to wait a bit before getting up to set the alarm so Kirsten would be deep in the arms of

Morpheus by then. He didn't want to wake her. All he had to do was stay alert for a little while longer. He had to make absolutely sure he didn't fall asleep. If they both missed their report time down in the lobby the crew would know for certain what had occurred. Privacy was essential.

Missing report time was *not* a desirable situation. Although most crews were aware of what took place behind closed doors on layovers, discretion was something flight attendants and pilots valued very highly. Not to mention the fact that missing a crew report time was stressful on everyone. If he and Kirsten failed to show up in the lobby, the rest of the crew would add two and two together in an instant and know they'd spent the night together.

Marvelous Mark would call his room and if he failed to get an answer, the next call would be to crew scheduling to request another first officer and the entire world would at that point be made aware that Kirsten and Pierre had slept with each other.

Naturally, he and Kirsten were adults and free to sleep with whomever they desired, but when their personal life interfered with the flight schedule, then the company had something to say.

He could not let that happen. He really didn't give a damn about himself being branded as a *Don Juan*, but he absolutely had to protect Kirsten. She was still on probation until the end of her first year with the company, and being exposed as having slept with a pilot and missing a report time were grounds for firing.

Pierre admired Kirsten's lovely face. She was even more attractive innocently sleeping there in his arms, totally nude and entirely sexually satisfied. He quickly thanked *The Force*, or St. Peter, or whoever was responsible for giving him this incredible gift.

I owe you big, whoever you are. I really do. Thank you. Thank you.

In the morning, they were going to have a busy day flying, with four legs on the schedule. He recalled they would end up in Madison, Wisconsin for the night. An alarming thought came to him. He couldn't remember if Kirsten was going to fly with him the rest of the day tomorrow, or if she was going to be switching pilots in St. Louis when they flew through there. The thought filled him with dread and sadness. He didn't want this to end. She was out cold, so waking her up to ask about her schedule the next day was not an option. She was sleeping like a baby. Dammit, he was sure she'd mentioned what her plans were, but for the life of his, he couldn't recall what she'd said.

He'd just wait until the morning to find out.

Once he was convinced sufficient time had passed and Kirsten was out cold in her sexually induced sleep, Pierre very slowly shifted her arms aside, inching away from her, then standing up he walked to the clock with the turquoise readout. Lifting it, he realized the damned thing was the typical hotel clock, too many buttons and not very intuitive. How the hell was he going to set it up in the dark and make sure the stupid alarm would wake them up?

Heck with it. He wasn't going to trust the fucking thing. He found it prudent to set up a wakeup call with the front desk instead.

He sauntered to the night table, lifting the telephone receiver, pushing the '0.'

A tired female voice responded, "Good evening, front desk. How can I be of assistance?"

"I'd like to setup a wakeup call, please," he said in as low a voice as he dared.

"Of course. What time would you like?"

Pierre rapidly decided their lobby time being eight-thirty, seven a.m. would give them ninety minutes to get ready. "Seven will be good. Thank you."

The front desk woman confirmed the room number and the time, signing off.

Now what?

He could stay there with Kirsten the rest of the night or he could leave now, return to his own room and go to sleep alone. The alarm was set. They were going to call her at seven. What the heck, what was he thinking? But of course, he was going to stay with Kirsten. Pierre pulled the comforter from the other queen bed, covering Kirsten with it very gently. He then climbed in bed next to her. She had fallen asleep on her back, with one leg stretched out in front and the other angled away. He reached over, pulling her closer to him. She felt limp and hot. Kirsten rolled easily against his chest with his help. Her face came to rest on his shoulder, her warm breath caressing his face.

All the religions in the world with their favorite concepts of Heaven could not match what he had in his arms at that moment.

He finally pulled the comforter over himself as well. She smelled of some sort of sugary scent he couldn't quite place. That was his last thought until the phone rang seemingly only two seconds later.

Jeesus!

PIERRE SLAMMED HIS EYES open not unlike a vampire in a horror movie, quickly taking in the situation. Kirsten was out cold, asleep with her head resting on his chest, one arm wrapped around him.

Oh, God, how he LOVED that.

They were both cozy under the comforter. And who the devil was calling? Was it wake up time already? It couldn't be!

No fucking way!

The damned phone kept on ringing. He developed homicidal thoughts about the damned thing. If the phone were alive, he sure as hell would want to kill it.

Pierre stirred, rolling away from Kirsten. He was up in a moment covering the distance to the phone in a blink, answering the call.

"Hullo!?" He croaked. Ugh, his voice sucked.

"This is your seven a.m. wake up call," the voice at the other end said. To make it even more annoying, it was the voice of a friggin' machine.

Pierre was disoriented. Already? Damn! That was one goddamned short night.

Kirsten stirred under the covers, her hands pulling the comforter away.

"Good morning!" she purred.

"Good morning, beautiful." She looked even better than he remembered from the previous night's adventure. In fact, she looked good enough to eat—again. There was some light coming in over the top of the room-darkening curtains. It was daytime. Definitely.

"What time is it?" Kirsten's sleepy blue eyes were fixed on him.

He was already hard first thing in the morning. This was a normal condition for Pierre. He'd long ago resigned himself to the reality that he must be under a gypsy curse or something equally dreadful, as he would wake up horny every morning of his life no matter what. Awful really, because most of his life he hadn't had anyone to share it with.

Kirsten didn't miss his erection. She smiled. "You're incredible."

"I'll show you just how incredible," he climbed back in bed reaching for her. Goodness! They may have just enough time for one quick frantic tumble.

"Not so fast!" Kirsten rolled away from him, jumping out of bed on the opposite side. She was fast and agile. "I gotta pee! And we have to work today!" she gingerly ran to the bathroom, providing Pierre with a delicious quick view of her bouncing rear end disappearing thru the door. She closed the door behind her.

Really?

That made him crack a smile. How coy.

After the night of passion they shared and she shuts the door?

That was funny. And God, what a splendid ass she had! The sight of Kirsten running for the bathroom lingered in his mind, like the images visible after staring directly into the sun for a second or two.

Life was good.

She was right, though. They had to get their butts in gear. He looked around for his pants. They were on the floor next to his shorts and her pants and underwear. He picked up her clothes, placing them neatly on the bed, then grabbed his own pants, slipping them on without boxers. They were a wrinkled mess, but who cared. He collected his shirt, boxers and shoes.

He had to return to his own room. Pierre wondered what the odds were of running into other crew members in the hallway this time in the morning. Probably not too likely yet.

The young pilot heard the toilette flush. He decided not to put on his shirt. He was only going a very short distance.

Kirsten opened the bathroom door, coming out wrapped in a white hotel towel. How could she be shy, after their passion hours earlier?

"Good morning again, *mademoiselle!*"

She walked up to Pierre, reaching on her toes, kissing him lightly on the lips. "Good morning."

"Did you have a good night?"

"Are you kiddin' me? That was the most incredible night of my life."

That was definitely sweet music to his ears, the song of the sirens. Incredibly, this girl knew how to say the right words to make him feel like a million bucks. He liked that. "Well, I got news for you too."

"What?"

"That was the most unbelievable night of my life for me as well. You are one incredible woman."

Kirsten reached up, circling his neck with her arms. Her white towel dropped to the carpet. She kissed him hard and passionate. Pierre wrapped his arms around her naked waist, returning the kiss. Then he moved his hands down to her buttocks, squeezing softly. Her cheeks felt cold and soft and so erotic. He was aware of his erection crowding her crotch through his pants. He wished he'd setup the wakeup call for five in the morning so they could've had another opportunity to make love. Too late now.

Kirsten broke the kiss. "Now you get your butt outta here, Mister, I gotta get ready!" She pushed him off.

He didn't resist or argue. Reaching for his clothing he walked out of her room, allowing the door to shut softly behind him. He found himself in the empty hallway, bare-chested holding his shoes and other items of clothing in his hand. Three doors down and he reached his room. Where in heaven's name had he left his room card? Oh, shit. If he didn't have it, he'd have to go down to the lobby and get another one. He fished in his pants pockets for the room card. Much to his surprise and relief, the damned thing was still in his pocket.

What were the odds? After a night like this, there was no way in hell he was going to remember what he'd done with the card. Finding the card had to be a good omen.

The green light in the card reader cleared his way into the room.   Pierre entered the chamber glancing at the two untouched beds, making the bathroom his first stop. After relieving himself he stood in front of the mirror.

Holy shit, look at those blood-shot eyes, time for Visine. And what the devil was that stuff all over his face?

His reflection in the mirror looked as if he'd been eating Krispy Kreme donuts. He closed on the mirror to get a better look.   Yep, it looked as if his entire face had been smeared with glazed sugar. What was that stuff? It suddenly came to him. He laughed out loud. That stuff was Kirsten! She'd been so creamy and wet. And now her delicious body fluids had dried up all over his face.

Pierre laughed again, running the hot water. He was somewhat childishly thrilled to still carry a taste of Kirsten with him.

Time for a shower and a shave. He took a short five-minute shower, briefly enjoying the steaming hot water rushing past his body. Yes! That was invigorating. He washed himself with a small pink bar of hotel soap. Man, he hated those little soap bars, they were so difficult to grab. After the shower, he stood naked in front of the bathroom mirror, wiping the water vapor with a dry towel.

His shoulder sported a nasty black and blue bruise the size of Kirsten's mouth. Boy, she'd really taken a good bite while making love. She was definitely a passionate one. A sexy little vampire.

He reached for his lemon-lime shaving cream, dispensing a handful of the white Gillette foam on his hand. With one practiced movement, he applied the lather to his face. His beard was more than a five-o'clock stub. Being of Basque blood he had very thick, tough hair on his face. He could only shave with razor blades. Electric shavers didn't work worth a damn on his thick beard.

He momentarily recalled the events of the previous night, reviewing with great pleasure the images that had been permanently engraved in his memory. He had made love to Kirsten. He still found it so incredible. She was an intoxicating young woman. And she had spent the night with him! Great Scott! He hadn't realized how much he'd missed female company, not to mention sex. And with her it hadn't been just the sex. He realized he was developing more than just a passing infatuation with his adorable colleague.

After shaving and drying himself, Pierre reached in his overnight bag, pulling out a pair of clean white boxer shorts. He stepped into them with a quick, elegant move. His dark uniform pants were still on the bed, where he'd placed them after returning from Kirsten's room. They were wrinkled, but not too unsightly. He pulled them on, since that was his only pair. Reaching back inside his overnight bag he pulled out a white T-shirt and a clean pair of black socks. His Bostonian black shoes came on next.

Al last, he retrieved a uniform shirt that had been professionally cleaned and folded at his local cleaners, medium starch, please. Pulling the shirt out of the plastic bag, Pierre noticed the shirt had many folds and it did look somewhat wrinkled. He transferred the epaulets from his soiled uniform shirt to the new one, then he put on the shirt, stepping up to a full-length mirror.

He was in great shape. By all means, it couldn't be any other way. Pierre loved his profession, and he was very aware that his career depended on his health. His FAA medical certificate was a very strict requirement allowing him to practice his profession. Consequently, he worked out every chance he got. He jogged outside on every layover, and if the weather was too inclement, then he jogged on the hotel treadmills in the gym. Sit ups every morning also helped. He smiled. The activities of the previous night kept him in shape as well. No doubt about that! He briefly smiled, wondering if there was any other more pleasant way of keeping a tight tummy shaped like a six-pack other than through vigorous sex.

He tied a Double-Windsor, adjusting his black uniform tie. After collecting all his belongings from the room and the bathroom, Pierre put everything away in his overnight bag. He strapped his flight bag to the wheelies, reaching for his uniform coat. One final glance at the mirror and he was satisfied at the sight of the airline pilot staring back at him in the dark blue uniform. He reached for his hat from the dresser. He loved the gold emblem of a world globe elegantly displayed on his hat. His airline not only was the best one in the world, it also definitely had class.

One final quick look at the room to ensure nothing was being left behind, Pierre placed his hat firmly on his head and left the room.

NINE HOURS LATER, MARVELOUS Mark parked the brakes of the big Airbus jetliner at the gate at Dane County Regional airport, in Madison, Wisconsin.

"Aaah, we're here! Take the rest of the night off," he offered again, magnanimously.

Pierre was too tired to laugh at the same idiotic joke. It'd been a long day for them, with four legs, four takeoffs and four landings. The only thing keeping him awake was the enormously enticing prospect of sharing a bed with Kirsten again tonight. He'd barely spoken a word to her all day. They'd exchanged glances at the hotel lobby in Minneapolis in the morning, but that had been pretty much it.

He'd spent the day wondering what she was thinking. Was she happy they'd met? Not to mention ending up in bed together? He'd gone back in the passenger cabin a couple of times to use the lav, but she hadn't been anywhere in sight. She'd probably been working the coach cabin, out of sight behind the curtain separating First Class from the Greyhound bus crowd, and so he'd not seen her. That had been disappointing.

Pierre packed away his iPad, headset and cell phone, standing up in the flight deck. He peeked at the passenger cabin as he slipped on his jacket. Kirsten was there, passing right by the flight deck door, exiting the airplane, giving him a quick look. Not a smile, just a quick look.

Pierre didn't wait for his captain. He just exited the flight deck, following the four flight attendants marching ahead through the terminal. He didn't catch up with them until they were at curbside, headed for the hotel van that was already there waiting for them.

"Wanna join me later?" He finally whispered in Kirsten's ear.

She looked tired. The fresh, flight attendant glamour-magazine look was gone. She and the other three young women appeared exhausted. Simply beat.

"Maybe not tonight," she pleaded, quietly. "I'm wiped. Really tired."

Pierre felt his heart sink. "Long day, eh?"

She locked eyes with him. "Yes, very long. You can say that again. Especially after last night."

He didn't say anything else.

Bummer.

His libido was alive and well and driving him totally batshit with desire. Why was she not as hot for him? He'd been planning on making love to her again tonight. He wanted to pleasure her until she melted like butter on a hot corn cob at a county fair. He was just dying to sleep with Kirsten in his arms. But regretfully, he had to admit the poor girl was obviously thrashed. Four flights in one day were a hell of a load. He was being a selfish shithead. Of course, she was tired. He handed his bags to the van driver, allowing him to lift them into the back of the vehicle after the four flight attendants had disposed of theirs.

Marvelous Mark appeared, joining his crew in the van. He climbed into the front seat next to the driver. Pierre had taken the seat next to one of the other flight attendants. He was a little disappointed Kirsten had not made any attempt to sit next to him.

Oh, well.

The ride to the hotel was short, through mostly deserted streets. Madison was not exactly a thriving metropolis after dark. The hotel was not nearly as luxurious as the Marriott in Minneapolis either, in fact, it was almost a motel. Two-stories, with outside balconies all around. The driver had a clipboard in front with six hotel key cards and a sign-in sheet. Marvelous Mark reached for the clipboard, signing his name on the roster, taking a card and passing the clipboard back. This procedure provided the crews direct access to their rooms without having to visit the registration desk in the lobby. The van driver would just drop them off as close to their rooms as possible.

Pierre handed the clipboard to the flight attendant next to him. One thing he'd noticed in the airlines was that some of the captains appeared to have absolutely no manners. Some of these guys would make an orchestrated effort to arrive at the sign-in counter ahead of the other pilots and flight attendants. They would sign for their rooms and then hightail it upstairs. No manners. Pierre had been raised allowing women to go first. In his mind, flight attendants had to be given the courtesy of signing for a room ahead of the men. A small gesture, really, but it was just common courtesy. Class was like fine embroidery, made up of thousands of small stitches.

Once all four women had signed the crew roster, Pierre accepted the clipboard back, helping himself to the very last key. He glanced at the sign-in sheet. The last room available was right next to Kirsten's. That was good.

And Marvelous Mark had taken the room on the other side of Kirsten's.

That was bad.

The van driver pulled up to the curb alongside the hotel, next to a glass door.

"You can use any of the room keys to get through that door," the driver instructed, exiting the van. By the time the crew had exited the vehicle, all their bags were lined up on the curb alongside the van. The crewmembers reached for their bags, tipping the driver the customary two bucks.

The tired crew headed for the glass door without saying a word.

"Is everyone on the second floor?" Marvelous Mark asked out loud. Airline policy prohibited crews from using rooms on the first floor. Safety was a serious consideration. This measure was not necessarily out of any consideration on the part of the airline, it was a clause in the union contract for pilots and flight attendants.

They all responded in the affirmative. The hotel didn't have an elevator. Everyone had to take the stairs up to the second floor. Not an endearing fun prospect after such a long day. The crew began climbing.

Before following the rest of his crew up the stairs, Pierre reached over, grabbing the wheelies away from the flight attendant closest to him, a brunette in her early twenties. "Let me help you with that."

The flight attendant didn't fight it. She gave him a tired smile, allowing Pierre to grab her bags. Pierre easily transported the two sets of luggage up to the second floor. He would've wanted to help Kirsten, but she'd gone ahead of the pack and he couldn't see her from where he stood. And this other soul was just as tired, so he was happy to help her. Reaching the second floor, he deposited her suitcase on the ground, allowing the woman to reach for the handle.

"Thanks, that was nice of you."

"My pleasure. Get some rest."

Pierre stared down the hallway. Only one other flight attendant was still visible entering her room. Everyone else was already in their rooms. Or most likely in their bathrooms.

He checked the numbers on the doors. His room was near. Once he found his room, he opened the door with the keycard, entering a typical small hotel room. Two queen beds and only one lamp on, providing soft illumination. Pierre lifted his suitcase onto one of the beds, placing his hat on the dresser and removing his jacket. His superstitious nature prevented him again from placing his hat on one of the beds. That was a definite no-no. Why tempt fate?

After relieving himself, he pulled off his tie, tossing it on the bed.

Now what?

He wondered if Kirsten was already climbing into her own bed. He was undoubtedly tired, but the deliciously sweet memories of the previous night kept him going generating rivers of stamina. He longed for more of Kirsten. He briefly considered calling her.

What room was she in? 406. Yea, his room was 405 so she was right there next to him.   He remembered the numbers had been increasing as he walked down the hallway. That meant her room was to the left of his from his balcony.

He walked over to the balcony window, shoving the green curtains aside, pushing open the glass and aluminum sliding door. He stepped outside. The night air was brisk. Pierre glanced at the silent parking lot below. Just a typical motel. Not a soul in sight. These Midwestern cities didn't kid around; it appeared everyone was in bed by ten at night.

He studied his balcony. It was separated from the balconies to either side of him by flimsy walls. He leaned over, concluding that he could easily step up over the rail and jump onto her balcony without too much effort. Actually, that wasn't such a bad idea. He really wanted to see her, but going out in the hallway was not a good plan. That idiot Mark had parked his ass in the room right next to Kirsten, so Pierre didn't really feel like going out in the hallway and knocking on her door. Without doubt, Marvelous Mark would show his face in the hallway if he heard Pierre knocking on her door.

Without any further consideration, Pierre stepped up on the railing, using both hands to hold on to the wall separating the two balconies. He swung his body around, landing on her balcony with a quiet 'thud.' The possibility of losing his grip and landing in a heap of broken bones two stories below never entered his mind.

He looked down at the parking lot, confirming that there was no one there and that his jump had gone unnoticed in the night. Just another cat roof-hopping in the dark.

He softly rapped on the glass of her sliding door, trying not to make too much noise.

What if she was already in bed and out cold? What the heck, he'd just go back to his own room then. He rapped again.

The green room-darkening curtain in front of him parted abruptly, her wonderful smile flashing at him from behind the glass. She took a few seconds to unlatch and open the sliding door.

"What are you doing here?" She was wearing only her white unbuttoned uniform shirt, nothing else. Her hair was hanging loosely over her shoulders.

What a sight. His heartbeat jumped.

"I came by to say good-night."

"You're crazy! Did you just jump the balcony?"

"Definitely crazy. Over you. And no, I didn't jump the balcony, I climbed up from the parking lot below."

"Sure you did."

Kirsten backed away from the sliding door, allowing Pierre to step inside her room. She looked incredible, with her white unbuttoned uniform shirt allowing a peek at her perfectly sculptured breasts.

He walked straight up to her, wrapping his arms around her waist, lifting her up a little, while his lips connected with hers.

She felt warm and smelled delicious. She always did. Her lips parted, allowing his tongue to enter her mouth. She tasted of toothpaste. He slowly ran his tongue between her upper front teeth and the inside of her top lip. Her arms came up encircling his neck.

He lifted Kirsten off the floor, delicately carrying her backwards towards one of the beds. He had a quick glimpse of her suitcase laying open on the other bed. Good! He didn't want to drop her on top of the suitcase. That would be funny as all hell but an instant mood killer.

She accepted his direction, letting herself be deposited on the bed. Kirsten separated her legs, allowing room for Pierre to join her on the bed. He climbed up on his knees, between her legs. He let go of her waist, sliding his hands inside her shirt. She had already removed her bra, so the palms of his hands were rewarded with the delicious feel of her warm breasts, cupping them, gently finding her nipples, rolling them with his fingers. Her nipples instantly hardening.

Kirsten moaned. Her back arched and she shifted her hips.

Pierre kissed her tenderly, using only his lips. Kirsten darted her tongue in and out of his mouth, encouraging more passion.

He let go of her nipple, running his hand down to his belt. Pierre hastily undid his black belt, unbuttoned his pants and lowered his zipper in one continuous motion. He stuck his hand down the back of his pants and boxer shorts, pushing both down towards his ankles. He remembered he still had his shoes on. He used one foot to wedge his shoe off, then the second one followed. Then he wiggled his hips, sending his pants and boxer shorts down past his knees. He was terribly excited—and no surprise there—hard as Italian granite.

He realized Kirsten was fully aware of what he'd been doing. She'd said nothing, she just laid there patiently waiting for Pierre to be ready, with her breasts exposed in the soft twilight and her thighs spread apart in anticipation of his arrival. She was not wearing any underwear.

The anticipation was killing him. It was so delicious, it was downright painful.

Although he was panting like a wolf in heat, Pierre resisted the powerful urge to just enter her and fuck her silly.

He could be inside her in less than two seconds. She was so ready for him, no doubt, but that would not be fair to her. Instead, he decided to be gentle and dedicate himself to what he knew was going to make her feel good. Kneeling alongside the bed, he lowered his face between her legs. He caught a glimpse of Kirsten looking down at him. Pierre gently caressed the inside of her thighs with both hands, feeling her warm skin. This time he didn't want to tease her. He immediately stuck his tongue between her lips, going inside her half an inch, as far as his tongue would go.

She gasped as his tongue parted her lips.

"*Aaah*," Kirsten approved, wiggling her hips.

He moved up, using his tongue to arouse her. He found her clit, helping himself with his hand, spreading her lips more so his tongue would have direct access to her center of pleasure. However tired Kirsten was after the long day, his stimulation and his caresses seemed to be working the magic getting her out of her daze.

Her abdominal muscles were tight as a tennis racket again. Pierre liked that, a clear indication that he was doing a good job getting her excited. Gee, tired as she was, it hadn't taken her long to get all turned on again. Kirsten's hands reached down for Pierre, gently clutching handfuls of his black hair. He licked her clit with more speed, encouraged by her growing excitement. His tongue urged her closer to an orgasm, her muscles tensing, spreading her legs wider inviting Pierre to lick her even deeper.

Pierre was indomitable. He only had one purpose in life at that moment, to continue stimulating this angel until she flew headfirst into a world of pleasure. But while she got there, he wanted her to enjoy the drive, not just the destination, as the cliché illustrated.

"Ohh, Gawd, Pieeeerre!" She suddenly cried, taking him by surprise. He hadn't been expecting her climax just yet. She appeared to tighten all the muscles in her body, using her legs to lift her hips off the bed, pushing her mound against his face with increasing force.

Yes! Pierre licked faster.

He decided not to use his fingers inside her since she was already climaxing. He'd missed the moment where his fingers would have played a significant role in triggering her climax. Inserting her fingers in her at this moment would not add much to her pleasure, and with her violent spasms, he was bound to scratch her and hurt her. That was definitely something to avoid.

Kirsten kept spasming and convulsing for what appeared an interminable length of time. Ultimately, her breathing began slowing down, her buttocks settled on the bed again, her hands releasing their grip on Pierre's hair. He briefly considered starting again, but Kirsten appeared to be totally knocked out. She was completely limp, although still breathing hard. There was no reaction whatsoever from her when he licked her soft outer lips with a couple of final brush strokes.

The long day and their lovemaking had wiped her out. Pierre sat up looking at her. Kirsten was a sight worthy of the Louvre museum in Paris. She was barely visible in the dim light of the room, yet even in the twilight she was pale and blonde and absolutely adorable. Her body was so perfectly proportioned, Pierre soaked in the pleasant proportions of her breasts, her waist, her hips. She was not just a woman; she was a goddess. Her eyes were closed and her chest still rose and fell at a fast pace, in the dissipating phases of her orgasm.

Pierre reached past her, pulling the comforter and the blanket and sheets over the sleeping Princess. Kirsten rolled on her side, assuming the fetal position, resting her hands under her face, as if praying.

The young aviator covered her up, climbing into bed slipping under the covers behind her. He moved slowly, so as not to bounce the bed and her with it. Her incredibly sexy ass and her back were being offered to him in all their beauty.

Spooning. What an exquisite concept.

He reached over, wrapping his arm around her, cupping her breast for a second or two. It was soft and hot. Pierre was still hard as a rock. He moved his hand down to feel Kirsten's butt, enjoying the intense heat radiating from her. He grabbed a hold of himself and directed his stubbornly hard member down towards the area where Kirsten's buttocks met. He might as well fall asleep between her legs.

She was soaked. He inched his hips forward in slow motion, using his hand to direct his member where he wanted to be. The tip of his manhood found the entry into Kirsten. Pierre moved forward a little more and with one slow, deliberate thrust, he felt himself entering Kirsten. Not that he had intended going inside her, but his primal instinct had taken over.

She didn't make a sound, but he felt her gently pushing her buttocks back against him. That turned him on something wicked. He pulled out and went back in, repeating the motion over and over. Kirsten began softly pumping her ass against him while laying on her side. It only took a few seconds for the incredible situation to drive Pierre to the edge of oblivion. Her derriere was such an incredible turn on for him. He thought she'd been satisfied for the night, but the motion of her ass against him told him maybe she still had some desire left in her.

Twenty more ins and outs and Pierre knew he was done. His body took away control from him, launching an orgasm he knew he couldn't stop no matter what he did. His lower abdomen tightened with great force, his body independently increasing the frequency of the thrusting in and out of Kirsten.

"OohGod, Kirsten!" he said, while rapidly pumping against her buttocks. He held on to her slim waist with both hands while his hardness emptied itself inside her. Kirsten thrust her rear end back, meeting his hard shaft one final time before going perfectly still.

Pierre allowed his head to collapse on the pillow next to Kirsten. His face touching her hair, breathing rapidly on her neck. He was done, wiped. Exhausted and satisfied. Wrapping his arms around this gorgeous sexy creature he decided to fall asleep like that—spooning. He reached down with his hand, feeling the exquisite form of her buttock. It was tight and taunt like a helium-filled balloon. And wet and slippery. His orgasm had overflowed onto her buttocks. He kept his hand there for a few moments, taking in the delicious sensation.

A thought crossed his mind. What about an alarm?

Oh, shit. Not again.

He didn't have his cell phone with him, having left it in his room. He could only hope Kirsten had made provisions for a wakeup call or set up an alarm clock. He was just going to have to depend on her. No way in hell he was going to return to his bedroom just now to fetch his phone. Pierre was enjoying her warmth and was deliciously satisfied, hugging Kirsten from behind, with his shaft still inside her. Like hell he was going to get up from this heaven and setup a wakeup call. At that point, he was willing to risk a no-show for the crew call in the morning. No, he couldn't risk Kirsten getting in trouble not showing up for crew call. Fuck it, he'd just stay awake all night and wake her up come morning.

Kirsten had stopped moving. She was firmly wedged against him, her exquisite hot buttocks squeezed tightly against his crotch. He was still hard and deep inside her, although he knew that as soon as he began to fall asleep, he would shrink and slip out of her.

The phone rang.

What the fuck?

Pierre came out of a deep sleep in an instant. It took him a couple of additional seconds to remember where he was. Holy crap, he'd fallen asleep! Kirsten's naked back was still pressed warmly against his chest.

The phone kept ringing.

He jumped up off the bed, moving fast to answer the stupid thing.

This was becoming a goddamn annoying routine.

"Hullo!?" he mumbled into the device.

"Good morning!" The unnaturally-cheerful robotic voice greeted. "This is your wakeup call!"

Aah, crap. He put down the receiver.

Kirsten was stirring, like a kitten, slowly turning to look at him. "Good morning, lover."

"Good morning, sweetheart. Sorry that woke you up."

"Is it time already? We have to go to work today, remember?" She slowly leaned up on one elbow. One of her beautiful breasts was uncovered, flirting with him.

"Unfortunately we have to."

She pulled the bed cover, wrapping it around her naked body. "Better scoot back to you room!" Kirsten stood, covering herself with the comforter, walking towards the bathroom, dragging the bedcover. She shut the door behind her.

Now what? Pierre checked the bedside clock. Less than an hour until they had to meet in the lobby. Great. He considered going out the front door into the hallway and returning to his room, but decided to jump the balcony again instead. He pulled on his pants then reached for his shoes, shirt and underwear. The sliding door to the balcony was still open from when he arrived. He stepped out into the balcony, realizing Kirsten was not in any hurry to leave the bathroom. Now the parking lot was busy, with cars moving about. He threw his clothing and shoes around into his own balcony, then climbed over wondering if anyone down below was going to see him and call the police.

That would be real interesting. How would he explain that?

Pierre returned to his unused room, going back in the bathroom and jumping in the shower, allowing himself the luxury of reviewing the events of the previous night. Damn, he'd made love to Kirsten again! Yet they'd not exchanged ten words. That had to change. He wanted to know everything about her. He also didn't want her to think he was only interested in sex and nothing else. She'd been totally wiped out after the long day, yet he'd still been able to pleasure her. That gave him a totally irrational feeling of tremendous satisfaction.

THE CREW MET IN the lobby forty-five minutes later. When Pierre showed up, Kirsten and the other three flight attendants were already there, smoking-hot cups of coffee in hand.

"Good morning ladies!"

The women greeting him appeared much more alive than the last time he'd seen them. "Only two legs today," he remarked. "Heck of a lot shorter day than yesterday."

"Thank God," one of the flight attendants replied, the brunette Pierre had helped with her luggage.

"Yesterday was brutal," Kirsten finally spoke.

"Were you able to get some rest?" Pierre asked her, with an intimate smile.

Kirsten shot him a pretend angry stare. "Yees, thank you. Eventually. How about you, how'd you sleep?"

"Wonderful," he stared in her eyes. "To tell the truth, I slept like a baby."

"You don't strike me at all like the type who would sleep like a baby," she replied. "Or let others sleep like a baby." Her blue eyes were mere slits.

The other flight attendants appeared oblivious to the intimate exchange taking place right under their noses.

"But you're still tired?" Pierre was enjoying the exchange. He really hadn't had much of a chance to converse with her in the room before bailing out. He was hypnotized by the sound of her voice. There was something about it that was in perfect harmony with him.

"No, I'm not tired. I slept enough. Once I finally got to sleep, that is." She was teasing him like a high school girlfriend now.

"Oh? What kept you awake?"

"An *incubus*."

"A what?"

"I know what *that* is!" One of the other flight attendants chipped in enthusiastically. "That's the demon who visits women in their sleep appearing in the middle of the night and has sex with you. And he's rumored to have an enormous ... *thingie*."

That caught the attention of the other women.

"Is that right?" Pierre knew exactly what an incubus was. He'd read enough literature to know the legend and the mythology of the incubus, but he decided to play dumb and see where this went.

The other brunette came alive, entering the conversation. "A thingie? You mean a hard-on?"

"Yeah, that's what she meant," Kirsten explained. "An incubus was generally identified by its unnaturally large penis."

"And that's what kept you up last night?" Pierre asked. He was amused. So now he was an incubus? He didn't really think of himself as having an unnaturally large penis, but if Kirsten thought so, so much the better.

"Yep, that's what kept me awake." She looked at him with a defiant smile.

"And did you enjoy the dream?" He didn't want the rest of the crew getting wind of his developing relationship with Kirsten, but he was enjoying teasing her. And she appeared to relish teasing him back.

"No, I didn't enjoy it quite as much as I could have, the visitor kept me awake when I wanted to sleep."

"The visitor? You mean the incubus?"

"Yes, I meant the incubus."

"Did you know 'incubo' in Italian means 'nightmare'?"

"No. How would I know that?" Kirsten was just a little shorter than the other three flight attendants.

"In Spain they say that he who is hungry thinks of bread."

"What's that supposed to mean?" She was immaculate in her dark grey uniform. Not one hair out of place, perfect make up.

How the devil did she manage to look so good this early in the morning?

He'd felt rushed just shaving and showering. Yet here she was looking like a Victoria's Secret catalog model brand-new, fresh out of the box.

"What's that supposed to mean? It means that if you're hungry, you will desire some bread. I guess if you dream of an incubus, you probably desire what he has to offer."

"You are naughty," she threw out, her eyes flashing defiantly.

"I'm not the one who brought up the incubus."

The brunette came alive. "Wait! Kirsten, you were visited by an incubus in your dreams last night and you wanted to get some sleep instead? What the hell is wrong with you, girl, are you insane?"

Kirsten addressed the brunette, whose name was Alison, while still staring at Pierre. "Yeah, that's coz I was tired. But let me tell you, a visit by an incubus can be overrated."

"Oh, I don't think so! Are you crazy, Kirsten? I could really use one of those visits, overrated or not!" Alison's eyes had a spark to them. "Next time he visits you, send him over to me if you don't want him!"

"Were you visited by this incubus friend of yours only last night?" Pierre asked innocently, "Or is that a routine occurrence?" Pierre scanned the lobby. No sign of Mark yet.

"Oh, this incubus friend of mine has paid me a couple of visits lately and he seems to be rather persistent."

"Is that a good thing?" Pierre teased.

"Yeah, it can be a very good thing," Kirsten added, provocatively running her tongue along her upper lip. Only Pierre saw it.

"You bet your ass, it could be a good thing!" Alison contributed again, oblivious as to the real nature of the exchange.

Pierre smiled, studying Alison for a moment. Well, here was somebody who hadn't gotten any for a while, that much was obvious. She was not his type, but she was cute. Hopefully, she'd connect with someone soon, someone who could scratch that itch for her.

"Here's Mark!" Alison announced.

The captain made his appearance pulling his wheelies. He didn't wear his uniform hat. His hair was still wet from the shower. Neatly combed, but wet.

"Good morning ladies!" He chirped. "Any coffee around here?"

Cripes, he really thinks he's a Sultan addressing his harem.

"Hey Mark," Pierre greeted back. "Sorry, old boy. No coffee anywhere around these parts. The girls already drank it all."

"We'll get a pot going once we get on the airplane," Alison offered.

"Is the van here?" Marvelous Mark ignored Allison's coffee offer, walking past his crew, heading for the front door of the hotel.

Pierre noticed the behavior bordering on rude, not happy with it.

Why couldn't these guys just practice some goddamned manners?

The flight attendants quickly organized themselves, grabbing their wheelies and following their captain.

Kirsten was the tail end of the Conga line.

"*Overrated, eh?*" Pierre whispered in Kirsten's ear, as she passed him on her way out of the lobby.

She didn't answer him, just grinned, her dimples illuminating her face.

"Overrated!? That was real clever. First chance I get I'm gonna spank your derriere, you little stinker! You won't be able to sit down for a week. And I will derive enormous pleasure smacking your cute little butt."

"You do that; you'll get in trouble. That's a Level Two security threat. Remember? 'Unwanted physical contact'? I'll have you arrested."

Pierre laughed out loud, attracting the attention of the flight attendant in front of Kirsten, who turned quickly to see the source of the laughter.

The International Civil Aviation Organization, known as ICAO, had issued guidance booklets for airline crews on how to deal with threats onboard airliners, and what Kirsten had quoted, a Level Two threat, was the type dealing with unwanted physical contact. These booklets were easily Googled on the Internet. Any unwanted physical contact with a crew member would most likely land the perpetrator in jail with a felony charge and a huge fine. Spanking definitely qualified as such.

Unless—of course—the spanking was consensual and done in the privacy of their own bedroom. Pierre made a mental note to revisit the topic. One day, he was going to give this little angel a good paddling. But definitely, only if she wanted it. That, he mused, would be highly entertaining and erotic. He felt himself getting hard at the thought. In his heart, he suspected she'd ultimately beg for it.

He followed the crew to the curbside, waiting patiently for the rest of the flight attendants to deliver their luggage to the van driver. Marvelous had already taken station inside the van, in the middle seat by the window. He obviously wanted to park himself next to one of his four young flight attendants.

Some things never changed.

Pierre waited until only he and Kirsten were left standing on the curb. "The security levels only apply when we're on the airplane, sweetheart, they don't apply when we're in bed. You'll still get your spanking."

"Tuff talk, eh?" She raised her eyebrows, smiling, then climbed inside the van.

The drive to the airport was longer this time. Traffic had appeared.

Pierre sat shotgun with the driver. Kirsten ended up sitting in the middle seat next to Alison, who was next to Marvelous Mark. The captain kept up a monologue with her all the way to the airport, obviously boring the bejeezus out of the poor girl. Once the driver dropped them off at the airport the four flight attendants and the two pilots marched as a team to the security line. They entered the lane labeled 'Known Crewmember,' advancing to the front and bypassing the TSA inspection.

Pierre considered the TSA one gigantic pain in the ass. As well as a joke. The government had wanted to reassure the American public that something was actually being done to protect them after the attack against New York, and the answer had been the TSA. Good intentions, perhaps, but totally ineffective. If anyone with real military training desired to get around the security at most airports in America, they could do so without as much as a second glance at the TSA.

But what the heck, the American traveling public felt safe because Big Brother was protecting everyone with the TSA. Pierre did not feel any safer.

Having everyone remove their shoes going through security was a fucking joke, far as he was concerned. In his opinion, all the TSA circus had accomplished was depleting the ranks of Walmart greeters by making them government employees.

He followed Marvelous Mark down the concourse, with the four women trailing behind them. Naturally, their gate was at the far end of the terminal. Never failed. The terminal was already packed with people, with every flight scrambling to leave within minutes of each other.

Pierre reviewed the past two days while walking alongside Mark. He and Kirsten had connected in every way a couple could connect. Well, physically at least. He was totally infatuated with her. They hadn't had too much verbal communication yet, but what the hell, their physical communication had been mind-altering. He couldn't ask for better. And he could sense she liked him as well. Or at least it seemed that way. He was mentally already making plans for their immediate future. He had to get her schedule so they could plan time together. And her phone number. Definitely. Christ, he hadn't asked her for her number yet? Great going. What an idiot. If they became separated, how in God's name was he going to find her? He felt panic.

Easy, just call Crew Sked and ask for the name of the crew on this here flight. Dumbass. He just wasn't thinking straight for some reason. He wanted to take her out to an elegant Italian restaurant for dinner, and take her shopping at the Mall; he would treat her to everything she desired he was going to spend an obscene amount of money on her. All sorts of exciting activities. Then there was Oshkosh this month. She may want to join him for a visit to the famous aviation gathering. The prospects were many and definitely exciting. Maybe he was jumping the gun, but having been without steady female companionship for three years had him acting like a teenager in heat. And he was so looking forward to exploring her mind.

The crew reached their gate, also known as '34B.' The gate area was crowded to capacity. All sorts of travelers sitting and standing everywhere, patiently awaiting their flight to Milwaukee. Pierre eyeballed the crowd. Young people sitting on the ground wearing headsets staring into their laptops, carry-on bags cluttering every corner of the place, a long line in front of the customer service rep at the counter. Not a single empty seat in the gate area. He observed sadly how nearly everyone in sight was engaged with some sort of electronic screen. Cell phones, iPads, iPods, laptops, etc.

Whatever happened to human interaction?

Marvelous Mark marched straight up to the counter, bypassing the long line of passengers waiting for service.

"Good morning!" Mark greeted, extending his airline badge to the customer service agent. The gate agent cut off her conversation with a passenger in midsentence, reaching for Mark's badge. She looked at it, checking the name on the ID against a page on her clipboard.

Pierre followed suit, flashing the customer service agent his own badge, followed by each of the four flight attendants, who did the same. The gate agent confirmed everyone was on the manifest, leaving the podium to unlock the jet bridge door. The crew descended down the carpeted jetway, arriving to a brand-new gleaming white and blue Airbus A321 for their flight to Milwaukee.

The pilots entered the flight deck, climbing into their respective seats. In airline parlance, each began 'making his nest.' Pierre placed his flight bag to his right, into the specially designed space. He pulled out his airline-issued iPad, snapping it into place right below his side window. He would use it to look at his charts and his manuals throughout the flight. His headset followed, plugging it into the airplane and inserting it in his ear.

The ritual each pilot followed to prepare the airplane for flight was the same every time they flew. The short hop from Madison to Milwaukee was about thirty minutes' flight time, followed by another hour flight down to St. Louis. After which, Pierre was scheduled to have three days off. He already had all kinds of plans he was contemplating with Kirsten. Aah, life was good. He forced himself to concentrate on the business of getting the airplane ready to fly, deliberately attempting to force the irresistible sensual girl from his mind.

"Can I get you guys something to drink? Coffee? Water?"

Kirsten was standing between the two pilots.

Forcing her from his mind? Yeah, right.

His heartbeat accelerated. "You're wonderful. I'd love a Coke." He turned to look at her, she had removed her uniform jacket and looked totally desirable in her white blouse, dark vest and red scarf. Ah, Pierre wondered, could that be the same white uniform blouse she'd worn last night when they made love?

Of course not, what was he thinking? That particular shirt had become one wrinkled mess. Kirsten usually worked coach, so it was a real nice surprise having her come up to the flight deck. That meant she was going to be working the First Class cabin. He might get to see her again during the flights. That boosted his spirits.

"I'll take that coffee you offered," Marvelous Mark answered.

"Coffee and a Coke," she chirped. "Coming right up." She left the flight deck without any sort of intimate exchange between them. No personal look. Nothing. Cold as ice.

Damn.

Pierre was a little disappointed. He returned his attention to the business at hand. The weather in Milwaukee stunk. Low ceilings with fog. And from the forecast it seemed the weather was not going to improve by the time they were due to arrive there. It was his leg, so he programmed the onboard computer—the MCDU—the Multipurpose Control and Display Unit, for the flight. Automation was very advanced on the Airbus, which he loved. He felt like Luke Skywalker, in the original Star Wars movie, flying the most advanced state-of-the-art machines in human history. Shit, he even had Chewbacca for a captain sitting right next to him.

Kirsten returned within a couple of minutes, handing him a can of Coke, a plastic cup with ice and a cocktail napkin with the Worldwide Airlines blue logo printed on it.

"Here you go," she said, smiling.

Pierre's heart missed a beat. His eyes momentarily connecting with hers. Volumes of unspoken words passed between them.

Then she turned, extending a Styrofoam cup of coffee to Marvelous Mark.

"Thank you, honey," he replied.

Kirsten rapidly retreated out of the flight deck without another look.

Pierre didn't like ice in his drinks, he felt ice diluted the flavor of whatever he was drinking, be it whisky, vodka or Coke. He looked for a place to ditch the ice Kirsten had brought him in the clear plastic cup. Nowhere to put it really. He placed the plastic cup in a small holder designed for it. What the heck, he'd just drink it out of the can. He knew then it was going to be a long day, trying to keep Kirsten out of his mind.

FORTY MINUTES LATER THEY were cruising eastbound at nearly 600 miles per hour, flying over a solid layer of smooth white clouds extending as far as they could see. The sky was clear and blue above the cloud level. An incredible view from the flight deck, one very few people ever got to see.

Pierre handed Marvelous Mark a small piece of paper, where he'd jotted down the weather in Milwaukee. He'd obtained that information on the radio from the Automatic Terminal Information Service being broadcast by Mitchell Field in Milwaukee. The pilots referred to it as ATIS.

Marvelous Mark read the report. "Looks like the weather is going to shit in Milwaukee."

"Yep. It's down to CAT III minimums already." Category III minimums, also known as CAT-three, was a weather condition where the visibility was down to almost nothing. The airline standard operating procedures dictated that in such weather the autopilots would have to fly the approach all the way down to the runway. The autoland system on the Airbus was so sophisticated that the airplane would also track the centerline of the runway during the flare and the rollout. It would even apply the brakes automatically after touchdown.

"CAT III, ah? You can go ahead and fly the approach, if you want," Mark generously offered.

Pierre said nothing, he just stared at his captain. Was he serious? Company procedures required that every autoland had to be flown by the autopilots under the monitoring eye of the captain, not the first officer. This was not meant to imply that first officers were incapable of monitoring an autoland, it was done this way because the airline wanted the crew to get used to one way of doing things. When a crew flew one of these approaches, they got very close to the ground in low visibility and consequently had little margin for error, consequently, it was safer to have the pilots always performing the same duties during one of these approaches.

By offering Pierre to fly the approach, Marvelous Mark was flagrantly violating company procedures. That made Pierre very uncomfortable. Without a doubt, Mark was doing it to be a buddy, a generous captain.

"I gotta go take a leak," Mark politely announced. "That coffee got me." He reached down for the intercom handset. "Your airplane and you got the radios."

"I got the airplane and the radios," Pierre acknowledged. Flight decks in airliners were very regimented, and this sort of control changeover was standard among fliers. That way there was never any doubt who was in charge of actually flying the machine.

"Kirsten, honey," Mark spoke into the handset, "I need to use the facilities, could you gals please come up and relieve me?"

Airline procedures required a flight attendant to be present in the flight deck with the pilot flying once the other pilot left the flight deck. That way, the pilot flying the airplane was not left alone. The idea was to protect the man at the controls.

Flight attendants hated the procedure. First of all, they really did not want to know anything about the pilots' bathroom habits. They also didn't want to be interrupted in the middle of their service by some idiot lacking enough common sense not to drink gallons of water. Once the pilots summoned them, two flight attendants had to make their way to the flight deck door. One of them would call the flight deck using the intercom, letting the pilots know they were ready.

Next, the pilot needing the visit to the lav would look through the door viewing port, confirming that the person standing outside the flight deck door was indeed one of their flight attendants. At this point, the door would open, and one of the two flight attendants would enter the flight deck. The departing pilot would then exit the flight deck, making an effort to keep the door open a minimum length of time. The second flight attendant would stand guard while the exchange took place.

This procedure had seemed ridiculous to the Europeans for the longest time, and none of their airlines practiced the routine, until a German Airbus pilot deliberately crashed his airplane full of passengers into the Pyrenees while his captain had gone out to the blueroom to relieve himself. Immediately following that crash, all the European airlines adopted the American procedure.

Another regulation called for the pilot flying to don his oxygen mask anytime the other pilot left the flight deck if the airplane was above 25,000 feet of altitude. Pierre thought about reaching for his oxygen mask, only to realize that it would not be necessary. They were cruising at 21,000 feet, hence the oxygen mask was not needed.

Marvelous Mark climbed out of his seat. He put his eye against the door viewing port lens, confirming that Kirsten was on the other side of the flight deck door, then he opened it.

The swap took but a few seconds. Kirsten entered the flight deck, shutting the door behind her with a 'click.' This procedure had originated after the terror attacks against New York. The idea was to have an additional body in the flight deck to protect the pilot flying the airplane. Good concept, although not really practical. A ninety-pound flight attendant would not present too much of an obstacle to a determined assailant.

"Hello, lover boy," she purred, walking up to Pierre, turning and seductively sliding her derriere on top of his lap.

Pierre was totally surprised by this. The autopilot was flying the airplane, so she was not directly interfering with the operation of the flight, but he still had not expected Kirsten to become a sexy kitten at the bat of an eye the instant she entered the flight deck. Not that he didn't like it, but it was just the wrong place to be playing games.

Kirsten placed her arms around his neck, pulling herself against him. Her lips found his and she felt hot and exciting, instantly rekindling all of the experiences of the previous night. Pierre wrapped his arms around her waist, enjoying the feel of her lips and the taste of her tongue, which she was using to explore the inside of his mouth.

Holy shit.

The kiss lasted for a long time, making Pierre uncomfortable. He opened his eyes, peeking past her golden hair at his Primary Flight Display on the instrument panel. Much as he was enjoying having Kirsten on his lap, and the exciting taste of her mouth, he was still in charge of an airliner with almost two hundred passengers. He had the responsibility for all these people.

Everything looked good far as the instruments were concerned.

"You are a gorgeous creature," he finally stated, staring into her eyes.

"So are you," she replied.

"I'm sorry, but this incubus doesn't have time to pleasure you at this very moment."

"Incubus? You liked that, eh? Oh, and exactly why are you unable to pleasure me at this moment? This thing has an autopilot, doesn't it? And you are an incubus, after all."

What was she suggesting, that they go at each other right then and there? And how could he make love to her in the flight deck? That could be a real challenge. He momentarily indulged in the fantasy, thinking about it. Maybe if she removed her undies and straddled him while facing him, yea, that might work. Naw, she'd have to lift her skirt way up around her waist in order to do that. That would take time, and time was something they didn't have. Mark would be back any second now. Although the concept was incredibly exciting, it was also totally asinine. There was absolutely no way in hell he was going to do anything as stupid as that when he was in charge of the airplane—what in God's pajamas was he thinking?

"Yea, it actually has two autopilots, although it's only using one right now, but I have to stay right here monitoring all that's going on, and you need to get your delicious little fanny over there."

"So, you don't want to fuck me?"

Oh, Christ.

"Believe me, I'd love nothing more. But we just can't do it right now."

Kirsten laughed, seeing the look of concern on his face. "Relax! I was just messing with you." She bent forward, kissing Pierre on the lips again.

Pierre bit her lower lip.

"Aaw!" Kirsten cried, jerking back away from Pierre. "You bit me!"

"And I would spank your butt if I had the chance to do so this very moment."

"Not nice!"

"You are a very distracting force, milady. You gotta behave yourself."

"*Milady?* How formal."

"Kirsten, behave!"

The intercom chime interrupted them. Marvelous Mark was outside the door, waiting to be let in.

"Bully!" Kirsten chirped, getting up from Pierre's lap, reaching down to his crotch, playfully pinching his phenomenal erection.

That just about sent him into orbit.

Too much of a distraction. He checked his electronic instrument panel to ensure all was as it should be, catching Kirsten straightening her skirt on the periphery of his field of vision. She stuck something in his hand before turning for the door.

Pierre looked down at the object. He was holding a pair of white silky panties.

Goodness gracious! She had removed them and given them to him!

His heartbeat jumped. That was a friggin incredible turn-on!

Kirsten peeked through the peephole installed on the door, confirming that indeed, Marvelous Mark was on the other side of the flight deck door patiently waiting to be let back in his office.

Pierre unlocked the flight deck door with the console switch.

Touching her smarting lip, Kirsten opened the door, allowing the captain to enter the cockpit, then she quickly stepped out, shutting the reinforced bullet-proof door behind her.

Pierre wiped his lips with the back of his hand, looking at it. Cherry red lipstick was smeared on his wrist. Dang, all he needed was for Marvelous Mark to notice lipstick on his lips right after Kirsten was in there. It wouldn't take a genius to realize they'd been kissing. That would most definitely not go down well with Marvelous Mark. Smiling, Pierre suspected Mark would probably have a bigger problem realizing he wasn't getting any than being angry at the potential risks to the flight.

Regardless, avoid conflict at all costs.

He admired the small totally sexy feminine undergarment in his hand, reaching for his messenger leather bag, discretely stuffing it away before the skipper had a chance to see it.

"All good?" Marvelous asked.

"All's well. No changes."

"Good! We better start setting up for the arrival. I got the airplane. You got the radio."

Pierre acknowledged. He then turned up the volume on the radio with the ATIS frequency. He copied it onto another piece of paper. Surprise, surprise. The weather in Milwaukee had gone down so low, it had just closed the airport.

"Mark, Milwaukee airport just closed."

"No shit?"

"Nope. ATIS just called it." Pierre was relieved because with the airport shutdown, he would not have to fly an approach that Marvelous Mark should have flown. That took him off the hot seat. He really didn't like doing anything that went against airline procedures when it came to approaches.

"All right, you've got the airplane and the radios, I've gotta call dispatch."

Pierre confirmed the command.

Marvelous Mark got on the other radio, talking to the company dispatcher.

Pierre took advantage of the break to review Kirsten's visit to the flight deck. She must've suspected Mark was eventually going to use the bathroom sometime during the flight. That's why she switched to First Class instead of working coach. Manipulating little angel, that way she could come up to the flight deck and be alone with Pierre. He smiled. Calculating little stinker. The realization pleased him enormously. Had the little rascal truly thought he was going to make love to her in the flight deck while Mark was out? Nice thought, but totally out of the fucking question. Of course, with the cockpit door locked,

Mark had no way to come back in and interrupt them. However, if the captain's request to return to the flight deck was not honored within a few seconds the man would go apeshit and then the situation could get real interesting. And besides, the cockpit voice recorder had it all on tape. Oh, great.

"I'm back."

"What's up?"

"We're skipping Milwaukee and going directly to St. Louis."

"No shit?"

"No shit. General Mitchell field is closed. Doesn't look like it's going to be opening up anytime soon. We're going to St. Louis."

"Fantastic!" That eliminated one leg from their day. They had been scheduled to fly a little under two hours that day, but because of the weather, it had now been reduced to one hour. Regardless, they were still going to see a paycheck for five hours each. Their union contract guaranteed that.

"So, we're bypassing Milwaukee?" Pierre smiled. The morning was turning out to be rather pleasant.

"That, we are. You want to ask ATC for our new clearance?"

"**WANT TO GO OUT** to dinner and a movie tonight?"

Kirsten stood outside the jet bridge, ready to head for the employees' parking lot.

Marvelous Mark and the other three flight attendants had already bolted away from the gate, not to be seen again.

Pierre still didn't have her cell phone number.

"You're sweet, Pierre. Not tonight. I have some errands to run, and I'm tired. I need to catch up on my sleep. You've been a bad boy. Didn't get enough sleep the past two nights."

"Bad boy?" He smiled. "You seemed to like it. What was it you called it, the 'incubus' visit?"

"Like it? I have no words. I loved it," she stated. "But I am exhausted."

"I don't even have your phone number." He was feeling disappointed. Now that he had three days off he wanted to spend as much time as possible with Kirsten. He knew a delicious German restaurant they could visit. They could go to the movies. And above all, they could make passionate love every hour of the day. He had a lot of stamina, that was true. Maybe he'd really wiped her out with their lovemaking of the two previous nights. "Gimme your cell phone number." He touched the screen of his Galaxy smartphone, bringing up the dialer.

Kirsten gave him her number, which he typed into his dialer, calling her.

When her phone rang, Pierre ended the call. "There, now you have my number as well."

"You are the most exciting pilot I've ever met," she replied. "The most exciting anything, really."

"You're adorable, Kirsten. You are a very special woman as well. I have become addicted to you."

She stared at him with a serious look.

Is your car in the employees' parking?"

"Yes, I have my car here. Do you want to come over to my place tomorrow?"

"To your place?"

"Where else? I already learned you don't enjoy sex in the cockpit."

The mention of sex got his attention. "I don't enjoy sex in the cockpit? You're gonna get your butt whipped. You knew I couldn't do that. Much as I wanted. I'd love to come by your place tomorrow, though. Just give me your address. What time?"

She smiled. "Around noon? I'll text you where I live."

"Noon's good. Are you too tired to drive? I can give you a ride home."

"That's sweet, but no. As I said, I have my car here. I can drive."

Pierre was still not sure any of this had really happened. Had the beautiful creature in uniform standing there actually spent two nights with him while he made wild love to her? His mind kept suggesting that nothing was real, that none of this had happened. It had all been a figment of his imagination. Totally unreal, really. And now she was ready to disappear.

They began walking towards the main concourse, both of them pulling their respective bags.

"Seems like two seconds ago you were standing next to me at *Viera's* in St. Louis."

Kirsten smiled. "It seems that way, doesn't it? And you did a lot of things in those two seconds."

"All of them pleasant, I hope."

"Oh, absolutely. Very pleasant. You've done something incredible to me."

Something incredible? He liked the sound of that.

"Like what?"

"I was a one-orgasm girl. My entire life I've been that way."

"Your entire life? You're only twenty-two. You couldn't possibly have that much experience."

"Wouldn't you like to know?"

"How old were you your first time?"

"My first time?" She thought for a moment. "Not that it's any of your business, but I was sixteen."

"So, anytime you've ever made love since you were sixteen you've only had one orgasm?"

"Yeah, if that even. Until two nights ago. You blew my mind. I didn't know I could come more than once. I was completely convinced more than one climax was a physical impossibility for me."

Pierre smiled, remembering Kirsten pinned down on the bed in the hotel in Minneapolis, violently pulling his hair in an attempt to make him stop. "I just had to unlock all the passion you have in you."

"I still don't know how you did that, Pierre, but I want more of it. So much more. Just not now. You've sucked all the energy out of me. I've gotta go home and sleep for thirty hours straight."

Pierre loved everything that came out of her mouth. *She wanted so much more?*

That in itself was an incredibly stimulating turn on.

They boarded the employee bus for the five-minute ride to the parking lot.

"Do you mind if I take a picture of you?" He wanted a shot of Kirsten in her uniform to link to her number on his smartphone.

"No! I look terrible. Why do you want it?"

"For your phone number."

"Here, I'll send you one you can use."

PIERRE DROVE HOME FROM Lambert Field in his 2001 English racing-green Camaro convertible. He'd found the car in a small town in Iowa, for a knock-out killer price. Only 9,000 miles in a ten-year-old car. His plans of eventually moving back to Phoenix had to include a convertible, so he'd found one. St. Louis was not really the place to own a convertible. The weather just didn't cooperate.

Drizzle running across his windshield reaffirmed his belief that convertibles were not designed for the Midwest. Taking Kirsten for a nice drive with the top down would have to wait for a dry summer day.

Kirsten, that lovely creature the gods had bestowed upon him. His mind reviewed at triple speed all the events that transpired between them in a short couple of days. He could see her naked skin, her blond hair scattered on the pillow. Kissing her in the elevator.

Friggin unbelievable. Thank you, God!

Pierre pulled into his parking space in front of the townhome he rented in St. Charles. With his generous income, he could afford to buy a house in town, but that was not going to happen because his plans to live in Arizona took precedence. In spite of the weather, there were some things he did like about St. Louis. It was a pretty town, Pierre loved the seasons and the trees, but he needed a change. And Arizona was that change. He'd gone to school there and now it was time to go back.

He also really liked that girl. He briefly wondered if the attraction was mutual to the degree that he felt it. Her going home just now after their trip puzzled him. He would've loved having her join him for the rest of the day and the evening. Hell, particularly for the night. Yes, that would've been wonderful. They could've slept together all night and he would've spoiled her. God, the thought of having her sleep in his arms without having to rush down to the lobby in the morning was a delicious thought, never mind the sex. He'd even imagined sleeping in front of his fireplace, his arms wrapped protectively around her.

And no wake-up calls.

He'd already planned a quick stop at Trader Joe's for some cheese, bread and wine. Ah, yeah, and some chocolates—the food of love. But the entire enchilada had just melted away and Kirsten had gone back to her own place. Somehow the equation didn't add up in his mind. She spent two nights on the road with him, making love and sleeping together, knowing they'd have to get up and rush out early both mornings. And now, now that they had time off, she chose to go home. What the devil?

His smartphone chimed, announcing the arrival of a text.

Kirsten

> What time you coming over tomorrow?

Pierre smiled, feeling instant excitement. He suddenly felt like a blasted high schooler, getting disproportionately excited because of a stupid text message from a new girl.

Pierre

Whatever's good for u.

Kirsten

Noonish?

Pierre

Sure. That sounds great!

Kirsten

My address: 23786 River Walk Apt 234 Creve Cour

Pierre didn't particularly like texting. Why couldn't she just call him so they could hear each other's voices? No doubt texting was definitely very handy on certain occasions, but he much preferred a phone call. Besides, he remembered they had already agreed on a time, why was she asking him again?

Pierre

> . Got it. Thanks. You in bed Yet?

Kirsten

> Not yet. Fed my aunt's cats, got out of my uniform. I'm gonna shower, have some cereal then I'm crashing.

Pierre

> Out of ur uniform? U walking around the house nude? Wait! I think I'm gonna hold on to that image.

Kirsten

> Wouldn't u like to know.

Pierre

> Now you're being coy. Send me a selfie.

Kirsten

> In your dreams.

Pierre

Nothing I haven't seen before.

Kirsten

And u may never again.

Pierre

Wait, did you say your aunt's cats?

Kirsten

Yes, I share a place with my aunt. She's also a flight attendant for us, I told u that.

Pierre

Will she be there tomorrow?

Kirsten

Relax, she's going out on A trip tomorrow afternoon.

Pierre smiled. Damn, Kirsten could read his mind. First thing that crossed his mind was how he may not be able to go after Kirsten with her aunt in the house. But if the lady was going out on a trip, then that solved the issue. Their two nights together had been the stuff that dreams were made of, and he still had a lot of fun things in mind he wanted to explore with Kirsten, but having an older aunt around could make things a tad uncomfortable.

Pierre

> I am relaxed.

Pierre

> I just didn't remember u lived with anybody

Kirsten

> My aunt's cool. You'll like her. She's dating one of our captains.

Pierre

> That's nice.

Kirsten

> Dave McMann. That's his Name. Do u know him?

Pierre

> No shit. Yeah, I know him.

Pierre

> Flew with him recently. A very nice guy.

Kirsten

> You're not letting me get my shower and my cereal. You are interrupting me, Sir. Gotta run. Til tomorrow!

Pierre

> Don't let me hold u up.

Pierre

> You'll see me in ur dreams, though.

Kirsten

> U wiped me out the past two nights. I need some sleep. Ciao!.

That short text conversation with her made him feel a lot better. She was just tired after all. She did have a demanding job. Pierre could not even imagine what it was like being a flight attendant and dealing with humanity every minute on the job. No way in hell he could ever do that. Putting up with people day in and day out, especially with the uneducated masses was very unpleasant, to say the least. He had to admit, he admired all flight attendants for being able to deal with that. He just plain wouldn't do it for five hundred thousand a year and any Ferrari or other high performance sports car of his choice thrown in to sweeten the deal.

He was a little tired, but not enough to warrant going to bed. What he would've liked would've been spending time with Kirsten, but since that was no longer an option for the evening, he might as well take care of bills, get his Camaro washed and hit the gym. Typical single airline pilot agenda for his day off. He walked to his fridge, where he'd posted his flight schedule for the month, double-checking to confirm that he indeed had three days off. Not showing up for a flight because one had misread one's schedule was a capital sin in the airlines, and he was not going to screw up like that if he could help it. He grabbed a bottle of Heineken, reaching for an opener.

After spending years without a girlfriend, he was having difficulty steering his thoughts away from Kirsten. He didn't want to come on too strong with her. He didn't want to scare her away. But now that he'd tasted the honey a woman like her had to offer, he was desiring—no, desperately craving so much more of the same.

And she said she wanted more as well.

The townhome was deserted. Steve and Del, his two roommates flew for Delta, and they weren't home. Their absence made the situation all the more tolerable when having roommates. They barely ever crossed paths.

THE FOLLOWING MORNING PIERRE drove to the exclusive neighborhood of Creve Cour. His dashboard-mounted Garmin GPS directed him to the luxury apartment complex at the address Kirsten had texted him. He took in the well-maintained green lawns and the mature trees in the apartment complex. A very pleasant environment, and also an expensive one. Plenty of parking spaces. Pierre maneuvered into a spot under the shade of an enormous oak tree. He stepped out of his car, locking the Camaro with his remote, smiling as the Italian air horn gave him a double tweet in confirmation.

He followed the numbers discreetly posted along the sides of the buildings until he found what he was looking for, apartment 234, second floor. He wore faded blue jeans, a black cotton T-shirt and white leather Adidas Stan Smiths without socks. A quick splattering of Paco Rabanne splash cologne completed the package.

Pierre rang the doorbell. His excitement meter was redlined and it began at his crotch. He'd forgotten the incredible sweet feeling of anticipation a desirable woman could bring into one's life.

Kirsten opened the door greeting him with a bright smile. "Hi Pierre!"

"Good morning," was all he could think of saying. He normally thought of himself as being quite eloquent, but the sight of her took his breath away. She was standing there wearing only a very *tiny* turquoise blue bikini. Her body glistening with tanning oil, perfectly proportioned by anybody's standards.

Eat your hearts out, Renaissance masters. You never painted one as exquisite as this!

He congratulated himself on his incredible good luck meeting Kirsten. It seemed to him no one had ever painted or sculpted any woman with such beauty, of that he was convinced.

Her golden-straw blond hair completed the totally sensual image of a gorgeous creature. Her blue eyes seamlessly matching the color of her bikini.

"Come in!" Kirsten held the apartment door wide open, stepping aside to let Pierre pass.

Pierre found himself at an impasse how to behave with her. Should he embrace her and kiss her right away? Or should he just walk past her and into the apartment? He didn't want to make Kirsten uncomfortable. He was dying to kiss her, but hesitated. Odd—really—considering they'd already gone at each other like minks and enjoyed a degree of intimacy reserved only for passionate lovers.

Kirsten solved the issue at once, reaching up with one hand placing it behind his neck, then, leaning on her toes she kissed him lightly on the lips. "I'm so glad you came!"

The bare skin of her waist felt wonderful against the palm of his hand, she was hot and slippery. She'd no doubt just come in from the sun.

Kirsten smelled of suntan oil and flowers. Pierre was fascinated. And good God, she was so attractive! This was the very first time he'd ever laid eyes on her barely-clothed body in bright daylight. Her skin was lightly tanned—a soft cocoa with a tinge of red. The red hue suggesting she'd been in the sun until a few moments ago. Tiny perspiration droplets adorned her body. Her blue bikini could not possibly hug her breasts more perfectly, and her shoulders could've been sculptured by Michelangelo himself.

She took note of his quick examination of her body, smiling in appreciation.

"Wow!" was all he could say.

She appeared pleased by his approval.

"Come! My Aunt Lisa is just getting ready to go on her trip. And Dave McMann is here too." Kirsten reached for his hand, pulling Pierre behind her. The familiarity of the gesture thrilled him.

He had another brief opportunity to glance at her body from behind and admire her perfect proportions. Sensual and tempting. Her bikini bottoms outlined the curves of her body like a glove. Her legs were strong, long and slender, and her ass was shaped like the most beautiful mandolin. He quickly looked up, detecting other people in the room and not wanting to be caught staring at Kirsten's rear end.

"Aunt Lisa, this is Pierre."

Pierre smiled, extending his hand. The woman in front of him in Worldwide's flight attendant uniform appeared to be in her late forties. Just a guess. Pierre had never been any good really at estimating people's age, especially women. She had a friendly smile and hazel eyes. He'd never met her before.

The flight attendant shook his hand.

"Hi Pierre! Kirsten's hasn't stopped talking about you since she got home yesterday."

Aunt Lisa stood a few inches shorter than Pierre.

"She hasn't?" He glanced at Kirsten, who had obviously not expected the comment. Or wanted it made. The aunt was gonna get it for this, no doubt.

"Yes, and I'm glad to finally meet you."

A man walked up behind Aunt Lisa, in a pilot's uniform.

"Hi Pierre!" the man said, offering his hand "Dave McMann. Remember me?"

Pierre recognized him instantly. Dave McMann, the line captain. They'd flown together not two months prior. Pierre was terrible with names, never remembering any. That was one of his life's curses, not being able to remember anybody's name. He was continuously trying to read other people's badges or if that didn't work, he would try reading their names on the crew tags attached to their flight bags.

"Of course I do. How ya doing, Dave? You guys going on a trip?"

"Yes," Dave McMann replied. "We buddy-bid so we can fly together."

Pierre couldn't recall whether Dave McMann was married or not. A quick glimpse at the captain's ring finger confirmed he was married.

The little shit.

Pierre hadn't been with the airlines for too long, but he was beginning to get the picture. Many of these guys evidently played around on their wives as a matter of routine.

"That's fantastic. How long of a trip?"

Dave McMann, a friendly sort of fellow in his mid-forties, was slightly taller than Pierre, and looked sharp in his airline pilot uniform. "A three-day trip, Pierre."

"With layovers in West Palm and then New York City," Aunt Lisa added. Flight crews assigned desirability levels to their layovers depending on which cities they were visiting. West Palm and NYC were held in high regard by most crews because those cities offered numerous and exciting opportunities for entertainment.

"We're just on our way out now," Aunt Lisa explained. "I'm just happy I got to meet you before we had to leave." Aunt Lisa flashed Kirsten a private look, smiling. Kirsten didn't seem to be enjoying herself very much at that particular moment.

Pierre found it amusing. Kirsten would probably wring her aunt's neck the next time they had an opportunity for some privacy.

Everyone shook hands again, then the two crewmembers departed the apartment pulling their crew bags behind them. Last thing Pierre wanted was to come across as judgmental. He was beginning to realize that spending sixteen or more nights on the road made pilots lonely, so they either embraced the bottle or some flight attendant.

Human nature.

Pierre finally had the peace of mind to look around and relax. The apartment was ample and nicely furnished. Lots of light, travertine marble floors. The big balcony glass doors were open and he could see part of a pool down below.

"Can I get you something to drink?" Kirsten was visibly more relaxed as well. That hadn't taken long.

"Sure. Thanks. I'd love a Diet Coke."

"Coming right up," she walked to the open floor kitchen, reaching for a Coke can from the stainless-steel refrigerator.

Pierre identified an expensive-looking set of Bose speakers sitting on the kitchen counter. Justin Timberlake's "Can't Stop the Feeling" permeated the air.

Pierre had an instant to admire her stunning body from behind again. He was blinking rapidly staring at her adorable little ass. His growing erection was now quite noticeable, although he hadn't caught Kirsten looking at it yet.

"Would you like some ice?"

"No, thanks. In the can is just fine for me. You've been out in the sun already?"

"Couple of hours."

"You're starting to get a tan."

Kirsten handed him the soda.

He popped open the Coke can, sipping the ice-cold cola. Pierre was terribly turned on being in the apartment alone with Kirsten. The unlimited possibilities open to them were incredibly exciting. There was something extremely sensual about being alone with her, something profoundly sexual. Everything in that kitchen seemed to smell like flowers. She was a sight too. The bright room showcased Kirsten's smokin' hot physique in all its splendor. Her body was exciting and erotic in its perfection, not a blemish or freckle anywhere. A porcelain doll if he ever saw one. He was hard as a rock, so ready for her. He momentarily wondered if sex was on the cards. Pierre rested the Coke can on a glass table, walking towards Kirsten. She smiled seductively, expectantly raising her face to him.

"Yes?" She asked, feigning innocence.

"Come here," his arms went around her waist. She felt silky and warm. He could see she was in excellent shape, her body was strong and taunt under his touch. The body of someone who exercised regularly.

Kirsten remained standing where she was, allowing Pierre to embrace her. She placed her arms around his neck, accepting his kiss.

Pierre felt Kirsten move closer to him as he kissed her hot lips. She had made contact with his body, and he was certain she was now feeling his hardened masculinity through her bikini bottom. The pressure of her lower body against his increased. She was pushing against him.

Yep, she had detected his erection.

Her tongue felt hot and exciting touching his as he travelled the inside of her mouth. She was practically hanging from his neck. She smelled of suntan oil and some sort of perfume and another scent. Kirsten scent. It was delicious. He was surprised at her strength. Pierre broke the kiss, backing away from Kirsten just enough to slide one of his arms behind her knees, lifting her up effortlessly, although her weight surprised him. For a relatively small girl, Kirsten was surprisingly heavy and solid. He liked that. Not an ounce of fat in her. She kept her eyes locked on his, as Pierre walked away from the living room towards the door he assumed was her bedroom.

"This your bedroom?"

"Yes," she replied, bashfully.

Her tacit acceptance of his intentions turned him on even more. *Finally!* There was really no doubt in anybody's mind she was surrendering to his desires and he and this goddess were going to be making love in just a few minutes! The anticipation was so pleasant around his crotch he just about dropped her. He'd been dreaming of this moment since they parted at the airport the day before.

He walked through the door carrying Kirsten in his arms, swiftly taking in the view of the king size bed and the tastefully decorated furnishings. The room was adorned mostly pink and white, with a delightful female feel and decor to it that he found very appealing. There was a big glass sliding door on one side, with a view of trees and other vegetation outside. He wondered briefly about Kirsten's neighbors—would they be able to see in her bedroom? Was her bed visible to anyone outside those windows?

He didn't want any of her neighbors having a clean line of sight when they were in bed. Scanning outside the windows he quickly confirmed there were no other buildings anywhere within sight.

Perfect.

Pierre briefly thought about Kirsten's aunt and her boyfriend, evaluating the odds of those two reappearing in the apartment for whatever reason. What if they forgot something and had to come back? They hadn't been gone that long. Aah, what the devil, if they showed up he'd just have to deal with them. He briefly considered shutting the bedroom door behind them, providing some privacy in case the aunt did show up, but he couldn't really reach the door while carrying Kirsten, and didn't want to interrupt the bond he had with her just yet. He walked all the way to the bed, gently lowering her onto an expensive-looking pink and white cotton feather comforter.

Screw the door and to hell with the aunt. He wasn't going to spoil the moment.

Kirsten reminded him of a classical painting, seemingly entirely relaxed resting there on her comfortable bed, staring at him expectantly, her eyes on fire, her blue bikini screaming at him, *'remove me!'*

Pierre smoothly climbed on the bed next to Kirsten, moving closer, kissing her again on the lips.

She tenderly placed her arms around his neck one more time, accepting the kiss. He could sense she was trembling lightly from excitement.

He liked *that.*

Pierre ran his hand from her shoulder to her breast, delicately caressing it as he continued kissing her. Her skin was now cold, the perspiration on her skin having instantly evaporated in the air-conditioned room. He felt her nipple hardening through the bathing suit fabric. That was breathtaking. Arousing her was incredibly exciting for him. He slowly ran the palm of his hand along her rib cage, reaching the bottom part of her blue bikini, along her hips. He kept his hand moving, caressing the lower part of her hip, continuing down to her knee. That's as far as he could reach while still kissing her. He returned his hand to her breast, smoothly slipping it under the bikini fabric. The fabric gave way easily, moving aside. Her breast was soft and warm and he found her nipple, tenderly squeezing it between his index finger and his thumb, rolling it gently. He immediately felt Kirsten's response to his touch, her tongue darting into his mouth faster, dancing around excitedly, her respiration accelerating.

Pierre abandoned her nipple, pulling Kirsten over towards him on her side, in order to gain access to the back of her bikini. Reaching behind her, Pierre found a lightly tied knot … gently pulling on it he released the garment from her body.

Kirsten rolled over on her back again, fixated on Pierre's eyes. The top of her bikini was now loose. Pierre grabbed the blue garment from the front, trying to remove it from her body in one slow tug. The straps resisted his pull, remaining stuck under her body, so he pulled harder.

Her defiant faultless breasts bounced free without restraint. Pierre had his first opportunity ever to admire them in full daylight. They were definitely shaped to perfection, the perfect size for him, not too big, not too small, and each nipple stood erect in its center. The color of her nipples was a soft pink, matching perfectly the color of her skin and the color of her cotton duvet.

Damn, had he actually just thought about the color coordination? He must be getting in touch with his emotional side! That was odd.

Pierre connected with her lips again, kissing her gently while his hand caressed her breasts. Kirsten began to show her arousal, softly rolling her hips evidently enjoying his advances. He paused for a moment, pushing himself away, stepping off the bed. He stood alongside it, looking down at her. Kirsten was obviously puzzled by the sudden, unwanted interruption.

This time he wasn't going to beat around the bush. No more clumsily removing his clothes while he was kissing her, like some dumbass teenager in the back seat of a car. Standing by the bed he methodically removed his black T-shirt, pulling it over his head, tossing it on the floor, his naked torso feeling the chill in the air. Kirsten's bedroom was ice cold from the air-conditioning. He momentarily wondered if he should change the thermostat. The room was really cold, way beyond comfortable. Kirsten was going to be nude any second now, and she would freeze in this meat locker. He wanted her to be content in bed with him for a long time, not shivering like a wet mouse. Maybe she had the thermostat set to walk-in freezer temperatures because the front sliding windows of her apartment balcony were wide open. Yeah, that would certainly ensure the bedrooms stayed cold.

He'd have to ask her where the thermostat was, then he'd have to explain his thinking. Naw, that would spoil the mood. Fuck it.

She was riveted on him, eating him with her eyes. His well-developed abs, slim waist and muscular shoulders held the sort of promise any woman would desire in a lover.

Pierre unbuttoned his jeans, pulling them down together with his boxer shorts in one well-coordinated motion over his slim, narrow waist. While he was reaching down to remove his pants he also removed his Stan Smiths.

He was so excited and erect that he once again had to make an effort to resist his urge to just slam into her. Patience and control. He had to maintain some sort of discipline. She deserved it. Kirsten momentarily discontinued eye contact to sneak a glance at his solid, erect member, before locking eyes with him again.

Like it? I hope you do, sweetheart, cos this is how I'm gonna be inside you in just a few more moments.

Pierre climbed back on the bed, advancing on his knees, his eyes still locked on Kirsten. She was beyond ravishing, God, she was an incantation, an apparition, a succubus, resting there, comfortable on her back, patiently anticipating unimaginable pleasures. Too good to be real.

No one, absolutely no one could look as good as you.

Balancing on his knees he reached out for her, placing his fingers on the sides of her blue bikini bottoms, pinching the material between his index fingers and thumbs, he slowly and very deliberately tugged her bottoms down past her knees, past her ankles and off the bed onto the floor, while Kirsten helped him lifting her hips slightly off the bed. Her shaved pubic area was decorated with just enough hair to be erotic. The fact that she was a true blonde did not escape his rapid scan. Reaching for Kirsten's ankles he separated her legs enough to allow his wide shoulders to fit between them. She contributed by easing her knees even further apart. He went down on his chest, moving his head towards her fleshy lips. She was ready, a soft moan passing through her lips as she tilted her head to the side, in expectation of being pleasured. Pierre went directly for her sex button, licking it once with steady pressure.

One single brushstroke.

Kirsten moaned in appreciation.

She was ready for him, exquisitely soaking wet. Wet and creamy.

All of a sudden Pierre was able to recognize that sugary smell.

Kirsten smelled like *cotton candy!*

That being one of his absolute most favorite sweets on the planet, Pierre was intrigued. Did she really have that scent, or had his brain assigned that fragrance to her because—just like cotton candy—he liked her so much. He'd have to think about that one later. Ask her what the name of her perfume was.

Pierre glided his hands under her buttocks, careful not to scratch her with his fingernails, lifting her towards his face. His tongue continued stroking her clit now with greater frequency. He had the perfect angle. Kirsten defiantly began rolling her hips left and right, attempting to get away from the absolutely delicious mind-boggling strokes.

Pierre held on to her buttocks with increasing force. She was not going to get away. Kirsten fought him, again reaching down with her hands trying to pull him off by the hair.

Pierre softly ran his hand across her belly. He wanted to feel just how excited Kirsten was. She was already tight as a board. Her tummy muscles were evidently already setting her up for an exquisite orgasm. The back of each of her legs rested solidly on top of his shoulders. Pierre knew Kirsten wasn't going to be able to keep her stomach muscles taunt like the strings of a Stradivarius violin for too long without slamming into an orgasm.

This time he was going to make her reach heaven quickly. She was already sufficiently aroused so she should climax soon, and he was not going to be able to keep up such intense licking much longer. Heck, the bottom of his tongue was still sore from their previous two nights together. He smacked her clit with his tongue, sending waves of pleasure radiating through her body.

He stuck two fingers in his mouth, soaking them in his saliva. Pierre inserted his left index finger in Kirsten's vagina, while his middle finger went inside her ass all in one smooth progressive motion, both fingers finding their way inside Kirsten simultaneously. Her sphincter relaxed enough to allow him entry, so he moved his hand in and out very slowly, stimulating sensations inside both her vagina and her ass. His index finger applied soft pressure to the inside of her pussy, favoring her G-Spot. Pierre was able to do all this without once missing a stroke on her clit with his tongue.

It seemed to him Kirsten was definitely agonizing with pleasure. She had gotten there pretty quickly. The rolling of her hips from side to side became progressively more violent, making it a challenge for Pierre to follow her with his mouth. She began to tremble, her body shaking uncontrollably. She clinched the comforter with her fists, her eyes closed. Kirsten's facial expression changed, making her appear to be in intense pain. She moaned with pleasure. Kirsten was losing control of her reality.

Pierre knew her body had decided it was time for her moment of pleasure.

Wow, that was quick!

"Ooohhh, my God!!" She wailed. *"Awww, Pierre!"*

He held on to Kirsten for dear life with one hand, her exquisite full buttocks allowing him a good firm grip. Her fingers firmly locked in his hair were distracting, but he decided to ignore the pain and concentrate on giving her all the pleasure he could. She had given herself to him, and he was going to reward her. He persevered licking her clit during the entire time she orgasmed. The pulsing of her ass grabbing and releasing his finger confirmed the intensity of her orgasm. That alone was incredibly erotic. He felt his tongue was going to fall off from all the activity, but he wasn't going to stop, not just yet, just a few more seconds. He loved the way her sighs sounded in her throat, how they grew shorter and coarser. Equally erotic was how she'd called out his name when she came.

At that point Pierre pulled away from Kirsten, reaching for her wrists in an attempt to disconnect her from his totally Kirsten-tousled mess of a hair. He managed to loosen her grip on his hair, getting back up on his knees. He observed the flush that had appeared across Kirsten's chest and how she was breathing in short, quick gasps. Her breasts stood perky crowned by hardened nipples. He placed both his hands on Kirsten's hips, applying pressure. "Turn over!" He ordered.

Kirsten was still shaking lightly in the final stages of her intense orgasm, not totally conscious, yet she did as he asked, turning around, resting face down on her stomach. She reached up, hugging one of her feather pillows, her striking perfectly-shaped ass fully exposed and accessible, vulnerable to his every desire. And his every desire at the moment was to fuck her hard. Pierre noticed the tan lines her bikini bottoms had branded on the sides of her derriere. The skin of her ass was several shades lighter than the rest of her. One of her cheeks exhibited in red the shape of his hand where Pierre had just held her.

He nearly came just from looking at Kirsten like that.

He gently reached down, resting his hands on the inside of her thighs, parting her legs a little more. Then he leaned forward, smoothly lowering himself on top of Kirsten's back, directing his incredibly stiff throbbing sex towards her buttocks. He felt the silkiness of her rear end against his belly, his member simultaneously slipping between her buttocks towards her totally soaked lips. He found her entrance and allowed himself to slowly, cautiously penetrate it, limiting himself to entering her only a little bit, perhaps an inch, just enough for an exploratory peek to ascertain he was in the right place.

Yes, her sensuous lips had slid aside, allowing him to slip in just the tip. She was hot, wet and willing and on her stomach. He was in the right place.

With one solid gradual forward thrust of his pelvis he went completely inside Kirsten, driving his meaty sword into her eager pussy from behind.

"Hmmm!" She approved, wiggling her ass.

Pierre was undeniably aroused in the knowledge that he'd already given her one delicious orgasm. There was something about his male ego that was very satisfied knowing he'd managed to please his woman. Now he was just dying to thrust into her, to fuck her blind until she begged him to come inside her. Keeping his weight on his elbows and knees he thrust in and out of her with increasing frequency, taking care not to slam into her too violently so as not to make her sore. His face moved close to her neck, feeling the silky touch of her golden curls caressing his cheek. He nibbled on her earlobe biting with gentle force, just enough to make her notice, breathing hot air in her ear, while pumping in and out of her.

Kirsten half-turned to look at him, an incredible sensual smile on her face.

"You're such an animal!"

"I thought I was an incubus," he whispered in her ear.

"Yes, you're an incubus, a demon, here to seduce me! *Fuck me, Pierre!*"

"I'll seduce you later. For now, I'm just fucking you blind!"

"Yes, you do that! You fuck me!"

Her words only served to turn him on even more.

God! She was so hot and exciting!

He picked up the pace, in and out. Her buttocks underneath him bouncing lightly with each thrust under the impact of his pelvis. He looked down, pushing himself up a little with his arms, becoming further aroused at the sight of his erect shaft going in and out of Kirsten, perfectly centered between her two mounds, her buttocks compressing against his lower body each time he pushed forward. Looking at that image increased his arousal tenfold, pushing him to the edge of orgasm.

He had total control of her, but he was going to lose control of himself.

Kirsten lifted her hips off the bed slightly, positioning herself better, offering her body for better penetration. Pierre shifted his body weight so he could lean forward, resting his hands on her buttocks.

He felt the situation starting to go out of control.

Dammit, too soon!

No! He wasn't going to come just yet. He stopped thrusting into her, reaching down pushing his index finger gently at the entrance to her anus.

"Have you tried making love this way?" His breathing was slowing.

Kirsten surprised him by rolling off from under him without a word, jumping off the bed and ambling to her airline overnight bag resting on a bench in front of her mirrored dresser. She dug in the bag, strolling back to the bed holding in her hand a medium-sized jar of Vaseline.

Pierre was rather surprised, and quite pleased, and very turned on.

Really?

He accepted the jar of Vaseline from her, opening it while Kirsten climbed back on the bed, positioning herself on her tummy in front of Pierre, spreading her legs and backing up into him. She was offering him her exquisite ass, no questions asked.

WOW! The entire event was too much, Pierre just about orgasmed right then again, barely keeping his sanity, concentrating on the Vaseline instead. This was so goddamned exciting he was stumbling. He removed a dab of the slippery, gooey stuff with his fingers, smoothly spreading it between her cheeks. His index finger found her ass again, slowly and most gently applying forward pressure he dipped his finger inside her, feeling her sphincter relaxing, giving way. Pierre ascertained some of the Vaseline on his finger had remained inside her, lubricating her opening, then he removed his finger, spreading the remaining lubricant on his throbbing cock.

He was more than ready to fuck her in the ass, oh, God he couldn't believe this.

Kirsten waited patiently for Pierre to enter her this way.

He used his hand to guide his erect cock to her tight entrance. His finger found her opening again, and his shaft followed. He glanced down, confirming that the head of his shaft was at the entrance to her ass, and began inching his hips forward, in expectation of sliding into her.

But it wasn't happening. Her sphincter was not allowing entry.

He felt Kirsten backing into him, trying to help, but for some unknown reason her body was not allowing him to go there. She was locked shut.

Pierre had no desire to force the issue. If he jammed into her, he would eventually slide inside her ass, but that would most likely hurt her and put an end to her sensual mood. He didn't want that. Yeah, he was dying to go inside her ass, a completely new and tempting experience with Kirsten, and the very idea aroused him something awful, but he wasn't going to hurt her no matter what his own desires were.

It was time to make a decision.

"Stay here," he said rather loudly. He jumped off the bed, practically running to her bathroom. He hung his hard cock below the faucet in the sink, running warm water over his enlarged member. A couple of squirts of liquid soap and some more water and he was ready. He dried himself with a pink towel hanging by the sink, praying the water treatment didn't prove lethal to his hard-on.

Pierre returned to the bed where Kirsten was waiting exactly as he'd left her, on her stomach with her ass in the air, totally vulnerable, poised to fulfill any of his desires.

He positioned himself behind her, directing his erection with his hand and finding her vagina this time. She was still soaked, so he entered her with one slow, continuous thrust. Kirsten moved her hips back and forth, helping him penetrate her better with each thrust. He'd been holding it off for too long. He knew that at a certain point his body would say *Enough!* And take control away from him. And that irrevocable moment was about to arrive.

His body began experiencing short spasms, at rapidly increasing intervals, so he pumped faster. He sank his fingernails into her buttocks, giving himself complete control over her body, pushing inside her as deep as he could, listening to the wet sound of their bodies slapping together. The immense pleasure became unreal ... agonizing.

He realized *IT* was going to happen. No way on God's earth to postpone it now.

The electricity began in his toes, traveling at warp speed to his crotch. He'd reached the point of stimulation where he no longer was in charge of his body. Pierre had reached the edge of the cliff, and he was jumping off into the void. Once again, there was absolutely nothing he could do to avoid having an orgasm. He was no longer capable of restraint; his body had taken over and he was just along for the ride. And what a ride! He looked down at Kirsten's blond hair, then basked in the visual pleasure of her buttocks receiving his uncontrollable thrusts.

"*Aaah, Kirsten, I'm cuming inside you!*" he said *sottovoce*, feeling the exploding arrival of what promised to be a tremendously intense orgasm. His hands full of Kirsten's ass tightened their grip on her butt cheeks as he felt his body begin shooting hot sperm deep inside her. He was now pumping in and out of her totally independent of any control he may have had.

The unbelievable electrifying orgasm lasted but a few seconds, but the intensity of their lovemaking left him breathing and gasping like a marathon runner. Again, she had done this to him, she had made him lose control. For the time being he was unable to formulate any conscious thought. Pierre allowed a minute to pass, then another. Pushing himself up and away he slipped out of Kirsten, noticing the red marks in the shape of his hands and fingers clearly visible on each of her buttocks.

Those marks confirmed she belonged to him!

God, he must've really grabbed her hard. He was amazed she didn't complain one bit.

Rolling on his side he reached for her, turning her around to face him, then oh so softly kissing her eyelids. He focused on the lovely creature next to him. She rested her face on his shoulder, delicately kissing his neck.

Pierre loved that. "You are incredible," he whispered.

She said something back.

"What?"

"Can you make me come again?"

He was surprised. Surprised and pleased. God, he'd really found the perfect girl! Her words were music to his ears. She wanted more?

Gawd!

"I'll be very happy to do whatever you want, sweetheart."

Pierre gently directed her to lay down on her back, shifting himself away towards the foot of the bed. His breathing was slowing. He positioned himself between her legs again. Kirsten abandoned herself in anticipation. His shoulders made contact with the inside of her thighs, spreading her legs further as he came closer to her pelvis. He felt Kirsten helping him, spreading her legs even more. She was wet and slippery.

Pierre ran his tongue along the inside of her thigh, slowly, gradually licking up towards her crotch. The sugary scent of cotton candy way more pronounced now. He inhaled deeply, savoring the delicious smell. It still blew his mind that everything about this girl was so attractive to him, her laughter, her looks, the way she catered to his every wish.

He licked further, but didn't touch her vagina or her lips when he came abeam them. Kirsten shifted on the bed, moving her pelvis towards his mouth when he was near her pussy.

Oh, no. Not so fast, my sweet angel. This time you're going to suffer the delicious agony of anticipation.

His refusal to comply with her wishes served only to arouse her even more. Her moaning began again.

He decided to build up her anticipation by switching to her other leg and tracing the inside of her thigh licking down towards her knee. He planted soft kisses on her skin in between licks.

Once he got close to her knee he reversed course, heading back up again along the inside of her thigh. As he got closer to her love mound he anticipated Kirsten was going to shift her hips again and attempt to direct his mouth towards her lips. And she did just as expected, but he refused to accept her invitation once again, running his tongue up towards her belly button, proceeding to insert his tongue in it. Kirsten shifted on the bed, in increasing sexual frustration.

Pierre reached under her with his two hands, cupping her butt cheeks in them. Her strong buttocks were slippery and wet. By God, they were indeed very slippery and very wet. He realized smiling that the wetness was not all Kirsten. He'd just come inside her, and some of his gift must be seeping out of her. The thought added a novel erotic angle to the situation. He couldn't remember going down on a girl after coming inside her.

Kirsten moved her hands to his shoulders, sparing his hair this time. She again applied pressure in an attempt to direct his mouth towards her hot, eager lips but Pierre wasn't ready to follow her wishes just yet.

Instead, he ran his tongue in small circles around her breast. He knew his saliva was going to become very cold very fast in the frigid temperature of the bedroom, affecting her sensitive nipples, so he opened his mouth wide, encircling her nipple and the aurora, fastening his mouth to her breast, delicately licking around her exquisite nipple.

He exhaled warm air, bathing her nipple with heat.

Pierre knew the moment he removed his mouth from her nipple she would experience uncomfortably cold temperatures on her breast due to the evaporation of the water vapor he'd smeared on it. He quickly reached for one of the pillows near him, placing it on her breast, protecting it from the cold. He left the pillow in place, covering her chest.

Enough. It was time to please her and give her what she wanted. He shifted, moving down towards her lips. This time he was not going to tease her. Shifting down, he used his fingers to separate her labia, exposing her engorged clit. His tongue went to work licking her opening from the bottom up. Kirsten shuddered, her hands applying renewed pressure on his shoulders. Her legs started to tremble.

"You are bad! Oooohhh!"

Pierre was now really feeling the tiny cut under his tongue. He had caused that cut by stretching his tongue out of his mouth too far and for too long over the past few days. Yet it didn't matter, Kirsten wanted more and he was going to give her more. He hadn't had a chance to recover from his own delicious orgasm just yet, but that was fine. They would sleep together once she was satisfied. He would hold her in his arms and just look at her, thanking St. Peter and his lucky stars for this astonishing gift. Kirsten rhythmically moved her hips in a circular motion, responding to his intense licking.

Pierre reached up with his hand, finding Kirsten's erect nipple under the pillow. He kneaded it and gently pulled on it, sending intense pleasure pulses down to her pussy.

Kirsten moaned, her breathing changing into short gasps.

Pierre circled her clit with his lips, using his mouth to generate powerful suction on her bud, then releasing it, then sucking again. Kirsten's abdomen muscles tightened up like a washboard in response. Pierre sucked again, this time Kirsten grabbed a hold of his hair.

Oh, great.

She pulled.

Pierre cringed, sucking harder, creating an unreal vacuum on Kirsten's clit which sent her moaning into the genesis of another exquisite climax. She thrust her pelvis hard against his face, exhaling hard and pulling his face against her clit.

"Ah, aaaaargh!"

Pierre switched to licking. Kirsten's body was spasming in short, continuous shudders, totally lost in pleasure.   Kirsten was only vaguely aware of his presence; her moans of approval could be confused with cries of pain. Her inner muscles clenching tighter and tighter with orgasmic passion, carrying her into a world of nothing but pleasure.

She eventually released his hair, pushing him off with both hands, away from her incandescent sex.

"Enough! Please! I give up! No more!"

Pierre did not perseverate. She appeared to have had enough indeed. Kirsten rolled on her side, into a fetal position, tucking her hands between her legs and against her crotch, whimpering and shaking. Pierre hugged her from behind, holding her tight against him.

Kirsten was still having short, delicious spasms, transmitting light tremors to his chest. She was soaked, slippery with perspiration. The intensity of her orgasm had hit her hard.

Pierre smiled, satisfied. That was it, then. So, spooning was going to be the last item on the menu for the night. Reaching behind him Pierre grabbed the duvet, bringing it over to protect their naked bodies from the frigid air in the room. He laid his head on the pillow next to Kirsten, her golden hair spread out in total surrender, caressing his face. She smelled of sex, of woman ... and incredibly enough, against all logic, of *cotton candy*.

Maybe her perfume had that scent. He'd have to ask her that.

He woke up hours later, surprised he'd fallen asleep without any warning. How'd that happen? Last he remembered, he'd been admiring Kirsten's angelic face. He hadn't changed position for hours and his one arm under Kirsten was totally numb. Pierre took a few seconds to get his bearings. It all came to him in a flash. His passionate and most delicious succubus was right there next to him, still out cold, in total abandonment, sleeping in his arms.

In his arms? *Ouch!* He realized he couldn't feel his arm. Impossible to know how long they'd been asleep. Turning his head a tad he noticed it was now night time. Dark outside. He had to get his arm out from under Kirsten. Doing so was probably going to wake her up, but he couldn't stay like this much longer. The lack of circulation in his arm had to be resolved. He pulled himself back inch by inch, away from her, while rolling his shoulders forcing his numb arm to break loose from under Sleeping Beauty.

Kirsten didn't even flinch. Once his arm was free, Pierre experienced a couple of minutes of intense tingling rapidly becoming severe pain. He bit his tongue not to scream. He didn't know whether to laugh or cry.

Holy mother of God! That was painful!

Eventually, circulation returned to his arm and he delighted himself admiring Kirsten's body in the twilight of her bedroom. He wished he had a camera to take a few pictures of her sensational body.

But wait, his cell phone had a camera!

Regrettably, Pierre had no idea where his cell phone had ended up. Most likely, it was somewhere on the floor stuck in his pants. On second thought, he really shouldn't take pictures of Kirsten without her consent. Maybe later, after developing some more familiarity, she would agree to pose for some shots under similar circumstances. Doing it with her sleeping and without her knowledge reeked too much of voyeurism. That was not him, he refused taking advantage of her vulnerability. God, but he would love having some nude pictures of her to carry around on his trips so he could privately admire her looks while she was not there with him.

He had absolutely no idea what time it was. He didn't have to work for a couple of more days, so he could just relax and spend the night with Kirsten. He couldn't think of anything else in the world he'd rather be doing.

Music was still playing out in the living room. Zayn's "Pillow Talk" melodiously filtered into the bedroom.

Pierre repositioned himself next to Kirsten. She was still on her side and hadn't moved since they finished making love, so he gently rolled her on her back. Kirsten momentarily half-opened her eyes, the beginning of a smile painted on her lips. He kissed her tenderly on the lips. Kirsten brought her arms up, encircling his neck.

"Good night, lover," she whispered, barely moving her lips.

PIERRE WOKE UP FIRST. The room was brightly lit. It was morning already. It took him but a couple of seconds to remember where he was. He listened closely for any sounds from the rest of the apartment. Nothing. Silent as a tomb. What happened to the music? Maybe the Bose system was on a timer and it had shut itself off.

Kirsten was next to him breathing very relaxed, on her stomach, her naked body covered with the cotton comforter.

He stirred, then shifted his weight away, bouncing her on the bed.

Kirsten gradually opened her eyes, appearing momentarily surprised at seeing him there. Captivating eyes, bedroom eyes, he thought.

"Good morning sleepy bones," he smiled.

"Hi!" She offered, transitioning from half-awake to fully alive, tossing the comforter aside, she jumped out of bed and ran for the bathroom.

"I gotta pee!" She announced, going in the bathroom. This time she did not shut the door behind her.

Progress, Pierre thought, smiling. This time she didn't want privacy. And she looked just as striking in the daylight.

He heard the toilet flush and the sound of water and cabinet doors opening and closing. Then spitting. Brushing her teeth, no doubt. *Damn*, he didn't have a toothbrush with him. He should've brought an overnight bag with the bare necessities. Yea, right—

that would've looked real good. Showing up at her doorstep with an overnight bag. Pretty presumptuous of him, assuming he was automatically going to be spending the night, no?

He sat up on the edge of the bed.

Kirsten strolled out of the bathroom, gorgeously nude, walking straight towards him. She placed her hands on the bed to either side of him, leaning forward, searching for his lips. Pierre met her and received a soft, sweet kiss from the nude goddess in front of him. He hadn't brushed his teeth yet, so he made an effort not to open his mouth. Her breath smelled of some minty toothpaste. Pierre jumped out of bed, heading for the bathroom. "Back in a second!" He explained. He had to relieve himself of that Coke she'd given him the previous day. He wondered if he should close the door of the bathroom. She hadn't closed it herself when she used the toilet. What the hey, he left it open.

After relieving himself and washing his hands he reached for some of her toothpaste to rinse his mouth. He thought briefly about using her toothbrush but decided against it. She may not like that.

Hello there!

He'd just become aware of his usual morning erection, incredible, considering his activities with Kirsten just hours ago.

His incredible animal-like sexual drive didn't cease to amaze him.

Kirsten was standing in front of the sliding door window, her back to him, when he rejoined her in the bedroom. She appeared to be in deep thought, looking outside. Pierre quickly burned that image of her from behind into his permanent memory. Kirsten had a perfect body, far as he was concerned, with graceful lines and sculptured proportions. He approached her, surrounding her with his arms. Her skin felt cold.

"Good morning Princess." He kissed her neck.

His solid erection found its way between her buttocks, slipping right under the apex of her legs, coming to a stop below her slippery, soft, hot lips.

"Wow!" she cried, stepping forward, forcing his shaft to slip out from between her legs. She turned, facing him. With her bare feet flat on the floor she was maybe five inches shorter than him. "Good morning, Pierre! What was that?" Her arms went up around his neck again, her eyes looking down at his hard cock. She inched forward, allowing his shaft to slide between her legs from the front, without going inside her.

God, but he loved the feel of her body!

"That was my good morning kiss, what'd ya think it was?" He teased.

"You're bad. And on the warpath again I see, uh?"

"If by that you mean ready for action, yep. Ready for you. Did you sleep well?"

"Sleep? I didn't sleep! I passed out! After all you did to me!"

Smiling, he placed his hands flat on her lower back, above the curve of her butt. "You didn't like it?"

Kirsten took on a feigned look of surprise. "What was there to like?"

"I don't know. So, the visit by the incubus didn't please you?"

"You are a little shit! No, a little demon. But of course, you pleased me. What did you think? You're so spoiling me. I never knew sex could be like this."

"Like what?"

She didn't answer for a moment, staring into his eyes. "Like what? You know like what! Absolutely mind-altering sex. Never ending sex." She shook her head. "How can I even begin to explain it? All I can say is you must be *very* experienced! You could make a lot of money selling your playbook to other men, Mr. White."

"I have no playbook. *You* are my playbook."

"See? That's what I mean. I rest my case."

Want to go back in bed and I'll show you a couple of other pieces of candy?"

She pushed him away. "Not in your dreams! I'm starved, take me to breakfast!" She took one last, quick look at his erection, patting it with the palm of her hand, then escaping towards her closet, in search of garments adequate for breakfast.

Pierre laughed. Went without saying he would've truly enjoyed making love and fucking her blind again, but she was right, he had to look after her in other ways too. And breakfast did sound good. He'd just have to live with his annoying morning condition, and why not? He'd lived with unsatisfied morning hard-ons most of his adult life.

HE DROVE THEM TO a cute little quaint restaurant near his neighborhood. One of those adorable small individually-owned places where the owner was both cook and waitress. Definitely not a boring franchise.

The place was named 'Charlie Brown,' tastefully decorated and picturesque, with eight tables. She liked it. The owner gave them menus, disappearing in the kitchen.

"*My!* Everything looks delicious!" Kirsten had slipped into black tights and a comfortable extra-large pink sweatshirt.

"She serves breakfast all day, if you prefer instead of lunch."

"Breakfast sounds dreamy. I'm going to have an omelet."

Pierre studied her attractive face, thanking his lucky stars for the tenth time that morning. He was already making plans for the rest of the day with her.

"When do you fly again?" He asked Kirsten.

"Tomorrow," she said, without taking her eyes off the menu.

"Tomorrow?" *Crap.* He'd somehow thought she had a few days off ahead.

"Yes, three-day trip. Overnights in Chicago and Las Vegas."

"Dang! I was thinking of asking you up to Oshkosh for the air show with me."

Kirsten looked up. "I've been to Oshkosh a few times."

"So you've been to the air show?"

"Yes, many times. That'd be sweet, but I gotta fly."

The owner-waitress reappeared. "You kids decide?"

Kirsten pointed at the menu. "I'll have the tomato and avocado omelet. Could I have that with sour dough toast?"

The woman nodded, jotting it down. "What would you like to drink, honey?"

Kirsten ordered an orange juice, large.

Pierre ordered scrambled eggs with a side of bacon, and some tomato juice.

"I have a wedding to go to next month. Wanna go with me?" She reached for his hand under the table, grasping it.

"That would be fun. Where is it?" He didn't have his schedule for the following month yet, but going anywhere with Kirsten promised to be fun and exciting.

"The wedding's gonna be in Milwaukee. First weekend of the month."

"I'd love going with you. Just text me the dates and I'll bid around it."

Everything in airline life revolved around bids.

Bids and seniority.

The day one was hired, the airline assigned the new pilot or flight attendant a seniority number. If there were fifteen thousand pilots on the seniority list already, then the new comer would be assigned seniority number 15,001. Everything depended on seniority, the types of airplanes one flew, the salaries one collected, the types of trips one could fly, domestic or international trips, the time of year when one could go on vacation.

Needless to say, if one was at the bottom of the seniority list, one would have to accept anything that was left over after the rest of the pilots had bid.

In other words, junior pilots sucked hind tittie.

"You planning on being a pilot your whole life?" She asked.

"You mean an airline pilot? Yeah. At least until I reach the retirement age of 65. How about you? You planning on being a flight attendant all your life?"

"No, I don't think so. If I get married I may wanna stay home."

"Married? You're a little too young for that, don't you think?"

"I'm certainly not! Why would you say that?"

"I mean, don't you want to taste a little more of what life has to offer before committing to someone?"

"Why can't I taste a little more of what life has to offer now and also after I'm married to someone?"

He smiled. "I guess you have a point, what I meant was, right now you don't have responsibilities. Which gives you more freedom. You can take off and go to Paris for breakfast tomorrow if you feel like it."

"Whenever I find the right guy, I'll still have all the freedom I want. We'll take off and go for breakfast in Paris together if we feel like it." She opened her big eyes. "Wanna go for breakfast in Paris with me tomorrow?"

He laughed. "Don't you have to work?"

"That could be changed."

"How?"

"Marry me. Then I'll quit and we can go together as man and wife with our passes."

That took him by surprise.

"You serious?" *Marry her?* Pierre considered the scenario. What would life be like married to Kirsten? He never really thought of these things when he dated a girl. Marriage?

The furthest thing from his mind. However, the concept did have a certain taste of honey to it.

"Am I serious? Look at you! One would think I asked you to do something unpleasant."

He caught himself. *Gak!* Was he that transparent? Had his expression displeased her? "No, no. That's not it at all. I was just surprised, that's all."

"Relax, I'm just fucking with your mind. I'm not ready to get married, and even if I was, I sure as all hell wouldn't want to be married to you."

That got his attention. "*What?* Why not?"

"Because you're a pilot, that's why."

"Oh? Last night you didn't seem to have any problems with my being a pilot."

"That was sex. Marriage is an entirely different story, honey."

Pierre had nothing against marriage, he just didn't think about it. Undoubtedly, at a certain point, with most girls the topic was bound to eventually come up. He had the impression many girls had marriage in mind from the second they laid eyes on you.

Kirsten as his wife? A little early to consider such a thing, but he had to admit the concept was more than a little attractive and it had its fascination. He was definitely infatuated with her. She was intelligent and funny, had a delicious body, and she knew how to use it. Know how to use it? She was a knock out in bed! And she was a flight attendant. A captain he flew with recently told him flight attendants made excellent wives to airline pilots because they understood the life of a pilot. Who else would put up with a husband being gone half the month?

"By the way, I had something I wanted to ask you."

She waited patiently for him to continue.

"Are you on any kind of birth control?"

Kirsten stared at him incredulous. She flashed him a serious look, shaking her head. "*Now*, you ask?"

He didn't know why he'd blurted that out. Yes, maybe he should've asked her earlier, but even if he'd thought about it, he would've avoided asking not to ruin the mood. The idea of using condoms hadn't even crossed his mind. After all, Kirsten was an educated, clean girl from the Midwest. It's not as if he was playing around with a prostitute in Amsterdam's red light district, where two condoms worn at the same time may not be enough to protect him from unspeakable STDs.

"Yeah, I'm on birth control. Relax, nothing for you to worry about."

Pierre wondered if he'd pissed her off. He hoped not, but one never knew. He assumed if Kirsten had wanted him to wear a condom, she would've said so. Damn, maybe he shouldn't have brought that up.

"When do you fly again?" She asked, in an obvious move to get away from the subject.

"Thursday. Four-day trip."

The friendly owner-waitress reappeared, depositing two delicious-looking plates in front of them. "Careful, these plates are very hot," she warned, adding more plates with toast, bacon and grits.

Pierre felt his mouth watering at the inviting aromas.

"*Bon appetit!*" He paused, allowing Kirsten to dig in first. Manners were essential in life, he contemplated.

He waited for her to take the first bite. Once she took her first bite he delighted himself with the flavor of his own scrambled eggs.

He was a little disappointed Kirsten couldn't join him for the fly-in at Oshkosh, but if she had to work, that came first. Attending a wedding with her would be fun.

"So, you wouldn't marry me, eh?"

She looked up from her plate. "Not in a million years."

"So I guess I'll just drop you off at home after breakfast, and be on my way."

"Suit yourself."

"Or I could drive you back to your apartment after we finish here and make wild love to you again."

"*Ha!* Dream on!"

He watched her assail her omelet with a voracious appetite.

FORTY-FIVE MINUTES LATER KIRSTEN shoved him hard, forcing Pierre to fall backwards onto her unmade bed.

"For God sake!" He had not expected it. He landed on his back, bouncing a couple of times.

She hastily stepped out of her black tights, jumping on the bed straddling Pierre. "Shut up lover boy! Don't say a thing!"

Kirsten unbuttoned his jeans, struggling to pull them off.

Pierre recovered from the surprise, deciding to let her have her way. Avocado must surely be an aphrodisiac. He was definitely amused that after breakfast she'd all of a sudden turned into a horny succubus.

"So, you won't marry me but you want me to be your sex slave and take advantage of me."

"Shut up, I said! Not a word!" She somehow managed to pull off Pierre's jeans and his boxer shorts, pitching them off the bed.

He was flat on his back on the ruffled bed, smiling at her aggressiveness. That was a new one! He enjoyed how she was taking the initiative. Pierre was already harder than a rock. Kirsten really knew how to turn him on. His fully erect member bobbed up and down when freed of his boxers.

Kirsten straddled him.

She wasn't wearing any panties.

He could sense her body heat radiating pleasurably against his crotch area.

Man, was she hot!

Kirsten placed one hand on Pierre's chest, shifting her hips to align her hot wet opening with his erection. Reaching below with her other hand she guided him into her vagina, lowering herself tantalizingly slow, impaling herself on his thick, hard cock, deliciously allowing the entire length of his shaft to slip inside her to the hilt. Her full weight was now resting on his crotch.

"Wow!" He definitely approved. He was stunned at how incredibly hot she was inside, and the feel of her buttocks resting on his lap was how he imagined heaven to be.

Kirsten stared at him for a few moments, not doing anything.

Then she lifted her hips up and down, slowly at first then provocatively increasing the pace, her inner walls milking him with a fury, violently grabbing and releasing his shaft in one continuous, agonizingly pleasant sequence.

Pierre was still a bit surprised at this New Kirsten. Thus far, he'd been the one calling the shots when they made love, but somehow the omelet had turned her into a delicious nymphet. Not that he was complaining, this was the most exciting girl he'd enjoyed for a long, long time. And he was unquestionably curious about what else she had in mind. He seriously wondered what the fuck they put in her avocado.

He caressed her breasts, rubbing the palms of his hands on them. Her nipples were erect and solid. So, he wasn't the only one turned on here.

Kirsten hadn't changed her rhythm. She was not too heavy, yet she felt pleasurably solid on top of him. And she was oh, so hot. He felt his balls tightening up, his stomach hard as a board. She was doing it, Kirsten was going to make him come. And goddamn, it hadn't taken her any time at all to reduce him into a pile of shivering Jell-O!

He breathed faster, releasing her breasts and grabbing her legs in mid-thigh. He used his back muscles and his legs to lift his pelvis up and down, lifting her as if she were riding a bucking bronco. He was strong, so she was having a wild ride. Kirsten had her nails buried in his chest, and was hanging on for dear life, her blond hair flailing wildly.

He was losing it.

Hell, fucking yeah! He was there. Waves of sweet orgasm hit him like a charging bull. He felt heat spreading from his balls to his chest, trembling starting in his feet, he could not stop it. The visual of Kirsten riding him while he shot his juices into her was erotic and delicious. His legs and back stiffened, elevating Kirsten off the bed. His body trembled violently, preventing respiration. Violent spasms of pleasure clouded his vision.

"*Oh, yeaaaah! Jumpin' sweet Jeesus!*" He spastically pumped in and out of her several times, feeling himself emptying deep inside her.

Then it was over.

"Whew!" He lowered his hips back on the bed, with Kirsten still straddling him. "What the Dickens *was* that?"

She smiled, flinging her hair away from her face with one hand.

"I thought I ordered you not to open your mouth, lover boy." She leaned forward, landing on his chest, moving her hips back away from him.

Pierre felt himself slipping out of Kirsten. They were both soaked again. He wasn't about to move. She had wiped him out. Her hair tickled his nose and cheek. He loved her weight on him. It was exciting and intimate. Somewhere, he found the strength to hug her and hold her against him. He turned his head, kissing her cheek, then her lips.

Hot damn, she had really sucked the life out of him.

He was the textbook definition of happiness.

Kirsten relaxed, allowing her body to become entirely limp on top of Pierre. She was fading rapidly. Pierre looked at her with tremendous affection and gratitude. Then he passed out.

PIERRE WOKE UP TO find Kirsten studying his face. She was resting on her side next to him, stretched out with her head leaning against the palm of her hand.

"Hello, lover."

He adored the sound of her voice.

"Hello Princess."

"I was just watching you sleep. You were smiling."

"That's cause I'm the cat who ate the canary."

She laughed. "And I'm the canary?"

He nodded, smiling.

"Well, then this canary is irrationally happy to have been eaten by the cat."

"So, am I still your sex slave?"

"You'll be that forever."

"Oh? I couldn't be that forever, remember? You said at breakfast you couldn't possibly be married to me."

"I changed my mind."

Pierre pulled Kirsten against his chest. "Come here."

She laid her chin on his chest, smiling. "What?"

"You changed your mind about marrying me?"

"Yes."

"That's wonderful, but what makes you think I would ask you?"

"That's easy. You like the sex."

Pierre laughed. "No, I like you, I like your smile, I love the sound of your voice, I like your looks. But the sex? Naah, it's all right—I guess—but nothing spectacular."

She punched him.

"Easy, tiger! You're bruising me! How am I gonna explain those bruises to my wife?"

Kirsten hit him again, only harder.

Pierre laughed, wrapping his arms around her, in an attempt to immobilize her.

"Not funny!" she cried, feigning anger.

"Relax, I'm just teasing you!"

She fought to break free from his hold, to no avail.

"Looks like your sex slave has you where he wants you now."

"Let me go!"

"If I let you go, you promise to stop hitting me and behave?"

She stared in his eyes.

"Yes."

Pierre released his grizzly hold on her.

Kirsten punched him again.

"You little stinker!" He sprang up, reaching for her, as Kirsten tried to put some distance between them.

"Oh, no, you're not going anywhere!" He quickly wrestled her nude body across his lap, face down. He managed to secure her arms, crossing them behind her back, immobilizing them with one hand. One of his legs went up over both of hers, holding her pinned in that position.

"Time for a spanking," he announced. He was aroused, breathing hard and on the warpath. Her act of rebellion had released thousands of Monarch butterflies in his crotch. He was so goddamn incredibly turned-on having her totally under his control.

"Don't you dare!" She warned, struggling desperately to break free. All her efforts were fruitless, he had her as immobile as a butterfly pinned to a display case.

Pierre smiled, admiring the rebelliousness of the adorable fighting bobcat he had securely trapped across his lap. Her gorgeous, sensual ass begging for a spanking.

He remembered he'd promised Kirsten a spanking for some reason or other, although he couldn't remember the details but now he had her at his mercy, and the temptation to paddle her butt was irresistible and delicious.

"Okay, the penalty for the insubordination of a princess in this kingdom is twenty spankings, milady. We shall commence."

"Don't you dare!" She pleaded, her butt desperately trying to swing away from Pierre's deadlock with renewed vigor.

He could sense Kirsten *knew* she was going to get paddled, she just wasn't accepting it.

He released her.

Kirsten pushed herself away, sitting up, her hair in disarray. Her big blue eyes staring at Pierre in surprise and relief.

"What? You chickened out?"

He laughed. I just want you to know, if I wish to spank your butt, I will do it."

"Bully!"

"I believe you wanted me to spank you."

"Did not!"

"Really? Seems to me you were really turned on."

"You have a vivid imagination, Pierre."

"Tell me you weren't dying in anticipation of my hand slapping your rear end."

Kirsten's cobalt blue eyes shone like a diamond illuminated by a strobe light.

"So, why didn't you spank me?"

He laughed. "I knew it."

"So? Why didn't you?"

"Because, Darling, from this moment on, you'll look forward to that time when I finally have you pinned down again and paddle your delicious rear end. But it will happen when I decide it will happen. In the meantime, I'll just keep you in suspense."

"You are a sadist."

"No, I just want you to endure so much anticipation, you'll beg me to spank you."

"Dream on."

Pierre laughed. "Okay. But when you're my wife be forewarned; I won't be able to resist smacking your exquisite rear end a couple of times a night."

"*When* I'm your wife?"

"If you're my wife."

"No, you said *when*."

Pierre smiled. The concept of having this fascinating, rebellious woman in his life forever was actually quite attractive. He was very surprised at himself. For someone who never ever thought of marriage, he was surely exploring new possibilities. Talking about Kirsten being his wife was turning him on, just like sex.

"Yes—okay—I said *when*. I'll admit, the idea of having you around permanently is quite addictive."

Kirsten became serious. "Having me around permanently? Is that your way of asking me to marry you?"

Pierre thought about this. Here they were, both nude in her bed after twenty-four plus hours of incredible intimacy. Was he asking her to marry him?

Maybe.

But he didn't want it to be this way. If he decided to make such a move, it would have to be done properly. He'd need a diamond ring, and a romantic dinner at an elegant restaurant, and soft music, and flowers.

"Yes and no."

She frowned. "What does that mean?"

"It means no. I'm not asking you to marry me right this minute, and yes, if I were to ask you, it would have to be done properly."

"Meaning?"

"Meaning I would have a ring for you. And it would be done in the proper setting." He couldn't read her. Was she disappointed? Relieved?

"And besides, I also feel you should have the opportunity to know me outside the bedroom a little bit better, before you decide I'm the one you want to spend the rest of your life with."

"I'm not so sure I understand what you're saying," she offered.

"Look, I never believed in love at first sight. I found the concept ridiculous. But ever since I met you, I'm unable to think of anything else but you. Is that love? I don't know, but I know that whatever it is, I like it. And I want to be with you every minute of the day."

She had her hand on his knee. "I changed my mind again. I wouldn't marry you in a thousand years."

"*What?* Why?" Now it was his turn to be confused.

"Because you didn't spank me."

FIVE DAYS LATER PIERRE still carried a taste of Kirsten in his lips. Her flavor was still there, sweet and exciting and electrifying. He was done, cooked, in love, in lust. She was his midnight fantasy.

All of the above.

Did he believe in love at first sight before meeting Kirsten?

Absolutely not.

Did he believe in love at first sight now?

Goddamn right he did.

Now he felt he was in love with her, totally infatuated, and happy as an angel fish cruising the coral reefs off the coast of Australia.

So, just to confirm, did he believe in love at first sight now?

Hell, yeah!

Pierre possessed a photographic memory, and had permanently engraved in it every second he spent with Kirsten. His memory put the digital camera in his smartphone to shame. He had replayed the 'story of us' tape in his mind many times over the last few days. Particularly the scenes where he was making love to that enchanting angel. After that incredible sexual marathon their first three days, they hadn't been able to connect again. Either she'd been flying or he'd been flying and their days off had not coincided. Holy Mongolian crap, he'd been dying to see her!

They texted every chance they got, but that wasn't enough. He wanted to see her, be with her, and of course, engage in steaming hot, passionate sex with her all day long. Talk about infatuation. Or was it really love? He smiled. Keep it at infatuation level for now? Probably too late for that.

"Worldwide three-fourteen, present heading, maintain three thousand until established, clear ILS runway Two-Eight Right approach. Tower at the marker."

The approach controller gave them their clearance to shoot the instrument approach into

Chicago. Pierre repeated the instructions, mentally preparing himself for the last part of their flight from Houston.

Time to put Kirsten out of his mind.

Glancing outside the windshield Pierre could see nothing but white. They were in the clouds, and although they were moving at close to 180 nautical miles per hour, looking outside provided no sense of speed or motion. Totally misleading to the untrained eye.

The baby blue and white A321 jetliner intercepted the localizer turning inbound towards O'Hare International Airport. The localizer was an invisible electronic beam airplanes tracked all the way to the runway.

His captain had setup the airplane for a full autoland. The airplane—baptized 'Fifi' by its pilots because pilots thought of airplanes in the female gender, and this was a French airplane, was ready to fly them all the way to the airport in weather so bad that even the ducks were walking.

Truly unbelievable.

Although he flew these airplanes for a living, Pierre had to admit that the technology still awed him. It stood to reason he understood how everything worked, but the guys still referred to it as PFM.

Pure fucking magic.

He could only imagine how his passengers would react if they knew that Fifi—the French girl—was flying them to O'Hare without either one of the pilots touching the controls.

Many of them would probably have diarrhea with blood at the thought. And next they would question why the jerkoff pilots were getting paid high salaries if they weren't even flying the damn thing.

Ahh, the importance of being ignorant. As long as the good folks in the back ignored what Fifi was doing, everyone could go about their happy lives.

Kirsten had spent the night at the airport hotel in Chicago, and she was still there. Pierre was going to spend his layover there tonight as well. Problem was, Kirsten was scheduled to leave the hotel in a little over one hour to work the late-night flight to Las Vegas. They had texted all day and initially agreed to meet in her room for a brief and much anticipated passionate sexual rendezvous, but the horrible weather in Chicago had delayed his arrival, and so now Pierre had doubts they would have any time together at all. The time they had planned on spending together had only been one hour anyway, which eventually had shrunk to thirty minutes due the weather. Traffic delays had now reduced that one hour to maybe ten minutes.

Very disappointing.

'Man plans and God laughs,' the Arabs said. How true that was, Pierre thought. He'd been dying to spend even a few minutes with Kirsten, but it just didn't seem it was going to happen.

"One hour?" She had questioned. "We're going to have just one hour together here in my room?"

"That's the best I can do. And that's only if the weather cooperates."

"Don't be crazy," she had insisted. "There's no need for you to bust your cute ass getting here so we can have a measly one hour together!"

Her surprising lack of enthusiasm had disturbed him. He'd be happy just spending ten minutes with her. One hour was a bonanza. But strangely she didn't quite seem to feel the same way.

He really had to get Kirsten out of his mind and monitor the friggin' airplane.

Fifi intercepted the glide path and the pilots configured the airplane for the approach, extending the flaps and lowering the landing gear. Fifi then slowed itself down to the approach target speed of 140 knots.

Pierre wanted to get out and push. They were going so damned *slow*. At this rate, he was never going to connect with Kirsten even for a couple of minutes.

Holy cripes on toast!

The way things were looking she'd be long gone by the time he arrived at the hotel. The thirty minutes Air Traffic Control had them holding over Joliet, Illinois, had sucked up his Kirsten time. Now he hated the town of Joliet.

With a passion.

The Airbus continued its descent, oblivious to the libidinous needs of the carbon-based life form inside.

A few minutes later, the ninety-ton airplane settled on runway Two-Eight Right, deploying the spoilers and applying the autobrakes.

Pierre grabbed a handful of thrust levers, pulling them back, activating the powerful reversers in the engines. The airplane decelerated to below 60 knots.

The ground controller gave them rapid-fire instructions directing them to their gate. The man sounded like an auctioneer.

The weather in Chicago was rainy, windy and gray.

Pierre retracted the flaps, going through his after landing flows. Their gate was a long way from the runway they were vacating.

By all means. Why would he expect anything to happen fast?

Pierre hoped Kirsten's flight to Las Vegas was delayed due to the weather. That would be a gift from heaven. Then, he could join her in her hotel room and kiss her, touch her, love her. For that to happen, however, her flight would have to take a gigantic delay. He smiled, resignedly. That was in all probability not going to happen.

His Galaxy smartphone chimed. He'd had it balanced on his lap.

Company policy absolutely prohibited the use of private cell phones in the flight deck while the aircraft was in motion.

What the heck.

He glanced at it.

Kirsten

Where are u?

Crap. They still had a long way to taxi. And then they'd have to shut down and hoof it over to the hotel van pick up point. If their van was already there, it'd take just a few minutes to make the hotel.

Pierre

Just landed.

They were taxiing in, still in what was known as the 'sterile cockpit.' Meaning no texting or talking allowed about anything not related to the operation of the aircraft.

He knew the captain he was flying with was very diligent, and the man was taxiing the airplane very conscientiously. Pierre could afford to steal a moment to communicate with Kirsten. She texted him again:

Kirsten

Doesn't look like I'm gonna see u. Leaving the room now. Heading downstairs.

Pierre cursed in a low voice. So much for their opportunity to get together. Ugh, all his efforts to make it to the hotel with an hour to spare had vaporized. He couldn't help but smile out of resignation. Heck, one can't force things in life. It'd been unwise of him to even think they were going to have an hour together, considering all the variables.

Pierre

> Sorry. Cursed weather.

Their gate came into view. It was drizzling. The skipper slowly maneuvered the A321 following the yellow line painted on the concrete leading to the gate. Pierre mentally reviewed his schedule. If he didn't get to see her now, they wouldn't be able to get together for another four days.

That sucked big time.

He'd had a taste of her and was desperate for more. Heroin withdrawal was chickenshit compared to the *Kirsten Withdrawal* he was experiencing.

He really wanted to spend time with Kirsten. Next month they were going to bid together and try to fly the same trips, although that was not a guarantee that things would work out in their favor. Regardless, even if he got to fly with her only half the month, that would be fantastic, and maybe they could also arrange to have days off together.

But that was next month. This month, they had no advantages. They just had to grin and bear it.

The captain brought the Airbus to a stop at the gate.

The Skipper shut down the engines and went through the usual procedures to secure the aircraft for the night.

This was it, layover time, end of the day.

Pierre rushed through his flows, wrapping up their last flight of the day. He hurriedly packed his headset, iPad and other miscellaneous personal items into his flight bag, standing in the flight deck putting on his jacket.

"I'm gonna run ahead and take a taxi to the hotel. I've got a friend who's leaving and I need to catch her before she leaves the hotel."

The captain nodded, barely registering what his copilot had said.

Pierre bolted out the door, pulling his wheelies.

He fought and dodged the O'Hare terminal crowds, cursing the mobs, finally exiting the building. He lucked out, flagging a cab right in front of the terminal, without any further delays. The cab driver didn't seem too happy when Pierre told him where to go. It was obvious the cab driver would've preferred a more substantial fare, instead of a five-minute ride to the airport Hilton. The driver pulled out into the traffic flow, cursing.

Pierre paid the man in front of the hotel, tipping him an additional five dollars. The guy still didn't look happy. The young aviator dashed past the front doors, entering the lobby. The place was crowded.

Then he saw her.

She was standing in the way back by the windows off to one side with the other members of her crew.

Hurrying over he couldn't help admiring Kirsten from afar, she was a sight to enjoy. Her uniform fit her perfectly, her hair was ready for a fashion magazine cover, and her porcelain face was flawless.

Pierre hadn't seen her in days, but the effect she had on him was the same as the first time he laid eyes on her at *Viera's* in St. Louis.

She was texting on her phone.

Dammit, she's already down here, all checked out of her room. Good-bye sex.

"Hi there!" She beamed at the sight of Pierre. "Pierre!"

The sound of his name from her lips rang like music in his ears, and made all his efforts getting there worthwhile.

He was dying to take her in his arms and kiss her, but recognized that public displays of affection in uniform were not necessarily the best of ideas. Not by any extent of the imagination.

Kirsten welcomed him, planting a soft kiss on his cheek, very European-style. Just two friends saying hello. She evidently had the same concerns about PDAs. And the flight attendants had to live with an even more severe code of conduct. Management flight attendants were often compared to the Gestapo by their peers, and rightly so.

A quick kiss on the cheek. Nothing more.

The rest of the crew barely acknowledged his presence, except perhaps a young flight attendant standing next to Kirsten, who appeared to notice him, checking him out.

"So sorry. Couldn't get here any sooner. The weather stunk."

"Relax, cowboy. I'll see you in four days."

The scent of her perfume rekindled the delicious longing for their intimate moments together. That pissed him off even more. He really *hated* the fucking radio fix over the town of Joliet, Illinois.

"You look so serious," she smiled.

Pierre shook his head. "Aw, So I guess this is it, I'll just see you in four days, eh?"

"I'll call you tonight," Kirsten noticed a couple of the other members of her crew starting to move. "I gotta go." She kissed Pierre in the lips this time, very softly.

"Have a good flight, sweetheart," was all he could think of saying. Using terms of endearment with Kirsten was easy to do, she was delightful. And by now he really adored her.

Kirsten walked away without responding, pulling her wheelies after her.

Pierre was left standing in the lobby, hypnotically following the sight of this incredible girl walking away.

Arghhh, he sure wished things were different, wished Kirsten had just arrived for an overnight with him. He would treat her to a nice, elegant, expensive dinner and then they'd spend the night making wild, passionate, steamy-hot love.

Soon as she disappeared from sight he snapped out of it.

Reality check, Bubba.

Time to go get a room.

THE ALARM WOKE HIM. God, he hated that thing!

He groggily reached for his smartphone, sliding his finger on its screen, effectively silencing it.

Time to go to work already?

Ugh!

He really hadn't slept all that great. He tried to remember what was on the agenda for the day. Two legs, one down to New Orleans and then on to New York City for the night. Pierre slowly sat up on the bed, wondering why the room was still so dark. His smartphone read 7:00 a.m. there should be light outside. Then he realized the room darkening curtains were still in place.

He used half an hour to shower and shave, carefully dressing for the day with the fastidious attention to detail a bull fighter would use.

Pierre made a mental note to ask Kirsten about that wedding next month. Was he expected to wear a tux? He'd have to line one up if that was the case. Shit, that meant a trip to the rental store to get fitted. Most of the guys renting tuxedos generally also rented the shirts for one night. Those shirts provided with the rental tuxedos were pure trash, garbage. They were made of cheap, thin cotton. If one was going to look decent, one had to invest a hundred bucks buying a fine tuxedo shirt. He planned on doing just that.

He wanted to look good for her.

Pilots and flight attendants normally stayed at two types of hotels during layovers, if the overnight was relatively short, around nine hours or less, then the company would put them up at an airport hotel, in order to minimize time wasted shuffling back and forth between the airport and the hotel. If the layover was longer, then the company contractually was obligated to accommodate the crews at downtown hotels, to provide its crew members with restaurant and entertainment options.

Pierre was aware that he was going to end up in New York City tomorrow. And the company was going to drive him down to his layover hotel in Manhattan for the night. He made a decision early the following morning he was going to take a walk over to the diamond district by 42nd street and buy Kirsten a gold necklace she could wear for the wedding. The price of gold had escalated something terrible, but he still wanted to do it. Many captains had shared with Pierre the fact that New York was the place to go when one wanted to buy gold or diamonds. You couldn't beat their prices, short of going to Sierra Leone yourself, which for all practical purposes was out of the question.

A beautiful necklace would probably cost him around five thousand. 85 or 90 grams of total weight in gold would make for a lovely necklace.

As a young man Pierre's uncle had pontificated to him, "nephew, never give women all the love nor all the money." Perhaps there was a lot of wisdom in those words, as he'd found out with Nicole.

But was Kirsten worth all the love and all the money?

Absolutely.

He had no doubt Kirsten deserved the gift.

Blasted, even if things didn't work out between them and she ultimately sent him packing, he felt she deserved a gift from him, a 'thank you' from the very deepest part of his soul, for providing him with so much happiness at a time when he really needed it.

He relished the thought of what her reaction would be when he gave it to her. Yeah, he was planning on dropping a lot of money for the necklace, but was totally thrilled with Kirsten and wanted to give her a valuable gift as a symbol of his feelings for her. Was it love that he felt for her? Or was it infatuation? Or just simple lust? What did it matter? Pierre didn't usually put labels on his feelings anymore. After the fiasco with Nicole, his ex, he'd become gun shy of that four-letter word, 'love.' He'd been 'in love' with Nicole, and where had it taken him? Precisely nowhere. So, using that word with girls was not something he was ready or willing to do again.

He liked Kirsten very much, really enjoyed being with her, was addicted to her body and her mind, found her funny and intelligent and hopefully the magic he felt when they were together would last for a long time. But was it love?

Who cared what it was called?

He'd noticed Kirsten wearing golden stud earrings with her uniform, so it should be safe to assume she liked gold.

Pierre was making a generous income as a First Officer, nearly two hundred thousand the previous year so he had more than enough funds in his accounts to cover the cost of the gift he wanted to buy for her.

Of course, he didn't carry that much cash with him. He'd just put it on his American Express. God bless his happy card.

There was so much he wanted to do for Kirsten. A hint of an idea began materializing in the distant corners of his mind. The diamond district where he was going to buy the gold also had diamonds for sale. What if he bought her one? An engagement ring? Was he a lunatic? He'd barely just started dating her. Pierre had lately become a firm believer in love at first sight, so why not now? Would she accept? He suspected she would. Was that what he wanted? He suspected it was.

Their conversation about getting married had been more than just casual pillow talk. Back then he'd decided that if he was ever going to marry, and if Kirsten was the woman of his dreams, then he'd have to ask her to marry him with a ring and flowers and all the other protocols which—in his mind—were important because they made women feel wanted and appreciated.

Yeah, the idea of a diamond ring was becoming more attractive by the minute. That would certainly change their lives. With that thought, and a smile on his face, he left the room headed for the elevator.

"YOUR LEG TO NEW Orleans, Boss," Pierre pointed out.

"That sounds about right," Captain Larry Reebie responded. Reebie was in his late fifties, had a small frame and whatever hair he still had was now predominantly grey.

They were back in what the men considered their office, the flight deck of another brand-new Airbus A321. The airplane smelled of metal and hot electronics and fine leather. The pilots' seats were covered in soft British leather, not unlike the upholstery found in the latest Jaguar sedans. The environment reeked of 'expensive.' And undoubtedly it *was* expensive, Pierre mused. His Airbus airliner represented a veritable smorgasbord of all the best the world had to offer. The finest metals, the most advanced electronics, the latest technology in plastics and fabrics and glass. Only the very best materials the world had to offer ended up in a jetliner. And this airplane cost *twelve hundred* times as much as a top-of-the-line Jaguar. Somewhere in the neighborhood of 130 million dollars. How was that for new-car smell?

That was one of the perks working for the best airline in the world. And the one making the most money, they were receiving brand new airplanes from Boeing and Airbus at the rate of four per week. Aahh, what a nearly erotic pleasure it was flying brand-new equipment.

Pierre checked out the view of the ramp below from his flight deck window. It was another wet Chicago day, rain and fog were going to be delaying departures from one of the world's busiest airports again. He observed a ramper covered in a blue raincoat sporting the airline's logo drive a luggage train up to the conveyor belt being used to load the bags on board. Two other rampers assisted, transferring bags from the luggage train onto the conveyor. The men were getting wet, the look on their faces one of complete determination, mixed with what could be interpreted as a touch of sadness. Pierre felt admiration for those men. What lives they had, lifting heavy bags in the rain for a living. And God only knew what they were getting paid. Probably not much. Meantime, he sat there in his air-conditioned flight deck, wearing a custom-made dress shirt and a tie, looking forward to some days in paradise with his incredible girlfriend.

Life was definitely not fair.

Airline pilots routinely alternated flying the airplane, taking the controls every other leg. That way, the flying was split fifty-fifty. First flight of the day on the first day of a trip belonged to the captain. From there on, the pilots just alternated legs. One pilot flew the airplane while the other monitored the operation and talked on the radio. In reality, both pilots were mentally flying the airplane at all times, but only one of the two manipulated the controls at a time. The airlines called this 'Pilot Flying' and 'Pilot Actively Monitoring.'

Pierre had brought the flight in the night before, so now it was the captain's turn to fly.

"You got the flight plan?" Captain Larry Reebie asked. Since he had to fly the next leg, it was his turn to enter the flight plan into the airplane's computer, the super sophisticated MCDU—Multipurpose Control and Display Unit.

Airlines *loved* acronyms.

Pierre handed the skipper a stack of printed flight documents clasped on a simple wooden clipboard. "Here you go." That paperwork had been given to the pilots at the gate, before walking down to the airplane.

Pierre grinned at the irony of a modest, wooden clipboard being used to hold together the paperwork for an ultra-high-technology modern computerized jet airliner.

The Captain concentrated on entering the information from the paperwork into the aircraft computer. The device was capable of navigating just about anywhere, and basically did everything a flight engineer and a navigator used to accomplish in the days when airliners carried four pilots. Now, however, thanks to the computer revolution, two pilots could do the work of four with the help of the on-board electronics.

Once Captain Larry Reebie finished entering all the data into the computer, Pierre accepted the clipboard back and together with the captain performed a route verification, ensuring that everything the skipper was asking Fifi to do was exactly according to plan. Entering erroneous data into the computer could very easily result in an accident or incident.

A male flight attendant entered the flight deck. "Hi! I'm Louis, you gentlemen would like anything to drink?"

Pierre was glad he'd finished the route verification prior to the interruption. He did not like it when the flight attendants or anyone else for that matter, interrupted his routine. Bad Karma. A simple interruption could generate a distraction with the potential to create an accident.

"Some coffee would be great," Captain Larry Reebie answered, turning to look at the flight attendant, giving him a smile. "Cream and sugar on the side would be nice, too."

The flight attendant nodded. "And you?"

"A Diet Coke and a bottle of water would be terrific. Thanks."

The flight attendant departed the flight deck leaving the door open. Pierre caught a glimpse of passengers boarding the airplane through the L-1 door. 'L' meant the door was located on the left side of the fuselage starting from the front of the airplane. The '1' merely indicated it was the first door out of four on that side of the airplane.

"So, down to New Orleans, final resting place of Katrina, and then back up to the Big Apple," Captain Larry Reebie stated aloud to nobody in particular.

Pierre liked him, he was an educated, gentle soul married to the same woman for decades and with two kids he could be proud of. "Final resting place of Katrina, how'd you figure that?"

"That's where hurricane Katrina went to die. Don't you remember?"

"Sure, I remember it hit New Orleans, I just didn't know that's where it went to die."

"Technically, once the storm hit land, it stopped being a hurricane. Its horribly destructive power diminished very rapidly over land. It went from a hurricane to a tropical storm rather quickly. That's why New Orleans was the final resting place of *hurricane* Katrina. *Storm* Katrina continued along its path of destruction after New Orleans, but no longer in the hurricane category."

"I'll buy that."

"Cool! I'll be happy to take your cash."

Pierre considered the humor rather infantile, but he still wouldn't hold it against Larry. He did like the guy.

"Morning, gentlemen."

Both pilots turned to look at the new guy.

"Was wondering if I could hitch a ride with you fellas down to New Orleans," he said, handing a jumpseat authorization request and an airline badge to Reebie.

The young man wore a TransCon pilot uniform and sported a Louisiana twang. "Sam Thomas," he said, offering his right hand. He was tall and dark, as in Black German. Caucasian but with dark hair and eyes.

Reebie accepted the paperwork, shaking the newcomer's hand at the same time. "Larry Reebie."

Pierre extended his own for a handshake. "Pierre White."

The newcomer reached over the center pedestal, shaking hands with Pierre.

Captain Reebie studied the paperwork the newcomer gave him, carefully comparing the information on the badge with the hand-written name on the form. "Glad to have you," he finally said, returning the documents to the man. "Looks like we're gonna be pretty full, you may have to ride up front with us."

"That's fine. I really appreciate the ride."

"Hey, a man's gotta get home any way he can," Reebie pointed out. "You can secure your bag over there, by the manuals."

Although most modern airliners only needed two pilots, the majority of the flight decks, or cockpits as they were called during the first ninety years of commercial aviation, usually had three or four crew seats. Two of those seats were for the pilots flying the airplane. The others were extra and were known as 'jumpseats.' Those extra seats were normally available so FAA inspectors could observe pilots in the performance of their duties to ascertain they were safe and following company procedures.

Airline pilots worldwide were allowed the use of the extra seats, known as 'jumpseats' to travel anywhere they wanted to go, depending on the agreements existing at the time between the different airlines and as long as no inspectors were occupying the seats. Protocol required pilots to ask the captain for authorization to use the 'jumpseat.' The captain would normally invite the 'jumpseater' to take a seat in the First Class or Coach cabins, provided there was an empty seat back there. But when the cabin was full, then jumpseat riders had to remain in the flight deck the entire flight. Not terribly comfortable, but how could anyone complain when it was a free ride.

Louis, the male flight attendant, returned with the drinks. Noticing the presence of the additional pilot, he asked the newcomer if he would like something to drink as well.

"No, thanks, I'm good." The TransCon pilot did his best to move out of the way of the flight attendant.

Pierre loved his job, but these past few days he'd been having a real hard time concentrating. His thoughts kept going back to Kirsten. Once again, he admitted he was definitely infatuated with the girl. Infatuated? Duh, he was head over heels for her. He liked everything about her. He was dying to spend more time with her. He wanted to spoil her, pamper her, treat her like a queen. And definitely spend hours and hours engaged in steamy, earth-shattering, passionate animal lovemaking with her.

In one word, he was in love with her.

There was—however—this annoying voice in the back of his head warning him to slow down. He'd been without a girlfriend for too long, hence he was vulnerable. He could easily get totally fucked up if he wasn't careful.

Did his presence in her life have the same impact as she was having in his? He hoped that was the case. So many days had passed since that first night they spent together in Minneapolis, Pierre was starting to fear it had all been just a product of his imagination. But indubitably, the hundred or so texts they were exchanging daily contradicted that absurd notion.

The insane flying schedules they both had were not conductive to spending time together. He smiled, maybe that crazy idea of being married to her was not so crazy after all? That way, at least they could be assured of being home at the same time when he was not on a trip.

Pierre balanced the can of Diet Coke inside his flight bag alongside his seat, removing the cap from the plastic water bottle and taking a couple of long drinks from it.

"How 'bout we do the 'Before Start' checklist, Pierre?"

"You bet." He inserted the water bottle into a small cylindrical receptacle designed exactly for that purpose. Pierre then reached for a white cardboard checklist resting on top of the glare shield.

"Before start checklist," he started reading. "Recorder ground control ..."

"On."

"Logbook and flight forms—"

"On board."

"Fuel quantity, verify twenty-five thousand six hundred required. Twenty-six thousand on board—"

Pierre read the other fifteen items from the printed card. Those were the 'killer items,' the ones that could kill you and your passengers if you overlooked any of them. Precisely why they were on the checklist.

"Before start checklist complete," he informed the skipper.

The jumpseat occupant got busy parking himself in the seat behind Pierre, buckling his five-point seatbelt and testing his oxygen mask with a hiss of escaping gas.

The male flight attendant stuck his head through the flight deck door. "You gentlemen have all your paperwork?"

"We certainly do," Captain Reebie responded. He was adjusting his seatbelt.

"All passengers are seated and all bags are stowed. Ready to close the cabin door."

"Go ahead and close it."

The flight attendant departed the flight deck, closing the door behind him.

Pierre reached down, pressing a square button on the center pedestal, locking the cockpit door. The horrible attacks against New York had made security a very real part of their lives.

This was the start of the 'sterile cockpit.' Once again, from that point on, until the flight reached 10,000 feet in the air, all conversation not related to the operation of the airplane was prohibited. The FAA had created the rule to prevent crew errors during high workload stages of the operation. Many fatal accidents had occurred because the pilots had been distracted by idle chatter during taxi, takeoff and climb. Baseball scores, casual flirting with flight attendants and discussions about home and garden had caused almost as many accidents as mechanical problems.

The closing of the main passenger door behind them made the aircraft shake, followed by the sounds of the jet bridge being retracted.

"Pierre, would you be so kind as to get us pushback clearance."

Pierre transmitted on the ground control frequency. "Ground, Worldwide six-five-one gate four bravo. Ready to push with alpha."

The ground controller immediately replied. "Worldwide 651, gate four bravo, clear to push."

"Cockpit to ground," Captain Reebie spoke into his mike.

"Go ahead Cap'n."

"Yeah, we're ready up here, cleared to push."

The tug operator below the nose of the airplane revved up his engine. A cloud of diesel fumes belched from the exhaust. "Cleared to push, release the brakes."

Captain Reebie stepped on the top of the two pedals in front of him, releasing the brakes.

"Brakes released."

"Clear to start engines one and two," the tug driver announced. His two walkers were checking out the wingtips of the Airbus as it began to move backwards so it wouldn't collide with any obstacles.

"Let's start engine number one," Captain Reebie instructed.

ONE HOUR LATER THE white and blue Worldwide Airlines Airbus A321 was cruising in clear skies, twenty thousand feet above the stratiform overcast below.

Pierre had his table pulled out in front of him. Since the Airbus he was flying had a joystick instead of a yoke, he was able to enjoy the convenience of a nice retractable table. His Toshiba laptop rested comfortably on it. He just *loved* Airbus airplanes.

Captain Reebie's HP laptop was also solidly resting in front of him.

Airline procedures and FAA regulations expressly prohibited the use of personal computers on the flight deck for purposes not related to the operation of the airplane.

You make stupid, unreasonable rules, Pierre pondered, people will ignore them. Throughout the history of airline flying, pilots had historically engaged in what they considered occupational therapy once they were cruising along at altitude. Reading a newspaper, sharing photos of that new sailboat, discussing the airline's labor contract, planning a new vacation to the Virgin Islands. All of these harmless activities kept the pilots awake and alert during long hours of cruise flight. Without these activities, sometimes it was very difficult to remain alert, particularly during a night flight.

With the advent of the computer age, all of the above activities became digital. Most crewmembers carried some kind of laptop with them. So, even in these modern times, pilots could still read a newspaper, share photos of their families or their toys and discuss labor issues. Only now they did all this on their laptops.

The jumpseater behind them didn't have a table, but he also had his laptop out, balanced on his lap.

The intercom chimed.

Pierre took the call. He listened for a moment.

"It's Louis. You guys want some lunch?"

"*Ooh la la,*" Captain Reebie expressed. "I'd love some."

"Sure, thanks!" the jumpseater joined in. "If you have enough for everyone, that is."

Pierre told the flight attendant they'd love having something to eat.

Two minutes later there was a knock on the flight deck door.

All three pilots closed their laptops, getting them out of sight.

"I can get that if you want me to," the jumpseater offered. He'd removed his uniform coat.

"Go for it," Pierre responded, glad the guy was there, saving him from having to climb out of his seat to go open the flight deck door. "Just look through the door viewing port first and tell me you see Louis out there, then I'll unlock the door."

The TransCon pilot placed his face against the door viewing port, verifying who was on the other side. "Ya, looks like Louis on the other side."

An electric solenoid cycled, unlocking the door.

The flight attendant in charge of all the others was known as the Purser. The flight deck door opened and Louis, the Purser, walked in, carrying three trays with crewmeals.

"I have a steak, turkey and a spaghetti Bolognese."

Airline regulations required pilots to eat different crewmeals at different times. This was intended to prevent both pilots from becoming incapacitated simultaneously in case the food was bad. Since the airlines rarely put identical crewmeals onboard, the pilots seldom consumed the same food. The timing, however, was another issue. Although, in theory, the pilots had to eat at different times, in real line operations, that never happened.

Hey, we're both hungry at the same time, Pierre liked to think. Ain't no way in hell I'm sitting here waiting for the other puke to slow-chew through his steak while my stomach is trying to kill me by digesting itself.

The jumpseater didn't have a table, but he found a small airline pillow at the back of the flight deck, placing it on his lap. He then rested his food tray on it.

The two pilots placed their crewmeals on the tables in front of them, digging in. The food was not bad, really, but after a couple of hundred crewmeals, pilots avoided them like the plague. Pierre often bought himself personal pan pizzas at the airport during the time they were on the ground. Or a burger, or a chicken sandwich. Anything but the horribly monotonous domestic crew meals.

Captain Reebie finished first. Having assaulted the steak dinner with a voracious appetite, he wiped his mouth with a paper napkin. "So, Sam, you going home?"

The jumpseating pilot swallowed a mouthful of spaghetti Bolognese. "Yeah, just finished a three-day trip yesterday."

Pierre noticed the guy had some Bolognese sauce on his shirt.

"Where's home?"

"Just outside New Orleans,"

"You finished your trip yesterday and just now you're going home? What happened, you couldn't catch a ride home last night?"

Captain Reebie reached back, placing his food tray on the carpet behind the center pedestal.

The jumpseater shook his head. "I spent the night in Chicago. My girlfriend's a flight attendant and it just so happened she had a layover there, so I stayed with her."

Pierre was instantly envious. Hot damn! He'd tried his best to have one lousy hour together with Kirsten, and it hadn't worked out. And this puke had spent the entire night with his girlfriend. Not fair.

Lucky bastard.

"You on the bus?" Pierre asked.

"Yes, but not on this one, I'm on the big one, the A350."

"No kidding? That's great. How'd you like that airplane?" Pierre was anxious to get off the 'little' bus, as they called the A321, and transfer to the big widebody, the A350, so he could fly to Europe.

Worldwide was hiring pilots every month and at such a fast pace, Pierre estimated he'd be able to switch to the widebody before too long, provided a pilot bid came out.

"Best job in the world," the jumpseater confirmed. "But someone's gotta do it," he added, in traditional airline jest, feigning resignation.

"Are you French?" Captain Reebie asked.

"French? No. Why?"

"You live in New Orleans."

The jumpseater laughed. "All sorts of people live in New Orleans, Boss. I happen to be Greek. I mean, my grandparents came from Greece."

"Greek, eh?" Captain Reebie turned to look at the jumpseater. "So your ancestors fought the Persian army of Xerxes at Thermopylae?"

"No, actually, those were the Spartans. Didn't you see the movie?"

"Yeah, I saw the movie. I thought it was the Greeks."

"No, not the Greeks. The Spartans were the warriors."

"Hey Larry," Pierre piped in. "You better get your ancient history straight. You're embarrassing me."

"These goddamn copilots are getting more insolent all the time," Captain Reebie joked.

Pierre decided he might as well offend everyone. "I heard the Greeks invented sex." He paused for some effect. "But it was the Italians who introduced it to women."

Captain Reebie laughed loudly.

"Very funny. A real knee-slapper," the jumpseater remarked, pretending to be offended.

"You said your girlfriend is a flight attendant?" Pierre asked.

"That's right. She flies for you guys. But I don't get to see her much because you guys are flying her tail off."

"Hey, at least you were able to catch up with her last night."

"Very lucky break for me. It doesn't happen very often." The jumpseater released his seatbelt. "You guys mind if I step outside to use the restroom?"

"Go right ahead," Pierre offered, reaching for the flight deck door unlock button. "Have one of the flight attendants ring us on the intercom when you're ready to come back.

The jumpseater left the flight deck, shutting the door behind him.

"So, you're gonna switch over to the big bus?" Reebie asked.

"Hmm, yeah. First chance I get."

"Itchin' to fly international, eh?"

"That's right. I like long legs. Coast to coast flights are all right, but I really don't enjoy short hops. Up and down several times a day is not for me. Just lazy by nature, I guess."

"You're gonna age faster flying across the pond."

"How do you figure that?"

"You mentioned you're planning on moving to Phoenix, right?"

"That's the plan."

"So, you're going to be commuting from Phoenix to New York?"

"Yeah, if that's where I end up being based."

"You'll be crossing eleven time zones every time you go to work. That, and the sleep deprivation when flying eastbound will age you. Haven't you noticed how most of our senior crews flying across the Atlantic look eighty years old?"

Pierre laughed. "Yes, I've noticed that. They all have white hair. You're saying that's due to crossing that many time zones?"

"That's exactly what I'm saying. If I were you I'd bid Miami or LAX and fly the South American routes instead. There, you won't cross that many time zones just flying up and down the coast of South America. And you will age gracefully."

"Yea, I may do that eventually, but I'm kinda looking forward to flying to London, Paris, Rome."

"You're single, right?" Captain Reebie didn't wait for Pierre to answer him. "You can find good-looking babes everywhere. You oughta see the Brazilian women."

Pierre had heard about the Brazilian women. A couple of captains had already shared with him how desirable they were, and how getting some of them to bed was not really all too difficult, if that's what one wanted. Those Rio de Janeiro hotel bars were swarming with girls, according to the old dogs.

"Yeah, I'm aware of that, but I'm not out hunting for good-looking babes. I've already got a girlfriend. One of our flight attendants, as a matter of fact."

"You too?" Captain Reebie shot him a sideways glance, smiling.

Pierre nodded. "Yeah, me too. She's a terrific girl. We've only been dating a couple of weeks."

"Sweet!"

"Tomorrow morning I'm planning on walking out to forty-second street to buy her a gold necklace. We're going to a wedding together and I want her to wear it."

"A gold necklace? Whew, she hit you hard. She must be some girl."

Pierre had a quick flash of Kirsten stretched out nude on her bed, her golden hair spread on the pillow, followed by an image of her laughing. "That, she is, Larry, she's very special to me."

"That wouldn't happen to be the 'friend' you were in such a hurry to meet yesterday when you bolted like a bat out of hell catching a cab ride to the hotel, would it?"

Pierre laughed. "No. Whatever gave you that idea?"

"Just asking, is all."

Pierre looked at the skipper, smiling. "Yeah, that was my girl."

"So, did you connect with her?"

"I did, but only for a couple of minutes."

"Bummer, disappointment!"

"That sucked." Pierre decided to keep the idea of a diamond ring to himself. Somehow, he suspected Reebie would question his sanity if Pierre shared that particular bit of information.

"I can imagine."

The intercom chimed. The jumpseater was outside the door, ready to return to the flight deck.

"I'll get it, I need to stretch my legs," Reebie offered. He released his seatbelt, stepping out of his seat, moving to the door. He glanced out the peephole, confirming that indeed, the jumpseater was outside the door waiting to be allowed in.

A minute later they were all back in their seats.

"They're landing to the south," Pierre pointed out, handing Reebie a piece of paper with the latest airport information for New Orleans Louis Armstrong International airport.

"So we're coming in over the lake," Reebie noted.

"Yep."

"I just *love* that approach at night, Reebie said sarcastically. "Freakin pitch black hole. Coming over the water at night provides me with no frame of reference whatsoever. I just feel like I'm floating inside a black barrel of oil, standing perfectly still," Reebie complained. "Very easy to end up in the water if one's not paying attention."

"I've flown that a few times. I know exactly what you mean."

"Thank God we're not landing in the dark today."

"Thank God," Pierre agreed.

"Years ago," Reebie continued, "when I was a young man flying 727s, I read about some crew who ended up in Lake Michigan during a night approach into O'Hare. They were in the same black hole and didn't realize they were sinking like a Texas shithouse. Flew smack into the water. That was before the days of altitude warning systems. In fact, I seem to recall that it was due to that accident that the FAA mandated that all airliners would have to be equipped with altitude alerters."

"Aah, the 'Dirt Alert'," Pierre joked.

"You guys hand-flew the approaches a lot more in the old days, didn't ya?" Pierre scanned the sky ahead. Blue and a million miles visibility and no other traffic in sight.

"You bet we did!" Reebie spat out. "None of this sissy bullshit being on autopilot the entire time. We *liked* to fly, so we flew."

Pierre smiled at the old dog bravado. "You must admit, Larry. When you're absolutely beat at the end of a long day, Fifi can do a heck of lot better job flying the airplane than we can. And she won't fly you into the lake either, black hole or no black hole. I think safety is a lot better today because of automation. One hell of a lot safer, I would say."

"I don't like all this automation. Shit, I don't even like using the cruise control in my Beemer."

Pierre was aware that some of the old-timers abhorred automation. They insisted on hand-flying the big airliners as much as possible, which was comparatively unsafe and not economic. Fifi could fly itself better and more efficiently than most pilots could. At all times. That was something worth remembering when one was exhausted and not thinking clearly at the end of a long day.

Fifi never tired, she never had a bad night sleep, never drank alcohol and didn't fuck all night.

"The company keeps buying all these high-tech airplanes for us. What, they think we don't know how to fly? We need the autopilot to fly them for us?" Freebie was getting worked up.

"Worldwide didn't buy these highly automated, top-of-the-line airplanes to make our lives easier, Boss. They bought them to make more money. The automation saves us money. If I were to hand-fly this here airplane from LA to New York, I would burn more fuel than Fifi would if she flew the airplane on autopilot without any control input from us," Pierre explained.

"Say I burn a hundred bucks more fuel than Fifi, then multiply that times six thousand flights a day. That's over half a million bucks a day. Almost two hundred million a year in fuel savings. Yeah, an added beneficial side effect of the automation is that flying has become a lot safer than it used to be, but bottom line, don't fool yourself thinking the company did it for safety or to make our jobs easier."

Pierre gulped some water from a bottle. "The company doesn't really give a rat's ass about our comfort or about safety. They are merely interested in the economic aspect of it. Sure, they'll spout all sorts of statements of concern to the media, alleging that their first and foremost concern is always safety. Bullshit. Their first and foremost concern is always money. It's the same with every airline in the world. They carry all sorts of insurance in case of an accident, hull insurance to replace the airplane, liability insurance to pay off the relatives, loss of income insurance to cover the money they lost by crashing an airplane."

Captain Larry Reebie responded with a grunt.

Time to change the topic. Pierre turned to look at the jumpseater. "So, your girlfriend's one of our flight attendants?"

"Yeah, yes. Typical flight attendant, wants to marry me and live happily ever after. I'm not really interested in marriage, though. She's great in the sack, and has great tits, but I don't really know if I'm gonna keep her around too much longer. She's becoming sorta of a pain in the ass."

Pierre was astonished.

Wow. A real gentleman.

What a total asshole!

'Real Gentlemen don't tell,' Pierre had firmly believed his whole life. This guy talked about his girlfriend like some men talk about the prostitutes they frequented. Not cool. Pierre studied the man carefully. He appeared well-groomed and intelligent. Yet, his statements were completely offensive. His poor girlfriend, probably thinking she'd landed a good candidate for a future together, and here was the asshole telling two complete strangers that she had great tits.

Pierre decided the guy was not worth a conversation. Shaking his head, he replaced his laptop on the small table in front of him, pushing the 'resume' button. A total dipshit. Obviously, the dude had no class. Who talks that way about a woman they love? Or even if he didn't love her, who talks that way about a woman they are dating. Or any woman, for that matter?

"Here, let me show you some real hot pictures," the jumpseater offered, reaching for his smartphone.

Reebie turned in his seat to look.

Pierre decided to ignore the man. Show them hot pictures of his girlfriend? Goodness, that just completed the image he had of the guy as a complete scumbag.

"I took these last night while I was fucking her," the jumpseater explained to Reebie, holding out his phone so the captain could see the screen.

"...I can't say I've ever met her," Reebie admitted. "But then again, her face's not showing."

The jumpseater hee-hawed, flipping to the next photo. "Here, you can see her face."

"...Aah, a very pretty girl," Reebie complimented.

"Fuck, yeah!" the jumpseater agreed.

Pierre could tell by Reebie's tone of voice that the captain was embarrassed. And why wouldn't he be? He was being shown photos of some chick in compromising positions, from the sound of it.

"Yeah, she's purty, ain't she? Check her out!" The jumpseater held out the phone for Pierre to see.

He was compelled to look. Ignoring the imbecile would just create conflict.

The girl in the screen shot was very beautiful indeed. At least her body was. Her face was not visible and she was in the middle of what appeared to be a steamy sexual encounter. To be expected. Why else would this idiot flaunt the pictures? So, the jumpseater had taken pictures of his girlfriend while he was having sex with her. Big deal. Many people did that, but not many people shared the pictures with strangers. The guy was a dick.

The jumpseater flicked the phone with his finger, advancing to the next picture.

Pierre froze.

There, looking back at the camera smack in the middle of sex, was Kirsten. She was straddling the man holding the camera, a look of intense concentration on her face.

His Kirsten.

He looked at the jumpseater and then at the picture again. No doubt in his mind. That was Kirsten. And the douchebag said he'd just taken those pictures last night.

Last night. Layover in Chicago. *Holy fucking crap!*

"Can I see that?" He managed to blurt out, his voice unsteady.

The jumpseater handed the smartphone to Pierre, who grabbed it unceremoniously. "Just use your finger to flip through the pictures," the pilot added, relinquishing the phone.

Pierre shifted in his seat, facing forward, holding the cell phone against his belly. He flipped through several more pictures, seeing his Kirsten in many different sexual positions, engaged in apparently hot steamy sex with this asshole seating in his jumpseat.

He was speechless. The situation was absolutely astonishingly unbelievable. His mind was telling him it couldn't be, yet his eyes were telling him otherwise.

He looked again, confirming that yes—that was her.

Pierre somehow had to have some of these pictures. Asking the dipshit for them would probably not work. Pierre rapidly figured out how to extract the pictures from this guy's cell phone. All it took were a couple of screen taps and then selecting his own cell phone Bluetooth icon. *Voila!* He sent himself five photos in but a few seconds. Thank God he kept his cell phone turned on in flight with Bluetooth enabled.

Once the transfer was done, Pierre turned back to look at the jumpseater, handing him back the cell phone. "Here you go, she is impressive. What's her name?"

"Kirsten! Been with her four months now. She's a dish, ain't she?"

"That she is," Pierre said, facing forward again, gritting his teeth.

Holy shit.

He spent a couple of minutes taking deep breaths. What he'd really love to do at this precise moment was hack this jumpseater into pieces with the flight deck crash axe. Or discharge his Glock's entire forty-caliber thirteen-round magazine into the asshole's shit-eating-grin. One problem was, he didn't have his pistol with him. Maybe a set of brass knuckles would do.

'... She has great tits, but I don't really know if I'm gonna keep her around too much longer. She's becoming sorta of a pain in the ass.'

Pierre was furious. Disappointed, frustrated and more than furious. His anger transferred to Kirsten. Okay, okay. How could he have misread her so bad?

What an idiot he was. And like a complete moron, he'd built all these expectations of her. Her betrayal had him gasping for air. Okay, he had to concede they hadn't said anything about exclusivity, true. So, he couldn't really consider it a betrayal. But he'd taken exclusivity for granted, why shouldn't he? He really thought she was as taken by him as much as he'd been mesmerized by her. She sure didn't tell Pierre she was dating anyone else. And not that she had to, but lying by omission was just as bad as lying to one's face.

And she'd just spent the night with this asshole? That was even more shocking. He couldn't help a silent laugh. She's been dating this Romeo for nearly *four months* and she hasn't caught on that he doesn't really give a shit about her? The way he spoke of her made that totally evident. Pierre suddenly wondered if the jumpseater had any inkling that Kirsten was two-timing him with Pierre. Probably not.

Ha! He was dumber than he looked.

Wow, he thought he'd satisfied her sexually, at least enough so that she could hold off until their next rendezvous. And then she ends up in bed with this guy in her hotel room just last night.

A devastating blow, to say the least. How about that?

This was unfuckingbelievable!

"You okay?" Captain Reebie asked, a look of concern on his face.

Pierre was jerked out of his reverie. "What?"

"You all right? You just went real quiet and weird there all of a sudden."

"Ah, no. I'm all right. Just thinking, that's all."

"Okay. Just checkin."

"You guys staying in New Orleans for the night?"

The shithead spoke.

"Naw," Reebie answered. "We still got another leg on to New York. Spending the night there."

"That's too bad. I could've shown you guys a small restaurant I know right by the Gulf. It's not a fancy place, but it's great. All they sell is shrimp and beer."

Paul considered how many ways he could kill the man with a bottle of beer.

"But I guess in New York you'll find plenty of places to eat."

Pierre thought of New York, tasting vomit in his mouth. His plan to buy Kirsten a gold necklace came back to mind. And a diamond ring. What an idiot he was. He tried to think of *anything* that could've given him a hint that she was two-timing him. Much as he squeezed every single last drop of memory from his brain, he couldn't think of a single hint Kirsten could've given him that she had another guy in her life.

Damn, she was good.

Was he just stupid? Being away from girls for too long, that's what it was. He was just out of practice. She had played him like the proverbial fiddle.

Outsmarted by a twenty-two-year-old.

Humbling, to say the least.

No way he was buying her anything now, much less a five-thousand-dollar gold necklace. That splendid plan simply disintegrated, deleted from the agenda.

The men got busy readying the Airbus for the descent and arrival into New Orleans. Pierre tried forcing the issue out of his mind. The Kirsten issue. Time to take care of business.

Wishful thinking. As expected, he wasn't able to get Kirsten out of his mind.

Who was he kidding?

And those photographs. He was itching to check his phone, see if the Bluetooth had done its job transmitting those photographs. The photos. What the devil was he gonna do with those? Send them to her? A picture paints a thousand words. He wanted to get a hold of the jumpseater's cell phone so he could delete the pictures of Kirsten. Or if he just destroyed that phone, then the asshole wouldn't have pictures of Kirsten to look at later. Pierre could just ask him for the phone and remove the card from it. If it had a card. Or maybe just 'accidentally' smash the damned thing against the center console. *'Ooops! How could that happen?'* he would say. My bad! Too obvious?

How could she pose for him like that, allowing him to take pictures of her? Another thought occurred to Pierre. Surely dipshit sitting behind him must have hundreds of other pictures of Kirsten in his own computer. He didn't just start taking pictures yesterday. So, destroying the prick's cell phone wouldn't guarantee that all of Kirsten's pictures had been wiped out.

Maybe he could kill him with the cell phone.

Frustrating as all hell.

And what were the odds that the one dickhead Kirsten was involved with would hitch a ride on his flight today? Astronomical. Incredible. Hard to believe.

Straight out of a Steven Spielberg movie.

She must've thought that since the guy was a TransCon pilot she was safe. The odds of a TransCon pilot and a Worldwide Airlines pilot connecting with each other were smaller than winning the Powerball. No way, that was just not ever gonna happen.

Until now.

"Why don't we do the 'Descent and Approach' checklist, Pierre?"

Reebie yanked him out of his thoughts again. Dammit, he had to get away from Kirsten and concentrate on doing his job.

"Descent and Approach checklist," he read it out loud, listening to Reebie's responses.

"Descent and approach checklist complete."

"Thanks, Pierre."

THIRTY MINUTES LATER CAPTAIN Larry Reebie set the parking brake at the gate, officially completing the flight. The whine of the auxiliary power unit was the background sound once the turbofans began winding down.

"And so, modern technology has once again overcome ignorance, fear and superstition," Reebie chanted.

The jumpseater stood up behind the two pilots, getting his bags ready to go. He had his coat back on.

"Thanks for the ride, guys. Really appreciate it." Reebie took the jumpseater's extended hand, shaking it. "Hey, our pleasure. See you again, someday."

The hand was then offered to Pierre, who ignored it, pretending to be examining his iPad, attached to his window.

The jumpseater, unperturbed, withdrew his hand, lifted his bags and beat it. He was out of the flight deck at the blink of an eye.

Pierre began preparing the airplane for their next leg to New York, thankful that Reebie was not questioning his rudeness.

Now what?

Was he going to ignore everything that had just happened and carry on with Kirsten as if nothing had taken place? Yeah, that was one option. In her wildest tequila dreams she had no way of knowing her boyfriend had hitched a ride with her newest lover.

Or he could confront her and see what she had to say for herself. There was no denying that was her in the pictures. Aah, live proof. But then again, why exactly was it that he thought he was entitled to exclusivity? Did he really have a right to be so angry?

Many things bothered him about this situation. The fact that she'd slept with this asshole after what they had together. Or what he *thought* they had together. Also, her dishonesty. He'd just seen her a few hours ago, and she had not even hinted at any of this.

Sonofabitch.

He didn't know what next. And he still had to fly this bucket to New York City. Better put her out of mind and get the show on the road. Oh, yeah, the pictures. Before getting more involved with the procedures required to prepare the airplane, Pierre reached for his smartphone. He touched the 'Gallery' icon, finding himself staring at five pictures of a nude Kirsten, engaged in intense sexual activity with Sam Thomas, *aka pieceofshit.* He stared at them for one minute straight. Yeah, she was so attractive.

And she didn't know the meaning of the word 'loyalty.'

Forty-five minutes later they had the airplane ready, the passengers onboard and were taxiing out headed for the runway.

His cell phone chimed.

Pierre glanced down at it, totally against company and FAA regulations.

Kirsten

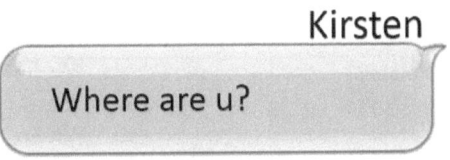

Where are u?

He glanced at his watch. She was probably already on the ground in Las Vegas.

He decided to ignore her, returning his attention to the business at hand. He felt like a complete idiot. Dammit, he'd promised himself he'd go easy with women. He could enjoy all that was good about girls without falling head over heels for them. He didn't need to be entrenched in a relationship in order to have some fun. And yet, his first time out without training wheels he had delivered himself gift-wrapped to Kirsten, and then slammed face first into a brick wall.

Fuck it. He'd think about it tomorrow. Right now, it was time to concentrate and fly Fifi to New York. Someone once said 'life was a comedy.' They were so right.

FOUR HOURS LATER THE tired crew caught the hotel van at JFK International airport. Pierre rode shotgun, strapping himself tight with the seat belt. These van drivers in New York City were friggin' maniacs. Pierre finally had a chance to check his text messages. The ride to the Lexington Hotel was over a half hour long, so he concentrated on his phone.

Kirsten

R u in NYC yet?

Kirsten

Let me know when u land.

Kirsten

I made it here ok. Text me when you land.

Kirsten

Helloooo?

Kirsten

Did u run into delays?

Kirsten

Let me know.

Pierre was dying to text her back, just ignore all he'd learned about what Kirsten had been doing, and allow life to continue. Shit, he could just hit the 'delete' button in his mind and remove the entire unpleasant episode forever. Then tomorrow he could stroll down to 42nd street after a good breakfast and buy her the gold necklace and perhaps even a diamond ring. Then she would be his. Then he could ask her to stay the fuck away from other men. Particularly other pilots. Then maybe someday in the distant future he would share with her what he knew about her and the jumpseater.

Sure, and continue sharing her with the other guy.

Totally out of the question.

His fingers tap danced across his smartphone's unbreakable glass screen to the photo gallery. He positioned his cell phone so no one else in the dark hotel van could see the screen, or the reflection of the screen against the inside of the van windows.

And there she was, Kirsten naked in the arms of the jumpseater, *aka asshole.*

He shook his head. No, this was too big to ignore. He'd always believed that one must not think about problems after dark. Things always look darker at night. Better wait until the new day arrived to see problems under a new light.

So be it, he decided. He'd stop tormenting himself with the situation and wait until morning to make a decision about Kirsten. In the meantime, she could wait all night for his texts, which were not going to come.

She would find that strange, no doubt. They'd been texting back and forth for days without interruption. Especially at night. If he quit cold turkey, she'd be alarmed. Not that it would make any difference at this point. In a million years, she would never guess that her boyfriend and her lover had met. Unless, of course, the jumpseater texted her telling her the names of the pilots on his flight to New Orleans.

Pierre smiled. No, that wasn't going to happen either. He'd be willing to bet the farm that the asshole jumpseater couldn't remember either his name or Larry's if his life depended on it.

Let Kirsten wonder what the heck was going on.

He would not contact her at all tonight.

Thirty minutes later Pierre ordered a burger with fries and a Coke from room service. He was tired and irritated. The emotional stress Kirsten had generated for him was far more exhausting than the actual physical wear and tear from a day of flying. He turned on the TV, only half-listening to the news. The next day they had scheduled one leg back to St. Louis, which was not bad, except it was a night flight, which he detested. Pierre was a morning man. He could be up at four in the morning and have tremendous energy all day, but come nine p.m. he started to fade. By ten he was ready for bed. So, flying at night was something he avoided like the plague. His cell phone chimed.

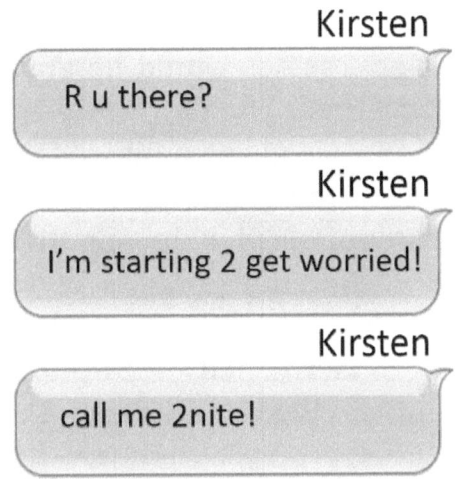

Kirsten

R u there?

Kirsten

I'm starting 2 get worried!

Kirsten

call me 2nite!

Pierre turned down all the volumes on his phone, except for the alarm. He was not willing to listen to his smartphone anymore tonight. He picked up the hotel phone by the bed.

"Good evening, front desk," a chirpy young woman answered.

"Hi there. I'm in room twenty-five-fifteen. Could you please hold all calls tonight? I need to get some sleep and I don't want any interruptions."

"Hold all calls. Of course. Have a good evening, sir."

He hung up, reaching for the TV remote. Might as well watch a pay-per-view movie. He would sleep in tomorrow. His mind focused on the arrival of his food and his choice of movies.

PIERRE STOOD BY THE window in his hotel room, staring out at Manhattan's cloudy and gray morning. He woke up at six a.m. not well rested but unable to sleep more. He could've used a Vicodin to sleep like a baby. Except if the 'Pee Squad' found the Vicodin in his urine, his ass would be grass as far as his career was concerned. The first thing he did was go look at his cell phone. He allowed himself the luxury of hoping against reason that the events of the previous day had been a result of his vivid imagination.

No, the pictures of Kirsten were still there, in wonderful, vivid high resolution.

Pierre felt the phone vibrate in his hand, announcing the arrival of a text.

Kirsten

R u there?

He typed back.

Pierre

> Yeah, I'm here.

Kirsten

> OMG, where have u been?

Pierre

> Got in late last night.

Kirsten

> I tried calling u. Front desk said u weren't taking any calls.

Pierre

> I was tired.

Kirsten

> U didn't text me.

Pierre

> 2 much on my mind.

Kirsten

> Call me.

He switched to the dialer, touching a picture of a smiling Kirsten. His phone dialed her number.

She picked up on the first ring.

"Are you all right?"

"Yep. I'm fine."

"What's going on? What happened? I texted you last night until very late."

"I'm sorry, I really needed to get some sleep." He still wasn't sure what strategy to follow with her.

"I was worried about you."

"Nothing really to worry about."

"You sound different."

"Tell me something."

"What?"

"How do you see me?"

"How do I see you? What do you mean?"

"I mean, am I just a one-night stand, or are you interested in me?"

"What kind of a question's that?"

"I need to know. Did I interest you as a passing fling, or are you interested in more than that?"

"Pierre, I don't know why you're asking me this, but is it tied to your being incommunicado last night?"

"In a way, yes."

"And why are you asking me this now?"

"Do you enjoy being with me?"

She paused. "Are you serious?"

"Yah, I'm serious."

"Well, what do *you* think?"

"I asked first." He was not too sure where the conversation was going. Did he want her still, or was he telling her to get lost?

Kirsten paused again. "I enjoy being with you very much. Do you have to ask? Can't you feel it?"

Were he cynically inclined, he would have texted her the photos at that precise instant. "Well, for the record, I also enjoy being with you very much. Do I satisfy your needs?"

"Pierre, what's going on? Why are you asking me all this?"

"Because I was under the impression that you and I fit together very well. You're the most glorious earth shaking miracle that's happened to me in a very long time."

"And is that a bad thing?"

"In a way, yes."

"Explain, please. You're not making any sense."

"Do you have a boyfriend?"

A pause.

"Why would you ask me that?"

"Simply because I hadn't asked you before. Our relationship has been a flash fire, and we've had relatively little chance to talk."

"And you want to know if I have a boyfriend? Would I be doing what I've been doing with you if I had one?"

"I don't know, Kirsten, would you?"

"Pierre, all I know is I love being with you. I think about you every second of the day and to be honest I'm not happy flying around the country when I'd much rather be with you."

Wow. That sounded really wonderful. Exactly what he wanted to hear from her a couple of days ago. But now it didn't sound so good because there was a fly in the glass of milk in the form of five pictures in his cell phone.

"Kirsten, I had a guy on my jumpseat yesterday going down to New Orleans."

She was silent for a moment. "And?"

"He was a TransCon pilot. He said he knew you."

This time the pause was longer.

"Oh?"

"He told us he's known you for four months. His name was Sam Thomas."

He thought he heard Kirsten gasp.

"What else did he say?"

Pierre was not real happy with her, but even so he didn't want to hurt her, he just wanted to know what she was thinking. "Well, he did say you were his girlfriend."

Kirsten paused for a long time. "He said that?"

"Yes."

Another long pause.

"It's partially true," she finally admitted. "We'd been dating but after I met you I decided he's not what I want so I've been trying to find a way to break it off with him."

"So, you saw him in Chicago?"

"Yes. He was there at the end of his trip so I asked him to come over so we could talk."

"To your hotel?"

"Where else? Yes, to my hotel."

"Kirsten, I never asked you whether you had a boyfriend. I just assumed you didn't since you ended up with me. Did you break up with this guy last night then?"

"I did, yes." Her voice had gone up by an octave.

"Did he stay with you for the night?" There, he said it.

She paused again. "Yes."

Goddammit.

If he was looking for any consolation, at least she wasn't trying to bullshit her way out of this. Pierre wasn't sure where the conversation was going, and he wasn't sure whether he should mention the pictures.

She'd spent the night with the asshole. *Jesus Christ!*

"I don't know what to say." He really didn't.

"He stayed with me for the night," she blurted out. "Not love, I didn't make love with him. It was just sex."

Just sex!? Holy shit. Just like that?

Pierre was shocked at her ability to express herself so matter-of-fact. *Just sex.* What, that was all right then? Should he rejoice and pop the champagne because she hadn't actually *made love* with the asshole? It was just sex, nothing more. What was the big deal? He was also raving jealous and momentarily considered hiring a private eye to track down the asshole in New Orleans so he could put him through a wood chipper.

"I'm so sorry, Pierre." Her voice was breaking up. "I didn't intend to do anything with him, but Sam became very emotional when I told him it was over, and one thing led to another. It meant nothing."

The jumpseater had become emotional? The dipshit probably didn't have it in him to be emotional about anything. It was all just an act, of that Pierre was sure.

Pierre wondered what the jumpseater would think if he heard Kirsten's impression of their sexual rendezvous the previous night. Maybe the reason the pukehead expressed himself in such a vulgar manner about Kirsten was because he was sore he'd been handed his walking papers?

That would explain his remarks.

"He's not a very nice guy, you know?"

"I realize that now. After I met you the contrast was just too much. He just couldn't measure up to you. I hadn't even seen him for three weeks."

"Were you ever going to tell me about him?"

"No."

"At least you're honest."

"What purpose would it serve?"

"None, really. Listen, I'm sorry I didn't talk to you last night. I was upset and didn't really want to talk about this after a long day. Dealing with problems at night is a really bad idea."

"Are you very angry with me?"

"I don't know. Don't know what to think. Yes, I'm angry. How could I not be? I see what happened, but I'm still freaked out."

"Can you forgive me?"

Just like that?

"I've already forgiven you. I'm just gonna need some time to digest all this."

"I'm so sorry, Pierre."

"We'll talk when we get home."

Don't hate me."

He didn't want to talk to her anymore. "I don't hate you."

I just don't think I like you.

And I don't like myself either for all the violent things I wanted to perpetrate on your boyfriend. What was I thinking? That's not me!

After they hung up Pierre jumped in the shower. Technically, she hadn't lied to him about the boyfriend because he'd never really asked. True, however, not mentioning that fact was an intentional omission, which was tantamount to a lie. He liked Kirsten a lot, but his confidence in their relationship had been severely shaken when he reviewed the five photos of her in his phone. So, she'd given the guy a pity fuck. What was she thinking? And he still couldn't believe the chain of events that had led to the discovery of her behavior. Meeting her boyfriend on their way to New Orleans was nothing short of incredible. Maybe Pierre should buy some lottery tickets. Yea, with his fucking luck, he'd nail the Powerball.

He needed some distraction to recover from the horrible taste of the last twenty-four hours. He needed to stay away from Kirsten for a few days in order to clear his head and decide on a course of action.

Maybe he should put a car bomb in the asshole's vehicle. An enticing idea. Yeah, right. Although the idea had its appeal, he wouldn't know where to begin. And what about the photos of her in his phone? He thought about what possible benefit could be gained by acknowledging their existence with Kirsten. None came to mind, but then again he was actually pretty furious, so he wasn't thinking straight.

Pierre wouldn't have minded learning that Kirsten had a boyfriend, although her not sharing this information with him was disturbing. But her meeting with the guy in Chicago when she knew he'd been rushing his ass to spend some time with her, that was too much. When he saw her in the lobby at the airport Hilton she'd just come down after spending the night with the prick.

Definitely not cool. Major league uncool.

Dammit, and he liked her so much. No, who was he fooling? He loved her. And now, it appeared their love died on the vine.

But no, this was pathetic, demoralizing, depressing. He felt his depression intensifying. He was an emotional wreck. Maybe he better rethink this entire scenario.

What a joke he was.

Someone hand him the rat poison.

Naw, it wasn't all that bad. He was still a professional, he still had an enviable job. So, it didn't work again with a woman. What was he gonna do, sit there and cry?

Like hell.

He was gonna go out and enjoy life.

New page, new day

Book Two

COTTON CANDY AND TANGERINES   MR Chevalier

Navy

Pierre walked down the terminal alongside Ray, with their four flight attendants trailing behind them. The city of Philadelphia was already sleeping. Their late arrival at the end of a long day was a tiresome event. The crew just wanted to get to the hotel and call it a day, although flying with Ray had been pleasant.

Pierre liked him. Ray was in his late fifties, gray-haired and dignified. A good Midwestern man. And he liked country music. Every time they took off in the Airbus, Ray would start singing Willie Nelson's 'On the Road Again.' His voice was not half bad either.

The blue hotel van was waiting for them at curbside. Pierre barely noticed there were other people standing around, patiently waiting for the van to open its doors. He was tired, rendering a good imitation of a zombie. He ambled over to the rear of the vehicle, waiting for the flight attendants to deliver their suitcases to the driver. After delivering his own two bags Pierre joined the others in the van. The weather was chilly and damp.

The van driver slammed shut the rear gates, coming around to close the two side doors. The man appeared to be cold since he wasn't properly dressed for the freezing weather.

The ride to the hotel was inconsequential, taking all of five minutes. Pierre was lost in thought during the brief ride. He half noticed the huge shipyard cranes protruding over them along the ride. They must build some big ships in Philadelphia. Once the driver pulled up in front of the hotel entrance his passengers scrambled to leave the vehicle. Pierre zombie-strolled to join the others waiting for their bags at curb side.

That's when she caught his eye.

Right in front of him was a most gorgeous creature, a young woman dressed in the uniform of an officer of the United States Navy. He didn't have too much time to take it all in, but he saw enough, the navy-blue uniform, the elegant white hat, the tie, the breathtaking face, her hair pulled up tight under the hat. The apparition must be in her mid-to-late twenties.

Whoa! She had his full attention. Zombie or no zombie, he couldn't let this one slip away; she was beyond stunning. How in Heaven's name had he failed to notice her while they were in the van? She must've been standing there next to the vehicle when he and his crew arrived, how come he hadn't seen her then? He was probably more tired than he thought. Pierre took two steps closer to her, taking a deep breath, gathering his courage.

"Long day?"

The gorgeous creature in the Navy uniform turned to look at him. She was even prettier up close. Her tired green eyes spoke of long hours on the road. "Yes," she smiled at Pierre. "A very long day."

Some kind of explosive 'force' flowed between them at that instant. The sonic boom it made was heard galaxies away. Hard to put into words, really. It was just there. He felt it in his mind and in his heart and in his groin. Navy girl momentarily taking a second look at him hinted that perhaps she was feeling the same energy passing between them, and perhaps had even heard the same boom.

Pierre couldn't tell the color of her hair. It appeared to be dirty blond, hard to tell in the artificial light and also she had most of it tucked up inside her white Navy hat. A quick scan revealed she was about three inches shorter than him with a very attractive figure. All the right proportions. Pierre had certain preferences when it came to women, just as he imagined every other man did. Deal breakers were women taller than he was. For some reason, that particular trait turned him off. A woman had to be of a lesser stature or equal to his own height when wearing high heels. Tall women could definitely be quite attractive, but he felt that most girls looked better when accompanied by men taller than themselves.

He thought of several movie star couples where the women were a head taller than their mates. Beautiful human beings—in his opinion—but they did look strange as couples because of the female's height. It just didn't feel right. He was a traditionalist, and for him, men had to be taller than their mates. Period.

Also, most of the pilots he flew with seemed to prefer women with big breasts. That was not the case with him, although he never shared this with the rest of the guys. He preferred medium to smaller boobs, or tits, or whatever they chose to call them. He never really dwelled trying to find the reason why. He just did. But of course, size didn't really matter to him. Same reason—he figured—why some folks loved the flavor of salty anchovies and some didn't. Not up to him to waste time trying to figure out why. It just was.

Regardless, in his mind all women were beautiful, no matter what the size of their boobs.

Pierre and Navy both recognized their bags on the curb at the same time, reaching for them.

"May I help you with those?"

"No, thanks, I got 'em," she said curtly, picking up her black bags.

Pierre waited a moment for Navy to secure her luggage to the wheelies, then they headed for the lobby together, side by side, leaving the rest of his crew behind.

"Where you coming from?" He hated small talk, especially when they had such limited time, but he really liked this woman, he was intrigued and attracted to her and desperate to establish a connection before she rode off into the sunset.

"Spain," she replied, approaching the registration desk.

"No kidding. What airline?"

She looked at him, resting her arms on the green granite countertop of the front desk. "No airline. Military charter flight. Had to stop four hours in Bangor, Maine. Something broke in the airplane. Horribly long day."

He liked the way she spoke in short spurts.

"Wow, compared to you I had a short day. Came out of Las Vegas."

Navy gifted him with a worn-out smile, apparently uninterested or unimpressed with Pierre's tribulations as an airline pilot. Turning her attention to the hotel clerk she registered for a room, was given a key and turned to go. "Well, good-night."

And then she was gone.

Holy shit. Just like that.

Pierre would've laughed but he didn't want to attract attention. Man, he must be giving out the wrong vibes, what'd he have, the plague? He was tired, but not *that* tired. For one brief instant, he'd had the illusion that they had connected through eye contact and that maybe they could find time to talk, but he must obviously be on crack because she just up and left.

The rest of his crew joined him at the registration desk. Two of the flight attendants on his crew were young and very attractive. One of the two, Tracy, a striking brunette in her mid-twenties had been flirting with him for the past two days, but he knew she was dating a check airman instructor who had taught Pierre in the simulator when he was a newhire.

Although Pierre found Tracy very attractive and enjoyed some light flirting with her, he knew better than to fool around with her. Instructors in the training center could make life extremely unpleasant for the less prudent. Hitting on the girlfriend of one of the instructors could turn into professional suicide at the bat of an eye. Even if it was the girlfriend who had initiated it.

Since he had to visit the Flight Training Center every nine months for training and checking for the rest of his career, he really didn't want to jeopardize his future by pissing off any of the instructors there. He'd been with the airlines long enough to learn that messing around with senior pilots' girls was a no-no. The simulator instructors for an airline could literally bust Charles Lindbergh during a check ride, if they really wanted to.

"Join us for a drink at the bar," Ray offered.

Pierre normally didn't drink too much, and even when he did, his own personal rules generally kept him from drinking on the road so he seldom joined his crews in bars, much less hotel bars, but Ray was a real nice guy and so he decided to consider it.

One drink wasn't gonna kill him, really, and he needed to decompress.

Pierre accepted his room key from the concierge, leaving the crew behind. The flight from Vegas had been uneventful, the weather had been pretty good and the personal pan pizza he'd bought at the airport in Las Vegas to eat during the flight had completely satisfied him, so he wasn't hungry at all. His room was like any of the other fifteen or sixteen hotel rooms he would visit during the month. Nothing overly exciting there.

After using the restroom and changing into jeans and a navy-blue Chemise Lacoste, Pierre ambled down to the hotel bar. On second thought, a night cap would do wonders for him. They didn't have to fly for another thirteen hours.

The hotel cocktail lounge was huge and dark and not very crowded. Christina Perri's *'Jar of Hearts'* was playing over the speakers. He absent-mindedly wandered towards the end of the very long bar. Several people were having drinks way at the other end, perched on tall stools.

"Pierre!"

He snapped out of his stupor. Ray and two of their flight attendants were already there, having drinks. One of them was Tracy. She smiled at him, resuming her flirting. The signal she'd been sending to Pierre all day was pretty clear, 'I'm available if you want me.'

Boy, and how he would love playing with her. He'd already launched his powerful imagination to explore the thousand and one things he would do in bed with her. Too bad she had chosen to date a check airman, Pierre thought.

Jokes aside, he had not inherited any wealth from his ancestors, he wasn't a successful business man and he didn't have millions in the bank from questionable sources. His career was all he had, and he sure as Dickens wasn't going to jeopardize it for a casual fling with a girl, no matter how incredibly attractive she was.

"Didn't know if you were going to come down," Ray greeted. "Look who's over there."

Pierre wasn't entirely sure what Ray was talking about.

"Uh?"

"Over there, Navy's over there." The captain nodded towards the other end of the bar, sixty feet away.

Pierre followed the nod to see what Ray was pointing at.

He was speechless.

There, at the opposite end of the bar, sitting on a stool was a dazzling woman all alone, making love to her red wine. Her full long blond hair cascading over her shoulders, with two spaghetti straps holding in place her cheerful white summer dress printed with colorful flowers. From the distance, his tired brain gave her legs an automatic 'A.'

It took Pierre a couple of additional seconds to realize what Ray was *really* talking about.

The woman sitting at the bar by herself was none other than the Navy officer! *His* Navy officer! Hot dog! Maybe the gods had not abandoned him just yet. She was out of uniform and she looked nothing short of spectacular. How in the name of all the planets had Ray recognized her when he didn't? And he'd walked right past her!

But yes! That was her! A second chance! An incredible second chance to meet the Navy angel! She had not gone straight to bed!

"If you'll excuse me," he said to his crew, removing himself from their company, zeroing in on the Navy officer.

The blonde girl saw him approaching, breaking into a smile.

"Hi," he offered. Not very imaginative, he kicked himself mentally. Maybe he really should consider signing up for a creative writing class. Then he wouldn't sound so much like a friggin' hillbilly.

"Hello again." She had apparently recognized him faster than he had her.

"Mind if I join you?" She looked dazzling with her hair down like that.

"No. I don't mind."

The sexual electricity he'd felt earlier began to flow again. Electricity or magic or whatever it was. He felt it. And he suspected she felt it too. No, he didn't suspect it, he knew it. Hard to put into words, but there was some immediate basic attraction there flowing strongly between the two of them.

Pierre climbed on the stool next to her. "I'm glad you came down."

"I needed to feel human again. Been desperate for a glass of wine all day."

"What's your name?"

"I'm Scarlett."

He noticed she didn't offer to shake hands. "Pierre." He also observed she'd applied some makeup, making her eyes even more striking.

"They didn't give you wine on the flight?"

"Military charter," she volunteered. "No wine."

"What were you doing in Spain?"

She sipped her dark red wine before responding. "I was stationed there."

"In Spain? I didn't know we had any Navy bases there."

"We do. I've been there the past three years."

"That's fantastic. I take it your Spanish must be pretty good?"

"*Más o menos.*"

"Impressive. What're you doing back in the States? Vacation?"

"No, I'm done. I'm going home."

"Done as in 'no more Navy'?"

"Yeah, done as in *I'm outta there.*"

"Had enough?"

"Pretty much."

"Where's home?" Pierre caught a scent of some delicious perfume. Sweet and delicate.

"Seattle."

"So that's where you're headed?"

"Yes. Was supposed to make it there tonight, but the delay in Bangor screwed me up. We got here too late to catch the United flight to Seattle. That's why I'm here, the Navy put us up in this hotel. Early morning flight out tomorrow."

"*What can I get you?*"

Pierre looked at the bartender, startled and annoyed at the intrusion. "A beer, Bud Light, please."

"Bottle or tap?"

He ordered a bottle. He would've liked to buy her a drink, but she already had the glass of red wine in front of her. Asking her if she'd like another would be pretentious and even a little premature, and it might piss her off. Too much like a cliché, the handsome stranger offering to buy the lady a drink.

"You fly for Worldwide?"

"Yes," he replied, wondering if she could detect the pride in his voice.

"Cool."

"How'd you like Spain?"

"Oh, at first I thought it was great. I loved it."

"You're not married?" He'd already checked out her left hand, taking note there was no ring on that one finger. No ring and no telltale white skin where a ring had been worn.

"No. Not married. Had a boyfriend."

"Had as in past tense?"

"Yeah. Didn't work out."

"A Spaniard?"

She nodded. "That he was." She looked away, pensive. "When I first got to Spain I really liked Spanish men, but ultimately ended up disliking them. They had too much antagonism and resentment towards Americans and American women in particular. We're just too damned independent and self-confident for them."

The bartender deposited a beer bottle on top of a napkin in front of Pierre.

"I had a Volkswagen bug. That's the car I bought when I first got there. Someone damaged my car, I think my boyfriend had something to do with it."

"He damaged your car? Why, because you broke up with him?"

"Too controlling. And yes, I guess he was behind the damage to my car."

Pierre was amazed. Two minutes talking to a complete stranger and she was already sharing intimate information. He'd seen that happen quite often around airports and airplanes. Why not pour one's heart out to a stranger you'll possibly never ever see again? There was something very antiseptic about baring one's soul like that. Nothing to lose, really.

"How long did you date him?"

"Almost two years," she sipped some more red wine.

"Did he want to marry you?"

"Oh, sure. He wanted the whole *paella*. Marriage, kids, a wife to provide for his needs. All of it in *his* terms."

"A little bit of a cultural clash, eh?"

"You can say that again."

"He wanted you to marry him, leave the Navy and stay in Spain?"

She looked at him. "In a nutshell, yes."

"I'm glad you found the strength to come down for a drink."

"I'm exhausted, tired of spending time in airports, and that military charter was absolutely hideous. This wine tastes like heaven to me at this very moment."

Pierre studied her face. She had the face of a cherub. She was—without question—nearly a *perfect* 'dream.' Beautiful proportions, petite nose and perfect teeth. A very attractive woman. He was tired as well, but being with her had triggered his adrenaline so he felt pleasantly energetic.

"Are your parents in Seattle?"

"Yes."

"They must be thrilled you're going home."

She sipped the last of her wine. "They are. Especially my little sister."

Pierre pointed to her glass. "Can you handle another glass of wine?"

Scarlett glanced at her empty glass. "Are you kidding? I would *love* it."

Pierre caught the bartender's eye, pointing to her glass, in the universal gesture of ordering more. "Are you hungry? I could order you some food."

"No, thanks. The wine will do."

He was impressed with her manners already. He didn't know if she'd had any food all day. Drinking on an empty stomach could be rather detrimental.

The couple of times their eyes met Pierre felt some type of force flowing between them again. A very strong force. Crazy notion, yet he was sure of it. Even as tired as they both were, some kind of beautiful magic was there. And no, he was not too old to believe in magic. Pierre truly believed that everything that was good in this world was powered by magic. Pierre firmly believed in unicorns, love at first sight and magic. He was also careful never to mention his views on these topics to anyone, lest the airline decide to finance a paid vacation for him at the local psychiatric hospital, fire his ass and notify the FAA of a mentally unbalanced pilot in need of electric shock therapy.

The bartender deposited another glass of red wine in front of Scarlett.

"What are you gonna do now?"

"What do you mean?"

"When you go back home. What will you be doing with yourself?"

Scarlett held the glass of wine at face level, staring at it. "I don't know."

"What did you do in the Navy?"

"I was in intelligence."

"Not exactly sure how that's going to apply to the civilian world."

She smiled, blowing his circuits. Her mouth was wide and friendly, and she also smiled with her eyes, squinting a little. "The civilian world. I hadn't heard that for some time. I think I'm going to welcome a change."

Pierre wanted to place his hand behind her neck and kiss her. Damn, he almost did it!

That would *not* go down well at this stage!

"What sort of change are you looking for?"

"Oh, just something different, something that can provide me with some satisfaction."

Pierre had his hand resting on his lap. Scarlett reached out, placing her hand on top of his. "This may sound weird to you, but on second thought, I'm dying for a McDonald's Quarter-Pounder."

He couldn't believe she had touched him. Her hand felt cool and moist. There was an eerie familiarity to her touch, as if they had been lovers for a long time. In another life, maybe?

"I don't really think we can find an open McDonalds anywhere near here this time of night. This area where the hotel is has a lot of shipyards but very few commercial businesses. Maybe these guys can make a hamburger for you."

"I didn't mean right this moment," she laughed.

My God, he thought. Her laughter was musical. He always thought women's laughter was musical, but Scarlett's was different. It had the ability of releasing adrenaline in his body when she laughed, same as when he listened to Wagner's *Charge of the Valkyries*.

"I've been out of the States so long, I'm just craving a real down-to-earth cheeseburger. That's the first thing I'm gonna do tomorrow when I get home."

Pierre laughed. "I can understand that."

"You have a boyfriend back in Seattle?" He hated asking that, terrified that she would answer yes. But he had to ask. No use wasting both their time if she was already involved with someone else.

SHE LOOKED PENSIVE. "I did, a long time ago. He's probably married now."

"High school boyfriend?"

"College. What about you? Married?"

He held up his left hand in front of his face, shaking his head. "Single."

"Who are those women over there? Part of your crew?"

Pierre sipped his beer. "Yeah, those are some of my crew."

"A couple of pretty women."

Pierre was amazed at how observant Scarlett was, considering she must be beyond exhausted. He wasn't sure what to respond to the pretty women comment.

"We've been flying together for two days. Tomorrow we fly to Los Angeles, then back home to St. Louis the following day."

"Neither one of those two interest you?"

Pierre was amazed. She went right to the point, eh?

He laughed. "No, I have managed to keep my distance from those two so far. How do you know they don't interest me?"

"Because you're here with me. What'd ya mean, 'keep your distance'?"

"Those two are already spoken for. They have boyfriends."

"Afraid of a little competition?" She smiled mischievously.

He grinned. "No, not really. But see, with so many unattached women available, I don't see the point in chasing one who is already in a relationship."

"How do you know there are so many unattached women out there?"

Pierre smiled. I meet unattached women when I'm working. I've also looked at a couple of online dating services.

"Naughty!"

"Naughty? Why?"

"Those are sex sites."

"No, they're not. What makes you think that? There are many respectable websites catering to perfectly normal men and women trying to connect.

"I'm sure."

"You doubt me? Woman of little faith!"

"They used to call those women 'escorts,' didn't they?"

Pierre laughed. "No, you're confusing two different things."

"Oh, yeah? Explain."

"A dating website is not the same as one of those websites advertising escorts."

"How are they different?"

Pierre sipped his beer giving himself a second or two to think. He laughed. "Lessee, escorts are call-girls, engaged in the business of sex. Dating sites on the other hand, are used by normal guys and gals wanting to meet. They're actually pretty helpful."

"How are they helpful?"

"Their software allows you to establish a bunch of filters so you won't waste time trying to connect with people you're not interested in."

"So you don't have to go to bars and meet guys."

"Precisely."

"Like we're doing right now." She pointed out.

Pierre laughed.

"Relax, I know about dating websites. I'm just giving you a hard time."

He stared at her. She did have such attractive eyes.

"You're going to earn a spanking, milady, if you keep mocking me like this." The instant the words came out of his mouth he flinched, thinking he'd overstepped his position as a casual acquaintance at a bar late one night in Philadelphia.

"That could be fun. But that's probably not such a good idea tonight. I have to get some sleep, and I'm drunk."

That could be fun!?

For the love of God! Obviously, Scarlett was totally unaware the effect her words were having on him. She was turning him on with her casual remarks. Pierre realized how much red wine she'd had. On top of a horrendously long day. No doubt, she was ready to hit the pillows. He considered his odds of ending up in bed with her, and given the circumstances, he gave himself a pretty good chance. Probably nine out of ten.

And then, he would spank her.

Yeah, right. That was just not going to happen. Not tonight, anyway.

He was many things, but a shithead he was not. Ending up in bed with Scarlett under present conditions would be an act of cowardice on his part. She was in no shape to make an intelligent decision about ending up in bed with a man she just met. Besides, with all the wine she'd had, he probably would not be able to please her anyhow. And, she wouldn't remember anything in any case. If and when life gave him the opportunity to make love to this very desirable girl, he'd really prefer if she could remember what took place between them.

Much to his own chagrin, he decided to give up his hopes of ending up between the sheets with Scarlett tonight. He all of a sudden seemed to have developed a feeling of protectiveness towards her. Strangely, he wanted to protect her more than he wanted to have sex with her. Have sex with her? Since when had he become such a prude? He wanted to fuck her silly, that's what he was really thinking.

Take that for being weird.

And besides, whatever made him think he was *Don Juan* anyway, considering himself attractive enough and intriguing enough to women they would want to jump in the sack with him after a twenty-minute conversation? He was really overestimating himself lately.

"Are you back from outer space yet?" Scarlett had been staring at him for God knows how long now.

"*What?* Sorry, I was just thinking—"

"Thinking what?"

"Thinking I'd very much like to see you again." There, he said it. Now time to cross his fingers and ask the gods of Olympus for their blessing.

"Me too."

No shit? Thank you, almighty Zeus! Thank you as well to the rest of you Magnificent Ones up there, Hercules, Achilles, Minerva, whoever had seen fit to help him with this enchanting creature.

The force attracting them to each other was real and tangible and it connected them silently. Pierre felt strangely at peace with the universe, totally content and happy with what was going on. She'd said 'yes'! Lady Luck was definitely smiling upon him tonight.

His eyes connected with hers. If indeed, the eyes were the window to the soul, then he really liked her soul. And everything else about her.

"What's your phone number?" He reached for his cell phone.

"I don't have one," Scarlett admitted.

"No number?"

"No, no cell phone. I just came from Europe, remember?"

Crud! She was right! How was he going to get in touch with her then? Email? Her parents' place?

Scarlett observed him going for his cell phone. "Take this number down. It's my sister's. Her cell phone."

Scarlett gave him the number, which he entered into his keypad.

"What's your sister's name?"

"Erin. I'll get a cell phone when I get back home. The one I had in Spain doesn't work here."

"What time's your flight tomorrow?"

"Six. Have to be in the lobby at four."

"Geepers. You're not gonna get much sleep. I better get you to bed."

Dammit, there he went again, saying the wrong thing.

"No, I mean, you better get back to your room and get some rest."

"I know what you meant." She smiled at him from behind sleepy, very suggestive eyes.

Pierre signaled the bartender for the check.

"I'll call your sister in a couple of days."

"That will be nice."

The bartender took Pierre's Visa card.

The wine had finally hit her. She looked as if she could pass out at any moment now.

He accepted his card back, signing the check.

"Shall we go?" He wasn't about to turn her loose at that point, with all the red wine in her she would most likely stumble and fall somewhere before making it to her room. Scarlett got down from her stool, holding on to his shoulder for support.

Pierre slipped his arm around her waist, holding her steady. Scarlett did the same, entwining her arm with his, placing her hand against his waist. They walked out of the cocktail lounge together, like two lovers at the end of a lovely day, walking to the elevator. Scarlett didn't say anything more. He was right, the wine had finally done her in.

Reaching her floor, her room was not too far from the elevator. He helped her to the door.

Scarlett turned, placing both her hands on his shoulders, then she offered her lips.

Pierre instantly decided he would not spend the night with her, but he sure could kiss her.

Scarlett's lips felt cool and tasted of wine. Her breath also carried the scent of red wine. She advanced her tongue, hesitatingly separating his lips with it. Pierre wrapped his arms around her waist, allowing his tongue to meet hers, losing himself in the most angelic thing God ever made, a sweet kiss from a beautiful creature. He could feel her soft crotch against his hard-on through her thin summer dress, sadly accepting the fact that was all he was going to experience tonight.

THE NEXT MORNING PIERRE could still taste the sweet, warm, soft, delicious wine flavor of Scarlett's lips. He'd been dying to go in her room and make love to her, but knew that Scarlett had not only been exhausted but also half-drunk from the wine. Not the best situation in the world. Plus, she needed to get up at four in the morning to catch her flight home.

No, overall, he'd decided to be satisfied with kissing her and allow Scarlett to get a few hours of sleep. He wanted her so bad, and he could sense she reciprocated, but above all he had to be considerate. Scarlett had been traveling so many hours, and then the wine. Although his sex drive pushed him to get in bed with her, he congratulated himself for having made the best decision. He felt he had protected her, despite his monumental hard-on and his indomitable sex drive trying to convince him otherwise. He had to admit not going in the room with Scarlett was probably one of the hardest things he'd ever done.

Back in his room last night he'd called the front desk, setting up a wakeup call for Scarlett. The front desk clerk had given him some lip about requesting a call to a different room, but he was eventually able to sweet talk the clerk. He didn't know if Scarlett had setup a wakeup call, and if she slept through her flight she would be very upset. Pierre also asked the front desk clerk to setup a second wake up call for himself at four am. He was going to make sure Scarlett was up in time. And not that he didn't trust the front desk people, but he also set his cell phone to ring at four in the morning.

His phone rang at four. That was downright painful. He then dialed her room, relieved when she answered it.

"Scarlett, it's Pierre, from last night. Good morning. Sorry to call you this early, I setup a wakeup call for you but wanted to make sure the guys in the front desk did call you. I don't want you to miss your flight." He realized he'd just waken her up.

"Thanks," was all she said. Fatigue was in her voice. She didn't sound very much awake.

"Don't go back to sleep now. Have a good flight. I'll talk to you in a couple of days."

"I won't. Thanks, bye." She hung up.

BY THE TIME PIERRE and the rest of the crew met in the lobby of the hotel, Scarlett was long gone.

Ray and the four flight attendants were already there waiting for the hotel van when Pierre made an appearance.

"Good morning, everybody!"

"Good morning to you!" Tracy chanted.

She was looking at him with an enigmatic smile. "You guys make such a cute couple," she threw at him.

Pierre considered that for a second, realizing Tracy probably thought he'd ended up in Scarlett's room after drinks last night. An understandable assumption, really, since Tracy saw them leaving the bar together.

He didn't respond to her comment, just smiled at her, let Tracy wonder.

Now, at 36,000 feet above Texas, he was intoxicated by the prospect of seeing Scarlett again. Tonight, he would be overnighting in Los Angeles, then tomorrow one leg back to St. Louis and he was done for ten days. He would've loved to just fly up to Seattle soon as he was off the trip, but realized Scarlett was going to need a few days to enjoy her family and get reacquainted with them again. His presence could create an uncomfortable situation for her, at least the first few days she was back. He would've loved texting her, but without a cell phone she was off the grid. Well, she did say she'd have one within a couple of days.

He'd jump on a plane and go see her five days from now. Pierre congratulated himself for his schedule. He'd accidentally finished the month with a chunk of days off. His current schedule required him to work only sixteen days per month, and the nice thing about it was he could manipulate his trips to have a lot of days off at any one time. His neighbors often asked if he ever worked. With fourteen days off a month, he could pile seven of those days at the end of one month and seven at the beginning of the next month if he chose to have long chunks of time off.

Pierre's flight schedule each month was regulated by the Federal Aviation Regulations, which prevented the airlines from flying the pilots too many hours without adequate rest. Unlike doctors in residency, who had horrendous fifteen-hour shifts back-to-back, airline pilots were protected by the regulations. Tired pilots made mistakes, and some of those mistakes had killed hundreds of passengers. Doctors, on the other hand, were not protected by the regulations. If a resident physician made a mistake as a result of fatigue, he could kill one patient. If an airline pilot made a mistake as a result of fatigue, he could potentially kill hundreds, including himself. It was the old breakfast analogy comparing doctors and airline pilots. When enjoying a breakfast of scrambled eggs and bacon, the chicken was involved, but the pig was committed.

He'd book a room at the crew hotel in Seattle on his trip over to see Scarlett. Crew hotels were mostly three and four stars, and they gave the crews special rates even when traveling on their own.

"So you connected with the Navy?" Ray asked. The sky was clear and they could see over a hundred miles ahead. Not a cloud in view.

"Yeah, thanks for pointing her out to me last night. I walked right past her and didn't see her."

"I realized you cruised right past her and kept going without a second glance."

"I owe you, oh, Great Master."

"Naw, you owe me nothing. You would've seen her eventually. Tracy did say she thought you're one big flirt, though."

"She did?"

Ray nodded. "What the hell, maybe she's just jealous."

Pierre laughed. "Tracy is a really fine girl. But she's dating Bill Nelson, one of our check airmen. I'm not going there."

"Oh, really? Didn't know that."

"I think she's engaged to the guy. She wears a diamond ring. I asked her about it and she told me it wasn't an engagement ring, she said it was a promise ring."

"Whatever that means," Ray philosophized. "You just gotta be careful, boy. Many of these beautiful, young and willing flight attendants we've been hiring are gonna be circling the wagons around you. You're that rare beast, my boy, a young and single aviator."

"I'm not that young."

"Are you kidding? You're a kid! Jeez, even many of our older flight attendants, the Dragons and the Remos will be after your ass in no time, trying to take you away from the Cupcakes."

"Dragons and Remos?"

"Dragons are the older ladies. Remos are the returning mothers."

"What the devil's a returning mother?"

"That's a flight attendant who got pregnant, went out on leave and is now back on the line."

Pierre laughed. "Damn! You guys have these gals all figured out, eh? And what in God's name is a 'Cupcake'?"

"Ha! Shit yeah. We got them all figured out. A 'Cupcake' is one of our young newhires. And just like the nurses with the residents in hospitals, our gals back there are going to haunt you in their never-ending quest to marry a pilot."

"I had one like that already. I thought I'd found my *Guinevere*, was making all kinds of plans with her, then it just blew up in my face."

"*Guinevere?*"

"Yes, the imaginary magical romantic love of King Arthur."

"*Guinevere*, you say? One of our flight attendants?"

"Yeah. I accidentally found out she was two-timing me."

"Oh, crap. That's never good."

"No. It wasn't good." Pierre thought of the five pictures he still had of Kirsten in his phone. He'd never deleted them perhaps out of some instinct of self-flagellation. A reminder that he had so easily fallen for a girl who perhaps wasn't for him. He'd never backed up those pictures to his computer, so if he ever lost his phone, the images would go with it. Pierre didn't use any Cloud service to back up his files. He saw it as a security risk,

Fair enough.

He still thought of her every so often though, wondering how she was, missing her dimpled smile and her sharp tongue. And definitely, her delicious body. In all honesty, he was realistic enough to accept he'd never get over Kirsten.

The sun was setting in the west by the time they shot their approach into LAX. They had to don their sunglasses to avoid being blinded by the sun, which made it tough reading their electronic displays in front of them. Not so terrible, really, considering they had setup the airplane for another full autoland, so basically they were not flying the approach, they were monitoring how Fifi flew the approach.

As they flew over the 405 freeway on short final Pierre observed the evening traffic down below. Bumper-to-bumper as far as he could see, from the Sepulveda Pass to right below them. He felt sorry for all those poor bastards, stuck in traffic, and probably stuck in jobs they detested.

He thanked God for making him an airline pilot.

"HELLO?"

"Hi! Is this Erin?"

"Who's this?"

"Hi Erin. My name's Pierre White. I met your sister Scarlett in Philadelphia a couple of days ago when she was on her way back from Spain and she gave me your number because she didn't have her own cell phone yet."

He really didn't want to sound like some weirdo stalking Erin or her sister, but it occurred to him little sis could get the wrong impression if Scarlett hadn't informed her of his existence.

"Oh?"

A short pause. "Jeez! Yes, hi! Wait! You're the *pilot?*"

Halleluiah. Thank you, stars!

"Yes. I'm the pilot."

"Awesome! She got her new phone already. Do you want the number? I can give it to you. She's very anxious to hear from you!"

Anxious to hear from him? Yes!

Pierre was ready with a pen and paper, relaxed on the sofa in his townhome in St. Louis. "Go ahead!"

Erin gave him the number. She sounded young and enthusiastic. "Scarlett said you two met in the bar of the hotel."

That didn't sound particularly romantic. "Yeah … well, actually no. We met in the van which drove us to the hotel from the airport."

"That's like, so cool."

"Thanks, Erin. I guess you must be happy having your sister back in town?"

"I'm thrilled. Everyone's happy now that she's home. You coming out here?"

Straight girl, wasn't she? Pierre smiled. Maybe he'd made a good impression on Scarlett after all. "Yes, I'll be coming out there sometime and have the pleasure of meeting you."

Erin giggled. "Call Scarlett, she's waiting for your call."

Really? That was music to his ears. He laughed. "All right, I'll call her. Thanks for her number. Very nice talking to you. We'll meet soon, I hope."

"I'll look forward to it. Bye Pierre!"

He smiled. Little sister had probably given away a little too much during the conversation. Somehow, he suspected Scarlett would be embarrassed if Pierre repeated the exchange with Erin verbatim.

He decided to wait a few minutes before calling Scarlett. Give little sister the opportunity to text a warning to big sister that the 'pilot' was going to be calling.

He finally rang the number. He was going to have to take a picture of Scarlett to insert with her number.

"Hello?"

The same feminine, exciting voice he remembered from Philadelphia. The lovely Navy girl sitting alone at a non-descript bar in the town of Benjamin Franklin, making love to a glass of wine.

"Hi Scarlett!"

"Pierre? *Hello!* I hear you called Erin."

"I did. Your little sister is very nice."

"That she is. How are you?"

"Wonderful, now that I'm talking with you."

"You're sweet," she laughed.

"Same voice too. Only sober."

"What? Shush! You don't have to bring that up."

"Hey, you needed to blow off steam that night. I'm glad I was there to hold your hand, so to speak."

"So was I. How much wine did I drink with you, anyway?"

"Oh, about two bottles."

"Get outta here! No way!"

"Just kiddin'. I think you did have a few glasses of red wine though."

"For real?"

"Yep."

"Uggh, no wonder I can't remember much."

"You can't remember anything?"

"You I remember. I just can't recall exactly what happened after the bar. Next thing I know, the phone rings and it's you waking me up."

"I setup a wakeup call for you at four a.m. I didn't think you remembered to do that when you first got to your room, and I doubted you did it after I delivered you back following the bar visit."

"So, why did you call me yourself then?"

"Insurance. I didn't know if those fruitcakes in the front desk would call you. I didn't want you to miss your flight home. Did you get a wakeup call from the front desk?"

"I'm not sure. First thing I remember was you calling me. Thank you so much for doing that for me. I would've missed my flight and that would've been real upsetting."

"And I did kiss you before I left your bed in the morning."

Silence at the other end.

Gotya!

Pierre laughed. "Relax. Not really. I wasn't in your room. Just teasing you."

"I wondered about that."

"About what?"

"If anything happened."

"You mean, you wondered whether I'd spent the night with you? All four and a half hours of that long night? After you had all that wine?"

"Well, I didn't know." She still sounded hesitant.

"I guess you'll never know, will ya?"

"Stop it. Seriously, be honest. Did anything happen between us? Did I do anything stupid?"

"What do you think?"

"I don't know, that's why I'm asking."

Pierre congratulated himself on his decision to be protective of her that night. "No, Scarlett, nothing happened. I made sure you made it to the door of your room and then you went in by yourself and that was it."

He wondered if she remembered their kiss.

"That was it, eh?"

"Yeah. You went inside right after I kissed you."

She took a few moments before she replied. "That I remember."

"But nothing more happened after that kiss, I promise."

"I believe you."

"Please know that it's not because I wasn't attracted to you. I was dying to follow you in your room, but you were in no condition to engage in a night of lust and passion with anybody."

"A night of lust and passion? *Yay!* You do have a way with words."

"I was more concerned about you getting some sleep and making your flight than I was about getting in your pants." Once again, he wanted to bite his tongue. What the rats was he thinking, saying that to her?

"Well, that's pretty refreshing. *Getting in my pants?*"

"Just a colloquialism. No disrespect intended."

"You're funny."

He exhaled. He really had to watch his words. Time to retreat.

"Please don't think I didn't find you very attractive and desirable. I did. Believe me, it took all my will power not to pursue anything with you that night."

"Pursue anything? You mean sleep with me?"

"Yeah, that's what I meant. I didn't think you were in the best condition to take it to a higher level that night."

"Thank you."

"For what?"

"For being a gentleman."

"I just wanted to protect you. Happy to be home?"

Scarlet paused. "Yes! I'm irrationally happy being home. Finally!"

"You staying with your parents?"

"Yes. Everyone in the family's been dropping by to say hello. I'm so happy being back in the States."

"Did you ever get that McDonalds burger you were craving?"

Scarlett laughed. "I sure did! Quarter-Pounder with cheese. *And* fries!"

"You wanted to go get one of those in the middle of the night in the shipyard neighborhood in Philadelphia."

"I remember that."

"Very happy you have a phone now."

"Yes, so am I. Went to the cell phone store the very next day after my arrival and signed up for one. Where are you?"

"I'm in St. Louis."

"Is that where you live?"

Pierre realized they hadn't really had much time to learn the basics about each other. Realistically, he wasn't really sure how much she remembered of their conversation at the bar that night. "Yeah, for now. I'm moving to Phoenix, in Arizona, next month."

"Wow. Why are you moving?"

"I like Arizona, went to school there. I'm looking for a house to buy there. Missouri is good, but I want to live out west."

"And if I remember correctly, you're not married?"

"Boy, you must've had a lot of wine that night. Of course I'm married, Scarlett. I told you I was a Mormon. I have three wives. Did you forget so soon?"

"You are silly."

"Would that be a problem?"

"What, you having three wives?"

"Yea. I could invite you to become number four."

"You must be smoking some funny stuff."

"Your memory does not fail you. I'm not married. I share a townhouse here with two other pilots."

"No girlfriend?"

Pierre smiled. Right to the point, eh?

"No, no girlfriend—at the moment, anyhow."

"Why not?"

"Had one for a brief period of time a while ago. Didn't work out."

"I'm going to be looking for an apartment myself," she said, changing the topic. "Soon as I decide what to do with the rest of my life."

"Are you entirely out of the Navy now?"

"Oh, yeah. I've been honorably discharged."

"So you don't have to do anything else with them?"

"Correct."

"Well, that must be a relief. Now you can concentrate on doing whatever you like, after four years of everyone else telling you what to do every instant."

"That's what I've been thinking."

"Can I come visit you?"

"*May* I come visit you?" She said.

Pierre was taken back. "You want to come here?"

"No, dummy. I'm just correcting you. The correct form is 'may I come visit you.'"

He laughed. "What are you, an English major?"

"I could be."

"May I come visit you?"

"No."

What?

"Are you serious?"

Scarlett paused for effect. "No. Just paying you back for the three wives comment."

"I could come tomorrow."

"Tomorrow? Don't you have to work?"

"No, I have fourteen days off in a row."

"You have what? Fourteen days off? You're kidding. Vacation?"

"No. I just laid out my schedule that way."

"You laid out your schedule to have fourteen days off in a row and it's not a vacation? How can you do that?"

Pierre smiled. That was always the question with non-airline people. "How much do you know about the airlines?"

"Not much."

"Airlines schedule our work days different from everybody else, Scarlett. If you're interested, I'll explain this to you the next time I see you."

"Sounds complicated."

"It really isn't. You'll see that when I explain it to you."

"It must be pretty nice, if you can line up two weeks off in a row. So, you want to come out here tomorrow?"

"I'd love to see you."

"I want to see you as well."

Yes!

"Where are you in the Seattle area? I'll need to book a hotel."

"We're in Bellevue."

"Do you text?"

"Yes."

"Could you text me your address?" Pierre had no friggin' idea where Bellevue was. He'd overnighted in Seattle several times with the airline, but always near the airport. One time he'd stayed at a Red Lion Inn near Boeing, in Renton. Beyond that, he was an *ignoramus* about anything to do with Seattle.

"Sure. I have text. I'll send you the address."

His adrenaline was pumping at a furious rate. *He'd see Scarlett tomorrow!* He could barely contain his excitement. So far he had controlled his enthusiasm not really expecting anything from her. One never knew with attractive women, they could go one way or the other without any apparent logic. And their brief time together at the bar in Philly was not really a concrete foundation for a relationship.

"I can pick you up at the airport," Scarlett offered. "I'll just borrow my mom's car."

"That would be wonderful!" He hadn't really given much thought to the logistics of his trip to Seattle. He'd probably need a rental car. But if she was going to pick him up, would he still need the rental? Probably not.

"What time you thinking of coming in?"

He had absolutely no clue. "Not sure. Have to go look at flights in the computer. Can I text you the flight information once I get it?"

"That'll work. Do you get to travel for free?"

Pierre knew most people had no idea about how travel benefits worked in the airlines. "Mostly, yes. If there's space in the cabin, then I get a seat in First or Coach. On the other hand, if the airplane's full, then I get to ride in the flight deck the whole way."

"What's the flight deck?"

"The cockpit."

"Oh."

"They used to call it the 'cockpit' but since the airlines started hiring female pilots, someone in HR opted for the politically-correct name 'flight deck' instead."

"And why was that?"

Pierre considered a delicate way of explaining it. "Aah, you see, in this era of totally absurd political correctness, the name 'cockpit' seemed to offend certain people. I don't really know where the word came from, but I'm guessing in the early days of aviation someone must've joked that the front office in the airplane was called that because it was a pit full of cocks. As in 'roosters.'"

"I see. As in 'roosters,' uhm?"

"Right."

"But now the females are taking offense at the use of the word 'cock'?"

"Yeah, I guess that's ... correct."

"That's funny and totally absurd!"

"I think so too, but it appears that the entire airline industry has switched to 'flight deck.'

"What percentage of the pilots are female?"

"Not too many. About four percent. Roughly 720 women out of 18,000 pilots at our airline."

"And they're willing to change the name for a handful of women?"

"Afraid so. Our industry is plagued with sexual harassment, political correctness and other absurd modern-day maladies."

"Is there a lot of sexual harassment going on in the airlines?"

"We do have more than the average industry."

"Didn't know any of this was going on. But of course, what do I know about the airlines?"

"Let me tell you a funny story. One of our female captains drew a trip with a female first officer and an all-female cabin crew. While they were at the gate, the captain got on the public-address system and made an announcement: 'Ladies and gentlemen, welcome to an unmanned aircraft!'"

Scarlett laughed. "Very funny!"

"I'll look at the flights and text you the information."

"Okay."

Pierre reviewed the images engraved in his brain of the time he'd spent together with Scarlett at the hotel bar in Philadelphia. Naturally, he didn't have a real clear picture of her face in his mind. But the sound of her voice had been enough to rekindle the powerful attraction he'd felt for her, and the captivating image of her sitting at the bar in the cheerful summer dress. His memory wasn't good enough to have retained an image of her face, but he did have the certainty that she was stunning and when he first saw her he'd classified her as a 'dream.' After the sad taste in his mouth Kirsten had generated, he was a little gun-shy with girls, leery of getting too involved too quickly.

Practice makes perfect, though. He'll just have to go easy with Scarlett.

THE WORLDWIDE AIRBUS A319 parked its brakes at the gate in SEATAC, the Seattle Tacoma airport serving both cities. Pierre checked the clock in his cell phone. They were one hour late. Thunderstorms in St. Louis had delayed departures. It had been a horribly long day for him. He'd initially scheduled the day off but then made the stupid mistake of answering the phone early in the morning.

It was Crew Sked. They were delighted to have connected with Pierre, the scheduler at the other end admitted. One of Worldwide's illustrious first officers had called in sick in the middle of a trip, leaving Crew Sked in a pickle. There were no more reserves available, so they had started calling pilots randomly.

Jeez, *that douchebag illustrious dipshit first officer* had almost screwed him.

Pierre was not obligated to answer his phone when he was not on reserve, but once he did answer the call, he was forced by his contract to accept anything the schedulers threw in his direction.

He was absolutely furious with himself. answering the phone had been a real mistake. His fear that they would stick him with a two or three-day trip right when he was going to Seattle dissipated once the crew scheduler informed him he would be done early in the day, early enough to catch the flight to the west coast. All he had to do was fly an out-and-back from St. Louis to Chicago.

Piece of cake.

Once he recovered from his anger he resignedly put on his uniform and drove to Lambert Field.

That trip to Chicago took a lot of his energy, but luckily he was able to make the flight to Seattle later in the day.

He'd texted Scarlett, notifying her of the delay. She'd been very understanding telling him she'd check on the flight's progress online. The sun had set an hour before his arrival in Seattle.

The flight from St. Louis had been very relaxed. Nearly five hours earlier he'd approached the crew, requesting the jumpseat, and the Skipper had welcomed him aboard and directed Pierre to take a seat in First Class. Aah, just the kind of music he loved to hear. Those lovely words: 'Grab a seat in First.' Riding in First Class was the way to go. Half the First Class seats were empty, so he selected a window seat in the front row.

Not one minute after he sat down a very polite flight attendant approached him.

"May I get you something to drink, Mister White?"

Dang, he was impressed. How'd she get hold of his name so quickly?

He ordered a Diet Coke. Although he was pretty sure the First Class cabin was not going to be full, the possibility always existed that the flight could fill up. A flight cancellation at another airline, for instance, could bump him back up to the flight deck.

Unfortunately, airline regulations prohibited him from returning to the flight deck after consuming even one single alcoholic beverage.

Hence, whenever he traveled he always waited until they were in the air before ordering an adult beverage.

The flight attendant pulled out his tray, placing a napkin on it, then deposited a Coke served in a real glass, not a plastic cup.

"Thank you!" He relaxed in the extra-wide leather seat, sipping the Coke. He couldn't shake the feeling of euphoria. He was on his way to see Scarlett. A flashing amber light in the back of his mind kept warning him not to get too involved at this stage. Remember Kirsten. Go easy. Baby steps!

Go fuck yourself.

Although he was still smarting from his experience with Kirsten, that was not going to keep him from seeking female company. Pierre didn't really need several girls in his life, he didn't need to have a girl in every port—or airport—so to speak. He just wanted a woman who could be his companion and lover. A girl dedicated only to him. A beautiful partner who wanted what he had to offer. And he would reciprocate, giving her loyalty and support and undying love.

Gawd, that sounded like a cheesy B-rated romantic movie.

Maybe Scarlett could be that girl. And maybe not. But he would find out. Destiny had given him the incredible second chance to get to know her when she went down to the bar in Philadelphia, and Pierre was not going to waste the opportunity. His life seemed to be full of second chances.

He removed his carryon bag from the overhead bin, waiting patiently for the other passengers to deplane. 'Hurry up and wait,' was the rule when arriving at the gate. The very nice First Class flight attendant brought his jacket.

"Have a nice stay in Seattle," she said, now a little less perky than when he'd boarded hours earlier.

"Thanks. You guys done for the day?" He accepted back his gray flannel suit jacket, feeling her hand still on it, helping him.

"Oh, ya. We're done. Time for a martini and some rest."

"Long day?"

She nodded.

Pierre estimated she was in her late fifties.

"Started in Miami this morning."

He performed a quick mental calculation. That represented almost eight hours of flight time for the crew. That was a long day, indeed.

"You live in Seattle?" The flight attendant asked.

"No, just visiting a friend."

The crowd began to dissipate, giving Pierre the chance to finally head for the exit.

"Thanks! Have a good layover."

He walked out of the airplane, following a couple of passengers up the jetway.

THE SIGHT OF SCARLETT standing there right outside the jet bridge took his breath away.

Lord 'a Mercy!

Although he hadn't kept a good image of Scarlett engraved in his mental flashdrive, he knew without a shadow of a doubt, that was her. His brain recognized her instantly. Much to his delight, she was far better looking than he remembered.

Her hands were casually half-tucked into the front pockets of her blue jeans. Her thick blond hair tied into some sort of pony tail and her emerald-green long-sleeved cotton blouse matched the color of her eyes.

Pierre broke into an enormous smile, pulling his bag behind him.

"Hi Scarlett!" He parked his bag off to one side, letting go of it.

Scarlett took one step forward, "Welcome to Seattle!"

She threw her arms around his neck, hugging him like an old friend, but not kissing him.

She was warm and smelled of baby powder. He enjoyed feeling the smooth skin of her neck against his face.

Pierre wasn't sure what to do, should he attempt to kiss her? Technically, they weren't lovers.

She gave him a peck on the cheek.

Aha! She did kiss him after all!

Pierre caught sight of the crew from his flight walking rapidly past the two of them, pulling their wheelies. The nice First Class flight attendant was there too, casting a quick glance in their direction.

Scarlett's smile was intoxicating. He noticed how white her teeth were. A goddess.

"Yow! You really get dressed up." She gave him a look from head to toe.

Pierre always wore a suit when he traveled. Grey flannel single-breasted with a white shirt, red suspenders and a paisley tie. He thought of it as his 'wet suit.' Commuting pilots who liked to have a drink or two at the end of a trip, couldn't do so while in their airline uniform, so they changed into their 'wet suit' before flying home.

Besides, he felt that if one had the opportunity to travel First Class, one had the obligation to look elegant and be an asset representing the airline. Also, he wasn't particularly fond of traveling in uniform because passengers had the terrible habit of wanting to engage him in conversation. Pierre did not enjoy conversations with total strangers when he traveled as a passenger. That was his own private time to read or write.

"I prefer to dress up when I travel."

"Does your airline require you to dress like this?"

"No, we don't have to wear a suit. I just have the habit."

They walked away from the gate. Pierre was instantly and pleasantly surprised Scarlett offered her hand so they could walk holding hands.

Like a couple of young kids.

At which point, the logical sequence of events was for him to become instantly aroused by the closeness to the beauty next to him, and find himself the proud owner of a gigantic hard-on.

Good grief.

SEATAC airport was huge. Pierre had no idea where they were going. He'd just let her lead.

"Did you check in a bag?" Scarlett asked.

"Ah, no. Just this carry on. I like to travel light. Were you able to borrow your mom's car?"

"Yes. I've got her car. My sister, Erin has a couple of her friends over, everyone's been in the Jacuzzi drinking wine all afternoon. I thought we'd be able to join them but your one-hour delay probably nixed it."

Pierre was both surprised and at the same time disappointed. The Jacuzzi? Rats! He would've loved that!

"Oh, no. I'm so sorry." Damn, he'd missed the opportunity to be with Scarlett in a Jacuzzi. He was more than sorry. He was disgusted. What bad luck. First night arriving in Seattle, he would've loved the sight of her in a bathing suit.

Thanks, St. Louis, I love your weather. Thanks for delaying my flight one hour with your inevitable thunderstorms.

Pierre smiled at her. She was wearing tennis shoes of some kind, so he noticed she was a little shorter than the last time they'd been together in Philly. Back there she must've been wearing heels.

"Your mom and dad home too?"

"No, they took the train up to Canada for the weekend."

That was a pleasant and unexpected disclosure. No parents around, eh? Pierre had made a reservation at the Hyatt in Bellevue, hoping he'd have some opportunity to be there alone with Scarlett.

"What do you have in mind?"

"For what?"

"Tonight. Since we already missed the Jacuzzi party. May I take you out to dinner someplace nice?"

Scarlett laughed. "No, no. we're going to my parents' place. Maybe Erin and the others are still there."

"Your wish is my command, milady."

He followed her lead to the parking lot. Mom's car was a white Honda Odyssey minivan.

Pierre stashed his bag in the back, joining Scarlett in the front passenger seat. She started the engine, carefully and slowly driving out of the airport parking garage.

"Good flight?"

"Excellent, thanks." He didn't want to tell her he'd sat in First Class. He didn't want Scarlett to interpret it as bragging.

"Can you believe you're here? Hey, we just met a few days ago." She turned to read his face.

Pierre laughed. "It's actually pretty wonderful."

His answer seemed to please her.

"Have you had a chance to visit with everyone in your family?"

"Oh, more than I bargained for. I've repeated my story so many times, I may just type it out and hand out fliers."

"Which story?"

"My adventures in Spain."

"Your mom must be happy you didn't marry in Spain."

"Happy? No. She's not just happy. She's *irrationally* deliriously happy."

Pierre wasn't sure what to say. He really didn't want to go there. Scarlett must've had some feelings for her Spaniard, no matter what took place at the end.

She drove very attentively, looking in the rearview mirror often and not going over the speed limit.

He was impressed. Pierre respected any driver, man or woman, who drove with care.

"But bottom line, you're glad to be home?"

"Very much so," she smiled.

"No regrets about the Navy?"

"Goodness, no. I did what I had to do. Now it's time to move on to something else."

"Who's over at your parents' place again?"

"Erin and her boyfriend Steve and their friends Emily and Nathan and some other girl."

"You tell them about me?"

"Are you serious? Of course I told them about you! They kept bugging me all afternoon to jump in the Jacuzzi and start drinking. Couldn't do that, I had to come get you."

"Thanks, sorry I spoiled your drinking."

"Quiet! How'd you like being a pilot?"

Pierre never knew how to answer that one.

I friggin love it!

It's the most fun you can have with your pants on!

They actually pay me for doing this!?

The single best job in the world, bar none!

Living the dream!

I fuckin' love it.

All the stereotype answers he'd heard over his years in aviation. Each and every one of them apparently designed to infuriate girls.

"It's a delightful job," he said simply. "If this is what you enjoy doing."

Scarlett gave him a quick look, as if not expecting such a simplistic answer. "Did you want to be a pilot since you were a little kid?"

"I loved playing with airplanes since I was three years old. I don't think I knew what a pilot was though."

"Three years old? You remember that?"

"I didn't remember what age I was, but I remember the house we lived in and my parents told me I was three years old when we lived there. And I played with airplanes."

"And now you're an airline pilot."

Pierre nodded. "Yeah, and now I'm an airline pilot."

"You're very lucky. Not many people have that ability to know what they're going to do with their lives from early on."

Pierre had heard that before. For the life of his he failed to understand how that could be. What, were most people just plain dumb? He always figured if he liked drawing and building things, he would've been an architect or an engineer. If he liked money and numbers, he would've pursued a career in the financial world. If he liked the sea so much, he would've done everything to become a ship captain. So why was it that so many people just wandered through life like a bunch of zombies, not knowing what to do with their lives?

His old football coach in high school once told him: "Don't believe that garbage about going out *finding* yourself! Go out and *make* whatever self you want to be!"

He had lived his life by those words.

"I know. I'm very lucky. This magnificent job gave me the opportunity to meet you."

Scarlett diverted her attention from the road, looking at him for a moment.

He wasn't able to read her body language just yet. Was she pleased? Did he sound too much like a blabber mouth?

Twenty minutes later she pulled up to the driveway of a large Pacific lodge-style home, monumental and surrounded by huge pine trees. Pierre took in the design, more like a rustic cabin. All woods, of different kinds. The walls, the railings, the steps, the balconies, all wood. Enormous house.

Money. And lots of it.

"Okay, I'm impressed! This is striking! What is it your dad does exactly?"

Scarlett set the parking brake, shutting off the lights of the Honda. "Dad's an engineer. He's been with Boeing almost thirty years."

Pierre was duly impressed. He had absolutely no idea what real estate cost in Seattle, or Bellevue, but he strongly suspected this house must be in the over a bunch-of-bucks range.

Definitely over a million. At least a million. Frankly, he didn't have a clue what real estate went for in this place. One thing he did know, however, the house was monumental.

Scarlett popped the rear hatch, allowing Pierre to go for his bag.

He briefly wondered if he should get his bag. He'd booked a hotel, so she was going to be giving him a ride there later. The bag could've just stayed in the car. "Shouldn't I just leave my bag in here?"

"Don't you have a bathing suit?"

He instantly felt his knees go weak and his blood begin rushing to his groin.

"... Yeah, I do."

"So bring the bag, silly." She smiled.

HolymotherofGod.

He obediently reached for his bag, following Scarlett up the steps to the front entrance.

Up close and personal the not-so-rustic cabin appeared to be more the size of a small inn.

Two or three million maybe?

Pierre followed her through the foyer. The place was impressive, two-story ceilings, with a mezzanine and a huge fireplace the size of a Volkswagen minivan. Not much in the way of illumination either, just some recessed lighting here and there. Overall, the place had a dark, cozy look, not unlike a mountain lodge. And tons of furniture.

"Whoa. This is a isn't a home, it's a ski lodge!"

She didn't answer him, instead she kept walking towards the back of the main room. Large glass doors and windows led to a small wooden patio behind the home. It couldn't be deeper than twenty-five feet, totally surrounded by a high wooden fence and thick forest.

The sound of voices and laughter could be heard coming from the patio. Pierre walked closer to the windows, getting a full view of an above-ground Jacuzzi with several people in it. From where he was it appeared there were at least three girls in there.

And he couldn't see any bikini straps. Wait! were all the girls nude?

Scarlett opened the big glass door to the patio, saying something to the group.

Soon as Scarlett shut the door again, Pierre observed the crowd in the Jacuzzi starting to get out. And yes, they were all stark naked!

He was fascinated. He watched two of the girls reaching for large white towels, wrapping themselves in them. Then he quit looking, since Scarlett was walking past him.

"Follow me," she ordered.

One last quick glimpse confirmed there were five people out there, all of them naked as jaybirds.

"Where we going?"

"Upstairs. To my room. Bring your bag." Scarlett led the way up a steep set of stairs.

Pierre obediently followed her hauling his bag.

Up to her room?

He was hopeful about whatever agenda Scarlett had in mind, and also terribly excited. He'd developed an uncomfortable hard-on when he first met Scarlett at the gate, and it hadn't improved. The pain in his groin was not getting any better. Since Scarlett was ahead, he quickly reached in his pants, shifting his erection upwards, relieving the discomfort. And they were going up to her room!?

At the top of the stairs Scarlett entered what appeared to be a bedroom, waiving for Pierre to follow her.

The room had high ceilings and parked smack in the middle was a California king-sized bed with four posts and a canopy. The place exuded femininity, all pink lace, pillows and thick plush beddings.

Straight out of Cinderella.

"Go ahead and change. I'll be back in a minute."

"Change? Into what?"

"Your suit, dummy, what else?"

Pierre felt like he did when he had a double shot of Irish whisky, light-headed yet euphoric.

Scarlett left the room without closing the door.

Pierre looked around. Definitely a girl's bedroom. It smelled lovely too. perfume or cologne or something equally soft. So, Scarlett wanted to go in the Jacuzzi after all! Did he win the lottery or what?

Since all the others downstairs appeared to have vacated the Jacuzzi, he wondered if they were all going to return and join him and Scarlett in the water naked, or had their escape been permanent?

What if they returned?

That could be uncomfortable.

Pierre had no problem with nudity, but being butt naked in some Jacuzzi with two other guys and four girls was not what he'd had in mind. Scarlett did ask him to change into his suit, so it was apparent that going in the Jacuzzi was on the agenda for the night. Whether the others would join in, who knew.

He placed his bag on the floor next to the bed, finding and removing a navy-blue nylon bathing suit that traveled with him. His grey flannel jacket was down in the Honda, where he'd forgotten it. He quickly removed his shirt and tie, suspenders and T-shirt. His shoes, pants and boxing shorts following. Pierre then slipped into his swimming trunks. He felt definitely weird, standing there in a strange bedroom with nothing on other than his bathing suit.

And needless to say, the embarrassing erection. Thank God his trunks were dark.

The fact that Scarlett had led him to her bedroom, and that her parents had gone out of town, suggested Scarlett may be on what could turn out to be a very pleasant program for the night. Could it be she was planning on spending the night together?

Not likely. Too soon. Definitely, too soon. But that was fine, just spending time with her was such a delightful prospect, he was in heaven. Especially the idea of going in the Jacuzzi!

But what if he was underestimating her and she had sex on her mind? Here! In this room! His erection got harder.

"Ready?" Scarlett had one of the large white towels wrapped around her. Her shoulders and legs were bare.

"You tell me what to do," he replied, once again, kicking himself for his lack of creativity. Why couldn't he come up with a funny or exciting reply, like they always did in the movies?

Because in the movies they hired a writer who had weeks to plan the script, you moron.

Scarlett started downstairs, with Pierre in trail.

He was still in some sort of shock. He would not have imagined in his wildest fantasies that on his first night with Scarlett in Seattle they were going to end up in a Jacuzzi together.

Incredible. Pierre wondered what he'd done in a previous life to deserve such an Olympian reward. And he liked her so much. He was fascinated by her. And if this house was any indication, she came from a good family, or at least a very wealthy one.

Walking through the living room Pierre noticed the silence.

"Where'd everyone go?"

"They left."

"What? Why?"

Scarlett approached a big wooden armoire next to the glass windows. "They had enough Jacuzzi. Going to get some dinner and then they're all going dancing."

"Did I scare them off?"

"No, dummy. You didn't scare them off."

"Was one of those your sister?"

"Yes, Erin was here."

That was odd. Nobody had been introduced. However, Pierre decided it was actually a break. Now he had to wrap his mind around the fact that he and Scarlett had the house to themselves and the Jacuzzi silently waited for them outside.

The possibilities were boner-level erotic and endless. He breathed faster.

He watched Scarlett adjust a pair of speakers so they would point towards an open window behind the armoire. The sound of a piano echoed from the speakers.

Classical music. And none other than Chopin, one of his Nocturnes, the one in E Flat Major, one of Pierre's favorites.

He definitely approved. Oh, did he ever. So, not only was Navy great-looking and sharp but also educated in good music.

Scarlett paused at a small built-in bar, selecting an open bottle of red wine, pouring two glasses. She took them with her.

"C'mon."

Pierre followed her outside, glancing at the wine bottle.

Chianti.

A delicious choice!

The air was very cold and damp.

Holy shit, Batman! It was cold! Seattle was definitely not Phoenix.

They better get in that hot water fast, or he was sure they were both going to die from hypothermia.

Scarlett carefully deposited the two glasses of red wine on a narrow wooden shelf behind the Jacuzzi then began lifting the two covers protecting the above-ground hot tub. Pierre rapidly got his hands on the covers, taking over from her, removing each one and depositing them by the fence. Damned things weighed a ton each. Steam came out of the hot tub. He then extended his hand to Scarlett, helping her up the wooden steps built into the side of the tub.

Reaching the third step, Scarlett let go of her towel, allowing it to drop, turning to face Pierre.

Pierre gasped, his eyes feasting on her splendid body.

Splendid body!?

She was so many light-years beyond just splendid. She was stunning, a Sports Illustrated bathing suit model if he ever saw one.

Scarlett had on a bright green and pink bikini with very high sides, emphasizing her curvaceous, bare hips.

She appeared rather pleased by his reaction—hesitating momentarily—her quiet defiance evident in her pose, then climbed up one more rung before stepping down into the tub.

That provided Pierre with an unexpected exquisite view of her mouth-watering bottom. His eyes opened wide. Her perfectly toned ass flexed as she continued into the Jacuzzi. His overactive imagination saw himself touching that ass and nibbling at it with his teeth.

Oh, God, please let him live long enough to do that.

He made a conscious effort not to let his jaw drop.

Scarlett stepped down into the smoking-hot tub, rapidly lowering herself in the water up to her neck.

Pierre followed her up the steps as fast as he could move, sticking his foot in the water.

The pain nearly had him screaming like a little girl.

Holymother, ooouch! Aahh! Holy bejeezus! HOT!!!

How in God's name had Scarlett managed to get in that scalding hot water up to her shoulders in just a few moments? The water was hot enough to peel chickens!

She flashed him a quiet smile.

The little shit was enjoying herself!

"Hot?" She inquired, innocently.

"No, what makes you think that?" Holy crap, his voice sounded so much higher than normal.

"Dunno. Maybe the look of sheer agony and pain on your face?"

"I don't know how the Dickens you got in there so fast. This thing is boiling hot!"

"It's not *that* bad," she was still smiling.

The little stinker had tricked him. Pierre took his sweet time, allowing himself to enter the Jacuzzi one inch at a time. Much as he was dying to get in the water with Scarlett, there was just no way he could do it any faster. He thought he was going to freak out and squeal like a pig when the water hit his crotch. And the entire time Scarlett was submerged in the water to her chin, intently watching him with those innocent green eyes. How in hell did she do it?

Finally, after what felt like an eternity, Pierre found himself immersed in the hot water, truly surprised he hadn't passed out or that his blood pressure hadn't tanked, killing him on the spot.

He immediately tiptoed under water towards Scarlett, doing his low-gravity moon walk, reaching for her. She lifted her arms out of the water, softly locking her fingers behind his neck. Pierre pulled her towards him, his hands firmly placed on both sides of her waist. Scarlett crouched with her legs open. Pierre fit nicely between her knees. His erection was still there—

or so he hoped—despite the freezing cold air and the scalding water. For a moment there he'd wondered if his precious family jewels would suffer irreparable damage due to the water temperature.

Goddamn. Well, worst case scenario, at least he still had his tongue.

Scarlett leaned forward, meeting his lips.

Pierre finally abandoned himself to the warm, soft texture of her mouth. He'd dreamed about this moment for several days, ever since he kissed her goodnight in Philly. Scarlett opened her mouth, licking his lips, entering his mouth in a hesitant exploratory voyage.

He felt a delicious ripple of excitement in his balls.

"Hmm, I could just eat you," she purred.

It was just as exciting as when they kissed in the bar in Philadelphia.

Only better.

Better because now she was not intoxicated or dead tired. Better because unless he was totally asinine reading the situation, she was hot and willing.

One of her hands moved up from his neck to the back of his head, running her fingers through his hair. Her tongue no longer shy, but darting in and out of his mouth, violently colliding with his, challenging him.

He was at the gates of heaven.

Unbelievable, at the blink of an eye, he'd gone from days of missing her and wanting her, to finding himself kissing Scarlett in a steamy Jacuzzi.

You must thank The Force or God or whomever is responsible for this incredible situation. Remember, even a dog knows how to be grateful.

Pierre allowed one of his hands to drift down to her bikini bottom. Softly feeling between her legs, he found the small strip of cloth covering her pubis, using his fingers to move it aside, he gently touched her sex flesh, feeling the exquisite smooth oily texture.

Scarlett didn't object.

Holy shit. He couldn't believe he'd just done that!

Her rapid breathing told Pierre he must be doing something right. He moved his hand down to his trunks, pulling out his throbbing erection sideways through one of the legs of his shorts. He moved forward towards Scarlett. She was up against the back wall of the tub, so she had nowhere to go.

He guided his erection towards her lips. Scarlett made things easier moving her hips forward to meet him. Pierre made contact with her, her bikini firmly held to the side with one hand, finding her entrance. Her mischievous green eyes locked on his. Gently but firmly, Pierre thrust his pelvis forward, confirming that he was entering her, a tiny little bit at first, then allowing himself one long push, feeling his shaft inch by delicious inch sliding into her pulsing pussy. She felt hotter inside than the water was. Hard to believe, considering the water was scalding hot.

Scarlett gave out some mixture of moan and exclamation, pulling on Pierre's neck with renewed fervor, shoving her hips forward.

She was perfectly lubricated, surprising Pierre. He'd read many women complaining about having sex in the water, claiming they couldn't stay lubricated enough to enjoy themselves. Well, that certainly wasn't the case with Scarlett. She was as oily and lubricated as Pierre could possibly imagine. And they were in the water.

He moved his hips back, removing his erection half way, then going back inside her to the hilt.

"Aren't you glad you came?" She said softly, with a playful, teasing smile.

Pierre continued going in and out of her at a slow but sustained pace. He laughed, smiling. His hands were on her hips. "Glad? I am absolutely thrilled. You are incredible."

Scarlett smiled. "So are you."

He kissed her, immediately feeling her tongue darting inside his mouth. He was so turned on he was going to explode.

"Wait," she pushed him away.

"What?"

Pierre felt himself slipping out of Scarlett. Remarkably, the water felt cold on his erection. Geepers, that's how hot she was inside!

She reached behind her back, unhooking the top part of her bikini. "Take off your suit."

Pierre didn't need to be asked twice, crouching in the tub he removed his trunks in less than one tenth of a second. He did so without having to stand. Somehow he suspected if he stood up the cold ambient air would flash-freeze his erection into oblivion. Scarlett removed both pieces of her bikini, reaching for

Pierre's trunks, plopping all three on the bench alongside the Jacuzzi, next to the wine glasses.

"This makes it much easier," she stated, satisfied, moving her hips forward, spreading her tanned, toned thighs offering herself to Pierre again. Her perfectly shaped breasts with their aroused nipples came in contact with his chest the same instant his shaft found her entrance. Air bubbles floated to the surface as a result of their bodies colliding. Scarlett brought her arms around Pierre with surprising strength. He held her around the waist, pulling her young, strong body towards him. His pelvis plunged his mahogany erection deep inside her. Scarlett's tongue conveyed her approval and pleasure by darting in and out of his mouth, still holding on to Pierre for dear life, breathing rapidly.

He momentarily thought if the others were to come back to the house just now, they would be treated to a unique show.

What was happening to him was hard to believe. He was making love to Scarlett in a hot tub, not one hour after arriving in Seattle. He liked to think he was blessed with a great imagination, but this reality far outdid anything he could've imagined. Scarlett was moving her hips in perfect synch with his, making the experience totally delicious. He went in and out, harder and harder. Water splashed against the walls of the tub, spilling outside.

There wasn't too much room to get creative. The Jacuzzi was not going to lend itself to other variations of love-making. He wondered if he was hurting her back, which was leaning against the plastic walls of the tub. That couldn't be comfortable.

"Wait," she said again.

He stopped kissing her. Her green bedroom eyes one inch from his, her warm breath reminding him of the smell of maple syrup. "Yes?"

"Let's go upstairs." She pushed him back, away from her.

Dang! She was strong!

For the second time Pierre felt himself slipping out of her body.

Scarlett stood, allowing him his first full nude view of her magnificent physique, standing one foot away from his face.

In the name of Obi-Wan Kenobi! Holy Jesus! She was stunning!

He was spellbound. No other way to put it.

Scarlett was perfectly proportioned, her perky full breasts and sensual hips magnificently balanced. He had but a brief moment to admire the erotic, strong woman standing there. Water rivulets cascading down all over her body. His mind was misfiring coming to terms with the reality that the deity standing in the Jacuzzi with him was the same very attractive girl he'd met at the bar in Philly. Her pussy was neatly shaved showing only a line of blond hair for accent.

Chopin's nocturne filled the air with its lovely piano.

Scarlett walked around him, feeling for the steps. Pierre enjoyed the opportunity to admire her exquisite ass and strong legs when she stepped up and out of the water.

Her dream legs got a nine on the scale of perfection. Her ass a ten. No, an eleven.

She was shiny and dripping water. Her nude body had a reddish hue to it, from the prolonged immersion in the hot water.

God, he loved that ass!

During the brief two seconds Scarlett passed in front of him he already imagined himself holding on to her waist just above the hips while going inside her as she laid on her bed face down underneath him. Man, his sex drive was out of control.

He observed Scarlett reaching for the white towel, wrapping it around herself.

"Well? You coming?"

Pierre jumped up, going for the steps, his cock jutting out proudly. He caught Scarlett's deliberate stare at his manhood. That both pleased him and blew his mind. More blew his mind. He was actually *here*, buck-naked getting out of a Jacuzzi after having been inside Scarlett!?

Somehow his reality was moving too fast, it was leaving him behind. It was becoming a *virtual* reality.

"Let's put the covers back on," Scarlett reached for one of the Jacuzzi lids with one hand, holding up her towel with the other.

"Here, let me do it."

The two vinyl-covered Jacuzzi lids were so heavy it took both of them to slide them back in place. Pierre didn't feel the cold anymore after the time spent in the steaming water. He was also a little self-conscious about his nudity. Scarlett was covered by her white towel, but he was cavorting in his birthday suit, without any modesty. Pretty friggin' amazing, really, considering they'd only spent about an hour or so together at the bar in Philly.

Scarlett reached for the two wine glasses. "Wanna grab our suits?"

"Certainly!" Pierre picked up his blue trunks, jumping into them with lightning speed. Then he followed Scarlett in the house, carrying her wet suit. The living room was still quiet, no visible sign of any of the others. They went up the stairs again, without saying much.

Scarlett turned right through a different door at the top of the stairs.

"Come," she waved.

Pierre followed her into a roomy bathroom. It was all wood everywhere, high ceilings with a huge white porcelain bathtub behind a curtain on the left. Scarlett approached the tub, reaching out, running the water. The very loud sound of the faucets spilling water filled the room.

Scarlett released her towel, letting it land at her feet. "Come here," she commanded.

Pierre removed his bathing trunks again in a blink, tossing them aside, approaching her and getting more aroused by the second. He obediently closed up on her, feeling her nipples against his chest and his erection against her crotch connecting with each other at the same instant. Her breasts followed her nipples pressing against his chest, while his cock found shelter in the 'Y' space right between her legs. His erection went so far under her, he could feel her buttocks. Her crotch was incredibly hot.

Scarlett kissed him again, hard, pushing her pelvis against him.

Pierre felt her fingernails digging into his back.

He reached down, grabbing both her buttocks with his hands, extra hard. He was going to make her yelp.

They kissed for two minutes, until the bathtub was half full.

Scarlett broke the kiss, moving her mouth down to his shoulder. She bit hard.

"Yeaow!!" He was very surprised. Didn't know how to take that particular quirk. She did bite him hard and kept at it for what seemed like an eternity! He silently laughed. Maybe that was her reaction to his cast-iron grip on her buttocks. He remembered Kirsten liked using her teeth on his bare shoulder as well.

Scarlett had made *him* yelp!

Pushing away from him, a grin on her face, she ordered. "Get in the bathtub."

He smiled, finding her bossy *persona* rather exciting and intriguing. He hesitated for a moment, remembering the Jacuzzi downstairs. What if this water was also near boiling point?

Aw, screw it.

He stepped into the bathtub. It was friggin hot, but not as bad as the Jacuzzi had been. This time he wasn't going to scream like a little girl. The water was only up to his knee. Not real deep. He sat down slowly, his shoulder throbbing.

Scarlett followed him without hesitation.

Once they were both in the water, she stared in his eyes, turning around. Without another word,

Scarlett got down on her knees and hands, her head pointing away from Pierre, leaning towards the faucets that were still filling the bathtub. Her head hung low, allowing her blond hair to enter the water.

Pierre gasped. He was incredibly aroused. Scarlett was a nuclear explosion. She knew what it took to drive a man crazy with desire. And she was built like a goddess from Olympus. He couldn't wait another second, advancing on his knees he barely felt the hardness of the porcelain against his kneecaps. Her beautifully-sculptured ass awaited him, elevated half out of the water, invitingly, and he wasn't about to be asked twice. He was so excited his balls were hurting.

OhmeGosh!

Scarlett was actually offering her hot well-shaped ass to him. He had dreamed of this from the moment he'd met her, but without much hope of it happening anytime soon. Now, sooner than he could ever imagine, he was presented with the opportunity to make love to this most incredible of all women, from the back, of all positions. He edged his knees forward between her legs, applying gentle pressure to the inside of her thighs, separating her legs.

Scarlett didn't flinch, she did turn back to glance at him, a lusty smile on her face, her lips parted, her hair hanging in the water.

Pierre used his hand to guide himself to her pussy. He positioned the head of his boner right between her lips, thrusting his pelvis and hips forward gently. He observed his shaft sliding into Scarlett effortlessly, stretching her with his thickness.

She gasped.

And in no time at all, he was inside her.

"*Ahhhh*," she voiced appreciatively.

Pierre took that as a 'fuck me!' He began going in and out of her at a much faster rate. He loved the sound his lower belly made when it slammed against her buttocks. Not unlike the sound of a butt being softly spanked. Incredibly erotic. Placing his hands on her hips, Pierre pumped in and out of her. He was in ecstasy, staring down at Scarlett admiring the shape of her shoulders, her slender waist and her delicious ass. The very sight of her left him weak. He dug in his fingers into her buttocks. Her earlier bite still ached— now it was his turn to make her squirm.

He gave her a playful yet brisk whack in the ass before massaging the sting away. She jerked sideways under the impact, but kept shoving her hips back against him—with a fury—without objecting.

Pierre was sure now. He'd died and gone to heaven.

His thrusting against Scarlett was creating tsunami waves in the bathtub, splashing everywhere, soaking the floor.

"Wait!" She commanded.

Pierre stopped.

"We can't do this here. We're flooding the bathroom." She pushed herself up on her knees, with Pierre still inside her. "Let's go in the bed."

The next instant his erection slid out of Scarlett from between her cheeks.

Good grief, this was becoming a habit!

Stepping out of the bathtub she reached for her towel, vigorously drying her body. Her knees were red from the bathtub porcelain bottom.

Pierre looked around for another towel. Nothing in sight. He stood there dripping. He would've drenched the bathroom if not for the fact that the floor was already soaking wet.

Scarlett opened a side closet, pulling out a neatly folded grey bath towel, tossing it to Pierre.

He caught it and put it to use. His erection was still at DEFCON 1, and he didn't think it was going to be downgraded anytime soon. He'd already had a taste of Scarlett twice tonight, and he was definitely ready for more.

"C'mon!" she commanded again, getting a hold of his hand, leading the way out of the bathroom.

Scarlett walked up to her canopied bed, briskly pulling down the feather comforter and sheets. She then climbed on the bed, positioning herself on her elbows and knees once again.

Pierre silently issued another fervent 'thank you.'

He rapidly joined her in bed. This time Scarlett had two fluffy-looking pillows under her face, and her knees were not on solid porcelain.

She had rapidly assumed the same position she'd had in the bathtub, her adorable ass lifted off the bed, her legs spread open, her breasts hanging down, awaiting him.

Pierre couldn't wait any longer, he approached her beautiful derriere with every intention of fucking her blind.

And that's when it happened.

The fatigue of the day, combined with the cold air outside and the hot water in both the Jacuzzi and the bathtub played a surprisingly dirty trick on him.

What the hell?

His erection fizzled. Gone. Totally shriveled up and died.

What the fuck? This had *never* happened to him. Not in a million years. Not in his lifetime.

He was on the bed, behind Scarlett, ready to fuck her into kingdom come, and instead his most loyal of all friends was betraying him, stabbing him in the back.

Et tu, Brute!!?

He was horrified and embarrassed. What in the world was he going to do? This could not be happening! He had to do something before Scarlett noticed! He reached for his dick, stroking it, desperately trying to get some life back. No reaction, it was as helpful as throwing a drowning man both ends of the rope. Good God, did Scarlett have an automatic defibrillator in her bedroom? Maybe he could zap his cock with it and bring it back to life? What'd happened? Why all of a sudden his pride and joy had gone on life support? He looked up, as Scarlett patiently waited there on all fours, looking straight back at him between her legs.

Oh, shit. She knew.

This wasn't happening. He stroked faster. Nothing seemed to be helping. What could he do? His cock was dead on arrival. This was a disaster of biblical proportions! The most humiliating moment of his entire life.

Scarlett smiled, sitting up. She very sweetly directed Pierre to lay down on the bed, pushing him back so he could recline his head on the pillows. She then collected her blond hair, placing it behind one side of her neck, getting it out of the way. Laying on her side, Scarlett proceeded to direct her attention to his cock. She delicately grasped his limp organ with her fingers, gently holding it, moving herself closer so she could bring it to her mouth. She surrounded it with her perfectly-sculptured lips, moving her head up and down slowly, sucking at the same time, using her other hand to caress his balls.

Pierre was not hard, but nonetheless he could feel Scarlett's very hot mouth wrapped around his dick. The feeling was incredible. And the visual even more so. For the life of his, he could not believe this gorgeous girl was actually sucking him in her bed.

And she was doing this after he'd failed her so miserably. Definitely the most embarrassing moment of his life.

Scarlett continued sucking him, her eyes observing his reaction, moving her head up and down rhythmically.

To his absolute surprise, he began to get hard. In a matter of a couple of minutes Scarlett had him totally erect and ready for action.

Pierre was speechless.

Speechless and full of gratitude. Instead of laughing at him she'd given him back his manhood. He loved this woman. He'd die for her.

Scarlett let go of his shaft, getting up on the bed, placing one leg over him, straddling Pierre with great care. She used her hand to guide his cock inside her, looking down at Pierre the entire time with an enigmatic, amused smile.

Pierre felt himself entering Scarlett, as she speared herself on his now incredible erection.

The return of the proud son?

Fucking unbelievable.

She was so well lubricated his entire cock was inside her in an instant. He absolutely adored the feel of her buttocks pressing against his lap, the weight of her body and the touch of her hands on his chest.

She began going up and down slowly, swirling her hips at the same time. She pushed her hips up and back.

"I'm going to fuck your brains off," she stated. "So, enjoy the ride."

That enticing image and her words turned his brains into scrambled eggs. Pierre was unable to say anything. She had him speechless. The way she had come to his rescue filled him with such gratitude. He wanted to take care of her, he wanted to love her and look after her every desire.

Scarlett grabbed his hands. They entwined fingers, clasping hands and continuing like that, with their arms in the air, with her going up and down, until Pierre felt an incredible feeling in his loins spreading everywhere in his body.

"Oh, Scarlett, I just so love being inside you," he susurrated, eyes mere slits in lust. A delicious sensation started to crash into him, starting in his

cock and spreading to his feet, what magic was this? This woman was an incantation.

He became aware Scarlett was making him come.

He howled, raising his pelvis off the bed, with his goddess on top of him. The immense pleasure he felt was not of this world. She had managed to get him hard again and push him into a delicious orgasm in a matter of a couple of minutes.

Pierre was unable to think straight, all he knew was Scarlett was riding out his orgasm with their hands clenched together, his body shaking and jerking.

He pumped up and down lifting his pelvis with frenetic strength, feeling Scarlett sucking him into her.

The mental satisfaction of knowing he was coming inside her was as fulfilling as the physical one. For this one moment in time, she was wholly, utterly, entirely his.

After emptying himself inside Scarlett he began coming down from the incredible high, allowing his body to settle and decelerate. Scarlett stayed right where she was, straddling him and still staring at him, studying his face with a big smile, their hands still gripping each other.

She had survived the rodeo without being launched across the bed.

"You are a muse. I adore you."

She smiled. "You're not bad yourself, Mister."

Pierre attempted to get up. It was her turn to get some pleasure.

"No, don't." She ordered, holding him down. "Just stay put." Scarlett lifted herself off, allowing Pierre's manhood to slide out of her. They were both soaked.

Scarlett carefully stretched herself next to him, pulling the white feather comforter over them. Pierre was on his back so Scarlett laid on his chest, reaching up to softly plant a kiss on his lips. She kept her head on his chest. He understood, she was unofficially calling an end to their lovemaking for the night.

Pierre had wanted to get up and give her some pleasure, but she had nixed it. That was impressive. And not fair to her either. He had stimulated her so much the past hour, and then she hadn't been able to climax. There was no question in his mind Scarlett was adamant about not doing anything else for the moment. Besides, he loved the feel of her body against him, her breasts pressing gently against his chest, the smell of her hair right under his nose. He'd go along with her wishes for now, but later on he would take the initiative and please her as much as he could. He was in awe how she'd handled the most horribly embarrassing moment of his life.

Holding Scarlett against him, Pierre felt an intense surge of affection for her. He recognized the feeling seemed to recur after making love to a beautiful woman. Was he so desperate for a woman to love that he gushed after every one he met?

No, this time it was different. Fact was, he wanted to take Scarlett home. He could feel her heart beating against his chest. He was in trouble, he realized he was already addicted to this girl. But on the other hand, how could that be? They really hadn't had that much time together at all. Was he just fickle? No, that wasn't it. Their spirits, or souls, or whatever it was were in absolutely perfect synch. He could feel it, and he suspected so could she.

What more could anyone ask for?

ONCE AGAIN, PIERRE WOKE up wondering where he was. The room was pitch black and his brain was rebooting. As soon as he fully regained consciousness he remembered Scarlett and their evening together. He was in her bed. Where was she? Reaching in the dark he touched her hip, she was turned away from him, laying on her side, her tranquil respiration confirming she was sleeping serenely.

Pierre didn't have a clue what time it was. The bed felt incredible, deep and soft. It was like resting on top of a giant marshmallow covered by a 600-count Egyptian cotton sheet. The room temperature was pleasant, if a tad chilly perhaps, but not uncomfortably so. His eyes were adjusting to the dark, his night vision returning.

Scarlett's nude body was right there next to him, provocatively available.

Should he let her sleep? He debated just lying there watching her in her slumber, but then decided he was going to wake her in a special way that she was going to love.

He slowly shifted his weight towards the foot of the bed, moving slowly so as not to bounce her. Reaching out for her leg he used the palm of his hand against her thigh, rotating one leg away from the other, the weight of her leg turning Scarlett on her back. Her skin felt cool and dry.

He paused, observing Sleeping Beauty peacefully enjoying being in the arms of Morpheus. Well, he was planning on taking her away from the god of sleep and transferring her into his own arms. One look at Scarlett and he knew that nothing else mattered.

Pierre pulled himself up slowly, inching towards her pubis. Her body was incredible; he was amazed at the beauty of her curves. Her thighs and buttocks meshed together in one perfect symphony of erotic continuity. The best sculptors in the history of mankind could never create something this magnificent. He felt himself getting very hard, delighted to find that whatever had nuked his performance earlier was probably fixed. He had to delete that horrible memory from his mind.

Hovering over her pussy he let one of his hands slip under her thigh, then he softly licked between her lips, one single, long, loving brush stroke. She smelled of sex. He followed through with his tongue, ending the stroke at the fold where her clit was hiding.

Gawd, he loved the way she tasted.

No sign of life yet.

He repeated his action, allowing some saliva to transfer from his tongue to her lips, making his tongue slide faster.

This time she stirred.

Good!

Pierre used his hands keeping Scarlett's legs apart, gently resting them on her upper inner thighs. He licked again.

And again.

Scarlett came alive.

Her clit made an appearance. Pierre switched his focus to her center of pleasure, stroking her gently with his tongue. He was now fully awake and determined to make her knees as weak as he could.

"*Wow,*" she sounded sleepy. "What're you doing?"

"Quiet. Just lay back and relax. I want to make you feel good."

Scarlett found his head with her hands, caressing his hair. "Whew, you are awake, I thought I was dreaming."

Pierre ran his hands from her hips to her knees, providing her with additional stimulation. He then placed his hands below her buttocks, gently applying pressure while licking her clit. He knew the air in the room was a little chilly, so he positioned his mouth covering Scarlett's lips and clit to prevent evaporating saliva from dropping the temperature around her sensitive areas.

Her hips moved up and down, slowly, acknowledging his touch. She may not be fully awake but at least she was conscious enough to feel his touch and react to it.

Pierre was half off the bed, but that was irrelevant. He was going to concentrate all his efforts giving Scarlett all the pleasure she deserved. There was nothing more imperative in his world.

"So, what got you so perky?" She asked.

"Quiet girl! No time for conversation," he managed to say between licks.

Scarlett didn't say anything else.

Pierre stuck his middle finger in his mouth, getting it wet, using it to separate her vagina lips, gently inserting his finger into her channel. She felt hot and smooth inside.

He felt her back trembling from his touch. His tongue was irrationally hungry for her. He increased the pace on her clit, tasting her, moving his finger in and out of her, gently, applying steady pressure on her G-spot. Scarlett was no longer dry, and it wasn't his saliva. She was excited, aroused, melodiously moving in synch with his continuous stimulation of her most deliciously sensitive areas.

She was soaking wet. And very creamy.

Pierre moistened the index finger on his other hand. Gently exploring the area between her buttocks, he found her ass, applying slow continuous pressure he entered her with his finger, feeling Scarlett tightening her belly muscles at the sensation.

Enough licking.

Pierre took her clit between his lips, sucking hard-on it.

He felt her ass reacting immediately, tightening its grip on his finger, then releasing it.

He sucked again.

Her sphincter repeated its erotic dance around his finger.

"*Oooh,*" she approved, breathing faster. Her caresses on his hair were becoming rougher, more passionate.

Pierre continued stimulating her in that way a few more times, then returned to licking instead of sucking.

"I want you so bad, don't stop!" she pleaded. Scarlett kept shifting her hips left and right, desperately seeking release from the continuous stimulation.

Pierre wanted to keep her aroused during a prolonged period, so when she came it would be completely satisfying. Scarlett, however, was giving signs of imminent climax. Sexual fluids gushed between her legs, her respiration now openly loud. Her adrenaline was rabidly at work, pushing her towards a world of pleasure on top of the giant marshmallow bed topped with the cotton sheet.

"I'm cuming." Scarlett suddenly muttered, as she tumbled over the edge of happiness, her body stiffening and shaking, trembling and spasming, she couldn't stop it.

Pierre felt her strong legs clasping on his shoulders, while inserting his fingers in and out of her in a steady rhythm, careful not to scratch her with his fingernails because of her violent shifting and shaking. Her sphincter and vagina trembling around his fingers confirmed she had been launched into an abyss of pleasure. His tongue remained on her clit, licking Scarlett in order to prolong a much-deserved orgasm.

Scarlett breathed rapidly, her body rigid, her toes curling under the furious attack on her senses.

"Ohmyheavens!" She half-whispered, her entire body wet from sexual desire and perspiration.

Pierre kept his face against her totally soaked lips, hugging her hips with his arms. He loved feeling her shaking and squirming against him, delighted to have finally brought her some pleasure.

A couple of minutes later—surprisingly—Scarlett appeared to be out cold. He had knocked her out, no question about it. He listened carefully. Her respiration seemed to have normalized. He considered waking her up and gifting her with another orgasm, but given how quickly she'd passed out, he decided to just call it a night. In fact, he wouldn't even move from his present position. He'd just go to sleep with his head between her legs. Terribly sexy. What more could he ask for? It was incredible, laying there in the dark with his cheek against her delicious lips. This was the adorable girl he met at the bar in Philly? He just couldn't believe how friggin lucky he was.

Once again, he felt an intensely overwhelming feeling of love for Scarlett. Was it love? Who knew. It was a feeling of thankfulness and protectiveness and affection that made him eternally indebted to her. She liked him, and she gave herself to him. He *owed* her. With that thought, he faded off.

Sometime during the night Scarlett shifted, waking him up. Pierre moved off, allowing her to roll on her tummy. She hugged one of the down pillows, drifting off to sleep again. He pulled himself up alongside her, pulling the comforter over both of them. The last conscious thought he had before passing out again was resting his hand on one or her sexy buttocks.

"GOOD MORNING GALLANT AVIATOR," Scarlett murmured close to his face.

Pierre came out of a profound sleep, taking a deep, satisfied breath. His brain restarted in an instant, he was in bed with Scarlett. Life was good. No, it was more than good. It was fucking spectacular.

"Good morning, beautiful."

"I was watching you sleep. You were smiling."

"Really?"

"Yes, I loved that. Wonder what you were dreaming," she added.

"I was reviewing our incredibly sexy night."

"And that made you smile, eh?"

"Yes, I was actually reviewing every minute in my mind, at half speed."

Pierre inched closer to Scarlett, gently placing his hand on her naked waist. She felt cold and silky.

"And did that make for a good movie?" Scarlett smiled.

"Excellent, actually. A real love story. In High Definition."

"I would've thought it more of a sexy story myself."

"That too." Pierre felt himself getting hard. Good grief! The Pierre morning 'curse' was at work again. Was he ever gonna be satisfied? Then he remembered the disaster of the previous night. And the way Scarlett had helped him recover.

He was starting to love this woman with a passion.

He fixed his brown eyes on Scarlett's. Then he reached for her hand, directing it to his rock-solid hard on.

"Whew, you sure recover fast."

Scarlett kept her hold on his erection, rolling over on her side, backing into Pierre. Spooning was the perfect position for morning sex.

Pierre felt Scarlett backing into him, her cool back pressing against his chest, her sensuous ass cuddling against his groin. She reached back between her legs, searching for his shaft, directing it to her silken labia. He willfully shoved his hips forward, feeling the tip of his cock entering her, immersing himself in the hot paradise between her legs. Pierre stuffed his big, erect cock into her willing pussy.

Just like that, he was back inside Scarlett, making love to her again, feeling her deliciously shaped buttocks dampening his thrusts. It was mind-boggling, nearly a religious experience. She moved her hips with him, silently giving him what he wanted.

Pierre was thrilled beyond words. He delighted himself with the feel of his throbbing hard-on separating her steaming hot inner walls. This was a gift from the gods.

He was in ecstasy with all the pleasure this woman was giving him. What more could he want?

Then it came to him. He was being a selfish shit. He wasn't gonna make her come like this! Yes, he was acting selfishly. He immediately stopped, withdrawing back away from her, pulling her over so she could lay on her back next to him.

Scarlett didn't say anything, her emerald green eyes staring at him, curiously.

"How about I treat you to the most delicious breakfast of your life?"

Scarlett appeared puzzled, her eyes widening. "Oh? What happened to all the passion?"

"It's still here, but I need to look after you before I take care of me."

She appeared to think about that. "I'm fine. Still a little sore from last night, but we can take care of you."

Pierre smiled. Aha! She was sore? He'd done the right thing. "You are an angel, Scarlett, a real darling, but we don't have to focus on me. You come first. I hate leaving this snug bed, but there are other things in life besides sex, and feeding you properly is one of them."

Scarlett gifted him with a bright smile and a burst of laughter. "Okay, I'll buy that, since I gotta pee." She jumped out of bed with youthful agility, prancing for the bathroom.

Pierre sat up on the bed, resisting the urge to laugh. She had to use the bathroom yet she'd welcomed his advances and had been willing to stay in the game until he satisfied himself. That was consideration beyond the call of duty. He gave himself an 'attaboy.' A full bladder was not conductive to passionate sex. Yet she'd been willing to resist until he was pleased. What an absolute unselfish doll! In the future, he had to be more mindful of her needs.

He got up, catching a glimpse of himself nude in her full-length mirror by the dresser. He was in great shape, his hours of working out evident in his six-pack and his powerful shoulders. He'd always been of the opinion that if he wanted to be involved with beautiful women, he should bring something to the table as far as physical fitness was concerned. He should be able to offer good looks if he demanded them.

Just like with race cars, looks always seemed to go with performance. He'd found that to be true with men and women as well.

Looking around in admiration at the obviously girly bedroom Pierre was inundated with a feeling of happiness. He'd been right when he met Scarlett at the bar in Philly, they had been attracted to each other from the first instant. This incredible night had confirmed it.

Now what? He loved being with this woman. He was already rapidly dreaming up plans for their future. She was not employed, which was perfect. He could invite her to travel with him. Cancun would be a fantastic first stop. As long as she didn't get a job they would have flexibility to travel. He had three weeks of vacation he could request. He'd combine those with days off between flights and open up enough time so he could get to know her intimately.

He smiled. That was stupid. He *already* knew her *intimately*, far as that was concerned. What he meant was, they should spend as much time together as possible so he could get to know her and spoil her and pamper her and treat her like a medieval princess. He'd bring it up to her over breakfast.

COTTON CANDY AND TANGERINES   MR Chevalier

SCARLETT PARKED IN FRONT of a small breakfast place named "The Encounter," the sort of quaint hideaway with a personality, a place only the locals frequented, simple, clean and not too crowded.

Pierre had changed into cream Dockers, a black T-shirt and white Adidas. He was terribly comfortable. He followed Scarlett entering the very cozy restaurant by the side of a hill. The place was adorable, wood and glass construction, typical Seattle. She had donned blue jeans and a yellow sweat shirt. She also wore white running shoes. Pierre was very impressed with her looks. She was built to perfection. Built for performance, really. Or like the old priest at his school used to say, built for sin, really. Amazingly enough, now that she was there with him fully dressed, he was painfully desiring to have her in bed again, nude, passionately receiving him inside her. He did have demanding sexual instincts beyond those of any normal man.

Scarlett selected a small table by an enormous glass window overlooking a green forest under an overcast sky. "How about here?"

Pierre pulled out her chair.

"Hmm, you do have manners."

He just smiled at her, not sure whether that was a compliment or a critique.

A young waitress brought them menus.

"What sounds good?"

"I'm ravenously hungry." Scarlett opened her menu, looking at the images with wide eyes.

"Geepers," Pierre pointed out, "Everything looks delicious."

He peeked at Scarlett over his menu. She was a stunning young woman, her ruffled buttermilk blond hair swayed in front of her face as she studied her menu. She chose not to wash her hair because blow-drying it would take too long and she was famished, so from the looks of it, her hair still carried in it the scent of their night of passion. Her hair had caressed his balls when Scarlett had sucked him back to life. That in itself was obscenely erotic. Particularly when thinking about it in a public place smack in the middle of ordering breakfast.

Argh, he had to get his mind out of the septic tank. Was everything in life just sex?

Bet your ass.

Undoubtedly, there were other wonderful aspects to life, but sex was so important. At least for him.

"What're you having?" Scarlett blurted.

"I'd like to have you for breakfast, sweetie."

She flashed him a smile. "You are bad—and besides, you already did."

Having Scarlett acknowledging he'd already gone down on her this morning made him crazy with desire.

"I'm having an omelet. Bacon and tomato. You?"

"Chicken fried steak. Biscuits and gravy. And a cream soda. Today is *National Carb Orgy Day.*"

Pierre put on a look of intense concentration. "You're gonna have to work your butt off to burn all those carbs."

"I intend to do precisely as much. That's why you're here."

He quickly processed the sexual innuendo. "I have no idea what you're talking about."

"Yeah, you do."

Pierre smiled. "That being the case, Scarlett, you better order a banana split as well. You're gonna need it."

"Is that a threat of things to come?"

"No. More like a promise."

"That's exciting and I can't wait to take you up on it. But I don't wanna spend the entire day in bed. I want to show you Seattle."

"We don't have to spend the entire day in bed. Your mom's car has a wide back seat, no?"

"You're naughty."

"No, just normal attraction for a goddess."

Scarlett's eyes sparkled. "You're too much."

"I can't seem to get enough of you."

The waitress materialized by their table. "Did you get a chance to decide?"

Pierre allowed Scarlett the chance to order first, then he put in his request for the omelet. He also asked the waitress to bring them some black coffee and water for Scarlett.

"I'm very happy I'm here with you," he stated, his eyes fixed on hers.

Scarlett reached across the small table, placing her hand on his. "So am I."

Her attractive green eyes spoke volumes.

"I was smitten by you the moment I saw you." Pierre knew honesty sometimes had a way of fucking things up, but he felt a strong bond with this incredible woman, and wanted to be crystal-transparent with her.

"I don't know what happened," she admitted. "I was surely not looking for it. Meeting you in Philadelphia was the last thing I ever expected. I left Spain to get away from a relationship."

"It was destiny. You and I were meant to cross paths."

"As in 'everything is predestined?'"

"Yeah, kinda."

"You believe in that?"

"In a way, yes. In other words, is everything that's going to happen in the future already been written?"

"What do you think?" She examined his face, searching for clues.

"I think it's an interesting concept, but many people are really bothered by it."

"I'm not. I'm willing to listen to any sensible theory."

"Not to change the topic, but do you have any commitments with job interviews or relatives these next few days?"

"Hmm, no. Why?" Scarlett raised her eyebrows.

"I know you just got back from Spain, and probably want to spend more time with your family, but I was thinking, could I interest you in going to the Mexican Caribbean with me?"

Scarlett rested her elbows on the table, cradling her chin in the palms of her hands. "You serious?"

"Dead serious. We could leave in two or three days. I have some vacation I could use. I can trade out of my next trip and we could fly down to Cancun. Imagine going to a magical island where you can swim with dolphins, lay on white sandy beaches and eat fried fish while drinking tropical juices laced with rum or gin during the day. At night, we could go dancing."

"What else could we do at night?" She had that playful look in her eyes.

"Whatever your heart desires."

"My heart is capable of desiring lots of things."

"Okay, I'll bite. At night we can make wild, passionate love on the beach under a billion stars, and you can learn what it means to be loved in the warm sea breeze of a tropical paradise while I make your knees weak."

"Whew. That sounds quite romantic and very interesting, although the beach part could be messy. Sand can be sneaky." She was still resting her chin on her hands.

The waitress reappeared with their plates. The colorful, delicious-smelling food interrupted the mood. They were both drooling inside their mouths from the incredible aromas.

"And here's your drinks," the woman placed water and coffee in front of them.

Pierre thanked her, a little bit disappointed about the interruption right when he was trying to get an answer out of Scarlett.

"*Bon appetit!*"

They dug into their food, concentrating on the flavors.

"I could take you to see the Mayan ruins in a place called Tulum," he continued, between mouthfuls.

He instantly wondered if telling her that was a good idea. She might not be interested in visiting some old ruins. In fact, that was surely a fuckup. What the devil did she care about some goddamned ruins?

"I've been the center of attention for my family since I got back from Spain," she related, after she was done chewing. "Every relative I have has visited me at least twice and I've had to repeat the same story over thirty times. The Inquisition is getting old. And everyone wants to know what my plans are for the future. It's getting annoying. I could use some time away. I do have some money stashed away in my savings account so I could pay for my part."

Pierre's heart soared. He felt the old familiar butterflies in his crotch. "I think we could probably go tomorrow, if you want."

"Easy, there, cowboy. I haven't agreed to anything; we're just talking about it."

"Let me check," he said, reaching for his smartphone.

Scarlett bit into the gravy muffins, observing the aviator with amused eyes.

"There's a flight tomorrow morning at eight, connecting through Phoenix. Gets us to Cancun at seven-thirty in the evening." He looked up at her, expectantly.

"Spur of the moment like this, it's gonna cost us a fortune."

"No, it's not too bad," he lied, staring at the $1,100 price tag per round-trip ticket in Business Class. A little white lie never hurt nobody. He'd be glad to pay that and more for the privilege of taking Scarlett on a fabulous retreat.

"I thought you could fly free," she asked.

"Yes, I can, but that's stand-by only, and for something like this we want to make sure we get on the flight."

"Something like what?"

"Short time window. We wouldn't want to waste time trying to get on a flight. When we arrive in Cancun we can stay at the Hilton. I've stayed there before; it'll knock your socks off. Then we can go to Isla Mujeres by boat and spend a few days there."

"You've stayed at the Hilton before? With who?"

Pierre smiled. A hint of jealousy? That was good, it meant she liked him. "Different girlfriends."

The look on Scarlett's face made him regret his comment. "Just kidding! I've stayed there before during overnights with the airline when I had to fly there."

"Real funny."

"Never been there with a girlfriend, if that's what you're asking." He hoped his little attempt at humor hadn't backfired. He still didn't know Scarlett very well. He better thread lightly.

"No, that's not what I'm asking. Curiosity, that's all. And in answer to your original question, yes, I'm game. How many days do you want to go?"

She wanted to go!

Pierre took a real deep breath. He felt adrenaline shooting through his body. Images of Scarlett and him in Cancun flashed across his mind like a slide presentation, each more beautiful than the previous, each more erotic.

He had awakened in paradise, and now the day had become even better, if that was at all possible.

"How bout we stay there two weeks?"

She laughed. "You're crazy! How can you get two weeks off? And besides, I don't have money for a two-week vacation."

"How about five days there then? And by the way, your money is no good. I'm inviting."

"No, you're not. I have my own money. And five days sounds terrific."

He wondered just how stubborn she was going to be about the financial aspect of the trip. There was no way he was gonna let her pay for anything. But, she could be insulted and refuse to go if he pushed her. Better play it safe.

"How about I pay for everything and then we just figure out how much it was and you give me half at the end?"

Scarlett studied him, her eyes regarding him suspiciously. "I can do that, I guess."

Halleluiah!

He'd just have to deal with the fight later, when he refused to accept any money from her. "Tomorrow sound good?"

She smiled seductively. "You are serious about this, aren't you? We're crazy! Why not?"

"Gimme me one second. I'll book the flights." Scarlett sipped her water, her sexy green eyes fixed on him over the glass.

Pierre booked two seats in Business Class on the morning flight with an airplane change in Phoenix. Scarlett deserved to be treated like a princess. A tad over two-thousand three hundred dollars' total. She was going to like this. He typed furiously, one-fingered.

Next he switched to the Hilton hotels website, booking a room for them for one night—their arrival night—at the luxurious hotel. He was able to obtain a fifty-percent discount with his airline employee number. They would wait until their arrival to Isla Mujeres to find a place there. This time of year, that wouldn't be too difficult.

Hot dog!

His credit card number was stored in his smartphone, so he paid for everything on the spot. His phone chimed, notifying him of the arrival of a text message from his bank. The text message warned him that charges had been made to his account.

Ah, but he so loved modern technology.

"We're all set, Scarlett! We are now booked on the morning flight to Cancun, via Phoenix, and I got us a reservation at the Hilton for the night." He decided to keep the Business Class a surprise.

"That was fast," she complimented. "Are we really doing this?"

"We sure are." He broke into a big smile. "Now we have to do some shopping."

"We do? For what?"

"Well, we're going to a tropical paradise, and I don't think either one of us owns any clothing adequate for the occasion. What do you say we get crazy and buy some clothes we can use on our trip?

And by the way, this was my idea, so I'm paying for the clothes, and the shoes, and the jewelry, and the hats, and the suntan lotion.

She locked eyes with Pierre. "I don't know what to say. My mother warned me never to accept any gifts from men."

"Even those you know intimately?"

"Do I know you intimately?"

"I don't know. What would you say?"

Scarlett smiled. "Maybe."

"I'll take that as a 'yes.' Allow me to spoil you then."

COTTON CANDY AND TANGERINES   MR Chevalier

Tiffany

Twelve months later Pierre was jubilant!

His bid to transfer to the bigger Airbus, the A350, was awarded to him for his December schedule, which was the following month.

But for now, he was in the Crew Lounge in Phoenix, enjoying a one-hour 'Practice Layover.' He'd brought in the flight from St. Louis and in thirty more minutes he'd be flying his gallant steed, his 'little' Airbus A321 down to Tucson for the night.

He was actually beyond jubilant. Looking at the computer screen again to ascertain he was not imagining things, it was right there in front of his eyes:

Crewmember name: *Pierre White, First Officer*
Scheduled Training: *A350 First Officer Transition*

The opportunity to fly much bigger airplanes represented great things to come. Very positive changes to his life. He'd been eagerly hoping his transfer to the big bus would come soon. The new enormous airplane he was going to eventually be flying meant he'd be going over the Atlantic to many exciting European cities, and also down to South America if he wanted. South America! And definitely, the pleasure of flying a big airplane was nearly sexual. Most pilots craved flying the biggest airplanes because of the technical challenge involved in operating such magnificent machines.

Contrary to popular opinion, bigger *was* better.

Also, Pierre was going to be getting a thirty percent pay increase—at least thirty percent. He'd have to go look that up in his union contract. That was frosting on the cake for Pierre. That salary increase was going to represent roughly five thousand dollars a month extra before taxes. Excellent! It occurred to him he'd be able to afford buying himself that classic Jaguar sports car he'd been desiring for so long. *And* pay for the maintenance on the damned thing!

Gemini! Life was good!

If only he had a steady girl, then things would really be sweet. After the disappointment with Kirsten he was having a difficult time trusting anybody. She'd left over a dozen Hallmark cards in his mailbox in Operations, apologizing and trying to repair the heartbreak she caused but Pierre was having a hard time going in that direction. He liked to think relationships were always at their best in the beginning, and if the best Kirsten had to give him in the beginning was having sex with her ex, then she was not for him. Too bad, he'd really liked her. No, he hadn't just liked her, he'd adored her. That's how he was, able to fall in love at first sight. And why not?

He'd become infatuated with her at lightning speed, so maybe he should've been a little less enthusiastic until he got to know her better. Often in the middle of the night in some layover hotel he'd consider giving their relationship another chance, reaching for his smartphone to text her, but deciding against it realizing his sexual urge was most likely driving his thinking. Thus far, he had resisted contacting her.

Thinking of her in the middle of the night in some unfamiliar city was sheer torture. The memories and images of their times together were hard to dismiss when he found himself alone in bed in the dark. It was amazing how he'd developed feelings for her in such an unbelievable short period of time. But that was the kind of girl she was, to know her was to love her. The sound of her laughter haunted him many a night.

PIERRE LOVED PHOENIX, AND his plans to purchase a home there were solidifying rapidly. He'd found a fantastic four-bedroom home in the exclusive neighborhood of Ahwatukee, south of the city. He'd already qualified for the loan with Chase, and was getting ready to make an offer on the property the next time he had a block of days off. His realtor was screaming at him to place the offer on the house now, or else he'd lose it, but he was in no hurry. If that particular house sold, there were many others on the market that would do just as well. The realtor was just in a hurry to land her commission.

It eventually occurred to him that the pay increase on the horizon could also allow him to buy a bigger home, but just as quickly dismissed the thought. A two-thousand-square-foot home with tile roof and an inviting swimming pool was plenty house for a single guy. That was all he really needed. Better he finds other uses for his money. Some sort of side business perhaps. He was not going to buy a 'monument to aviation,' like so many pilots before him had done. Traditionally in the airlines when First Officers—or copilots—first upgraded to captain, their pay ballooned, and the very first thing they did was either build or buy an enormously expensive home.

"How's the weather down there?" Dean Bular asked. Dean was his captain for the three-day trip they were on. The man was in his mid-fifties and reasonably pleasant.

"Weather in Tucson's good, same as here."

"I got the paperwork. Nothing to write home to mamma about. I'm gonna get me a hard copy of the release."

Captain Dean Bular, like the rest of the aviators in the employ of Worldwide Airlines, received his paperwork for each flight through an email message sent to his company email address directly from dispatch. The paperwork was extensive, consisting of all the flight planning information needed, winds aloft, fuel consumption, notices to airmen, and weather reports. He was able to retrieve the email and look at the documents on his company-issued iPad.

Until the advent of the 'electronic flight bag,' as the iPad was known among fliers, pilots received all their documentation in paper form. Once the iPad became the primary information device, then the dozens of pages of information were no longer printed.

Pierre loved thinking of all the rain forests they were saving, since his airline had over six thousand flights a day, and each flight required nearly fifty pages of paperwork. That much paper was the equivalent of a small forest destroyed every twelve months.

However, older airline pilots—the senior dogs— still preferred having something on paper, so the company provided printers all over the place for this purpose. Pilots could simply use Bluetooth to connect their iPads to the printers, which could provide them with a hardcopy of the documentation, if they were so inclined.

The younger pilots had been raised with all sorts of screens in their lives, computers, cell phones, iPads, etc., so most didn't feel the need to print anything.

Pierre was of this new generation of airline pilots, but he'd learned from some of the old flyers that computers *could* fail, and if everything went to hell in a hand basket, having a hard copy of the flight plan was always highly desirable. Pierre felt the old-timers were not raised with computers, but they sure as pie had an oversupply of common sense.

The young pilot marched out to the Airbus 321 parked at the gate. He'd probably be in training over Christmas and New Years for the new airplane, but that prospect didn't faze him one bit. Pierre suspected going to school around Christmas was probably one of the reasons he was able to get that bid to the big Bus in the first place. Most pilots didn't like attending training over the holidays, but since he had no wife or kids, it didn't bother him one bit.

He walked into the flight deck of the modern airliner with a grin on his face. He was going to be flying wide body jets based out of Los Angeles in the very near future!

What more could he ask of life?

Pierre thought of Scarlett again, missing her, wishing she were still with him. Sadly, that was all wishful thinking. She was now married and with a little girl, and he'd probably never have her again as a friend or lover. A very sad thought. Their trip to Cancun had been pure magic. Magic and fun. And incredible sex.

He'd really thought she would be his partner for life, but things had slowly fallen apart. Scarlett, as it turned out, didn't like motorcycles, or sailing, or scuba diving or many other activities dear to his heart, all of which he could live without, but she particularly disliked guns, and that was a serious problem.

Pierre owned a couple of guns and he visited a local range a few times a month to stay sharp because he was allowed by the US government to carry a firearm in the flight deck.

Pierre belonged to the FFDO program, the Federal Flight Deck Officer program created after the attack against New York.

The purpose of the program was to deputize airline pilots as federal agents, allowing them to carry guns in the airplane when they flew. This was intended to be the last line of defense against any person attempting to hurt the pilots of an airliner, so they could defend themselves against acts of criminal violence or air piracy.

Participation in the program was voluntary, and Pierre felt he had an obligation towards his passengers to protect the flight deck against attempted breach.

Scarlet had adamantly objected to his ownership of firearms as well as his participation in the program. She had demanded he drop out of the program and get rid of his firearms.

At first Pierre thought she was joking, but when he realized she was dead serious, he found himself at a crossroads, forced to make a painful choice. Scarlett or his ability to protect himself and his passengers? That was a hard one. He really cared for her, and wanted her in his life, but there was no way under God's earth he was going to give up his responsibility towards the people who trusted him with their lives every time he flew.

If some crazy nut ultimately gained access to his flight deck at some point in his career as an airline pilot, the last line of defense available to him would be his FFDO pistol. That weapon could very well mean the difference between life and death for him and his passengers.

Add to that Scarlett's dislike of most of his favorite activities, and things began to fall apart like a cookie in a glass of milk. She had her own likes, most of which he found agreeable and enjoyed doing with her, but she was not going to back off about the FFDO program. Staying together under those circumstances was a recipe for disaster. Consequently, one rainy evening they had a sad, tearful conversation in a restaurant by the Sound in Seattle and called it quits. They were both realistic enough to see how neither one of them was going to yield to the other.

SEVENTY MINUTES LATER CAPTAIN Dean Bular parked the brakes at the gate in Tucson.

"I guess we're done for the day," he said, reaching for the checklist.

"Yeah, it's been a long one, Boss." Pierre felt tired and hungry. He tried to recall if there were any fast food restaurants near their layover hotel. Man, in all honesty, he couldn't even recall which hotel they were going to use. It'd been a long time since he'd flown into Tucson.

"Where are we staying here?"

The Skipper looked at him. "The Ramada Inn, isn't it?"

"Don't know. Haven't been here in ages."

"Yeah, it's the Ramada. Good hotel."

Pierre collected his headset and iPad, storing them inside a leather messenger bag he carried with him.

The captain silently read the "Secure" checklist, basically shutting down the airplane for the night. "Don't remember any place to eat nearby," the old timer pointed out.

"I was wondering about that," Pierre replied. Great, eleven o'clock at night in Tucson, and he'd have to order an overpriced burger from room service. *If* they had room service at such late hour, that was. Boy, he couldn't even remember if Ramada Inns had restaurants? Most hotels had candy and soda machines for the worst-case scenario, but Pierre was in no mood to visit those 'food simulators.'

The two pilots exited the flight deck, pulling their overnight bags. Pierre wore his hat. Although the airline no longer made use of the hat mandatory for the pilots, Pierre felt it was part of the image. Really, some of his peers walked down the concourse without a jacket and no hat. How could they expect to be taken seriously by anyone? It had taken one hundred years of commercial aviation to gain respect, and some of these bozos were destroying the image of the airline pilot with one single stroll through the terminal looking like a taxi driver from Brooklyn.

Would a motorist give a cop respect if the motorcycle highway patrolman walked up to the window wearing a Hawaiian shirt and flip flops?

Their four flight attendants had exited the airplane a few minutes ahead of them and were sitting in the gate area waiting. That pleased Pierre. Sticking together as a crew was good. The entire airport appeared deserted. Not another soul in sight. The annoying racket of an industrial-strength vacuum cleaner was the only sound disturbing the silence.

Pierre was grateful the gals had waited for them. Too often nowadays flight attendants didn't wait for their pilots at the end of a long day. Lately, the flight attendants exited the airplane, leaving nothing but dust behind them, in their desperate need to go sit down in the hotel van. He didn't blame them, but it was not real courteous. Pierre liked to think of the crew as a team, although in real life that was not the case much anymore.

Crew schedulers had to deal with incredibly complicated algorithms when they built the flight schedules for the crews. He and the Skipper changed flight attendants several times in one day, so they never knew how long they had together. The pilots could start the day with a crew of women and finish the day with an entirely different crew, one which could consist mainly of male flight attendants. Pierre didn't have anything against male flight attendants, matter of fact, he respected them greatly for the jobs they did. Not easy dealing with people all day long. But he still preferred the company of women, and that would never change.

PIERRE TOOK ONE LONG look at his flight attendants, something he always did automatically whenever good-looking women were in sight. Four of them, all looking tired. Yep, dealing with humanity did that to you. Pierre observed each woman individually. The first two were 'peaches.' No interest there. His own personal guidelines preferred women to be an 'orchid' or a 'dream' to hold his attention.

The third one scored nearly a perfect 'dream.'

A perfect dream?

How could that be? He studied her more carefully. Yep, she was a 'dream', no doubt about it.

Lessee, pretty face, attractive brunette, nicely proportioned body—as much as he could judge with her in uniform—a little over five-foot-tall, proportions definitely within reasonable parameters. Overall, a very attractive lady there.

Yeah, he reaffirmed his first impression of the lovely female.

How had he missed her? She'd obviously been with them all the way from St. Louis. Dang! He'd had no idea she was even onboard. The answer of course was simple—she must've been working the coach section in the back of the cabin. The three flight attendants working the coach section never stepped forward of the First Class curtain. Much less enter the flight deck.

The young woman lifted her eyes, looking straight at Pierre.

She had clear eyes, probably blue. He was a little startled by her direct stare. He wasn't expecting it.

He decided giving her the 'Tom Cruise' smile would be too much at this time of night. Instead he smiled at her without flashing his teeth.

She smiled back in kind. No big bang smile from her either.

Hot dog, it worked!

That was good.

Initial contact successful!

The crew began to move.

Pierre timed his walking speed to end up alongside the attractive brunette.

All seven crewmembers proceeded down the concourse. A couple of Hispanic men were operating vacuum cleaners on the carpets near some of the gates.

The terminal was indeed void of other people. Certainly, no passengers in view anywhere at that time of night.

Pierre took in the view outside the huge terminal windows, dozens of airplanes from many of the colorful airlines operating in America already parked at their gates, their crews long gone, most likely already asleep in their hotels. He wouldn't be surprised if they were the last crew to bring in a flight tonight.

"Tired?" he addressed the brunette walking alongside him. He noticed her profile was definitely a knockout. Incredible profile when viewed up close like this. She reminded him of some famous actress or model, but he was too tired to think about it.

"Not too bad," she responded.

This time she gave him her full smile. Her voice was young and musical.

"Were you with us all the way from St. Louis?" he had to ask.

"Yes." She appeared a little surprised.

"I'm Pierre," he gave her his warmest smile. Shaking hands was not real practical right at that very moment since they were both pulling wheelies. If he tried to shake her hand he'd have to stop, which would force her to come to a screeching halt as well. That would attract the attention of the other five crewmembers, pretty much announcing to the entire crew that Pierre was making a move on one of them.

That late at night, the other crew members had absolutely no patience whatsoever for anyone's romantic interests, they were so exhausted they were likely to bite Pierre in the jugular if he made them stop.

Consequently, there would be no hand shaking.

"I'm Tiffany," she smiled again, looking in his eyes just a little bit longer this time.

Wow, he liked her voice. "So did you start in St. Louis?"

"No, we started in Atlanta this morning."

"Were you working coach?"

"Yep, all three legs."

"I didn't see you in Phoenix."

"I stayed on the airplane. Took a short nap."

Well, that explained why he hadn't seen her. "You been here before?"

She nodded. "A couple of times."

"We staying at the Ramada?"

"Yes."

That was the extent of their conversation until they reached the van.

Bags were handed to the van driver, disappearing from view into the back of the vehicle. Pierre followed everyone else entering the van. He tried being courteous letting everyone else climb aboard ahead of him. By the time he got to the door he wasn't able to sit near Tiffany. He was still wondering how he could have missed such an attractive woman. He'd have to make it a point going back in coach to meet all the attendants on every flight.

He really wasn't in the mood to pick up anybody, but Tiffany had that 'certain something' which caught his attention. Call it sensuality, call it femininity. It didn't matter. She was very attractive, no doubt. Attractive enough—in fact—to make his fatigue rapidly disappear.

The ride to the hotel was fast through mostly empty streets. Once there, the crew congregated at the back of the van, claiming their bags and giving the driver the usual two-buck tip.

The tired crew entered the lobby, approaching the front desk.

Tiffany, the 'dream' brunette walking alongside Pierre spoke to him in a subdued voice, trying to keep the conversation private.

"Want to go swimming?"

Pierre wasn't sure he heard right. What? Swimming? The air was darned cold to go swimming! This amazing woman was asking him if he'd like to go swimming? That was totally out of left field.

His fatigue evaporated.

"*Sure!* What'd you have in mind?" No one was ever going to hold him accountable for passing up a good thing.

"They've a hot tub here. It's really nice, out in back by the pool."

A hot tub? Ah, that explained it. He'd been erroneously thinking swimming pool.

That truly sounded inviting. Pierre was dumbfounded at the situation. Tiffany radiated sensuality and excitement. And she sure didn't have any problem being direct! And she obviously found him attractive, or she would not have asked. Images began forming in his mind of the many pleasurable possibilities opening up for him tonight, totally out of the blue.

Food? Who cared about food?

"That sounds great. How long do you need?"

"Five minutes?"

The crew checked in at the front desk, obtaining their room assignments.

"What room you in?" Tiffany asked. She and Pierre had been the last two to get rooms, doing everything deliberately slow, allowing the rest of the crew time to get lost.

"I'm in 1301."

"I'll meet in your room in five," Tiffany confirmed, smiling provocatively.

Holy smokes! The gods must be smiling upon him tonight, first he finds out about moving up to the big Bus, and now this!

Something suddenly occurred to Pierre.

"Wait! I don't have a bathing suit!" He'd just remembered he hadn't packed one. He felt like an idiot. An opportunity like this and he didn't have a suit. What the hell was he thinking? The hotel store—if there even was one—was surely closed for the night, so he wouldn't be able to buy a suit.

Would asking her if she was interested in skinny dipping be interpreted as being a little too forward?

Yeah, right.

Tiffany stared at him silently for a moment. "Don't worry, I've got one you can wear."

What? "What do you mean, you got one?"

"I have a pair of waterproof shorts that are huge on me. They should fit you all right. I'll bring 'em."

Waterproof shorts? Her shorts? He sighed. Might as well give it a try. "Fantastic. See you in five."

Pierre entered his room in the dark. Turning on the bathroom light he went straight to relieve himself, then removed his jacket and hat. His tie and shirt following on the bed. Shoes and T-shirt next.

He was euphoric. Tiffany was so attractive and he was actually going to enjoy the hot tub with her. What an incredible way to end the evening. Hopefully, the rest of the crew would simply go to sleep, without visiting the pool area at all. He wondered what the chances were they would end up together for the night? Better not go there. If it didn't happen, he'd be disappointed. Although if it did happen, it would be heaven on earth. He hadn't been with a woman for too long, and he most decidedly needed the touch of a sexy female and the opportunity to get to know one.

A knock on the door snapped him out of his contemplation.

"Hello?" He opened the door.

Tiffany stood there with a white hotel towel wrapped around her body.

Pierre felt it was safe to assume she wore her bathing suit under the towel.

"Here you go," she handed him some garment.

"Come in," he held the door for her, admiring her naked shoulders and her lovely legs. A very pretty lady, he mused. No, not just pretty—so beautiful. Her dark brown hair tumbled loose on her shoulders.

Tiffany walked in, sitting on one of the beds, checking him out without saying another word.

Pierre rapidly considered what his next move should be. Remove his pants and put on the suit right there in front of Tiffany? Naw, a little too bold. He could go in the bathroom and shut the door and change in there. Or he could leave the door open. He opted for the last choice.

"Back in one second." He went in the bathroom, removing his pants and boxer shorts in one quick movement. He could sense Tiffany's presence not five feet away. That was exciting, standing there in his birthday suit with a pretty woman sitting on his bed. He felt himself getting hard. Oh, crud. That was going to be awkward if she noticed. Too early in the game.

He stepped into the shorts. They were big on him. How could Tiffany wear them? His erection had bloomed.

She was sitting in the same place when he stepped out of the bathroom. His erection was in full force, but he tried to camouflage it pulling it straight up and also counting on the dark color of the shorts hiding any details. Christ, just like a fucking kid. For an adult man, he sure had a lot of hang-ups.

"It works!" Tiffany exclaimed, standing up from the bed. For a moment Pierre thought she was referring to his hard-on.

"It sure does. Thanks!"

"Let's go!"

PIERRE FOLLOWED TIFFANY OUT of his room, walking alongside her down the corridor. She said she'd stayed in that hotel before so he might as well let her lead the way. He felt a little stupid walking down the halls wearing only an oversized bathing suit, barefoot and without a shirt. No way this suit belonged to Tiffany. It was huge on him. Maybe it was her boyfriend's? He did check her ring finger. Nothing there, so that was good. No fiancé and no husband, from the looks of it.

He was delighted and excited being there with her. She was very pleasing to the eye and apparently attracted to him. Her coming up with the bathing suit suggestion was unquestionable evidence she really wanted to spend time together. When he informed her he didn't have a suit, she hadn't taken 'no' for an answer.

He couldn't really look at her in detail while walking side by side, although he was eager to enjoy looking at her gorgeous face again. The hallways were deserted. Most hotel guests were already in bed at that hour.

The couple finally reached an outside door, walking out onto a huge pool area. Pierre surveyed the setting. Not too much vegetation, typical of these hotels in the desert. There was a large palapa structure at one end, housing what looked like an in-ground Jacuzzi, surrounded by several queen palms and seemingly acres of cool decking.

Tiffany walked straight there.

Yep, that was the famous hot tub.

There was some dim lighting in the area, but overall it was pretty dark and cozy.

And totally solitary.

Tiffany had her back to him. She dropped her towel, revealing a sexy glittering silver one-piece bathing suit. Revealing also how the bottom of her suit had climbed between her cheeks, allowing Pierre a momentary view of her perfectly shaped nude buttocks.

He inhaled deeply, breathless at the sight of her alluring rear end, conscious of his unbelievable hard-on. What an incredible body!

He resisted the painfully strong urge to reach out and squeeze ... or spank ... or caress her.

Tiffany stepped down into the tub, taking a long pause at each step, slowly getting adjusted to the water temperature. She finally submerged her entire body, turning to look at Pierre.

"You coming?"

He'd just put one foot down on the first step. Damned thing was friggin' hot!

"On my way."

Her sensual smile was unbelievable. His hyperactive imagination could never produce anything quite as sexy. Tiffany had beautiful teeth, straight out of a toothpaste commercial. He could see beads of perspiration beginning to form on her forehead, her unblinking light blue eyes fixed on him, following his progress as he made his way into the tub. He hadn't yet decided if it was written that he was going to have wild animal sex with her in the hot tub or not, but regardless, he'd first have to get in it.

Tiffany waded backwards to the opposite end of the Jacuzzi, bumping into an underwater bench. Pierre descended into the steaming hot water inch by painful inch, moving towards her with eventually only his head above water. *Sweet Jeezus, it was hot.*

"Hi," she said, smiling, feigning innocence.

He waded within a foot of her face.

Now he knew who she resembled. The main actress in one of the new Star Wars movies. Or at least he thought so.

Tiffany didn't reach out for him, her hands still under water, probably resting on the bench seat.

Pierre wondered, should he reach for her? Tiffany was still sitting there with only her head above water, but she didn't make any effort to touch him or encourage him. He didn't want to upset her, and since she was not taking any initiative, Pierre backed off another foot or so.

"You are so tempting," he teased her.

Tiffany looked at him for a few seconds without responding. "So are you."

There! The ice was broken! "I'm so totally turned on being here with you." He couldn't think of what else to say. He cursed that stupid teenager trapped inside his body.

"Stop talking and kiss me."

That popped his circuit breakers. For heaven's sake, he was really out of practice. Smiling inside, he propelled himself forward again, this time making contact with Tiffany. He reached for her waist underwater, finding her breasts instead. He felt their fullness in passing, his finger touching her nipple pulled a tiny reaction from her, startling her, his hands moving down to her waist.

Tiffany leaned forward, offering her hungry mouth.

Pierre closed his eyes, intent on enjoying the taste of Tiffany without any visual distractions. When they connected, her provocative silky lips felt hot and soft. As their lips touched she immediately opened her mouth, but her tongue remained inside.

She smelled of cacao. Hot chocolate. Incredible.

Pierre kissed her very softly, allowing his tongue to gently brush her lips without entering her mouth.

Tiffany finally encircled his neck with her arms, drawing Pierre to her. Her arms felt soft yet conveyed the impression she was very strong.

Pierre felt the softness of her full round breasts compacting against his chest, feeling his erection touching the bench seat. Tiffany was sitting back away from the edge, so their pelvises could not touch, even thought he was there right between her legs.

He was terribly aroused. He'd die to make love to her here and now, but he still wasn't sure he should try that. They'd just met less than thirty minutes before, and he was not terribly comfortable with her body language just yet. They hadn't spoken much either, so it was evident she was hot for some passion, if nothing else. And that was perfectly fine with him, but he just didn't want to upset her. And besides, having sex in the tub was probably not the best idea. This was not their very own private backyard and some dumbshit night watchman or over-diligent front desk clerk could very well make an appearance, ruining the mood and even getting them in trouble.

The airline would love that.

They broke the kiss but remained within an inch of each other.

"I'm glad we're here," she whispered. He again smelled chocolate in her breath. Milk chocolate.

"So am I. You're incredible."

"How 'bout we go back?"

"Sure." Back where? His room? Hers? Without any further discussion? Was this really happening? They hadn't been there three minutes and she was already interested in going back to the room? Could life be more perfect? But without any doubt, he'd go back wherever she wanted. He was just hypnotized, like a deer in the headlights of the incoming Budweiser delivery truck.

"Come on, then." She pushed him back, out of her way, treading water towards the steps.

Pierre followed closely, getting a second opportunity to admire her adorable little ass when she stepped out of the water. Tiffany threw the towel over her shoulders, turning to wait for him.

Pierre joined her on the deck, placing his own towel on his shoulders. The air had gotten pretty cold. They hadn't been in the hot water long enough to properly insulate themselves against the cold night air. Tiffany reached for his hand.

"C'mon."

They departed the Jacuzzi area walking hand in hand towards the building, with her leading.

Like a couple of teenagers in love, he mused.

He loved it.

The only thing making him self-conscious was his incredible erection projecting forty-five degrees ahead of his trunks. Notwithstanding all his exterior self-confidence and A-type personality, deep down, he was still ridiculously shy.

TIFFANY LED THE WAY to *her* room. He liked her choice. That was perfectly okay with him. It seemed to Pierre girls were always more comfortable going to their own rooms for extracurricular activities. Nothing wrong with that, whatever made her the most comfortable.

She used her key card to let them through the door, pulling him behind her by the hand, going straight for the only queen-sized bed in the room. He heard the room door closing behind them. The room was illuminated by light spilling over from the bathroom, providing an atmosphere of intimacy.

Tiffany climbed on the bed, discarding her towel on the floor.

Stretched out on her back she reached up to her shoulders, grabbing the shoulder straps of her one-piece bathing suit. She slipped out of her suit with a move worthy of the best ballet dancer in the world, lifting her hips off the bed, pushing the silver bathing suit off with one foot.

Pierre stood over her thoroughly bewildered. His vivid imagination on steroids would've been incapable of imagining the beauty of what was taking place. All he could do was stand there admiring her stunning nude figure. Tiffany had the body of a slender Marylyn Monroe. Breath-taking gorgeous. His heart was beating at warp speed. His cock was bursting at the seams.

He could hardly believe he was in this room with this deliciously erotic human being, who had obviously chosen him as a partner for the night. For the love of God, how lucky could one man be?

Pierre realized she was waiting for him, reclined on the pillows, looking at him in perfect silence.

Wake up, you dumbass!

The game was on, they had crossed the line, this was really happening. He removed the extra-large shorts she'd lent him, feeling his freed erection bounce up against his lower belly. Even in the dim light he was able to see Tiffany's longing eyes fixed on his hard-on.

Play ball.

He climbed on the bed, slowly approaching her on his knees and elbows.

Tiffany separated her legs further, giving him room to approach her.

Pierre pulled himself all the way up to her face, placing his hands on her boobs. They were cold and damp and deliciously sexual.

"*Yes, they're real,*" she said, defiantly.

"What?"

"They *are* real, Pierre."

Her breasts were large, so he assumed her statement was motivated by some past experience. Some former moron lover must've suggested she had implants, which would have consequently pissed her off. So now she logically felt the need to make that remark up front.

"I never doubted it. They're beautiful. You are beautiful."

He caressed her fully erect nipples and the skin around them with the palms of his hands. She was just as aroused as he was, no doubt about it. Pierre was high as he imagined a cocaine high would be. He couldn't believe what was happening. This happened to others, but not to him.

He vacillated for a second or two, mapping his next move.

"Come here and fuck me," Tiffany ordered, reaching for him. She was already breathing in short gasps.

He'd considered going down on her and pleasuring her first, but she was pulling him with such strength indicating she had other plans. She'd obviously already made up her mind what she wanted next. Her body was cold and still humid from the hot tub.

Okay. He could always pleasure her with his tongue later.

He was already between her legs, resting his weight on his elbows and knees. His face was directly above Tiffany's when he felt the tip of his shaft making contact with a part of her that was hot and wet and yielding. His mighty sword stabbed her, sinking to the hilt.

Her deep breath intake was music to his ears.

HE WAS AS FAR inside her as he could possibly go. She was sooo hot inside, the contrast was totally erotic, both their bodies still cold and damp on the outside from their little Jacuzzi adventure. Their eyes were locked, and he felt and saw Tiffany take a deep breath when he filled her.

"*Oh, Pierre!*" She wrapped her cold hands around his neck with a passion, moving her hips slowly in a circle.

Pierre was so damned excited by this incredible woman; he began to worry he may not last very long if she kept this up. She was turning him on beyond belief and she'd thrown his game to the dogs, so to speak. No foreplay at all, she hadn't allowed him to do anything to pleasure her before entering her. She was damned hot, that was for sure.

Losing control and coming inside her this early in the game would be completely unacceptable, he was not a teenager on his first rodeo. Time to take over.

He moved back, feeling himself slipping out of Tiffany.

"Don't," she protested, trying to hold him where he was.

He ignored her, moving down.

Her hands went to his shoulders, as he lowered himself on the bed until his mouth was in line with her labia. She didn't have a chance to fuss anymore before he was on her clit, stroking it with his tongue, his hands grasping her curvy hips.

Tiffany hesitated but in a few moments seemed to accept the fact that he was in charge, at least for the moment. Her lack of further resistance suggested she was going to accept whatever Pierre had in mind for her. She stopped resisting and in a few seconds, she was grinding her pussy against his face while moaning quietly. She reached down to her crotch with both hands, using her fingers to spread her lips for him. With that, she was able to completely expose her clit to his tongue. Pierre reached up with both hands, cupping her breasts, rolling her nipples between his fingers.

She was so aroused her body began shaking in short spasms, more and more frequently, her respiration increasing in rate, breathing in short gasps.

Pierre inserted his index finger between her very wet lips, separating them, gaining entrance into her deliciously tight vagina.

Tiffany reacted to his touch arching her back and exhaling loudly.

He could tell she was enjoying his touch from the way her hips began pumping up and down, faster and faster, reacting to his finger at play deep inside her.

Tiffany obviously knew how to direct a lover to please her, using her fingers to open her lips wide open, exposing her clit and giving Pierre a clean shot at it.

He kept applying continuous vigorous paint strokes with his tongue, inducing small tremors each time his tongue connected with her ultra-sensitive center of pleasure.

Her breathing accelerated, confirming the gradual increase in arousal she was experiencing.

"No! Stop!" She commanded, pushing his face away.

Pierre stopped. *Now what?*

Tiffany used her elbows to pull herself away from his grip, turning around on the bed, getting on her knees and elbows in one quick move.

It took Pierre all of one second to realize what the game plan was. Tiffany had positioned herself on all fours, offering her sensually delicious exquisite ass to him.

HolymotherofGod.

She pegged his arousal meter. Few things in life turned him on more than a seductive woman positioned like Tiffany was, totally vulnerable, trusting him blindly in anticipation of his next move. He was decidedly partial to that position. Pierre got on his knees, inching up towards Tiffany. He positioned himself against her from behind, placing his hands on the sides of her buttocks. He used his knees to further spread her legs apart. Looking down, he confirmed that the tip of his shaft was perfectly aligned between her cheeks, aimed at her lips. Her buttocks still felt cold from the chilly air outside.

Oh, God, what a turn on!

He thrust his hips forward, feeling the tip of his cock entering Tiffany.

"Hmmmm..." She moaned, in appreciation. She moved her hand down to her pussy, contributing to their love-making with some very familiar self-stimulation.

Continuing his thrust, he relished the feeling of knowing he was deep inside her. Pierre loved making love like this. Tiffany was an incredible turn on. She must obviously enjoy it this way, since she initiated it. He liked this position so much because he got to have her under his total control. And that excited him something crazy.

Tiffany swayed her hips left and right very gently, before switching to a back and forth rhythm.

Pierre began slamming in and out of her faster and faster. He could feel his balls bouncing against the general area where her clit was, his hands full of Tiffany's ass.

"No," she ordered loudly, then—more gently—"*Slow!*"

That surprised him. He'd never encountered a sex partner who didn't enjoy being slammed from behind at a fast pace.

He instantly slowed. If that's what Tiffany wanted, that's what he was going to provide for her. He slowed his speed considerably, hoping he was pleasuring her the way she preferred. It didn't take him long to realize making love to Tiffany in slow motion was even *more* exciting than just ramming into her. By doing it slowly Pierre could actually *feel* the walls of her vagina moving out of the way to let his shaft enter her.

Unquestionably delicious.

Admiring her sexy shoulders framed by her rumpled brown hair was also exciting as all hell.

It was just too good to be real. It turned him on so much he began listening to the alarms being sent by his balls, warning him he was going to lose control and explode.

No! He needed to pleasure her first. Against all instinct, he pulled out again, rolling Tiffany over on her side with one hand.

She allowed herself to be pushed onto her side without objecting.

Pierre moved over quickly, positioning himself between her legs, rolling Tiffany on her back.

She didn't make a sound.

Pierre lifted her legs over his shoulders, placing his face against her pubis, holding each leg with one arm, immobilizing her. He dove down into her pussy, finding her clit and giving it his full attention, licking it with a fury. She'd made it clear she liked it slow when she was on her knees, but he knew she was going to enjoy herself at whatever speed he decided to lick her.

Tiffany made a feeble attempt to fight against his hold, but she didn't have a hope of turning herself loose from his iron grip.   She reached down in resignation, using her fingers once more to delicately spread her lips open for him.

Pierre dedicated his attention to her delicious pair of sensual lips, his imminent urge to orgasm having been successfully interrupted and under control.

Tiffany tried to wiggle out of his arms again, but she was no match for his biceps. Each one of his strong arms was wrapped around one of her legs, keeping them apart.

"You are terrible!"

She was breathing rapidly.

He couldn't answer her and keep licking at the same time, so he said nothing.

Tiffany was shaking continuously now. Pierre kept the rhythm with his tongue. He was not going to let her go. She was going to lose herself in the pleasure of his lovemaking.

He began breathing faster. Using his tongue on Tiffany was a real work out. He consciously paced himself so he wouldn't burn out before she was satisfied.

Pierre caught a glimpse of Tiffany's face. Her eyes closed, her lips parted, breathing hard.

Good.

He continued concentrating his attention on her clit, holding her with his arms, preventing her from interrupting the magic flowing between them. She was not going to distract him this time.

Tiffany was making erotic little sounds, something between a moan and a whimper. Her body was now continuously shuddering, waves of small quivers coming uninterrupted. Pierre's face was soaked.

Man, was she wet. So beautiful.

He was determined to satisfy her. If it took an hour, he was going to send her into orbit. He was so grateful having this opportunity to make love to an angel. Tiffany was an angel, far as he was concerned.

"Ah, God!" she cried, lifting her pubis off the bed, placing her hands on Pierre's head. She applied force to his head, directing his tongue a little lower, towards her vagina.

Pierre went along with her desires, abandoning her clit, switching his attention to her lips. He inserted his tongue inside her pussy, as deep as he could, then he dashed in and out, trying to apply pressure on her inner walls from the inside.

Pierre marveled at how deep he could insert his tongue inside Tiffany.

He definitely must've been a frog in a previous life.

Tiffany let out a few gasps, tensing all her muscles. Her spasms became violent making it a challenge for Pierre to follow her with his tongue.

Her body tensed, autonomous reflexes radiating from the pleasure center in her brain taking complete control of her actions. She called his name again, attempting to wrap her legs around his shoulders, still fighting his grip.

Pierre accompanied her orgasm with his tongue all the way. He never let go of her, maintaining a firm grip on Tiffany's legs, enhancing her pleasure to the point where she surprised him by beginning to sob quietly.

Pierre didn't let go of her until he was sure Tiffany had felt each and every single drop of the pleasure he was giving her. Her body was still producing involuntary short tremors and her quiet soft sobs persisted.

He heard her sigh loudly, her hands relaxing the hold on his head.

Pierre waited a few minutes, letting her enjoy her moment of post-pleasure, then he pulled up positioning himself alongside her on the bed.

Tiffany appeared to be out cold. The sobbing had subsided. She ended up on her back, with her eyes closed, with what he'd like to interpret as a smile across her lips. She was finally breathing normally. Pierre admired the perfect beauty of her face. Her elegant nose was just the right size for her face. Her eyebrows naturally painted below her forehead didn't seem to have any make up. Her face was a *perfect* 'dream.' No question about it. She was the kind of tantalizing woman one only saw in magazine covers or beauty pageants, so pretty it hurt.

He gently reached over, depositing a soft kiss on her cheek.

Tiffany stirred, partially opening her eyes, turning to look at Pierre through half-closed lids.

She gifted him with a shy smile, turning her body away from him, rolling on her side, facing away from Pierre. She then reached behind with her hand, exploring and finally finding what she was looking for, his hard manhood.

Pierre was in disbelief. Where'd she get the strength? He thought she was out for the night. Her stamina was truly an unexpected and most delightful surprise.

Tiffany shifted her hips back, moving her body closer to Pierre while gently gripping his shaft, pulling it towards her rear end, directing him until she had him aligned at the entrance to her lips, from behind.

She inched closer to Pierre, shoving her hips back a little further, forcing his cock to part her lips, entering her quite easily because of her incredible lubrication. Tiffany's hand reached back around his hip, pulling him against her body, his hipbones comfortably parked against her warm, soft ass.

Pierre was ecstatic. He couldn't believe the delicious pleasure Tiffany was providing him. The joy she was giving him. Not only the incredibly erotic feel of her hand on his erection, or the unimaginable enjoyment of being inside her, but the fact she was willing to continue the evening until he climaxed. She could've as easily gone to sleep and enjoyed the satisfaction he had brought her, calling it a night.

He had pleasured her, and now this angel resting on the bed in front of him was offering herself to him, in retribution.

His intentions had been to just lay there watching her sleep, but in view of what she was doing, he abandoned himself to the pleasure of the moment. Placing one hand around Tiffany's narrow waist he slowly thrust his hips forward, pushing in and out of her slowly and gently, becoming more aroused by the instant. The silky feel of her buttocks against his pelvis each time he pushed was building up the *crescendo*, taking him to the brink of an orgasm. Although she appeared to have been knocked out by her own climax, Tiffany somehow still managed to find the strength and the interest to move her hips back and forth in a perfectly synchronized act of passion.

It didn't take Pierre long to approach the point where he lost total control. His body took over for him, thrusting in and out of Tiffany without any conscious effort on his part, it was doing it on its own, his heartbeat increasing at breakneck speed. He felt the fuzzy, warm tingle starting in his toes. At the same instant, waves of intense pleasure emanated from his balls to his chest to his limbs. He knew he was starting to come inside her, and the very thought excited him beyond words, if that was possible. He exploded, gripping her hip with great strength, pulling her towards him, letting Tiffany know without any doubt he was coming inside her and she belonged to him.

She held on to Pierre with the one arm she had reaching behind her. Her juices squeezed out around the sides of his cock as he plunged into her

Pierre felt pulses of pleasure radiating in every direction from his crotch. His body shaking with uncontrolled passion, accelerating the rhythm of their lovemaking.

His brain had gone into lockdown; he couldn't think of anything other than Tiffany.

Then it was over.

Still breathing fast, he was overwhelmed with feelings of gratitude and intense fondness for this incredible girl laying with him. Pierre could die right now of happiness. He smiled privately. Those feelings seemed to be his eternal emotional response to sex.

Every little thing that you do, girl, I'm amazed by you.

He leaned over, planting a soft kiss on Tiffany's cheek. Her head was turned too far for him to reach her lips.

He felt himself slipping out of her.

Pierre reached for the bed cover, pulling it up from the bottom of the bed, gently covering Tiffany with it, admiring her nude sensual body in the twilight of the room. She was so hot he had no words to describe her.

There wasn't enough slack to also cover himself with it, but it didn't matter. He laid down behind her, in the perfect spoon position. His pelvis resting against her buttocks, his chest caressing her back. He softly wrapped his arm around her, holding her gently against him. Pierre was irrationally happy having this incredible woman sleeping with him in this position. Her body was warm, and getting hotter by the second where they came in contact with each other. Pierre loved sleeping in the heat of a woman's body, and Tiffany was—at the moment—fulfilling his dreams.

"Good night, Tiffany," he whispered.

There was no response.

Tiffany was totally unconscious. Out cold. Her breathing had stabilized, and he could feel her lungs expanding and contracting against his chest. A long duty day with the airline and then half hour of intense passion had wiped her out.

Pierre took a deep breath, remembering they were on a layover, and tomorrow they'd have to fly again. After an instant of brief panic, he recalled their departure from the hotel was not scheduled until sometime in the late afternoon. That was a wonderful relief, he didn't have to get out of bed to setup a wakeup call or program one into his smartphone. Which by the way, right off the top of his head Pierre had no idea where the Dickens he'd left it. He smiled. What the devil did he care about his dumb phone. He was in heaven, right where he wanted to be, in bed with a muse sleeping against him.

So, fuck the phone.

A couple of hours later something woke him. The room was faintly illuminated by light spilling out past the bathroom door, which was cracked open, but the window curtains didn't show any light. Consequently, it was still the middle of the night.

It was Tiffany, she was stirring next to him.

"Wow, what time is it?" She asked groggily.

Pierre had absolutely no idea.

Tiffany pulled down on the comforter, kicking it away. "It's hot in here."

Pierre helped her remove the bedding covering her legs. "I don't know what time it is. But it's still dark outside."

Tiffany leaned against Pierre. "That was wonderful," she whispered, reaching down with her hand, exploring her crotch.

"Oh!?" She lifted her hand up to her nose, smelling then tasting it with her tongue. "You came inside me," she said.

Pierre said nothing. Hers was more of a statement than a question, and he wasn't quite sure what to respond.

"I don't usually screw without a rubber," she stated matter-of-factly.

Pierre was somewhat taken back by the statement and her use of the verb 'screw.' He considered that word very far from 'making love.' Somehow that word didn't fit the image he had of Tiffany. Stupid, really, he was nothing but an incurable romantic.

"But you are really special," she added. "So that's fine."

Pierre was unsure what she meant by that or what was going through her mind. Was she unhappy he'd come inside her without a condom? The topic had obviously not been addressed during their passion. He should've thought of that. What an idiot he was. What exactly made him think she was on birth control? And what if she wasn't? He had to stop taking things for granted, or he was going to get himself and some girl into a world of trouble.

"When our trip's over I wish you could come over to my place so I could cook you some spaghetti," she offered, moving up on the bed, resting her head on two of the pillows. "Come sleep with me," she groggily patted the pillow next to her.

Pierre joined her, admiring her porcelain doll face, accepting a quick sweet kiss good-night from her. "I gotta get some sleep," she explained, moving closer to him, resting her face on his arm, throwing her arm over Pierre's chest.

She smelled of baby powder and sweet sex. Tiffany closed her eyes and within a couple of minutes she was out of this world again.

Pierre took advantage of the opportunity to feast his eyes. He admired her full, silky brown hair, wondering once again what good deed he must've done in a previous life to deserve this.

Holding a sleeping Tiffany in his arms, his mind revisited earlier thoughts. What if she got pregnant? Great timing, Pierre, thinking about it after the deed was done. God, there were so many different angles to this. If Tiffany got pregnant, would she want to have a baby? Would she want to discontinue the pregnancy? If she did have a baby, would she want to continue flying? Would she even want to have him in her life?

All these were questions keeping him awake. He made enough money to take care of her and a baby without Tiffany having to work ever again if she so desired. But what was he thinking? Marriage? Living together? Too many options. He was drifting off to sleep. He barely knew Tiffany. They'd just met not three hours ago. Totally insane to be thinking along those lines.

He did like her a lot, though. She was so attractive, and decidedly fantastic in bed. But they hadn't really exchanged too many words. What was she like? Would she even like him enough to partner up? Pierre, decided to abandon such thoughts until morning.

One thing was for sure, no matter which direction this went, Tiffany would have his full support. She was not alone. She'd shared her bed and body with him, and he was not going to abandon her in the morning. She was trusting him, sleeping in his arms, and he was not going to let her down no matter what.

Rest well, sweetheart. You have a man looking after you.

He fell asleep feeling strongly protective of her, basking in the warmth of her embrace.

PIERRE OPENED HIS EYES. He was in a hotel room. But where?

He hated waking up not knowing where the devil he was. This happened to him a little too often, which was disturbing.

Tiffany!

Looking right and left, the bed was empty. He sat up, just in time to hear a toilet flush.

She was up.

Just then Tiffany walked out of the bathroom, not a stitch on her. Her dark hair in total disarray.

Pierre couldn't help admiring her sensual, feminine body before meeting her eyes and her glorious smile.

"Good morning!" She offered, in a voice so sweet it reminded him of a lullaby. She had not missed his examination of her perfect body. Her smile, however, conveyed approval. "See anything you like?"

"Ha! Beauty should always be admired, once exposed, love."

Pierre already had a hard-on. For the love of Zeus, didn't his hormones ever take a rest?

Tiffany approached the bed, leaning down, placing her lips on Pierre's.

He hadn't brushed his teeth yet, so he was self-conscious about kissing her. He kept his mouth closed, returning a brotherly kiss.

"Did you sleep well?" Tiffany proceeded to sit on his lap. He had part of the comforter covering himself, so she couldn't see his erection. She felt a little heavy but he could handle her weight without any trouble. He simply nodded, since he didn't want to speak this close to her without brushing his teeth first. But with her sitting solidly on his lap, Pierre didn't have a hope of sneaking off to the bathroom.

He looked away from Tiffany. "Ya, slept great! You?"

Tiffany smiled at his attempt at modesty. "Like a baby. You're quite a lover, Pierre."

She gave him a roguish smile. "Wanna use my toothbrush?"

He nodded.

Tiffany laughed, pushing herself away from his lap.

Now he could escape to the bathroom, except for the small detail that he had a monumental hard-on discreetly tucked under the comforter.

Hell with it.

Pierre stood, in his fully erect glory, walking straight for the bathroom. He didn't even cast a glimpse at Tiffany. No way under God's blue sky she had missed his boner, though.

"I love watching you walk around the room naked," she voiced, a little loud.

Pierre found her toothbrush and toothpaste. He rapidly applied some green goo to the toothbrush, brushing his teeth with a fury. A quick rinse and he was ready. He walked out.

Tiffany was sitting on the bed, her hands leaning on the edge, her knees close together. Her breasts perked up with the enthusiasm of youth. She took a long adoring look at Pierre's hard-on. Then she looked at his eyes, smiling.

"Wow!" Was all she said.

"I'm not naked. I'm nude." He wasn't too sure he should approach her now and have an erotic morning session, or just talk.

"Ya? What's the difference?"

"Nude is sensual. Naked is not."

"Oh? How do you figure?"

"Naked is unprotected and vulnerable. Nude is: 'Look at me in the eyes, sweetheart, because I want to make love with you.'"

"And you're nude?"

"Yes."

"So you're sensual?"

"Correct again."

"And you want to make love to me?" Her eyes had acquired a light of their own.

"Yes."

Pierre saw her glance at the clock in the cable TV box. "I don't think that's such a good idea, Honey. Did you see the time?"

TWO HOURS LATER THEY were on the airplane. Pierre was preparing the Airbus A321 for its flight back to Chicago.

Tiffany entered the flight deck, placing her hand on Pierre's shoulder. He glanced back at her. Her dreamy eyes flashed a smile, acknowledging the events of the night in lovers' cryptic code. She had a neatly folded piece of yellow paper in her hand. He accepted it, not looking at it right away. The ship's captain, Bular, sitting three feet from Pierre might have noticed the exchange, but said nothing. Aah, the great value of a discrete man, Pierre thought.

"You guys want something to drink?"

Bular asked for three bottles of water.

Pierre requested a Diet Coke.

Tiffany exited the flight deck without saying anything else. Pierre was aroused, feeling himself getting hard. Shoot! He would definitely have to stick his hand down the front of his pants to straighten himself out. No way could he fly like this, it was too distracting and uncomfortable because his seat belt was a five-point design, with one strap coming up between his legs, and a huge buckle hitting him right in the crotch.

He unfolded the yellow piece of paper, careful to do so without any sudden movement which would attract the captain's attention.

Call me
206-543-xxxx

Pierre smiled, inserting the paper in his chest pocket. In typical brain-dead fashion, he had failed to get her cell phone number. What the fuck was wrong with him? He had a night worthy of *One Thousand and One Nights*, and he failed to do anything so he could repeat it. He really liked Tiffany, no doubt about it, but he was sexually satisfied, at least for the moment, and when he found himself in this condition, his brain appeared to stop functioning.

Looking back at Tiffany, he found himself with so many questions. Where did she live? Did she have a boyfriend? A husband was probably not in the picture, since she didn't wear an engagement ring nor a wedding band. He quickly Googled her area code in his smartphone, learning that it belonged in Seattle. Aha, so that's where she probably lived. Most flight attendants naturally had cell phones with the area codes of their home towns.

Seattle was practically a walk in the park from Phoenix, that was a fact. About two and a half hours one way, if he recalled correctly. He'd flown that route before. So, if he wanted to see her again he'd have to catch a flight out there. Not too bad, really. It could have been much worse, she could've been from Vermont, making her geographically undesirable.

They didn't get much of a chance to talk after they woke up. He'd returned to his own room to shower and their conversation had been practically nonexistent once they gathered in the lobby with the rest of the crew. Tiffany probably had a hundred questions to ask him as well. He texted her.

Pierre

> Thanks for the number. I forgot to ask you for it. You are an Angel. Where do you live?

Pierre

> . You done when we get to Chicago?

He didn't have much faith she'd be able to respond anytime soon, since they were already boarding passengers, but at least he'd established a line of communication with her.

MONTHS PASSED, AND THEY didn't connect again. He texted Tiffany a few more times, but she never responded. Pierre became involved with his multiple activities during his time off, motorcycling, sky-diving, going to the movies. He eventually accepted the fact Tiffany was just not interested. His earlier concern about her being pregnant evaporated after a few months. He figured she would've told him if she'd been expecting.

The next time destiny arranged to have their paths cross she was working as a marshaller and ramper for the airline. She was one of those flight attendants who had chosen to be cross-utilized. That meant they could elect to work shifts as flight attendants, or drive one of the trucks used to pushback airplanes, work in reservations or staff any of the ticket counters if they decided to bid the position for the month. The airline allowed for a number of its flight attendants to be cross-utilized, as an experiment.

One sunny hot summer day Pierre was in Seattle, pushing back from the gate on a flight to LAX, when he heard Tiffany's voice on the intercom.

"Bye, Pierre!" She said simply. Tiffany had somehow, incredibly, recognized his voice on the maintenance intercom.

It only took him an instant to recognize her voice. He was thrilled to hear from her. Tiffany was one of four rampers assigned to his flight, pushing him back from the gate and making sure his wingtips didn't hit anything.

"Bye, Tiffany!" He responded, making a mental note to call her that night from the hotel. He caught a quick glimpse of her from the flight deck, wearing a blue jumpsuit. She looked great, her hair swaying in the breeze. Her attractive figure triggering memories of their night together. He could see she was feeling the heat out there, her face glistening with perspiration and the back of her jumpsuit totally soaked.

Later that night Pierre tried calling her from his hotel, but she didn't answer and so he just left her a voice message.

She never called back.

Months later, Pierre was on a layover in Ontario, California, on his way to have dinner at a nearby local burger joint when he ran into Tiffany again. He was walking out of the hotel, opening the main lobby glass door to the street, when Tiffany came in with a couple of other flight attendants, coming face to face with him. They locked eyes, but neither said one word. She just continued past him into the lobby.

Pierre wondered why he hadn't said a thing either. He had no explanation, other than maybe he'd lost interest. He still found her very attractive, but for whatever reason, she had decided to distance herself from the pilot. They never really had much time together to stimulate each other mentally. Theirs was just a passionate interlude between two beautiful people who just so happened needed the same thing at a particular moment in time.

Fair enough. He could live with that.

Amanda

Long friggin day. Pierre was tired. *Get it together*, his brain warned. One o'clock in the morning and they were still a little over half hour from landing in Denver. They were going to be starting their descent any moment now. Three legs had been longer than he cared to fly in one day. After partying the previous night at his buddy Mike's wedding in Dallas, he'd caught an early morning flight to Los Angeles, arriving just in time to catch his two-day trip.

First leg to Phoenix hadn't been too bad, but then he'd flown to San Francisco and finally on to Denver, for a total of five hours' flight time. Too goddamned much flying for one day, particularly after dancing and eating and partying at a wedding into the late hours of the night. Pilots used to be protected by government regulations. If they flew too long they became fatigued, and so the Federal Aviation Regulations prevented this by imposing limits on the number of hours a pilot could fly or just be on duty. But recently, the government—in its King Solomon wisdom—had changed those regulations, making it very difficult to follow them and understand what was required.

It went without saying that Pierre was very careful not to drink twenty-four hours prior to showing up for work. Basically, that had prevented him from having even one drink at the wedding reception, but so what? He was never going to get caught with his pants down—so to speak—when it came to booze.

Too little sleep was a definite detriment. According to the new regulations—FAR 117—as they were known, it was Pierre's responsibility to determine if he was too tired to fly.

Yeah, right. Put the fox in charge of the hen house, see what happens.

Fatigue was just like drinking alcohol. A simple comparison claimed each hour on duty was tantamount to drinking one Bud Light. One gets the picture.

Pierre was now up around nine Bud Lights, far as fatigue was concerned.

Time to call it a day.

"So, when are you going on the Big Bus?" Captain Hank Hilton asked.

Pierre had never met the man, never flown with him until now. "December."

"Going to school over Christmas, ah?"

"Yeah. I am thrilled. Can't wait to get on that thing. Best Christmas gift the company could've given me."

"You're gonna be moving up pretty quickly here, I hear we're hiring a bunch of new pilots."

Pierre was not much in the mood for conversation, he was tired, and would've preferred some silence but if Hank was feeling talkative, Pierre had to humor him. Flight Deck Protocol lesson 101. The captain felt like talking, his first officer had to listen. There was no way out of it. Just one of the basic rules of life in the flight deck.

They would be descending below 10,000 feet soon anyhow, and at that time the conversation would be over. Sterile cockpit rules below ten thousand, no extraneous conversations below that point was the rule. Thank God.

Hank Hilton was a union pilot, one of those unselfish, dedicated men every pilot group needed. His involvement with union business contributed to making Pierre's life safer, more relaxed and way better compensated. If Pierre hadn't been so tired, he might actually like the guy. As it was, Hank had been somewhat irritating all day, thanks to his constant need for conversation.

"That's correct. All those brand-new pilots the company's hiring behind me are pushing me to where I wanna be. The Airbus 350 has been flirting with me for a long time. I can't wait to fly international."

"They're gonna put you in Los Angeles?"

"Yeah. I was really surprised to get LA. I thought I was gonna be stuck in Philadelphia or New York."

"That should work out pretty good for you then." Captain Hank Hilton was in his late forties, former ex-Marine, strong as a bull and a damned good pilot.

"Ya. Commuting from Phoenix to LA should be a piece of cake."

Pierre could discern a glimmer from the lights of Denver in the distance. They were still over the Rockies, so the ride was not real smooth. Clear air turbulence over the mountains had them rock-and-rolling for the past hour. They'd had the seat belt sign on, but that time of night not too many passengers were bound to be walking around anyhow.

The intercom buzzed, announcing a call from the cabin.

Hank picked up the handset. "This is Hank." He listened for a moment. "Okay, come on in."

"One of the gals wants to come up," he said. "Wanna confirm?"

Pierre wondered what the flight attendant wanted. He slid his electric seat back all the way, releasing his seatbelt. Aah, it really did feel good stretching his legs after hours in the seat. He looked through the door viewing port lens. One of their flight attendants was standing out there. A little too dark to see any details really. "That's her," he confirmed, tentatively anyhow.

Captain Hilton pressed the door unlock button on the center pedestal. A 'clack' confirmed the solenoid had released the lock.

The door swung open as Pierre ambled back towards his seat. He sat back down, reconnecting his seat belt.

"Hi guys," a pleasant young feminine voice echoed in the flight deck. "Just wanted to know if you fellows wanted something to drink for later."

Pierre turned in his seat to look at the source of the voice.

The flight attendant was a delicious brunette. She stood there still wearing her serving apron. She was so pretty. Even in the dim lights of the flight deck Pierre could admire the beauty of her delicate features. Brown hair and very pale skin. No way to tell the color of her eyes. Too dark in there. In her mid-twenties maybe? Damn, he hadn't noticed her before, how could he miss someone that pretty? Where the heck had she been hiding?

"I'm fine right now, thanks," was all he could think of saying. He really wasn't thirsty, having downed two bottles of water over the past few hours. Nice of her to ask, though. And somewhat unusual. Maybe she just needed a break from the passengers.

"No, I mean for *later*?"

It took Pierre a few seconds to catch on and realize what she *really* meant.

"Oh?"

Captain Hank Hilton beat him to the punch. "Thank you, honey. I'll gladly accept some Scotch—for later. Johnny Walker Black, if you have it."

Pierre felt like a dumbass. Obviously, she wasn't talking about *right now*. She was asking them if they'd like some adult beverages *for later*, in the hotel.

What a dumbshit he was. How was he going to extricate himself from this one and not sound like an idiot? "Just kidding," he laughed. "I'd love some vodka.

Thank you!" He gave her his best smile, taking advantage of the moment to admire her looks one last time.

What a doll. Man, the company was starting to hire some really good-looking flight attendants.

"Scotch and vodka," she repeated. "Coming right up!" The flight attendant turned and walked out of the flight deck, closing the door.

Captain Hilton reached across the pedestal, pushing the door lock button, electrically securing the flight deck door once again.

"You think she's gonna bring the bottles up here?" Pierre was suddenly concerned. Having liquor in the flight deck was an absolute no-no.

Captain Hilton laughed. "Relax. She's not that stupid. Obviously, she's not bringing any booze up here, she was just being cute. Besides, we're not letting her back in here until we're on the ground, just in case she only has two brain cells."

Pierre pondered that. He didn't even know why he'd asked her for the vodka. In the first place, his own personal rules dictated no booze while on the job, layover or not. Although if he hadn't asked for any booze, Hank would've looked at him with great suspicion. Pilots trusted each other with their lives, depended on each other, and also expected to drink with each other, when given the opportunity. A non-drinker sent out all sorts of alarms among the pilot group.

Airline regulations absolutely forbid crew members, pilots and flight attendants from removing any liquor from the airplanes—ever—under penalty of termination, but that was another one of those silly rules that were unenforceable. Reality was, First Class passengers were allowed to drink anything they wanted, totally free of charge. Since there was no way of knowing how many free drinks the flight attendants had served in First Class on a given flight, it was relatively easy for the gals to take some of the cute little bottles home after each flight. All they had to do to cover their butts was forge the log.

Pierre knew some flight attendants had literally *hundreds* of the little bottles stashed in their apartments. The only way to get caught was if someone spilled the beans to management about a particular crew stealing the alcohol. Then the company would have a surprise welcoming committee at the next airport, meeting the crew and asking to search their belongings.

Many flight attendants had been nailed by the company under those circumstances, yet the practice continued. Seldom were pilots caught in the middle of the booze scam because they generally didn't carry the little bottles with them. The flight attendants usually carried the evidence all the way to the hotel.

"Got everything in the box?" Pierre asked, referring to the Multi-Purpose Control and Display Unit keypad the Airbus used for flight management and navigation.

"Sure do. Why don't we brief the approach?"

This was the captain's landing, for which Pierre was grateful. He was tired, and much preferred being the pilot actively monitoring than the pilot flying. Few non-pilots realized that the two aviators sitting in the front were both mentally flying the airplane at all times, but only one of the two was actually handling the controls. That concept helped safety by providing redundancy. Sort of like having two surgeons performing an operation, but only one of the two wielding the scalpel.

HALF AN HOUR LATER they were finally parked at the gate. Denver International Airport was already settling down for the night.

"We done for the night, Boss?" Pierre joked.

"I would say so."

Both pilots packed their equipment and belongings into their bags. Pierre wasn't even hungry; he was just tired.

They secured the airplane for the night, pulling their bags up the jet bridge, entering the terminal. The flight attendants had already departed the gate area. Pierre saw them a couple of hundred feet ahead of them, headed for the van pickup spot.

"What time do we go tomorrow?" He asked. It was close to two a.m.

"I think the schedule says four p.m."

Pierre did the math. That translated into a fourteen-hour layover. Assuming one hour at each end for transportation, that left him with twelve hours to do as he pleased. Not bad. At least it wasn't one of those despicable eight-hour layovers. Those left him with a mere six hours to do as he pleased. That sucked. He was lucky to get five hours sleep on one of those.

The airport was practically deserted. Pierre wondered if any other flights would be arriving yet tonight.

The flight attendants were already sitting inside the Hyatt hotel van when Pierre and Hank joined them. The driver was standing by the rear gate, waiting to store their bags.

Pierre handed over his overnight bag to the man, but he kept his leather messenger bag. He had his laptop, iPad, passport and wallet in it, not to mention his credit cards and a couple of hundred dollars in cash. That bag he kept close by.

The four flight attendants waited in the dark for their pilots. Hank sat shotgun, so Pierre took a seat on the edge, by the door. The Hyatt Regency was a good twenty-three miles away, but at least now he could relax and let his thoughts wander. He'd be real happy saying good-bye to the little Airbus. He liked to fly, but these narrow-body airplanes flew just too many landings for his taste. He'd be glad to leave this type of flying to the newhires. He liked the idea of having one-leg days. Say Los Angeles to London, for example. Or Los Angeles to Paris. Yeah, that was a gentleman's job. That was the right dose of flying for his taste.

Fly one long leg, then go have dinner at some respectable restaurant. Yes, that was his idea of what he wanted his life to be.

Many of the schedules on the little Bus had four or five legs a day. That was just too much flying.

He faded into a short power nap on their way into town.

The sound of the side door slamming open woke him up.

Holy shit, where the hell was he?

He regained orientation in a matter of seconds, realizing he'd fallen asleep on the way into downtown Denver. Since he was sitting by the side door, he should be the first one out. He briefly wondered if any of the others had noticed he'd passed out. That would be embarrassing. He stepped out of the van, unsteadily walking towards the back, not fully awake yet.

The rest of the crew followed.

Pierre accepted his bag from the driver, tipping him the habitual two bucks, then turned away from the others, heading for the front desk.

He was the first one at the registration and manners be damned. The friendly clerk behind the desk provided him with a door card and a room number written on the little envelope containing the card.

Pierre didn't look back, he simply found the elevators, pushing the button for the tenth floor. Nice hotel, deep carpet. Great smell of lemon furniture oil.

His room was wonderful. Two queen beds, immaculately ironed sheets, six large pillows, an enormous flat screen TV, and someone had actually pulled down his bed covers, setting a cellophane bag with chocolate chip cookies in it.

A classy act.

He stripped down to his pants. The air was cool and smelled of flowers. He wondered what deodorant the hotel room maid had used.

He relieved himself, washed his hands and face and stepped back in the room.

The hotel phone rang.

It had to be the front desk guy calling for something. No way crew scheduling was going to ring him this time of night.

"Hello?"

"Pierre?" A woman's voice.

"Yeah?"

"It's Amanda! I've got your vodka. What'd ya like with it? Coke? Soda?"

That totally confused him. *Holy Jesus! He'd totally forgotten about her!*

"Aah, straight is good." He'd had no idea her name was Amanda.

"All right, I'll bring ice. Or do you want to come to my room instead?"

Pierre rapidly analyzed the options. She had already made up her mind to visit his room. Better not change anything. "No, I mean, you can come over here if you want. Whatever you prefer."

"Be there in two," she said, and hung up.

He'd be damned! The lovely brunette flight attendant had totally escaped his mind. He hadn't even seen her on the way to the hotel. Just how tired was he? He must be totally exhausted, to forget about something like this.

And now she was on her way to his room with some vodka? How did she find out his room number?

He rapidly put his white T-shirt back on, surveying the room. Not too messy.

A rap on the door told him Amanda was there already.

How the devil had she arrived so quickly? Pierre went to the door.

She was even more gorgeous out of uniform. Her loose hair was thick, dark brown and appeared soft. He resisted an urge to smell it. She had bedroom eyes, no doubt about it, the color of cognac and at half-mast. Her breasts full and frisky hiding behind a white cotton T-shirt. Was she wearing a bra? Hard to tell. She stood there on his doorway holding a plastic bag. Her provocative hips were the ideal size for Pierre, in her black jeans she looked tasty enough to eat. Damn, without any question, he would love to fuck her. He was instantly disturbed at the direction of his thoughts.

God, he had to get his mind out of the gutter.

"Hi!"

"Hi Pierre!" She walked in the room, leaving a scent of citrus behind her. He definitely liked that perfume, or cologne, or whatever it was. Amanda walked straight between the beds, proceeding to empty the contents of her bag on the night table.

Pierre had a good opportunity to admire her looks. She wasn't too petite, which he liked. Maybe five foot five or six? And so exquisitely built. He was amused by how fast she had taken over. She'd just marched in the room and taken the reins. She retrieved two cans of Coke from her bag, and two glasses. Where did she get those?

"You like Coke with your vodka?" She stacked eight miniature bottles of Absolute vodka on the night table, courtesy of Worldwide Airlines.

"No. no, thanks." Pierre was hypnotized by her presence. It was just too unreal. Here was this gorgeous creature preparing drinks for them on his night table. And even more incredible, he was willing to accept the drink and join her, against all his own personal guidelines. He was violating one of his cardinal rules, no drinking on layovers.

Regardless, primal instinct ruled, and to hell with everything else.

He was fucked. She was so damned sexy, and she moved like a cat. He just stood there, watching her. No way was he going to offend her by refusing the drink. Refuse the drink? He'd dance with the devil to kiss her.

"Ice?"

"Uh?"

"Do you want ice with your drink?"

"Oh! No, no thanks. No ice." She'd even brought ice in that bag!

Amanda poured three miniature bottles into the one glass. She extended her arm, offering him the drink. "One neat vodka coming right up."

She then sat on the bed across from Pierre, pouring some Coke into her own glass. "Your name is Pierre?"

"Yes. How did you know?"

"It's on the crew list."

"And you're Amanda?"

"That's me."

"Thank you for bringing these." He sipped from the glass. *Holy shit*, that was pure vodka, no question about it.

"You're very welcome. I dropped off the Scotch with Hank on my way here."

"Whoa. You *are* efficient!" That made Pierre feel just a tad less guilty. If the captain was in his room sipping Scotch, then it couldn't be all that bad, could it?

"I aim to please." Amanda turned to the bedside radio, tuning to a station playing Van Morrison's *Brown Eyed Girl.*

Pierre was speechless. She was a real I'm-in-charge kinda girl.

"Sorry I didn't say much to you during the day, to be honest, I didn't even know you were back there."

"No big deal. I should've come up front earlier to say hello."

"We don't have many opportunities to visit with you all much anymore."

"In training, they warned us repeatedly not to go up front at all."

"They did? Why?"

"The instructors claim you guys aren't very nice and we should keep our distance and avoid you."

Pierre guffawed. "Right. We're gonna eat you for lunch. In all honesty, we really are quite nice. I think what's going on is some of the more senior flight attendant instructors don't want you to have any fun. Since they're too weathered to interest any of us anymore, they also don't want you to have contact with us at all."

"That figures. I've heard from some of the more experienced flight attendants that in the old days they went up front in the flight deck all the time. they even smoked cigarettes up there with you guys."

"I don't know about the smoking part; I haven't been around long enough to remember when they used to do that."

"How long you've been with the company?"

"Three years. You?"

"Same. I'm on my third year."

"Where are you from, Amanda?"

"I'm from Tucson."

"No kidding? I live in Phoenix."

"For real?"

"Yeah. Ahwatukee."

"I know where that is. You're just this side of South Mountain."

"That's true. You born and raised in Tucson?"

"Yes. Mom still lives there."

"Your dad too?"

"No, dad passed two months ago." Her voice cracked.

Damn. That was not good. "So sorry to hear that."

"Thanks. I just can't believe he's gone."

"Were you real close?" *What a dumbass thing to ask her, of course she'd been close, it was her dad.*

"Yes."

Pierre sat on the bed across from her. "What happened?"

"He had cancer."

"I'm so very sorry, Amanda."

"It's been hard." Her eyes teared up.

Aw, heck, now he'd blown the mood.

Way to go, Pierre!

Oh, well, might as well at least try to give her some emotional support. Not sure how he could do that, though. The loss of her dad was such a terrible tragedy no words were going to help her.

Pierre moved over next to her on the bed, placing his hand on her shoulder. "How old was he?"

"Not old. Forty-three."

Shit, he was young.

"I'm so very sorry, Amanda."

He downed the vodka in his glass, his throat catching on fire, not knowing what else he could say to her.

Amanda raised her glass, drinking the contents in one long gulp.

Dang! She could drink!

He didn't see how many of the little bottles of vodka had gone into her Coke. Pierre was right away starting to feel the effect of the booze. He hadn't had much to eat, so the vodka was already making him lightheaded. Amanda reached over grabbing two additional miniature bottles from the table. She skillfully uncapped them, pouring the contents of one into his glass, the other into hers. She added some Coke to hers.

Pierre was excited sitting next to her. Her body smelled of that unknown citric fragrance, stimulating his senses. Amanda was as pretty as a porcelain doll, and he was itching to kiss her and feel the warmth of her body. He was touched by her misty eyes. How he wanted to place his arms around her, telling her everything was gonna be okay. But he knew he couldn't do that because everything was *not* going to be okay. Her dad was gone and that was not going to change.

He drank the vodka straight like a shot. The stuff—again—burned his throat on its way down. He shouldn't be doing this, but it was really very exciting, hitting the vodka with this great-looking woman in the room with him. He was at a loss about what else to say. Words couldn't possibly mend the wound she had at the loss of her Dad.

"Would you mind terribly if I kissed you?" He finally gathered enough guts to ask her.

The next second he wondered if he'd really said that.

Amanda looked at him, her eyes still moist. "Only when it rains," she said.

Pierre had absolutely no idea what she meant by that. He reached for her, placing his hand behind her neck, looking for her lips. Her warm breath smelled of Coke.

He was very aware that alcohol enhanced the desire but affected the performance when it came to sex. He repeated that to himself every chance he got. Had he had too much to drink?

Her lips were cold from the ice in her drink. Pierre found her kiss soft and passionate. He was enchanted. Amanda reached up, placing the palm of her hand on his cheek.

Pierre was mesmerized. What had attracted Amanda to him? No idea, but he was aroused and kissing her and that was all that mattered. He pushed her back towards the pillows. Amanda willingly stretched herself on the bed.

Pierre laid down next to her, still kissing her. He reached down, finding the single button on her jeans. She allowed him to unbutton her, continuing their kiss as he grabbed her zipper, pulling it down.

"Hold on!" Amanda sat up, pulling at her white T-shirt. In a moment, she had removed it. Her magnificent breasts adorning her white bra presented an erotic landscape for Pierre to enjoy.

He followed suit, pitching his own T-shirt on the floor. Amanda was so desirable and so hot, his hard-on was ready for action. Reaching lower, he grabbed the sides of her black jeans, pulling them down.

Amanda accommodated by discreetly lifting her hips. The pants came off, joining his T-shirt on the carpet. Amanda wore white panties, not bikini-style. In fact, Pierre hadn't seen that particular style for some time. The sides of her undies were about three or four inches wide. And they fit her so well. Her hips were strong and sensual. He kissed her some more, nibbling very gently at her lower lip. He was definitely feeling the effect of the vodka. That bothered him. He wanted to remember every single detail of his time with Amanda, and he knew the vodka would mess things up. Too late now. He had broken a second cardinal rule, never engage in sex while under the influence.

Amanda's tongue found her way inside his mouth, darting in and out, telegraphing the unspoken message that she was now just as turned on as he was.

She pushed him off momentarily, holding Pierre off just long enough to remove her bra and panties.

Duh! He should've done that! He should've undressed her all the way. He blamed the liquor for it. He wasn't thinking straight. The liquor and the fatigue. Bad combination.

Pierre was excited as all hell though. looking at Amanda's nude figure through the vodka fog. She had a young body, worthy of admiration. Her breasts were deliciously round, and as real as any he'd ever admired. He was dying to go inside her, there was no longer any doubt in his mind that's what she wanted. Rapidly reaching down Pierre unbuckled his black belt, removing his pants and boxer shorts and shoes all in one quick, suave motion,

He tentatively explored Amanda's crotch with his hand. His fingers found her silky, well lubricated lips wet and hot. She was so ready for him. He felt her hips shifting at his touch.   Pierre pondered whether he should go down on her first, but decided against it. Amanda was wet enough and from the way she was kissing him, she was just as aroused as he was. And probably a little drunk as well. She had to be drunk. She was smaller than he was, and she'd had the same amount of vodka.

No way she wasn't smashed.

He positioned himself between her legs, slowly. Amanda helped him, moving her leg out of his way once he'd vaulted it. She then spread her other leg, presenting her open slick wetness to Pierre.

He didn't need to use his hand to guide himself. Staring into her hungry brown eyes he moved his body closer to her, feeling his shaft connecting with her soft lower lips, enjoying the incredible sensation of sliding inside Amanda, inch by delicious inch, spreading the inside of her walls with his solid erection. It happened so fast and so naturally, he thanked all the stars in the universe for the special moment. Amanda was sizzling hot inside, and her eyes were nailed on his, unblinking. She knew his erection was fully inside her. She had to know. Undoubtedly she knew.

Pierre felt her arms around his neck, her heels on the back of his thighs. Gad, her heels told him Amanda was wide open just wanting for him to fuck her into oblivion.

Time to cater to her wishes and provide her with some pleasure.

He slowly came out of her nearly all the way, then pushed forward again, filling her completely. He repeated the motion, but this time he remained at the entrance of her vagina, allowing merely the tip of his cock to stay inside her.

Amanda waited in anticipation for his next thrust, but Pierre remained still.

He then entered her another inch or so, backing out again. He repeated the tease a couple of more times.

"Meanie!"

He laughed. "What?"

"You are mean! Don't play dumb, come here!" She pulled him towards her, lifting her hips high, forcing his shaft deep inside her. Pierre gave in. She was hot as steam and so was he, although the vodka-induced haze was starting to screw things up. His awareness of time had been affected. He'd no idea whether he'd been making love, fucking, screwing or whatever, with Amanda for a minute or an hour. The vodka made him not give a damn about time, one way or another.

She was making sweet, delicious sounds, confirming her pleasure each time Pierre impaled her to the hilt. The sounds were dim enough that he couldn't tell if she was actually saying something or just moaning from enjoyment.

Pierre had read somewhere how women detested men who buried their faces in their necks during sex. It was just too impersonal. Women liked men looking at their eyes while they were engaged in sexual passion. Why that came to mind just at that moment, he'd no idea.

He wanted this to be special for Amanda so he opened his eyes, two inches from hers, staring into her soul. He loved being this close to a woman, and Amanda was all woman. She was so good-looking, and seemed intelligent, although they hadn't exchanged too many words. He didn't need too many words to determine she was a sharp girl. The way she had taken upon herself organizing the liquor while they were still on the airplane.

That was all part of the attraction.

He also loved the way her body felt underneath his.

Amanda was the perfect size for him and the perfect temperature and the perfect mate. She was exciting and hot and delicious and she smelled fantastic.

And he was fucking drunk.

Her devilishly defiant eyes were an inch from his, unblinking, as he went in and out of her. His exhaustion from flying all over the country had magically evaporated. He was now at his best. Or at least he thought so. It was probably the vodka creating the delusion.

Pierre wasn't sure exactly how, but from one second to another, he was no longer inside Amanda, and she was no longer under him.

He was now on his knees, and Amanda was on all fours facing away from him. He opened his eyes wide, to clear his head. Hot damn, the vodka had hit him harder than he'd anticipated. He had absolutely no recollection how or when they had changed positions. Her great-looking ass being offered to him was enough to sober him up momentarily. A seductive sight, an erotic gift, if there ever was one. She was just waiting there for him to enter her.

Yes, this he was definitely enjoying. At least his hard-on was still there. The booze didn't seem to have affected it. Thank God for that. At least for now.

He inched his way forward, feeling the world spinning. Holy shit, too much vodka. He shouldn't have had so much. Stupid, stupid move.

He used his knees and legs to separate Amanda's legs from behind, approaching her inviting lips with the tip of his cock.

Before he could make contact, Amanda surprised him, reaching back between her legs, grabbing his erection. Her hand was hot, and her touch was incredibly exciting.

Pierre expected her to guide him towards her vagina, but instead he felt himself being pushed a little higher. Amanda was directing his erection towards her ass.

Whoa! Drunk or not, he recognized what she had in mind. She wanted him inside her ass!

Yes!

The very thought elevated his arousal half a dozen clicks. That was going to be extraordinary. Ha! That was the understatement of the night.

Was the idea exciting!?

Did Pinocchio have a wooden dick?

He was ready to please her all night, no matter what her preferences were, and it seemed that what pleased her also turned him on. Going in her ass was unquestionably a good place to start. The thought that she was offering herself to him on all fours was major league anticipation. It was exciting enough to penetrate the fog in his brain caused by the vodka. He could feel an incredible sensation in his balls, a delicious ache in his groin, similar to the sensation he felt when approaching orgasm.

He felt himself making contact with her very sexy tight little ass. Amanda let go of his shaft, apparently satisfied that she had positioned him close enough and he could find his way home from there.

"Be gentle," she said.

She waited expectantly for Pierre to enter her.

No doubt in his mind what she wanted. *Oh, yeah!*

But wait! Pierre was inebriated but common sense still prevailed. He couldn't go inside her like this. She was dry.

He resisted the urge to just slam into her.

That wouldn't do it! And he had no Vaseline or any other sort of lubricant with him. He hesitated for a second wondering what he could use, trying to remember what he had in his shaving kit. Hair conditioner or shampoo perhaps? No, terrible idea. That would burn her.

Of course. The solution was so simple.

He lowered his head, placing his face between her cheeks. Her body felt hot and taunt as the cords in a violin. She was in such good shape. Extending his tongue, he immediately found her opening, teasing it, releasing saliva inside her. He applied as much saliva as possible around her tiny opening, then he put some on his hand, spreading it on the tip of his phallus. It may not be Vaseline, but it would make everything so much easier.

Amanda hadn't moved, she still waited patiently on all fours for Pierre to enter her.

Pierre straightened up on his knees again, inching forward, aiming his cock at her ass. He softly placed his left hand between her buttocks, finding her opening with his thumb, gently slipping it inside her puckered entrance, preparing her for bigger things to come. He finger-fucked her a few times, removing his thumb and using his hand to direct his cock towards her now wet opening. This was exciting beyond thoughts. Variety in sex was the name of the game in his mind, and Amanda was demonstrating a wonderful appetite for diversity.

He just *loved* that!

Pierre felt himself at the precise spot here he wanted to be, gently applying forward pressure with his pelvis. There was some initial resistance but with a little more pressure he immediately felt the tip of his shaft sliding inside Amanda with barely any friction.

He was inside her ass.

"Hmmmmm," she whimpered.

Yes!

Looking down at her was exciting beyond words. He very slowly moved his hips forward until his pelvis met with her buttocks. He could see he was not inside her to the hilt, some of his erection was still visible between her cheeks, not having gone inside her. But that was as far as he was gonna go. No way to penetrate her any deeper, her buttocks prevented it.

That was good enough though. He pulled back, feeling the heat inside her body on his cock, then pushed himself back inside her. Amanda pushed her ass back towards Pierre, attempting to synchronize their ballet.

He had absolutely no clue how long he fucked her like that. At one point, he came out of the fog, realizing he was making love to a muse, a woman who must be a product of his imagination, because no one could be as beautiful as Amanda. Could this be a *déjà vu?*

Looking down at his shaft sliding in and out of her ass made his head spin and question his reality.

How long had they been going on? And was this really happening?

He didn't know. The goddamned vodka had dulled his brain.

Realizing he was going to orgasm inside Amanda if he pumped inside her even one more time, he withdrew from her. He was just too hot. Pierre was not going to be able to control his body one more second if he kept looking at that delicious ass. Reaching down he pushed her hip sideways, making her lie down on her side.

Amanda didn't say a word.

Pierre got up, walking to the bathroom. He wanted to continue making love to her, but he had to wash first. He wasn't about to go inside her vagina just yet. He may be drunk, but he still knew enough to protect her.

Glancing back, he saw Amanda moving over to the other bed.

Pierre ran the water in the sink, not sure which faucet was hot and which was cold.

What did it matter.

He stuck his resilient erection under the flow of cold water.

Holy crap it was cold!

It didn't matter. Reaching for the little yellow hotel soap bar he washed himself, feeling the water changing from cold to warm to hot. He flipped the faucet to full cold. Scalding his precious jewels was definitely not on the menu. The ice-cold water felt good on his shaft.

He rinsed off the soap, reaching for a white towel hanging by the sink.

His hard-on was still there, still proudly at attention, having survived the washing. That was a joyous revelation and he felt enormous relief.

Pierre left the bathroom, finding Amanda laying crosswise on the other bed. She saw him coming, slowly separating her legs, reaching out with her arms.

Her body was hot and soft, despite the chill in the room from the air conditioner. Pierre gently lowered himself on top of her, keeping the bulk of his weight on his elbows and knees, feeling the erotic softness of her boobs against his chest. He inched his way up, until he felt the heat from her crotch against the tip of his shaft. Amanda was very wet, soaking, so he was able to slip right inside her with one slow, continuous push. No sound came from her. Amanda felt delicious. She was very hot around his cock. It must be a strange sensation for her, Pierre thought, feeling his ice-cold dick going in and out of her hot body.

"You are such a terrific lover," she said softly.

Pierre was delighted hearing that. What man wouldn't be? Whatever he was doing to her through the vodka fog obviously met with her approval. She must be drunk too, he mused.

"Be careful," Amanda whispered in his ear, as he gently went in and out of her. "I'm not on anything."

Pierre wasn't really sure what she meant, since his brain was not firing on all cylinders due to the booze. He kept fucking her with increasing energy. The effect of the vodka had not worn off at all, so he was having difficulties remaining clear-headed. She was delicious, a savory partner to say the least. What an incredible terrific woman she was.

Amanda reared and moaned under him.

It suddenly came to him. "Do you want me to get a condom?" He vaguely remembered he didn't have any with him. But he still had to ask. Worst case, they'd have to stop. If it came to that, he'd just go down on her.

"No. I'll be all right. Just be careful. I want you skin to skin. Keep going!" She ordered.

Pierre was very turned on, enjoying the delicious ache in his groin.

"Hold it!" She pushed him off using her hands on his chest.

Now what!?

He paused.

Amanda wiggled up, away from him, causing his cock to slip out of her. Had she changed her mind?

"You lay down," she sat up, getting on her knees.

Pierre had no idea what she had in mind, but whatever she wanted, he was game. His head was spinning so he was not sure he wanted to argue.

Amanda pushed him over on his back, with his head resting on the pillows.

"My turn," she announced.

Pierre watched her straddling him, his hands going to her thighs. Amanda reached below, guiding his shaft, placing it where she wanted it.

Pierre felt Amanda settling, transferring her weight from her knees to his lower body. He was inside her again. God, what a woman! Or what a girl, or whatever. He was drunk.

Amanda placed her hands on his chest, supporting herself while raising and lowering her hips, sending incredible electric sexual current from her body to his.

Her eyes remained in contact with his every second. She was carefully watching his reaction each time she moved up and down.

Pierre was ecstatic.

Amanda suddenly stopped their lovemaking. She just sat there on top of Pierre, with his cock deep inside her, appearing to savor the moment.

"No wife?" She asked, holding his ring finger between her index and thumb.

Pierre caught his breath. "No. no wife. How about you? Husband?"

Amanda shook her head. "Boyfriend."

"Where is he?" Pierre was both delighted and disturbed. Amanda obviously liked him enough to have sex with him, but she was taken. Dammit.

"At home," she said simply. "I haven't had a one night stand since I was in college."

A one-night stand? Aha! That's what he was? "Is that bad?"

"No," she began moving again. "It's not bad. You're actually pretty hot."

She didn't say anything else but started milking him again.

Pierre enjoyed the heavenly sensation of having Amanda ride him. She was passionate and beautiful and he loved having her legs spread to either side of his hips.

Was she as drunk as he was? She had to be. His head kept trying to spin off into some distant cliff. Pierre couldn't recall how many drinks he'd had. For that matter, he couldn't remember how many Amanda had either. Shit, he had no idea what city he was in either. Who cared, life was good.

Next thing he knew, Amanda was back underneath him, with Pierre furiously thrusting in and out of her. He shook his head. When in Batman's name had they switched? He had no recollection whatsoever. Amanda was holding on to him with great force, grinding her vagina against his crotch with a fury.

She was really turned on, writhing, moaning and rearing under him, her breath coming in gasps as she clutched him.

Pierre increased the speed of his thrusts, feeling his balls slamming against Amanda, while a wave of heat radiated from his crotch up to his chest. His abdomen tightened up like a washboard. His primeval instincts removed him from the driver's seat, taking full control of his body. He was coming. His pumping in and out of Amanda became an orgasmic, frantic reflex, programed by nature to continue pumping until every drop of his semen had been injected inside her precious opening. His breathing was frenzied and he realized he was squeezing Amanda's boobs during his orgasm, pinching her erect nipples. He opened his mouth wide, gasping for big gulps of air, his cock deep inside her.

It did not last too long, but it was powerful and it was exquisite and he was having a rough time coming down. Pierre took another deep breath, slowly regaining control of his body. His pumping slowed, then stopped.

Amanda didn't say a word. She was under him hanging on for dear life, her teeth clenched, drenched in sweat.

Pierre slowly shifted his position, working against the tight grip she had on his body. He managed to back away enough to slip out of her. It was her turn to have some pleasure. He had to provide it for her before she passed out from vodka and exhaustion.

He moved himself down to where he could reach her delicious center of pleasure, but his fogged in brain told him nothing was going to work. He licked Amanda a few times around her clit, without any visible results. She didn't make a sound, or react in any way to his touch.

Pierre made a conscious effort to lift his head. It weighed a million pounds and the goddamn room wouldn't stop spinning.

That's when he realized Amanda was out cold. She had passed out on her back with her head turned to one side. Her arms up above her head, resting on the pillow. The fatigue of the day, the explosiveness of their passion and the vodka had finally overwhelmed her.

Pierre shifted again, this time reaching up to kiss her. Her lips were hot, but he got no reaction from his kiss either.

The vodka had finally knocked her out, he concluded. He wrapped his arms around her soft hips, resting his head on her mound.

He passed out.

WHERE WAS HE? PIERRE opened his eyes, taking in the curtains, bright light entering the room around the edges. He was in a hotel room somewhere. Okay, that much was clear. Lifting his head felt like the most horrible of all migraines.

What the devil?

He remembered.

Amanda was next to him, on her stomach, hugging a pillow, only half covered by the sheet. She was out cold.

He had to find out what time it was. The clock on the night table said one-thirty. Man! He remembered crew call was at three. They had an hour and a half to be downstairs.

Amanda was breathing very tranquil. Her mouth-watering derriere inches from his face. Pierre touched her butt cheek, deriving enormous pleasure from the sensation. He placed his lips on the soft skin of her buttock, kissing it. Then he nibbled gently on it.

His head felt horrible and his mouth tasted like cotton. Ugh.

He ran his hand up inside Amanda's thigh, reaching the soft apex of her legs. Her lips felt soft and warm to his touch.

She stirred.

"Good morning Sleeping Beauty."

Amanda turned. "Good morning."

"You passed out on me."

"I did?"

"Yes. After a wonderful night making love."

She didn't respond. Instead, Amanda slowly got up, heading for the bathroom.

Pierre felt himself. He was hard as tropical wood again. No kidding? Aaah, his morning curse. Regardless of how satisfied he'd been just hours before, his manhood was ready for action again. He must be a genetically-altered specimen. Maybe they messed with his DNA at the hospital when he was born. Why else would he possess this indomitable sex drive?

Would Amanda be interested in some morning sex? First he'd better hit the bathroom and brush his teeth though. He couldn't remember every detail from last night, but the highlights were surfacing in his memory and they were delicious.

He heard the toilet flush and the sink water running.

What were the odds he was going to end up in bed with such an incredible woman? He shook his head, smiling. The planets must all be lined up, or his favorite Greek goddess must be smiling down on him from her advantage point on Mount Olympus, or something like that.

Maybe he shouldn't have read all that Greek mythology.

Amanda returned from the bathroom, climbing in bed next to him. Her disheveled brown hair gently caressing her sexy bare shoulders.

"You said you were going to be careful," she stated, accusingly. There was no doubt from her tone she was pissed.

Pierre was speechless. Oh, crap. He had some vague recollection she'd said something about him being careful, but he had no recall of what he'd replied. The reality of the moment hit him all at once. Amanda was pissed at him for coming inside her. Amanda's worried expression said it all.

Oh, God, he was hung-over, and now he'd blown it. Stupid. Stupid! He really didn't know what to say.

She left the bed again, leaving Pierre sitting there with his totally wasted hard-on.

He heard the shower running. Damn, what an idiot he was. He should've known better than drinking that vodka. He barely remembered coming inside her. That would've never happened if he'd been sober. No way was he going to go against Amanda's wishes if she was concerned about not wearing protection. He seemed to remember she'd said something about wanting him *au naturel.*

Now what? He liked her a lot, and he had to do everything within his power to fix this. Amanda did say she had a boyfriend. Man, that was going to make things complicated. What were the chances that she could've gotten pregnant with just one event—if that's what was on her mind? He had no idea. Naturally, wishful thinking put the odds at slim to none.

But reality told him otherwise. All it took was one time to get someone pregnant.

The shower stopped. They'd have to talk about this. Pierre was a lot of things, but a jerk he was not.

Amanda could depend on him for whatever the future held. He barely knew her, but he could sense she was a good person and was definitely interested in getting to know her better. He was raised to be a gentleman, and that included never leaving a damsel in distress. That probably rang corny as all hell, but he didn't care. If a woman liked him enough to share her body with him, he was not going to be a complete jerk and leave her on her own in the middle of a crisis.

He had created her distress and now he had to fix it. He'd no idea how he was going to fix it though.

Amanda walked out of the bathroom nude, with a towel on her head. Not a trace of modesty.

He loved it.

"I'm gonna go in my room to get ready."

Pierre struggled to find the right words, experiencing a sinking feeling in his stomach. "Wanna talk?"

"No, not now." She didn't smile. Barely looked at Pierre.

He watched her pick up her clothes, stepping into her pants. Next, the white T-shirt came on. She picked up her bra and shoes, bundling them against her chest.

Pierre saw her turn and head for the door, totally dumb founded. Amanda opened the room door, leaving without saying another word. She took the towel with her.

Holy shit.

Pierre was mortified. He'd needed to verbalize his thoughts with Amanda, but apparently, she was too distressed to talk. He'd have to connect with her later, when she was less stressed.

Uggh. Life sure had a way of switching from deliriously happy to fucked up beyond all recognition at the blink of an eye. He headed for the shower with a pained expression.

"ONE LEG TO ST. LOUIS and we're done!" Captain Hank Hilton announced.

"Yeah, then I have five days off."

"You lucky bastard, how'd you manage to do that?"

"I'm a careful bidder." Pierre had finished preparing the airplane for the one leg back to their base. He was going to be flying the airplane now, since Hilton had flown it into Denver.

Pierre was not happy. Amanda had not spoken to him at all after leaving his room. She'd intentionally avoided him in the lobby of the hotel and had kept herself withdrawn and private during the ride to the airport. She'd walked ahead of him with the other flight attendants without saying a word. Once they reached the airplane she'd gotten lost in the rear of the cabin almost immediately.

Not much of a chance to talk to her in private with the rest of the crew around either.

Shit, he didn't have her phone number or email. He would have to get that before he lost sight of her. It occurred to him he had no idea where she was based. Or even what her last name was!

How could he fumble the ball so badly? What in heaven's name was he thinking? He couldn't blame all that solely on the vodka either.

"Would you guys like some waters?" A female voice asked.

Pierre turned in his seat. One of their other flight attendants was standing there between their seats, holding four bottles of water. She was middle-aged and had a charming smile and gentle eyes.

Pierre liked her instantly.

"Yes, Please!" Captain Hank Hilton replied.

"That sounds wonderful! Thank you!" Pierre uttered, accepting two bottles from her. "What's your name?"

"I'm Hilda!"

"Nice meeting you, Hilda." He offered his hand, which she accepted.

"If you get a chance, would you mind terribly getting me a can of Coke? I'm addicted to the stuff."

"Glad to. I'll get it right now." She disappeared from the flight deck.

"I'm surprised you drink Coke," Hilton observed.

"Oh? Why wouldn't I drink Coke?"

Hilton hesitated. "Seems to me your generation of politically correct, social media addicts, only drinks bottled water. Oh, yeah, and seven-dollar designer coffees from Starbucks."

Pierre couldn't help smiling. "That's what you think, eh?"

"Don't get me started."

"Started with what?"

"Us older guys are not very impressed with most of you, young pukes."

Pierre laughed. "And why is that, if I may ask?"

"Not you, but most of the new younger pilots don't cut it in my book." Hilton glanced at Pierre's wrist. "Most of your generation wear digital watches, for Chrissake, they don't drink whisky and don't chase pussy. How can I trust men like that?"

Pierre looked at his analog Omega Flightmaster watch with pride. He'd bought the damned thing on eBay for almost $4,000. Just one of the few ridiculous luxuries he truly coveted in life. He raised his arm, displaying the watch to the Skipper.

"This one is analog. And I do drink whisky, although I prefer vodka."

Hank studied the Omega. "That's a nice watch. Haven't seen one of those in a long time."

"And I chase women whenever I get the chance," Pierre concluded.

"Hey, I did say not you, remember? No offense."

"None taken. However, word has it around the line that you older guys have to carry Viagra in your flight bag, in the extremely rare case you might get lucky."

Hilton laughed. "*Touché!*"

"Here you go," Hilda returned to the flight deck, holding out two cans of Coke.

Pierre accepted the cans, thanking her profusely. Going out in the cabin while they were in flight was a real pain in the ass for the pilots, so they tried to stock up on drinks right up front. Of course, so many drinks eventually mandated trips to the lav, which was another pain in the ass.

"Hilda, can I ask you another favor?"

The flight attendant squinted, puzzled. "Sure! What can I get you?"

"Could you get me the crew list with the names of all the flight attendants?"

Hilda paused, expecting Pierre to elaborate on why he needed the list. When no further explanation came, she agreed to go get it.

"Doing some hunting?" Hilton smirked.

"No, I just need some information." That was nondescript enough. In other words, none of your business, buddy. One thing Pierre treasured was his privacy. Particularly when it came to the women in his life.

Unlike most of the guys he flew with, he didn't feel the need to brag about his exploits. He saw women as private, delicate creatures, and when one opened up to him, he treasured the experience, not willing to share it with anyone else. He thought of women as flowers, beautiful and scented, giving joy to those around them. Even when a flower died, it could still be beautiful among the pages of one's diary, there forever to be enjoyed and remembered *privately*.

"Guess we're about ready." Hilton proclaimed. "How about we do the 'Before Start Checklist'?"

Pierre reached for the checklist.

Five minutes later, the flight deck was ready. All they needed now was word from the flight attendants that all passengers were onboard, seated and their possessions stowed.

Hilda appeared again. She gave Pierre a printout of the crew list. "There you go," she offered. "Anything else I can get you?"

Pierre studied the printout. It was a list of the flight attendants on his flight. Only last names were visible. There was only one name with the first name initial 'A.' Her employee number was listed as well. And her last name was Mullins.

Great!

He would most likely be able to locate Amanda through the company crew computer with this information.

"No, thanks, Hilda. You are wonderful, thanks for your help."

"They're all seated and the bags are stowed. Okay to close the cabin door?"

Hank Hilton nodded. "Go ahead and close up."

Hilda left the front office, closing the door behind her.

Pierre felt a little better having the information. Amanda was obviously rather upset about their episode last night, and must have decided not to speak with him at all. He wanted to make things right with her, and certainly, his responsibility as a man was to follow up with her in case she did get pregnant.

No doubt in his mind that concern was the reason behind her behavior in the room when she left. What were the odds? Maybe not very high, but nonetheless, it was his job to calm her. Good God, he had to be more careful. Last thing he wanted was traumatize Amanda over one night of wild passion. Pierre had a good friend, one of the managers for Crew

Scheduling. She would provide him with Amanda's cell phone number.

Then what? Should he text Amanda? No, way too impersonal. The other two options were calling her or investigating where she lived and paying her a visit. Calling her might not work, too easy to just not pick-up the call from an unknown number. If he left a voicemail, Amanda could decide not to respond. Yea, much better do it in person. She said she was from Tucson. He could show up at her place but that might freak her out. And wait! She did say she had a boyfriend!

Ugh, things were getting complicated.

With Amanda having a boyfriend, that changed the playing field. Pierre considered that maybe the best idea, given the circumstances, would be to get a very nice card at a gift shop. He would put his feelings in writing and let Amanda know that he was willing to meet with her, talk with her and do whatever it took to ease her mind. Up to marrying her? That was a good question. Would he be willing to do that over a night of passion?

Maybe. He'd have to give that one some more thought. He just was not going to let her deal with the situation alone. If she wanted his emotional and financial support, he would be there for her. Now the trick was going to be how to put that in writing without offending her.

He could either mail the card to her home address or drop it in her employee mailbox at work. No, home address was a bad idea. What if the boyfriend intercepted it? He'd no idea if they lived together, but he wasn't about to risk getting her in trouble. He'd better use company mail. He'd find out where Amanda was based, then he'd jumpseat there and drop off the card in her mailbox. Argh, that could easily take him two days traveling, depending on where she was based.

Indeed, if Amanda decided to just talk to him once they arrived in St. Louis, that would make things so much easier. He had no idea what her schedule was. She and the other flight attendants could very well go on to another destination after St. Louis.

Pierre sighed. Why did he have such a tendency for getting himself into complicated situations? He was like a human magnet for trouble.

Amanda was a lovely woman, he found her quite attractive indeed, and their steamy episode had made her all the more interesting, but for Christ's sake, they'd had all of one 'date,' and she was already generating all sorts of drama. If she really didn't want to talk with him, Pierre could very easily just get lost and forget about the entire episode.

Tempting as that may be, disappearing was not the decent thing to do. He needed to talk to her. He'd do whatever she wanted, but they had to talk. Getting lost was what cowards did.

And Pierre was no coward.

Book Three

Jessica

Pierre was irrationally happy. He was finally in his dream job, flying the airplane he'd always desired and now—at last—based out Los Angeles. The commute from Phoenix to Los Angeles was a piece of cake, with tons of flights between the two cities at all hours of the day. His new home in Arizona was wonderful. He had all he needed there.

He went to work four times a month, flying long international flights. Each time he went to work his trip was three days long. That took a total of twelve days from his month, leaving him with eighteen days off to do as he pleased.

If he just had a steady girlfriend, he'd be the happiest guy in the world, but oh, well. He already had more than most men ever dreamed of having, so he'd just have to be patient and keep searching for that special girl to fulfill all his dreams. Or at least some of them. He never imagined finding the perfect soul mate would be such a challenge.

He took a moment to admire his office, the electronic flight deck of the Airbus A350-200, one of the most advanced airplanes crossing the skies. Who else could claim to have such high-tech surroundings? He often felt he was living in the middle of a science fiction movie.

They were descending into the London area, with their 253 passengers after their nearly eleven-hour flight from LAX. Pierre was alert and charged with adrenaline. He'd had a three-hour rest in the Crew Rest Facility already, followed by four cups of black coffee. He'd never been a night person, and these all-nighter flights to Europe were somewhat of a ball-busting challenge for him.

Didn't matter. The rest period and the coffee had brought him back to life enough to do his job.

"It sure's a beautiful day out here today," Captain Sam Pedigo remarked, admiring the blue skies with scattered clouds.

Pierre liked Sam Pedigo. The captain flying with him was the quiet type, which Pierre preferred. Nothing worse—far as he was concerned—than being stuck in a flight deck three feet from a Chatty Kathy for eleven hours.

Ugh, that was horrible. The only comparison he could come up with was Chinese water torture, or Guantanamo torture, or whatever.

Sam had flown for the Navy, was a proficient aviator and was nicely educated, so their conversations—the few they had between them on the long flight—were mostly interesting.

"Sure is beautiful. Not very often do they see such clear weather around these parts," Pierre agreed. He'd been flying the London route six months now, and only twice before he'd arrived to find clear weather over the elegant capital of the United Kingdom.

On these transoceanic flights, they carried a third pilot in the flight deck. In aviation vernacular, the official title for this third crewmember was 'International Relief Officer,' or IRO. The airline assigned this third pilot on long flights over eight hours in length. Having a third crew member assigned to a flight made life significantly easier for the other two pilots. Once the airplane reached its cruising altitude, the pilots took turns having breaks. The airline provided a crew rest area for the pilots just behind the flight deck in these new airplanes, complete with two bunks, a sink with running water, and darkening curtains. There was also a second—if larger—crew rest area for flight attendants in the back of the airplane, above the galley area. The crews jokingly referred to that crew rest area as 'The Love Boat.' The innuendo being that extra-curricular activities actually took place there between crew members.

Pierre knew this was hogwash. He'd flown with hundreds of flight attendants, and none had ever shared with him having had sex in the crew rest areas. Hollywood was very fond of pushing the 'Mile-High' club concept, suggesting everyone was having sex in the airlines and that anyone having sex in an airliner became a member of that club. That was a truly ridiculous concept.

Pierre smiled.

Given the miniature size of airline seats being used in commercial aviation today, and the horribly high load factors every airline was enjoying, it was basically impossible considering having sex in the cabin of any airliner. Perhaps one could sneak a quickie flying First Class on some long-distance night flight, but even that was highly dubious.

The very concept was a joke. Having sex? Really? What a laugh! When distances between seats—called 'pitch' in airline lingo—were so tight one could not open one's laptop on the seat tray, and the bald spot of the passenger sitting in front was smack under one's nose, there was really no room to engage in complex sexual gymnastics. It was really sad realizing how bad service had deteriorated in the airlines. The seats kept getting smaller all the time, and the pitch kept being reduced to the absolute minimum. In pre-deregulation days, there was enough space between rows of seats for a passenger to be able to walk out of his seat and go use the lav without having to disturb the other two passengers sitting on the same row.

Today, in the sickening airline environment predominant all over the world, the center and aisle passengers had to step out in the aisle to permit the window passenger to exit on his way to the blue room. There just wasn't enough room for two pairs of legs to fit between the seats.

This was no way to treat people. Pierre strongly felt that the government would ultimately have to intervene, forcing the airlines to change their ways by establishing a minimum seat size and pitch.

Naturally, that would reduce their profits because seats would have to be removed from the cabin, so the airlines would most certainly fight like cornered rats.

Another Hollywood favorite, two passengers having sex in the bathroom—the lav, as the crews called it. With the current paranoia about terrorism, a horny couple locking themselves in the bathroom would risk the wrath of God in exchange for two minutes of pleasure. Fearful passengers would report them to the flight attendants as suspected terrorists assembling a bomb in there. The flight attendants would notify the pilots, who would declare an emergency and land at the nearest airport, where the FBI would drag the horny couple to the nearest police station for interrogation.

Pierre had yet to see a couple go in one of those miniature bathrooms and have sex.

"How about the Descent and Approach checklist?" Captain Sam Pedigo requested. The man would be handling the landing, since they were on the first leg of their three-day trip.

Pierre reached for the checklist, reading it out loud, listening for the appropriate responses from his Skipper.

ONE HOUR LATER, THE fifteen crewmembers found themselves in a private Greyhound-style Scenicruiser bus stuck in London morning traffic. They had managed to land in Heathrow within minutes of their scheduled arrival, so now the entire crew had over thirty hours in London before their return flight to Los Angeles.

Thirty hours to do as they pleased. These were the thirty hours the flight attendants lived for. This was the honey and wine part of their jobs. Free time in London with free hotel and money to buy meals and play.

Not too many people in the world ever enjoyed such an opportunity even once in their lifetimes, let alone four times a month.

Pierre hadn't had much of a chance to check out his flight attendants before they took off out of LAX, because when he arrived onboard he'd immediately busied himself with the preparations for the polar flight. He'd gone back to the First Class cabin twice during the flight to help himself to some water bottles. That had also been the opportunity to check out the flight attendants working First Class.

He'd been sadly disappointed.

Again.

Pierre was starting to realize these transoceanic flights didn't have too much to offer him in the way of opportunities with women, something he craved above all else. These flights laid over in some of the most exciting cities on the planet, and allowed the cabin crews and the pilots to rake up lots of flight pay with just a couple of legs.

Unfortunately, these advantages made the trips highly desirable, which meant only the most senior flight attendants and pilots could hold them.

To Pierre, the significance of all this translated into the simple reality that most of the flight attendants working these flights were old enough to be his mother—or grandmother. He liked those gals, they were generally very sweet to him, and he admired their determination, working with the traveling public all those years. But he just wasn't interested in any sort of romantic interlude with them, preferring women closer to his own age, or younger. He was always on the lookout for potential play partners during the London layovers, but so far he was batting zero. He, of course, didn't expect to end up in bed with every attractive woman he met, just having someone to wine and dine and laugh with was rewarding enough, but these past six months he hadn't had much luck.

Much luck? Shit, he hadn't had *any* luck.

An awful dry spell.

Also, often enough on these London flights, many of the flight attendants were male, which stacked the odds against him even further.

So, why did he insist on flying these trips? Good question. He'd been asking himself that for a couple of months now. He'd tried a couple of trips to South America with the same results. Very senior crews and no opportunities to meet desirable girls.

Next month he was going to bid trips to Copenhagen and Amsterdam. He found the women in those countries particularly attractive, so he was planning on a shift of strategy. Enough trying to connect with non-existent flight attendants. He'd try connecting with Scandinavian girls at clubs instead. That might provide him with better results. One of the

International Relief Officers flying with him had suggested that alternative.

The only times he'd even seen young flight attendants working his international flights was when they were called out of reserve. When one of the scheduled cabin crew called in sick, Crew Scheduling would use one of their reserves. Unfortunately, these younger women nearly always worked the Coach section, so Pierre seldom got to see them, much less meet them. Most of these reserves were new-hires, still on probation, and they were very intimidated by the senior flight attendants working the flights, so the brand-new recruits did their best to blend in with the landscape, and Pierre rarely had access to them.

Once they reached their layover hotel as a crew, it was practically impossible to connect with one of these reserves because they would simply disappear.

Pierre had eventually realized that if he wanted to meet all kinds of flight attendants closer to his age, all he had to do was switch back to the little Bus, the A321, and fly mostly domestic legs. New hire flight attendants were going to be flying the least desirable airplanes and routes. He realized now that was the case, but he wasn't quite convinced going back to domestic flying was the way to go. He liked the big airplane he was on, the pay that went with it, the layovers in exciting cities and he particularly enjoyed flying long legs. Going up and down several times a day was not for him. Let the Southwest boys do that, since their business model revolved around flying multiple legs in one day.

Meeting young, available, good-looking flight attendants was becoming a challenge, but so what. He was perfectly capable of meeting young women elsewhere. He just hadn't pursued other alternatives just yet. He had an insane sex drive, loved women, and felt he had to always be on the lookout for a partner or life would pass him by. Kind of like a shark, if he didn't keep swimming, he'd drown.

Extricating himself out of the somber mood, he started thinking of his plans for the day. First thing, he was gonna take a three-hour nap. That was mandatory.

These trips were a bitch. His flights would generally put him in Europe early in the morning, but for him it was midnight in Phoenix. If he went to bed for eight hours after landing in Europe, he'd totally screw himself up for the following day, when they had to work the return flight to Los Angeles. He had to take that three-hour nap, then force himself to get out of bed and spend the rest of the afternoon and evening on the same schedule as the Londoners. At the end of the day, he would go hit the sack at the same time as the rest of the Brits.

Then, and only then, would Pierre allow himself to sleep for eight hours.

Okay, so what did he want to do after his nap? A visit to Harrods, the legendary department store was in order. Pierre had an eye out for the Indian mahogany screens they sold. He'd been meaning to buy one of those the last couple of trips, so he might just do that. He'd have it shipped back to the States, since he couldn't very well take it on the airplane with him.

Harrods was very accommodating providing shipping assistance to its customers. There were also many restaurants in that store, so he'd have fun finding one for an early dinner.

He noticed the crew bus had reached Buckingham Gate, the street where their hotel was located. The bus had seating capacity for sixty passengers, but only the fifteen crew members occupied it. Pierre had ample time to study the members of his cabin crew during their trip from the airport. He intentionally sat all the way towards the back of the bus so he could have a good view of the flight attendants. Unfortunately, on this flight none of his cabin crew met his requirements for dating. The crew of ten flight attendants was composed of three males and seven females. The women all appeared to be in their late forties, if he was any judge of age. None of them interested him as potential layover play partners.

So, no cigar for you today, *Don Juan Pierre*, scourge of non-existing young flight attendants.

That was really no surprise there. The last ten trips he hadn't met one single woman sparking his interest with the exception of the one flight where he thought he'd linked with a new-hire flight attendant on this same London layover. He apparently overestimated just how attracted she was to him. She talked to him all the way into the city, flirting and coming on like the proverbial sex kitten, only to perform an impressive disappearing act during their thirty hours in London. Pierre understood. He wasn't her type. Some things in life were pretty black and white.

He could accept that.

No hard feelings. That happened. But he was still a little hurt and disappointed he hadn't been able to at least interest her in some fine dining experience at one of the lovely restaurants in the city.

She must've thought he was only interested in bedding her. Well, too bad if she thought so and probably that was the reason why she got lost. Pierre would've been thrilled to just enjoy her company and give her a good time, sex or no sex.

The bus stopped in front of the St. James Court, an exclusive luxury hotel a couple of blocks from Buckingham Palace.

The crew exited the bus, patiently waiting for their bags on the sidewalk.

Pierre thought the bus driver was probably from Bangladesh or India, judging from his looks and his outfit. A real smiler. The guy emanated positive energy, opening the side cargo doors below the windows of the bus, he handed out the bags to the crew. Pierre reached for his wallet, pulling out a ten-dollar bill. This guy deserved it, if nothing else, for his incredible smiling *persona*.

He held back until the last of his crew had started for the lobby, before placing the ten in the hand of the driver. He didn't wish to appear like a braggart with the rest of his crew, tipping five times the going rates. "Thanks, buddy."

"My pleasure, sir!" The smile got bigger.

Pierre suddenly felt very lucky, walking into the elegant lobby of the hotel in his dark navy blue airline pilot uniform, feeling proud of who and what he was. He was looking forward to thirty hours in that magnificent capital. He issued a silent *'Thank You'* to *The Force,* or the gods, or whomever had seen fit to bless him with his existence. He could've just as easily been born somewhere else and be the driver of that crew bus.

The lobby was long and elegant, which he greatly appreciated. Pierre truly enjoyed staying there. Fine marble and dark woods and all the elegance of the old British Empire.

He so approved.

The rest of the crew ahead were rapidly dissipating, headed for their rooms. Pierre received a warm 'Good morning, sir,' from the Englishman behind the front desk. He gave the man a VISA card to keep on file for incidentals, accepting it back after it had been scanned.

After receiving the room key from the hotel employee, he made his way to the elevators. His entire crew had disappeared already. Hot damn, they sure went in a hurry.

Pierre rode the elevator up to the fourth floor, enjoying the feel of the deep carpeting and the soft classical music being piped through hidden speakers. The elevator was small—barely one third the size of American hotel lifts. All dark wood and mirrors.

His room had a single queen sized bed exquisitely adorned with four huge white pillows and two smaller baby-blue pillows matching the duvet, which was white with delicate blue patterns. The carpet was patterned white Berber and two wall lamps illuminated the room, one on each side of the bed.

Pierre lifted his bag, plopping it on the bed. The effect of the four cups of coffee was starting to wear out and he felt the exhaustion of two in the morning Phoenix time. He may be in London, but his body didn't know that. His body was on Phoenix time and it was begging him for eight hours of sleep. He stripped down to his boxers, hanging his uniform pants and jacket in the closet. After relieving himself of all the coffee, washing his face and brushing his teeth Pierre pulled down the blue covers, crawling into bed. In a way, he was kinda glad he didn't have a girl in bed with him. He was just so friggin tired.

His last conscious act before passing out was setting two alarms in his smartphone, intended to wake him up in precisely three hours.

THE ABSOLUTELY ANNOYING ALARM chime from his smartphone finally registered in his subconscious, bringing him out of REM sleep. He hated that sound, why was it still going off?

Pierre woke up rapidly, reaching for his cell phone. He had to shut the goddamn thing off.

His hand reaching for the buzzing smartphone smacked the device off the wooden night table, sending it flying somewhere nearby, still buzzing.

Oh, shit.

Pierre threw off the covers, rolling out of bed, still only partially conscious. The stupid phone was still blaring, two feet away. He reached for it, strongly tempted to impale the offending cell phone against the corner of the night table. He just hated the thing.

No, good as it would feel destroying the cell phone, he really didn't want to spend half a day in London searching for a replacement. He controlled his anger, finally silencing the damned thing. Pierre sat back on the edge of the bed.

Oh, man, crazy Matilda, he felt like crap.

Taking a deep breath and exhaling loudly helped a little. His head was exploding, his body screaming for more sleep. This was no news to him. It was a foregone conclusion. Every trip was the same, he'd wake up after three hours feeling like a rabbit ran over by a semi-truck on some lonely highway in Texas.

He just had to overcome the perfectly justifiable desire to crawl back under the covers and die. These were the toughest ten minutes of his trip.

Shaking his head and feeling nauseous, he forced himself to get up and go splash water on his face. He then ran the shower, removing his shorts standing there naked in front of the mirror. He was in great shape, no question about that. Strong shoulders, narrow hips and powerful arms. He had hair in all the right spots. Pierre was aware the females of his generation much preferred shaved Chihuahuas to hairy apes, but there wasn't much he could do about that. He was not Scandinavian, he was Basque, and he had hairy arms, legs and chest. Not too much, but enough. Some of his contemporaries shaved everywhere, something which Pierre was not about to do.

Too much flippin' maintenance. He figured girls would just have to like him as he was.

Girls? What girls? There were no girls in his life.

Steam filled the bathroom fogging the mirror. Pierre pulled the curtain aside, stepping under the hot shower.

THE PILOT EXITED THE elevator, feeling partially alive again. The shower had washed away the sleep and invigorated him. He hadn't shaved again, so he sported a very interesting five o'clock shadow. Or was it an eight o'clock shadow? Or a ten o'clock shadow? Aah, to hell with it. He had no idea. Too many time zones to figure that one out. He just didn't feel like shaving, period.

He counterbalanced the unshaven look by wearing an elegant dark blue blazer over an open-collar starched white dress shirt. This was London after all, so he gave up the comfort of jeans for a pair of grey slacks and swapped his comfortable Adidas for a pair of black Bally Wabler leather loafers.

His outfit promoted self-confidence, making him feel good. He'd towel-dried his hair after washing it twice with his Aloe shampoo.

The hotel lobby was not crowded for three o'clock in the afternoon.

Pierre saw her at once.

A young woman standing at the reception desk talking to the concierge.

He slowed down his pace, studying her looks.

She was *hot!*

Blond hair, cream-colored pants, white blouse, what looked like a cashmere tan sweater casually thrown over her shoulders. Nice posture. And from the side she appeared to be somewhere between an orchid and a 'dream.' He still couldn't see her face very clearly. Her golden hair prevented a clear look.

Pierre was instantly interested. Was she a flight attendant? Certainly, not one of his crew. Were other crews staying in the hotel? Of his own airline or others? He had no idea. All he knew is she was incredibly attractive and he had to find some way to connect with her. Quick, what could he do? He couldn't just walk up to her and say 'hello,' could he?

No, that would be stupid and lame. Also, she could be European and not speak English. Language could be a definite obstacle.

Well, whatever he was going to do, it had to happen within the next few seconds. He couldn't just stand there gawking at her and if he continued walking, no matter how slow, in a couple of more seconds he'd be past her.

Without further thought he walked up to the registration desk, standing three feet from the gorgeous woman, pretending to be waiting for the concierge to finish with her.

She noticed him briefly before continuing her conversation with the hotel man.

Yes! She was speaking in English.

Argh, he had but a couple of seconds in which to think of something to say to her. She would be done with the concierge any second now, and then he had to get her attention. Standing this close to her he noticed she wasn't as tall as he was. Perhaps two inches shorter.

He heard her mention 'Harrods.'

Bingo!

Pierre cleared his mind, straining to hear what she was saying to the concierge. It appeared she was trying to get directions to Harrods!

The Brit behind the desk was trying to convince her to catch a cab but she was not biting.

He gathered all his courage, interrupting their conversation.

'Excuse me, you going to Harrods?"

The woman turned to look at him. She was so damned good looking! Pierre was thrilled at how beautiful she was. Looking at her face-to-face took his breath away.

"Yes, I'm trying to get some directions here but I don't seem to be getting anywhere."

She sounded exasperated, but her radiant smile contradicted her tone.

"I'm going there right now. I'll be glad to show you the way if you want."

Pierre estimated her in her late twenties, maybe. Light blue eyes and a fine nose, *a la* Candice Bergen. And she had two dimples on the sides of her mouth that made her irresistible.

"You would?"

Her smile was adorable. He sucked in a quick breath.

"Be glad to. Were you asking him for a map?"

The Brit behind the registration desk remained silent. Exquisite British etiquette prevented him from participating in a conversation between guests.

"No, I was just trying to get directions, that's all. He's suggesting I take a taxi, but it's such a beautiful afternoon I'd much rather walk."

Pierre was enchanted with the melodic sound of her voice, soft and yet clear. "You American?"

"Can you tell?"

That smile again.

Pierre corresponded with a friendly smile. "Yeah."

The young woman nodded. "California."

"I'm from Phoenix," he extended his hand. "I'm Pierre."

She hesitated briefly, accepting his handshake. "I'm Jessica."

Her handshake was firm, her hand cold.

Pierre nodded at the concierge. The man didn't flinch.

"Want to head in that direction now?"

"Sure!"

Pierre decided to ignore the concierge, pointing towards the street. They walked away from the front counter, pausing at the main door of the hotel, allowing Jessica to pass first. He then led the way along the sidewalk.

"That guy was determined not to give you directions, wasn't he?" He positioned himself, walking on the street side of the sidewalk, the way he'd been taught as a young man, always protecting the lady.

"No," her blue eyes flashed with humor. "But he was determined I was going to ride a taxi to Harrods," she laughed, smiling a perfect smile, those dimples driving him crazy.

"English bulldog stubbornness, eh?"

"I suppose."

"What're you doing in London? Vacation?" He would've liked having a couple of minutes just to look at her. She was very attractive, but he had to settle for quick furtive side glances as they walked side by side. She had bright yellow blond hair, flowing long enough to reach just below her collar, and he could sense an exotic smell, some delicate perfume. He imagined himself feeling her hair against his face.

A 'dream.' Definitely a dream.

Pierre couldn't believe his luck. For months, he hadn't been able to connect with anyone even partially interesting, and now here he was, walking the streets of London with what appeared to be the perfect dream girl, an apparition. He was praying he'd be able to keep her interested in him.

"Vacation? No, I'm not on vacation. I'm working."

Working? At what? She was an incredibly pretty woman, Pierre decided not to venture a guess what her job was. "What do you do?"

"I'm a flight attendant," she offered.

No way!

His eyes got bigger. "Really? For which airline?"

Jessica turned to look at his eyes. "I'm not with the airlines. I'm a corporate flight attendant. I fly in a private jet."

Pierre was dumbfounded, that wouldn't have occurred to him in a million years. A corporate jet? Holy tamales! "Really?"

"Yes, a Gulfstream 650."

Pierre was duly impressed. Unlike other airline pilots, he kept up with the latest corporate jets, and the Gulfstream 650 Jessica just mentioned was by far the latest and the hottest business jet in the world. That airplane could fly just about anywhere, it had such range. And if he remembered correctly, its price tag was in the neighborhood of 65 million dollars.

"Who do you fly for?"

"Capital Corporation, out of Carmel."

He'd never heard of it. "No kidding! That's one impressive airplane." Whoever Capital Corporation was, they had money. And lots of it.

They came to a crosswalk. "Hang on for a second," he gently held on to her arm for an instant, making sure she had stopped.

Jessica gave him a puzzled look.

"While you're here in London make absolutely sure you look at *both* sides of the street before crossing. They drive on the opposite side here, and at home you're used to checking out your left first, but here that doesn't work. If you look to the left first, you'll step right in front of a car or a bus coming from your right."

"Oh?"

From her look, Pierre suspected Jessica had not thought of that yet. "By looking at both sides, you're just making sure you cover all the bets."

"That makes a lot of sense." She deliberately looked to both sides.

They crossed the road, still walking side by side. Pierre wondered briefly what her hand would feel like if he held it.

Much as he was dying to touch her, no way in hell he was going to risk it at this point. That could really freak her out.

"So you flew out here from California?" He asked.

"Yes—no, we stopped in DC before flying out here."

"When did you get to London?"

"Just this morning."

Pierre knew the shortest way to Harrods, but he decided to take the longer path so they could stroll in front of Buckingham Palace. It was indeed a beautiful day, with the temperature around sixty degrees. He couldn't ask for better.

Love was in the air.

"Have you slept at all?" Jessica appeared bright eyed and bushy-tailed, surprisingly so for having flown all night.

"Yes, I took a couple of hour nap."

He searched for her eyes.

Pierre didn't detect any red in the Persian blue of her eyes. Visine?

"You did get two hours between the sheets? That was smart,"

Jessica laughed. "The pilots I'm flying with told me to do that. I was just going to hibernate in my bed until tomorrow, but they advised against it."

"They were so right. If you'd stayed in bed all day, you'd be up all night tonight. And tomorrow you wouldn't be worth a nickel."

"It was hard, getting out of bed after just two hours of sleep," she laughed. "It was *really* hard, almost painful."

"I know, I did the same thing."

Jessica stared. "You did? Why? What do you do?"

"I'm a pilot with Worldwide Airlines. Just got here this morning myself."

Jessica gave him a long stare, sizing him up and down. "A pilot? Whoa, that is so coincidental."

"You're staying at the St. James with your crew?" Pierre asked.

"Yes, we're all staying at the same place. Mr. Kaufman, our boss is staying there as well. He likes having his pilots close at hand."

Pierre was amazed at his good luck. A flight attendant! That meant she was free to do as she pleased while in London! What an incredible piece of Karma. Jessica was very pretty, no—striking, and she appeared quite intelligent. In all honesty, she looked more like a model. He would like nothing better than to have her for a companion during the entire layover. What more could he ask for? His imagination had already jumped ahead to the potential magic the night could offer him with this gorgeous woman.

Don't do that, dammit! Enjoy the moment! What's the matter with you!? Remember, you're just a normal man, you're not Don Juan Tenorio, women are not going to just melt at your feet, you dumbass.

"How long you gonna be here?" They were approaching the front gates of The Palace.

Jessica took in the view of The Palace; it was truly magnificent. The English were endowed with an incredible ability to make everything look elegant.

Jessica changed direction, heading for the fence. "We're here for two days. I've never been here before, is this the palace?" She appeared in total awe.

Pierre followed her towards the black fence surrounding Buckingham Palace.

"Yes, this is it. Magnificent, eh?"

"It sure is," she agreed.

Pierre smiled, enjoying her look of amazement. That was always the reaction the first time anyone admired the Palace on their initial visit. And justifiably so, the place was splendid, fit for kings. Literally.

"Is The Queen in there?" she asked.

Pierre was impressed with Jessica. She looked so much like a little girl standing there, admiring one of the most engaging sights in the world.

"I don't know if she's in there right now, but if I understand correctly, that's where she lives."

"Wow, this is awesome."

They walked slowly across the front of the Palace, admiring the meticulous grounds and the Guards of the Household Regiment standing at attention like wax statues.

"I've seen this on TV, but it's so much more impressive in person."

"It is one of the most magnificent representations of the British Empire."

"Impressive. How far is Harrods from here?"

"A little less than half a mile."

"I'm starved; you think there may be a place to get something to eat there?"

Pierre felt his stomach grumble at that exact moment. "Oh, yes, they have lots of places to eat. We'll find one that suits you. What were you planning on doing at Harrods? Just browse?"

"No, I'm looking for a bathing suit. I saw one online and if they have it in my size, I intend to buy it. I also wanted to see the store. It's quite famous."

"Bikini?" He regretted the instant the words came out of his mouth. That was a little too personal.

"No, a one-piece. Haven't worn bikinis for quite some time."

He bit his tongue not to ask her 'why?' He couldn't imagine any possible reason why she couldn't wear a bikini, since with her body she could easily be a model. "It's a nice store to go visit, but—are you aware of their prices?"

"Yeah. They are pricey."

Pricey? Bunch of fucking thieves, is what Pierre really thought.

"Just to give you an idea, a formal shirt can sell for about five hundred dollars."

She glanced at him. "A what?"

"A man's dress shirt."

"For real?"

"Yes," he nodded, gravely. "Same shirt with better cotton in Hong Kong will go for about forty bucks. Custom-made."

Jessica didn't give any indication she was impressed by his comparison. Pierre could only begin to imagine the price tag on the flippin' bathing suit.

"What airplane do you fly?" Jessica asked, abruptly changing the subject.

He wondered how educated she was on commercial aviation. "The Airbus A350."

"Wow," was all she said.

He still wasn't sure Jessica knew what airplane that was.

Pierre had already checked out her ring finger. Nothing there. Naturally, he could just ask her if she was married, engaged or had a boyfriend, but he got somewhat of a kick acting a little like James Bond, having obtained some information about this very desirable woman without her knowledge. And why not? Quite fitting, actually, being in London, home of 007.

"You fly to London much?"

"Yea, this month about once a week."

"That's a lot!" She stated. "You said you're from Phoenix. Are you based there?"

"No, I'm based in Los Angeles. I fly out of LAX."

"How long you've been with Worldwide?"

"I'm on my third year."

"And you're already flying international?"

Pierre wondered how she knew anything about the requirements airlines had for flying international routes. "Yeah. We're hiring about seven hundred new pilots each year and that translates to me being able to fly international. You could say I lucked out."

"So now you have enough seniority to fly the big jet."

"That's correct. You seem to know a lot about the airlines."

Jessica smiled. "I dated an airline pilot once. He taught me a lot."

Pierre wondered what else the pilot dude had taught her.

He estimated she was in her late twenties. And the more he saw of her the more gorgeous she became. While waiting to cross a street, he had a brief glimpse of her rear end. She was built for pleasure, no doubt about it. The cream pants outlined her ass just magically. The fabric of her pants caressing that magnificent body very seductively.

Pierre was unquestionably attracted to her, physically and mentally. He liked her spontaneity and he liked her body. What a combination. What a stroke of luck. If he'd taken five minutes longer to appear in the lobby, he would've missed her.

"You married? Boyfriend?" He felt obliged to ask. Of course, he already knew she wasn't married, but he had to ask.

"No, not married. I once was."

He waited for her to continue. She didn't.

"No boyfriend either?"

She gave him an enigmatic look. "Not at the moment."

Halleluiah! That was music to his ears. Yes! Let the angels play their celestial trumpets!

Time to change the topic, things were getting sticky. "How many flight attendants on your crew?"

"Just me. We only operate with one flight attendant."

Pierre had flown a corporate jet prior to getting on with the airlines, but he'd never carried a flight attendant. The little Sabreliner he'd flown didn't have very long range, like the airplane Jessica was flying.

"So it's just you and the two pilots at the hotel?"

"Yes, and our boss."

"How come the other two guys didn't come out with you?"

"I prefer to explore on my own."

"So you're saying I blew that one for you, eh?"

Jessica smiled. "No, you didn't. it's nice meeting someone new. I spend way too much time with those two guys already."

"Are they married?"

"Oh, sure, they're both married. Sometimes their wives come with us on some of the trips."

Pierre had marveled about her pilots. How could they let a fairy-tale girl like this slip out of their hands? Being married explained it. Maybe.

"Are *you* married?" Jessica asked.

Pierre didn't wear a wedding band, and Jessica appeared too smart to have missed that. He chuckled. Was she giving him a taste of his own chocolate?

"Not at the moment." He was going to add 'no girlfriend either,' but decided against it.

She laughed. "Do you have a girlfriend?"

It was his turn to laugh. "No. I don't have a steady girlfriend, not at the moment."

"You're not married and you don't have a girlfriend?"

She appeared pensive.

Pierre laughed, remembering what Kirsten had once said to him over a Margarita cocktail.

"And no, I'm not gay either."

Jessica appeared surprised by his statement. She laughed, "why would you say that?"

"Just to make things clear."

"I wasn't thinking you were gay."

"For the record, I like women."

"How old are you, Pierre?" She obviously had no problem getting personal.

Pierre liked her. She more and more seemed to be that rare combination of looks and brains. "I'm thirty-three."

"You said you've never been married?"

They were on Brompton Road approaching Harrods.

"Nope. Never been married. Close a couple of times, but didn't go through with it. It's just a little hard for me becoming involved with women in a serious relationship. Most women back home in Phoenix working professional nine-to-five jobs are leery of getting involved with me because of my work schedules. Quite often I fly on weekends, which is when they have days off, and then I have multiple days off when I'm not flying smack in the middle of the week, when they're busy with their careers."

Jessica nodded in understanding. "I can see that."

They came to a stop in front of a majestic building.

"This is Harrods?" She directed her attention to the impressive six-story building with multiple display windows and green awnings.

"This is it!" Pierre realized he was really hungry. Last time he'd had anything to eat was when they had reached cruising altitude about an hour after departing from Los Angeles, two lifetimes ago. No wonder he was famished.

Jessica gawked at the largest luxury department store in London with obvious admiration. "This place is huge!"

"Jessica, would you be interested in a late lunch, early dinner, whatever you want to call it, and shopping afterwards? Or do you want to go look at some of the departments first?"

"I am hungry," she commented.

"Let's go eat first, then. I know just the right place. You're gonna love it."

"Okay."

Pierre wanted nothing more than to hold her hand, establishing some kind of body contact with her, allowing electricity or magic to flow between them, but he just couldn't gather enough courage to do it. Dammit, he was acting like a little kid. Fact was, he liked Jessica very much, but he was hesitant to put their newly found connection at risk. What if she didn't like his touch and decided to continue her exploration of London on her own?

Aw, what the devil.

He reached out, grabbing her hand, pulling her behind him heading for the elevator bank.

Jessica's hand was warm and dry, and thankfully she didn't object to his touch, on the contrary, she responded to it, by squeezing back.

He liked that. *Ho-ly angels, did he like that! He felt ten feet tall. Such a little inconsequential act, but it made him feel great!*

Pierre took her up to the fourth floor, to the world-famous *The Georgian Restaurant.*

Stepping out of the elevator they found themselves facing an elegant dining establishment with delightful hand-painted ceilings adorned with stained glass images. They were met by a gracious host who directed them to a burgundy leather-covered booth with a round table luxuriously set in white linen. A cognac glass with two red roses swimming in water adorned the center of the table.

Jessica slid in the booth and he took the chair directly across from her.

"I'm speechless," Jessica finally stated.

"You like it?"

"Like it? *I love it.* This is a department store restaurant? My God, it's awesome!"

Pierre was delighted they were both dressed so nicely. He knew from past experience The Georgian had a strict dress code. He may be just an ordinary man dressed in a navy-blue blazer, but seated next to Jessica she made him look like a dark, mysterious stranger meeting the heroine of some exciting romance novel.

She hadn't objected to his hand-holding. That was unquestionably a good sign. Definitely a good sign.

He answered her. "Not really, it's not merely a department store restaurant, just like Harrods is not merely a department store, this is a rather famous restaurant here in London. This place is almost an institution."

"This is going to be expensive," she said, lowering her voice.

Pierre liked her even more. Her preoccupation with spending too much of his money was awfully considerate. "It's not as bad as it looks. And after that long walk, I feel you're entitled to some luxury."

She gave him a long look. Her face was that of an archangel, so enchanting, her brownish eyebrows contrasting with her blond hair, her alluring lips a vivid pink, poised as if pouting. Jessica didn't say anything, she just fixed her eyes on his.

"Good afternoon."

Holy batshit! Pierre just about jumped out of his pants.

A waiter in a white coat was holding menus for them hovering over his right shoulder. The server had flat out surprised the bananas out of him.

"May I offer you a glass of wine or some other beverage of your choice?"

Pierre felt the adrenaline shot circulating through his bloodstream. Damn, the guy had really startled him. And why was he so goddamn jumpy? Being with a female made him that unsettled?

He accepted a wine list, extending it to Jessica. "Would you like a glass of wine or anything else to drink?"

She accepted the leather-covered list, looking at the waiter. "A glass of Rosé would be great."

"We do have a *Pascal Jolivet.*"

"That will be perfect. Thank you," she returned the wine list.

"And for you, sir?"

"Perrier water, please."

"Right away, sir."

"Perrier?" Her tone was one of amusement.

"I have to fly tomorrow."

"That's right, the airlines are pretty strict about that, no?"

"They are, yes. But *you* can enjoy some wine if you feel like it. You don't have any restrictions on drinking, do you?"

"No. No restrictions, I just can't show up drunk."

"All right, I'll make sure we limit your drinking to one bottle then."

"The way I am right now, with hardly any sleep, If I drank an entire bottle you'd have to carry me back to the hotel, Pierre."

"I don't think I'd get very far carrying an unconscious, beautiful woman in my arms through the streets of London."

"And why not?

"The British police may want to know where I found you."

"Just tell them I'm your girlfriend and I ate too many liquor-filled chocolate-covered cherries at Harrods."

What an imagination.

However, the part about her being his girlfriend had an exciting, delicious ring to it.

"Jessica, if you woke up in my hotel room tomorrow you'd never believe me if I gave you the story about the liquor-filled chocolate covered cherries."

"Who said anything about waking up in your room?"

"You did. If I told the police you were my girlfriend they'd expect me to carry you all the way back to our room. If I didn't take you to my room and the cops tailed us, then the entire story would become highly suspicious and we could end up spending the night in some cell at Scotland Yard."

"Whoa, and I don't suppose they put men and women together in the same cells at Scotland Yard, do they?"

"No, somehow I don't think these incredibly proper Brits would go for that."

"Then please don't carry me back to the hotel."

He laughed. This was getting exciting.

"This store is out of this world. Just so you know, it has over 300 departments."

"So I guess we're not going to see them all today?"

Smiling at her he shook his head. "Not even close."

Pierre still couldn't believe how his luck had turned. A couple of hours earlier he'd been lamenting the lack of available females among his crew, making plans to hit the clubs in Denmark, and now, here he was, sitting across from a girl who could be a model, in one of the most exclusive restaurants in this vibrant city. And she seemed to like him. Lady Luck was being extremely accommodating.

"In reality, is Harrods really outrageously expensive? I know they're pricey, but what do you think?" Jessica asked.

"Depends. They do have a wide range of goods for sale. You can buy things here from all over the world, and the prices vary from a couple of bucks to hundreds of thousands."

"I don't know anything about this place. Other than I found a bathing suit online that caught my eye."

"Oh, this store has quite a history. I heard the guy who owned it, his son was dating Princess Diana. His son and the Princess were killed in the car accident in Paris, remember?"

"That was awful."

"Yes, it was. This is the only store in the country still selling real animal furs. They have received an awful lot of static for that."

The waiter reappeared, placing an empty wine glass in front of Jessica, filling it from a small crystal carafe. He then deposited a bottle of Perrier water and a glass for Pierre.

"You live in Carmel?"

"Yes."

"Born and raised there?"

"No, born and raised in Woodland Hills, near LA. I moved to Carmel for this job."

"I know Woodland Hills. I was raised in Sherman Oaks, San Fernando Valley."

"I thought you said you were from Arizona."

"That's where I live now, so I call that place home. But I came out of Sherman Oaks."

"What a small world!" She raised the wine glass to her lips, gently sipping it.

"Cheers," Pierre offered his Perrier glass to Jessica.

She extended her arm, producing a melodic crystal ding when clicking glasses. "Cheers."

"How long have you been a flight attendant?" Pierre surveyed the restaurant with one quick glance. Not too crowded yet.

"Three years."

"All three with this same company?"

"Yes."

"What were you doing before?"

"Modeling."

Woo-hoo, he knew it!

Such an incredibly attractive woman had to have been a model. Pierre was delighted his instincts had been right on target.

"Really? Yeah, I can clearly see that. That's probably why I can't take my eyes off of you."

She smiled. "You are nice."

"Who did you model for?"

"Nobody in particular. All sorts of random contracts."

The annoying growling from his belt area reminded him they hadn't ordered any food.

"Want to look at the menu?"

Jessica opened the leather-covered menu, studying it.

"Do you feel like fish? Pasta? Steak?"

She didn't answer him right away. "They have trout here."

Pierre rapidly scanned his menu, confirming her choice. "Yep. That sound good to you?"

Jessica nodded. "I love trout."

"Good! Why don't you order one, you'll probably love it. All their food here is fantastic."

The waiter seemed to materialize alongside their table, as if beamed down by Scotty, of the *USS Enterprise*.

"Have you decided on some dishes?"

Almighty, that was the second time the man had snuck up on him. Pierre would not make a good James Bond.

He ordered the trout, glazed with garlic and honey for Jessica and some halibut cooked in lemon-scented butter for himself. The place was pricey, but not extravagantly so. And the atmosphere more than justified the prices.

"How much do you fly?" He wanted to know.

Her white blouse was open at the collar, showing a small gold crucifix hanging from a thin gold chain.

"It varies. Sometimes we take three trips a month, some months we don't go anywhere the entire month."

"Do you keep track of the hours?"

"Do you mean the hours I fly?"

"Yes."

"No, I know I'm supposed to, but I never do. You have to keep track of your hours, right?"

"I do, yes. We are very tightly regulated about how much we can fly. These days I'm flying about twelve days a month. Can't fly more than a thousand hours a year."

"I know that's how you do it." Jessica sipped some more of her wine.

"You said you were married once?" Maybe he shouldn't touch on the subject, but he was curious. Who had she married? And what sort of imbecile would divorce a girl like this?

Jessica put her glass down. "Yes, I was married for a year when I was twenty-eight."

"When you were twenty-eight? You don't even look twenty-eight to me now."

"I think I like you. No, I'm actually thirty-three."

"No kidding? When's your birthday?"

She told him.

"Hey! You're merely four months older than me. Incredible!" He was truly surprised. She looked much younger than his thirty-three years. "Who was your husband?"

She hesitated before answering. "He a was screen writer, producer for television. Not a nice man. We got married in Tahiti. He turned out to be a real jerk."

Pierre understood. "Was he older than you?"

"Yes."

"It didn't work out, eh?"

"No. I realized I'd made a mistake and got out of it."

"Did you have any kids?"

"No kids."

"Sorry to hear about that."

"Life happens."

Two waiters showed up with hot food.

Already? Pierre was impressed. What, they already had everything cooked in the kitchen? How was it possible to prepare food that quickly?

The ceremonial food-serving was a show all in itself. Pierre enjoyed watching the fussing and attention to details professed by the waiters. Jessica appeared pleased.

Once the waiters uncovered the fish, the delicious aroma permeated the entire area, making them both salivate like dogs sitting outside a butcher shop staring at the meat hanging from the hooks.

The conversation paused while they devoured their food with great *gusto*.

"How's your trout?"

"Delicious," Jessica said, after taking a sip of her wine. "How's yours?"

"Excellent."

"What'd you order?"

"Halibut."

"Pierre, how come you're not married?"

Whoa! Change of direction!

Aah, the age-old question. "I was a late starter."

"Meaning what?"

"I didn't get on with the airlines until I was thirty. Before that, I spent a few years building experience so I could qualify for a job with the airlines."

"How'd that prevent you from getting married? Didn't you have a girlfriend?"

"I actually did, yes, but see—things don't work so easily when a man doesn't have an established career."

"I'm not following you."

"When I had girlfriends I never considered marriage. I never had adequate income to support myself, let alone a girl. Besides, I felt I was always too young to be considering marriage. Then at one point I did get involved with a girl I considered marrying, but since I didn't have a career, I had nothing to offer, so that crashed."

"Okay … then what?"

"I decided to put myself out of the game until that time when I could actually have something to offer. I dedicated myself entirely to flying, not allowing myself to get serious with any one girl."

"So you had girlfriends."

"Yes, of course. I just didn't allow myself to become emotionally involved."

"That's unusual."

"Maybe, but I had to stay focused."

"But you're on your third year with Worldwide now."

"Yes."

"And now you have the means to afford a wife."

He knew where she was going. "Yes, now I have a career and I have an income, so you're probably wondering why I have not gotten married yet."

"Yes—and?"

"I'm not on a mission to get married. I like being single. I also enjoy women, don't get me wrong. Female friends are terrific, and by all means, I need the same things everyone else needs, love, affection, sex. I just haven't found the right person, that's all."

"So you've been dating."

"You can call it that, here and there."

"Have you dated mainly flight attendants?"

"Some. I've also dated outside the airline. It just hasn't provided me with a friend I want to keep forever."

"I haven't dated much either."

That surprised him. Pierre would've thought such an attractive, intelligent woman would have a long line of suitors doing back flips to get her attention.

"How come?"

"Disappointed, mainly. I've had a few relationships but they just don't seem to pan out."

"Have you dated pilots?"

"Yes, a few."

"Didn't your mother warn you not to date pilots?"

She laughed. "No, should she have?"

"A four-year-old boy once said to his mother: 'Mom, when I grow up I want to be a pilot!' To which his mother responded—son, you can do one or the other, but not both!'"

Jessica laughed.

Pierre was fascinated by the sound of her laughter. He realized he had a tendency of going head over hills for any new woman he liked. Once he was hooked, everything the woman did was adorable. That was something he had to learn to control. But on the other hand, how could he not fall head over heels for

Jessica? One hour after meeting her, and he still hadn't found one thing about her he didn't like. She appeared fun, intelligent, and charismatic, looked like a model and was probably a volcano in bed.

Pierre discreetly observed Jessica's table manners. She was well-raised, no doubt. He didn't really consider himself a snob, but table manners were very important to him. The way she delicately held her utensils as far from the tines as possible, spoke volumes. She cut one piece of fish using her knife, lifting it to her sensuous lips. Then she'd cut a second piece, repeating the act.

Pierre had dated girls who exhibited atrocious table etiquette. Of course, most of the guys he flew with were complete slobs, but he wasn't interested in dating *them* so manners didn't count.

"So this really is your very first time in London?"

Jessica finished chewing before she replied. "Yes. Never been here before."

Pierre admired her divine neck. Jessica's proportions were amazing. Her sexy devilish eyes puzzled him. She seemed to be studying *him*, and making her own assumptions. He wished he could read her thoughts.

"You've been here in London a lot, haven't you?" Jessica sipped her wine.

Pierre stared into her smiling blue eyes. "Yes, lately I've flown a lot of these London trips. "

"You're so lucky! You get to have time to enjoy this city!"

He wondered how much he should share with her. If he told Jessica about his disappointment with the cabin crews flying these trips she was bound to think he was merely a player looking for some action.

But then again, honesty was always, definitely and by far the best option.

"I'm actually going to stop flying these London layovers." He waited for her reaction.

Jessica brushed her hair from her face. "You are? Why?"

He told her.

Jessica's light blue eyes squinted. "I understand. So, that's why you came down to the lobby by yourself. I always thought airline crews did everything together on layovers."

"Ya, I didn't have anybody I particularly wanted to hang around with."

"There you have it, I'm happy we ran into each other, then."

Her statement triggered a shot of adrenaline through his body.

She was happy they connected?

He thought, *hot dog! His instincts were right, she liked him! Goddammit, he was a self-confident man, he flew jets for a living, he had to knock off acting like a teenager in love, what the hell was wrong with him?*

Jessica kept studying his eyes, which was turning him on something fierce. Pierre suddenly became aware he had a painful hard-on under the table. Good grief. He'd have to reach down there inside his pants and straighten himself out before they could walk anywhere.

Incredible. He desired her, no doubt about it, but what had she done to generate such a boner?

Nothing really, merely her presence across from him was working some sort of mystic magic affecting him dramatically. That, and her voice. And unquestionably, his imagination was working overtime trying to picture what she'd look like nude, stretched out on his bed. Sometimes Pierre felt like a starving kid from some African nation, when it came to sex, he just craved it, never seeming to get enough.

He wanted her badly, it was not just a casual, passing whim, it was an ardent desire and it was burning him, pushing aside all thought, reason and caution.

"I'm delighted we ran into each other, Jessica." He fixed his gaze on her attractive blue eyes. Jessica didn't blink, she just stared right back with a hint of a smile in her eyes.

"Wanna try my trout?" She held out her fork, with a morsel of steaming fish speared on it.

Pierre was surprised and enchanted by the gesture. There was an exquisite intimacy involved in eating out of her fork. He opened his mouth half way, allowing Jessica to feed him the bit of fish.

It was delicious, hot and moist with a hint of garlic.

She retracted her hand with the fork, smiling. "Like it?"

"It's incredible!" Pierre admitted, after swallowing.

"Want to try my halibut?"

Jessica shook her head. "No, thanks. I want to enjoy this flavor."

"We'll ask where we can find your bathing suit and go get it after we're done here."

She merely flashed a smile with her perfect teeth, gently raising her wine glass to her full lips, looking at him.

Pierre once again allowed himself the totally imaginary mental pleasure of contemplating having Jessica in bed, totally nude, being able to explore every inch of her body with his tongue, wondering what she would taste like.

Wow! Down boy!

He had to mellow out or he'd scare her off. Of course, there was no way Jessica could possibly know what he was thinking, but then again, what if he was transmitting his desires through some other form of communication? What if his body emitted some unknown chemicals Jessica could smell and become instantly aware of his thoughts? He'd read about that somewhere, what was it they called it? Pheromones? Apparently, their existence had not been confirmed in human beings yet, but what if something like that actually existed?

Extremely farfetched, Pierre admitted. However, the eyes were the window to the soul, and the way she kept looking at his eyes, well, who knew?

"Do you have roommates, or do you live by yourself?" Jessica asked.

"I'm alone. Just me. I had roommates while I was based in St. Louis, but when I moved to Phoenix I decided I wanted my privacy." He wondered if her curiosity extended to the possibility of her visiting him in Phoenix. He laughed. Man, he was thinking ahead.

He'd just met her and he was already projecting her visits to Phoenix.

"How about you?"

"I live alone. I own a little home near Carmel."

Pierre evaluated what it would take for him to go visit her in Carmel. He could fly into the Monterrey Peninsula airport or San Jose. He'd have to check the company computer to find out what flights went straight there out of Phoenix. That was him, the eternal chess player, already planning his next move.

"I don't like roommates either," she added. "My mom lives not too far from me."

"Your dad too?"

"No, my dad lives in France. Parents divorced when I was thirteen."

"Sorry to hear that." Pierre was amazed by how many people he met in his daily life who were divorced. Didn't anyone test drive the car before deciding to buy it anymore?

"That's just how it is," Jessica observed. "What about your parents?"

Pierre felt a pang of guilt. "Alive, still married. They live in Scottsdale." He always felt slightly self-conscious telling children of divorced parents that his own folks were still married, alive and well and enjoying life together.

"You're lucky," she said simply. "Your dad a pilot?"

"No, he's a retired physician."

"Anyone else in your family a pilot?"

"Nope, I'm the sole weirdo."

"Why'd you say that?"

"I wanted to fly since I was a little kid. I stayed focused and was able to do it."

"And that makes you a weirdo?"

"You see, in my family they're very traditional, you have to be a doctor, an architect, engineer or economist. All the other professions just don't exist. Airline pilot is like being a firefighter or a race car driver, they look at it as more of a hobby, really. Something one may wanna do when one is just a child. A weirdo for stepping out of the basket."

"I've taken flying lessons," she blurted.

That got his attention.

"No kidding—you have? Why?"

"What do you mean 'why?' because I like to fly, why else?"

"That's cool! Do you have your private pilot's license?"

"No, but almost."

"How many hours do you have?"

"A little over forty."

"Have you flown all your cross-country flights?"

"No, I'm missing some of those."

"You have to fly a cross country flight of 100 nautical miles with your instructor and then another one of 150 nautical miles by yourself. Have you flown either one of those?"

"Not yet. Remember I told you I dated an airline pilot?"

Pierre nodded. Apparently, he had more in common with the alluring woman across from him than he'd imagined.

"His name was Eric and he was also a flight instructor. While I was dating him, he taught me how to fly. Things didn't work out and I went my own way without finishing all the requirements for my license."

"That's great. I mean, it's great you like to fly, not that things didn't work out between the two of you. Have you flown since?"

"I know what you meant. No, I kinda stayed away from flying lessons after Eric and I split."

"Sorry that didn't work out for you. Were you serious when you were dating him?"

"Serious? You mean were we contemplating marriage?"

"Yeah, I guess that's what I meant."

"Maybe we did, at one point."

Pierre was convinced the guy had to be a fool. Who else but a fool would give up such a woman?

"Things didn't work out. I got pregnant and he didn't want me to have the baby."

Whew.

"That pretty much ended it between us. I terminated the pregnancy and moved on."

Pierre was dumbfounded. First, by her sharing such personal aspects of her life with him. Then by the dumb sonofabitch doing that to her. That sucked donkey balls. What man would do that? And the way she so coldly stated she'd 'terminated the pregnancy' gave him a chill. Of course, that was her option, which he supported and respected, but he couldn't help being awestruck by her courage. Pierre had always been of the opinion that the choice to have babies was entirely up to a woman.

Her body, her choice.

Anyone who disagreed with him on this topic he simply wrote off as an ignorant unsophisticated country puke from the remote regions of the Appalachians. Or a frightened religious zealot.

"Once I got this job I promised myself I'd get my license, but I just haven't gotten around to it."

"I'm a flight instructor," he stated. "I could teach you." Pierre thought of the cost. He'd be delighted to have Jessica as a student, something he would do for free. Flying with her would be exciting and stimulating, and it would provide him an excuse to see her again. Considering where she was in her training, he quickly ran a mental estimate of twenty hours of dual instruction and ten hours of solo still required for her to finish. A very rough estimate, but that would represent almost five thousand dollars in aircraft rentals, maybe more.

Not a problem, he could pay for that without a hitch. That amount was probably a huge sum for her, though. He'd no idea what she got paid, but it couldn't be that much, considering she was a corporate flight attendant.

Pierre held his tongue, resisting the strong impulse to offer her the free flight training. That was a little premature and it could have her running for the hills in one second flat. A little too intense.

Jessica took another sip from her nearly-empty glass wine, studying him. "If I ever decide to finish my flight training I'll make sure to look you up."

Her off-handed dismissal of his offer was somewhat disappointing. Time to switch to another theme. Pierre put down his fork. "Would you like some dessert? Another glass of wine?"

Jessica laughed musically. "No, no. Thanks. I'll pass on both. I need to stay sober so I can buy a bathing suit."

Pierre smiled, agreeing with her. More wine may not be the way to go. They were both already fatigued. He remembered the night of passion he'd spent with Amanda long ago, and how drunk he'd been. Right after that night he'd promised himself he'd go real easy on the booze anytime a girl was involved.

"Why the French name?" Jessica wanted to know.

"I'm half Basque."

"Oh? As in Basque terrorist?"

"No. As in 'Latin lover.'"

She laughed. "You think so, uh?"

"No, I don't think so. I *know* so."

"Pretty cocky, eh?"

"No, just realistic."

That left Jessica studying him in silence, a grin on her face.

He caught the waiter's eye, half raising his hand. The waiter sprang in their direction.

Pierre asked him for the check. He liked the way Europeans ran their restaurants, waiting to present the bill only after being asked. Back home in the States he was continuously annoyed by the irritating habit waiters had of depositing the bill on the table half way through one's meal.

Different customs, he understood that.

He paid using his American Express card. Pierre was delighted he was able to treat Jessica to such a splendid late lunch.

"Should we?" He stood, pausing to permit Jessica to go first. "We need to investigate where to go find your bathing suit."

TWO HOURS LATER, THE couple strolled along Hyde Park, on their way back to the hotel. The park, one of the largest in London, extended past the main entrance to Buckingham Palace.

"Tired?" Pierre walked alongside Jessica, not holding hands. After lunch he'd shied away from holding her hand. There just hadn't been an opportunity to do it nonchalantly. Such a juvenile little gesture, and yet, he hadn't found the nerve to do it. For an adult man, he sure had a lot of hang-ups.

"Yeah, I'm starting to fade." Jessica carried a Harrods bag containing her new turquoise bathing suit.

"You hungry again?"

"Heavens, no," she laughed discreetly. "I'm still very satisfied from the lunch. Thanks again for that."

"You liked the Georgian?"

"That was splendid! A terrific restaurant. Thank you so much for taking me there."

He liked that.

Pierre congratulated himself again. Inviting Jessica there had been brilliant.

"You are most welcome, *mademoiselle*."

"I love Harrods. I see how it's gonna take several visits to see all of it. So many departments."

Pierre had to agree. He'd been to the famous department store half a dozen times already and hadn't really seen but a fraction of what it had to offer. He did notice most of their electronics cost far more than their counterparts back home, though. Jessica had found the bathing suit she wanted, at an obscene, exorbitant price. Pierre was not well versed on the price of bathing suits for women, even back in the States, but paying six hundred dollars for one seemed a bit extreme. Undoubtedly, Jessica would look stunning in anything, expensive or not.

While they were in the store he'd considered paying for the suit and offering it to Jessica as a gift, but once again that was a little bit too forward, and he suspected it would make her uncomfortable.

Traffic was loud in the streets of London, as the sun began its inexorable descent towards the horizon. Pierre couldn't help wonder what was up next. What was going to occur once they were back in the hotel? He really wanted more time with Jessica, but had to accept the fact she was tired. If he just said 'good nite' to her in the lobby, when would he see her again? Tomorrow? He had plenty of time in the morning to do as he pleased before reporting for his flight. But would she be interested? Breakfast together would be a good consolation price, but he much preferred spending more time with her now. He just didn't want the day to end.

Those thoughts raced through his mind the closer they got to the hotel.

The lobby was not crowded, an elegant piano bar to one side offered the comfort of cream sofas adorned with gold and royal blue pillows.

"Wanna have one last drink before turning in?" He asked her.

Jessica glanced at the elegant bar. A bartender was the only other person in the area. There was no piano player.

Pierre noticed her hesitation.

'C'mon, one drink. It'll help you sleep."

"Very well, just one."

Victory! A few more minutes together! He hoped he hadn't sounded like he was begging.

The sofas were plush and comfortable. A waiter made an appearance taking their order. Lemonade for Jessica and a Coke for Pierre. No booze this time.

"I had a good time," Jessica commented.

"So did I." She sat next to him, her mischievous smile still present. Pierre was enchanted by her. What an absolutely delicious, hot, exciting woman.

"Want to have breakfast in the morning?" She asked.

Pierre was delighted to hear her say that. He'd been trying to think of how to connect with her again in the morning. He had no idea where the hotel restaurant was, since he'd never visited it. He'd have to find out from their waiter.

"I'd love to."

The waiter brought their drinks, placing them on cocktail napkins on the glass coffee table.

"When do you fly out?" Jessica asked.

"Tomorrow late afternoon." Having met Jessica, he was not all that thrilled about the idea of leaving her alone in London an extra day by herself. She was easy pray for thousands of predators in that city. He wanted to stay back and protect her. Which was absolutely not possible.

"Going back to LA?"

"Yeah, nonstop."

"Then home to Phoenix?"

He nodded. "I don't have another one of these trips until the end of the month."

"That's ten days away. What do you do between now and then?" Jessica raised her lemonade to her lips.

"I'm off those days. When do you get back?"

"Day after tomorrow."

"I have a proposal for you."

"Is it decent?"

He snickered. "Of course."

"Then I'm not interested."

What?

Jessica laughed. "You should see the look on your face just now."

He tried to recover. "I can think of several *very indecent* proposals."

"I'm sure you can. So, what'd you have in mind? Along the decent kind, that is."

The birth of sexual bantering between them? That was exciting. "If you insist."

"Oh, but I do."

He gave her a slow smile. "How would you like if I flew you down to Los Angeles on an airline flight, meet me there and we can rent a Cessna and fly to Catalina island for lunch. I'll give you dual instruction during our flight to the island if you want, then I'll fly you back home."

"In the Cessna?"

"No, silly. In the airline. Flying you to Carmel in the Cessna would take me eight hours round trip. Not practical. I'll buy you an airline ticket."

Jessica rested her chin on the palm of her hand, her elbow on her lap, studying Pierre, her lips parting. "You want me to fly down to LA so then we can fly all the way to Catalina together."

It was a statement, more than a question.

"Yes. If that sounds like fun." Pierre couldn't read her. Was she attracted to the idea? He prayed she was. Otherwise he'd have to come up with an alternate plan to see her again, and that would sound too much like desperation. Maybe he should've thought about this a little longer before opening his big fat mouth.

Jessica had a radiant glow about her. "Okay."

Pierre's eyes widened. He laughed spontaneously. "Wonderful!" He didn't know what else to say. What he really desired was to kiss her, but once again this intriguing woman was throwing off his game. He was uncertain what her reaction would be to his advances. So far things had been progressing very smoothly, and he wanted her to be comfortable with him. Being too aggressive might discourage her or send her scurrying for shelter.

"Hey Pierre!"

He looked up into the smiling face of Sam Pedigo, the captain on his flight.

"Sam!" Pierre stood. The skipper was dressed in casual tan Dockers, pink Polo shirt and Gucci loafers.

Sam Pedigo smiled at Jessica, obviously awaiting an introduction.

"Sam, this is Jessica."

"Hi, Sam." She didn't offer her hand, sipping from her lemonade instead.

"Sam is the other one-third of our crew."

"Want to join us for a drink?" Pierre asked, praying he'd just go away. What timing. Although Sam was a likeable guy, Pierre had no desire to have him around just now.

"No, thanks. Don't want to interrupt you kids. Just saw you sitting here and came by to say hi. I'm headed upstairs for some sleep."

"Did you get dinner?" Pierre felt relieved. Sam was a good guy after all. Especially since he was getting lost in the next couple of seconds.

"I did. Walked to a Kentucky Fried Chicken across from Harrods."

"You had KFC for dinner in London?"

Sam smiled, embarrassingly. "Yeeah. Not very original, am I?"

"How was it?"

"Terrible. Overcooked."

"Try some fish and chips next time." Pierre was amused. Some of these guys flying with him just lacked the spirit of adventure. Sam had flown in the Navy, so he should be comfortable in foreign countries. KFC? Really?

"Well, nice meeting you Jessica. See you tomorrow, Pierre." The pilot departed, headed for the elevators. He was tall and slim.

"That's who you're flying with?" Jessica squinted her eyes.

"Yeah. Not a bad guy."

"Why did you say he's the other one third of your crew?"

"We have three pilots on our crew. Captain, First Officer and International Relief Officer."

"Oh?"

"The IRO—as we call him, is the third guy up front. On these long flights we have a third pilot so we can split the flying three ways and maintain legality as far as time on duty."

"Meaning?" She was shaking her head.

"Meaning the flight from LA is too long for just two pilots. We would become illegal two thirds of the way here."

"And that means?"

Pierre tried remembering if corporate pilots had to observe flight time hour limitations.

"That means legally this flight could not be conducted with just two pilots because we would exceed allowable flight time limits imposed by the FAA. Does that make any sense?"

"Sure. Who's your third guy?"

"His name's Phillip. Haven't seen him since we checked in."

"So it takes three of you little boys to fly that Airbus?"

"No, the airplane can be flown with just two pilots," he decided to ignore the dart. "We have the third little boy along just for legality reasons."

"I see." She finished the last of her lemonade. "I better get some sleep."

Pierre felt a curtain of disappointment descending over his world. He waived at the bartender, requesting the check.

"Where are you planning on wearing your new swim suit?"

Jessica smirked. "Don't know yet. I'd thought maybe Cancun."

"You planning a vacation there?"

"Never been there. I think it would be quite fascinating, though. Wanna go with me?"

Pierre felt a fluttering of butterflies in his belly.

Would he want to go with her to Cancun?

Is a duck's ass water tight?

"To Cancun? *Sure!* You bet!"

Dammit, he had to control his enthusiasm. He was acting like a lunatic. Cancun with Jessica was a delightful, exciting thought. No, it was an incredibly arousing idea. His imagination was already racing at warp speed transporting them to a solitary white sandy beach in Isla Mujeres, near Cancun, admiring Jessica walking into the warm ocean wearing her new Harrods suit, ripping it off her body and throwing her on the sand, making wild love to her. Oh, God, the possibilities were endless and all of them erotic.

He had to make sure no sand got between them.

"Have you been there?" Jessica wanted to know.

"Yes, a few times."

"Do you like it?"

How could he begin to tell her about the place where the gods went on vacation? Cancun was Pierre's favorite destination on the planet. The warm white sand and the turquoise waters framed against the green jungles were enough to make him feel in paradise. Throw in a sexy, intelligent woman, and life became heaven on earth.

"Yes. I love it. And so will you. Everything about that place is fantastic. The ancient Mayas used to claim that's where their gods went on vacation."

"That's poetic."

"Not too farfetched either, Jessica. The place is really spectacular. Sun and beach during the day, then magnificent exotic dining and dancing at night."

"Sounds promising. Just dining and dancing at night?"

Pierre squinted his eyes, smiling mischievously. "Among other things."

"*Among other things, uh?* Sounds interesting, definitely."

"I'd love taking you there for the premiere of your new bathing suit."

She smiled, obviously amused.

Taking her to Cancun? Jesus Christ, he had to back off! He was coming on so strong Jessica was going to go hide in the hills, never to be seen again. Really, honestly, he had to make an effort to slow down.

"I really like your name," Jessica offered. "*Pierre*—I love the sound of it."

Pierre wondered about that. She liked his name? That was interesting. He momentarily wondered if Jessica was a real blonde. Not that it made any difference to him one way or the other, blonde or brunette, Jessica was a stunning woman. Just natural curiosity.

The waiter returned with the check.

"Thanks for the lemonade," she stood.

Pierre gave the waiter his VISA card. Jessica was jumping the gun, the puke still had to go ring the card, then bring it back for him to sign. He didn't want Jessica taking off on him from there. He wanted to see her to her door. He had to quickly come up with something to delay her.

Honesty was always the best policy.

"Don't go yet. I want to walk you to your room."

Her eyebrows went up.

"Just walk you to your room. Nothing else. I promise. Just let me get my card back."

"Okay." Jessica agreed with an enigmatic grin.

Pierre wondered what the odds were for Jessica to end up in bed with him tonight.

He suspected pretty close to zero. But then again, he'd found himself in the same situation before, and the women had surprised him. Would Jessica surprise him? Somehow he doubted it. She seemed too much in control, nerves of steel, that sorta thing.

The waiter returned the leather card holder, waiting for Pierre to sign. He scribbled an undecipherable signature.

"Let's go," he paused, allowing Jessica to lead the way.

The lobby was beginning to fill, hotel guests pouring downstairs from their rooms in anticipation of elegant dinners awaiting them elsewhere in the city.

"I can't believe Sam had dinner at KFC," Pierre laughed, following Jessica in the elevator.

"You really think he did that?"

"Absolutely. I believe him."

"That sounds horrible."

"I bet it was."

"Thank you for our dinner. Or was it late lunch?"

"Late lunch, I would say, and you're very welcome. And I'm actually the one indebted to you for accompanying me."

The elevator arrived on the seventh floor with a melodious chime.

"Here we are." He allowed Jessica to lead the way again. As she stepped out of the elevator ahead of him Pierre had the opportunity to study her well-formed body, her adorable posterior, admiring the styled blond hair softly caressing her shoulders as she walked. The tingling in his groin announced the arrival of another monumental hard-on.

Oh, for crying out loud ...

The thick luxurious carpet cushioned their progress until she stopped in front of a door, Jessica reaching for her purse.

"This is it," she announced, her arrogant sensual lips parting slightly.

Pierre wanted to pick her up, carry Jessica inside and spend the next eight hours pleasuring her with one thunderous, uncontrollable orgasm after another.

But without a doubt, if he did that, he wouldn't be worth a shit for his flight back to LA.

But regardless of his libido, somehow he suspected that was just not gonna happen. Not tonight.

Instead, he gave out a heavy sigh. "I had a great time. Thank you for coming with me." His hands were in his pants' pockets.

Jessica closed the distance between them in a blink, placing her warm and willing lips on Pierre's. Her hand found the back of his neck, pulling him towards her. Her deep sensual kiss astounded him and pleased him in rapid succession.

That was so unexpected and pleasing, he was dumbfounded.

Jessica inched closer to him, her body merging with his.

She felt hot and soft and Pierre realized in the far recesses of his mind that Jessica must be feeling the presence of his bulging hardness against her crotch. No way she could ignore that one.

Her passionate, smoldering kiss was incredible, her soft tongue lashing his, colliding inside his mouth.

Pierre encircled her limber waist with his arms, strongly holding Jessica against him in an iron embrace. Now he was sure she was experiencing the feel of his hard-on against the apex of her legs. He was incredibly turned on.

Jessica placed both her hands on his chest, pushing him off, ending the kiss. "Good night, Pierre."

She backed away, her room card in her hand.

Good night, Pierre?

Pierre promptly release his hold. "G'nite, Jessica," he gasped, his ears ringing.

Her alluring smile as she turned away made him consider following her into her room.

"Talk tomorrow," she whispered, opening the door.

He'd only had a moment to act, and he'd lost the courage.

Jessica slowly shut the door, keeping her eyes fixed on Pierre until the last second.

The 'click' announced to his overworked libido that it was over. No Jessica tonight.

Pierre stood there staring at the room number.

Holy shit.

What just happened?

What if she was looking at him through the viewing-lens? Better not just stand there like a dumbass. He began walking towards the elevator.

Taking a deep breath, he realized he was both delighted at having met her, and totally frustrated at having to end the night like this. This just was not fair!

She liked him! No question about it. Or was there any doubt? Would she kiss him like that if she was just saying 'thanks for dinner?'

He doubted that. Pierre was disappointed about the outcome. She didn't have to work tomorrow; she could've stayed up with him talking or making love all night and rested all day. Yet she chose going to bed alone.

Bummer. Major bummer.

What was it she had said? 'Talk tomorrow?' Well, at least there was some hope there. What was it about women? How could they turn off sexual desire at the flick of a switch? That was cruel and inhumane.

Pierre rode the elevator down to his floor. On the other hand, looking at the positives, he'd spent the day with an angel, one he could consider geographically desirable. Carmel wasn't all that far from Phoenix, so to speak. She could've just as easily been from Maine, in which case any sort of a relationship would've been doomed from the start.

And from the way it was looking to him, Jessica had agreed to his idea of flying to Catalina. That, in itself, was a major victory. Considering they'd just met a few hours ago. And besides, at the end of the day, whatever had given him the idea that all women would end up in the sack with him the first time they met? Was he perhaps becoming a little too full of himself? Presumptuous? He was no goddamned Casanova.

The raspberry taste of Jessica's lips lingered in his tongue. How could she taste like that? Lip gloss? And she had kissed *him!* That had been a nice kiss. And so totally unexpected.

And boy, did she know how to kiss! Pierre wondered if her sexual abilities matched her kissing abilities. If that was the case, she was one super-hot lady, a real knockout. He'd better start thinking of something else pretty quickly, or his throbbing erection was going to prevent sleep for the next few days. How was he gonna fix this? Take a cold shower? That sounded awful. Go jogging? Not in London. He'd never done that. An American jogging along downtown

London in the middle of the night was bound to get arrested.

What the hell, he could just relieve himself in the shower.

He realized he didn't have Jessica's cell phone number. What was wrong with him? How could he forget such a basic thing? Soon as he got back in his room Pierre threw his coat on a bed and dialed her room number on the house phone.

"Hello?" Her voice sent delicious electrical pleasure signals to his groin all over again. Incredible, how a woman had the power to do that to him through a mere phone call.

"Jessica? It's Pierre."

"That didn't take you long."

"I'm sorry to bug you, I know you're tired, but I forgot to ask you for your phone number. One never knows what could happen in the middle of the night, and if we became separated for some reason, I'd have no way of contacting you."

"Gee, you do think ahead." She gave it to him. Pierre dialed it directly into his cell phone keypad.

"Anything else?"

"Uhm. No, nothing really we can do by phone."

She laughed. "Good-night, Pierre."

He put the phone back on its cradle. A delicious feeling in his groin confirmed what he was about to do was sensible. After all, he'd just spent the most fantastic afternoon with this creature, and he could feel the flow of force between them. No, he wasn't going to be a Milquetoast, a timid, a wimp. What was the worst that could happen? She could tell him to get lost.

Pierre walked out of his room, determined to show some guts. After all, he was the man, wasn't he? And by God, he was a pilot! He wasn't too sure what the heck that had to do with anything, but it sounded good. The way he was feeling at the moment, he could wrestle a salt-water croc with a pocket knife.

The elevator ride back to her floor seemed to last forever.

He rapped on her door.

Seconds later, Jessica cracked the door open, the security chain preventing entry.

"Pierre?" her confused blue eyes appeared puzzled yet also somewhat pleased.

"Jessica, I need to talk to you for a sec?" In the foreground, her queen-sized bed stared back at him with unspoken promises of lust and pleasure.

She didn't answer, instead, she shut the door on his face. Pierre heard the chain unlocking inside. The door opened again. Jessica stood there wearing only her unbuttoned white shirt. White bikini lace panties visible below. His knees went weak. Pierre took a deep breath. The nude cleft between her voluptuous breasts was sensuously in full view right in front of him, her tiny gold cross resting peacefully between her boobs. Her shapely well-toned legs looked just as sexy as he'd imagined, her flowing hair cascading across her shoulders. She didn't have too much light in her room, so that was all Pierre could see in a split second. And she just stood there like that, half nude.

He had a monumental hard-on and a delicious ache in his groin. Oh, by the great goddess Venus, he'd made the right choice!

He moved against Jessica, firmly gripping her sexy waist with his powerful hands. "Come here," he commanded, bringing his lips down on her hungry mouth.

Jessica embraced him, slowly opening her mouth, offering no resistance, accepting the kiss.

Pierre lifted her with ease, carrying her into the room, and laid her on the queen-sized bed, where she sank into the soft comforter. There was nothing he wanted more in the world than Jessica at that moment.

The door clicked shut somewhere in the distance.

"Wait," she whispered seductively, an inch from his face.

Her breath was warm and still had the delicious aroma of raspberry from before.

"What is it?"

"Is this going to ruin our friendship?"

What? Ruin their friendship? Why in God's name would she ask that?

"No, it's not." He hoped he sounded confident and assertive enough for an Alpha-male.

Apparently, she liked his answer, because she resumed kissing him.

Just how turned on was he? Was his heart racing? Where those goose pumps real? Was there a delicious ache in his groin?

Well, he was undressing a hot, ready and eager woman.

Bet your ass he was turned on.

Jessica was on her side, cuddling against his chest. Pierre reached down, his determined fingertips finding the edge of her panties, lowering them past her buttocks, the back of her thighs, the back of her knees, her ankles, pulling them off one leg at a time. He tossed them away from the bed. He removed her white shirt next, sending it flying after the panties. The room temperature was perfect, Pierre wanted her to be comfortable nude, not freezing or uncomfortably warm.

Jessica rolled over on her back, bringing her arms around his shoulders. Pierre was overjoyed, he could feel she was alight with desire, her breath coming in gasps as she clutched him. They had kept their distance for too long that afternoon, although their mutual attraction had been evident and surprisingly powerful from the very beginning. It was time to let themselves go. Jessica positioned her body underneath Pierre, giving him the clear message she was already desperate to feel him inside her, spreading her legs to accommodate him.

"*I'm gonna make you love me,*" she announced, in a no-nonsense tone.

That caused a flow of excitement through his groin. Without any additional ceremony, Pierre impaled her slowly with one manly fluid stroke, feeling his mahogany-solid erection slipping deep inside her. Jessica was soaking wet, slippery and hot. She wordlessly urged him to go deeper, lifting her pelvis against him, bringing one of her legs around to the back of his leg, using the ball of her foot to caress the back of his knee.

He squeezed a handful of her buttocks, sinking two more inches inside her.

Pierre was fascinated. Kissing him, Jessica opened her mouth as wide as he'd ever experienced with any woman in his life. Her skillful silky tongue plundering the inside of his mouth with intense passion. Pierre had never before felt such a delicious aggressive assault from any woman.

The level of pleasure was downright agonizing. Her hips rocked from side to side as he plunged in and out of her, still dumbfounded by her unashamed, insanely passionate kissing. Her grip threatened to squeeze the life from his body. Pierre was overpowered by lust. He really wanted to take his sweet time with this woman, but she was so full of passion it was driving him senseless. And she was wrestling him like an antelope in the grip of a lion.

He used his hand to feel his cock going in and out of Jessica. He loved the feel of his shaft burying itself inside her. Touching himself sliding between her lips was an incredible erotic happening.

In the name of the stars! The early warning sweet sensation of an impending orgasm unexpectedly sent electric signals from his crotch to his brain.

Already!? No fucking way!

Good God, he had to slow down, or the entire episode would end in a minute or so, with him exploding inside her like a young kid on his first make-out session. His rapid arousal was firm testimony of just how fast she was turning him on. He was absolutely crazy about her.

But losing it like a teenager in love was absurd.

That was not going to happen if he could help it.

"Hold on," he muttered, gasping for air.

Jessica let out a long sigh. "What?"

"Get on top," he articulated.

"What, *now*?"

"Yes." Pierre propped himself up on his elbows, moving away from her.

"Okay," Jessica eased her grip.

Pierre felt the specter of the incoming orgasm vanish from his balls. He positioned himself on his back, his head flat on the queen bed. Jessica slowly straddled him. Pierre was speechless at her beauty, her milky perky breasts smoothly bobbing sideways as she reached down, finding his hardened manhood, guiding it to her hot pussy. She lowered herself onto his solid shaft, voraciously devouring every bit of him.

Pierre felt her weight on his lower body, so sensual and hot. He played with her nipples, softly rolling them in his fingers, loving the view of her disorderly hair and her glistening eyes.

Jessica rode him with delicious determination. She had her hands on his chest, supporting herself, moving her hips back and forth without lifting her body one inch. She fucked him passionately, never taking her eyes off Pierre even for one second.

Pierre was incredulous. Here he was, making love to Jessica on her bed, something he'd considered totally out of the question just an hour ago. Like a complete defeatist idiot, he'd even considered masturbation after she sent him packing.

Jessica stopped moving.

Now what?

He had absolutely no idea what she had in mind next. Why did she stop?

While fixing her eyes on his with nearly scary determination, Jessica suddenly squeezed her vagina muscles with incredible strength. Pierre felt her insides squeezing his cock with a force he'd never felt.

Holymothersuperior!

How could that be possible? He'd no idea women could control their muscles to such a degree. That was something nobody had ever done to him, ever.

Jessica repeated the feat again, a conniving smile forming on her eyes and lips. She knew the effect her actions were having on the pilot.

The sensation was so pleasurable he didn't want it to end, pushing his hips up against her crotch he lifted her off the bed.

Jessica shifted forward, causing his erection to slip out of her. She moved further up, her eyes still locked on his face, until her slippery vulva covered Pierre's mouth.

Aha! That was a new one!

Her clit was in the perfect position for him to please her. Pierre tasted her sweetness, loving the slippery feel of her skin. She definitely smelled of coconut water. His tongue separated the tiny lips protecting her love bud, licking her rapidly, holding her thighs with his biceps. Jessica stared down at him with a serious expression. Or maybe just an expression of ecstasy. Having her like that, with her legs on either side of his face was so exciting. Having her squatting on his face was a definite ten on his majestic scale of arousal.

She gave out short cries of delight, shaking under the attack of his tongue.

Pierre had a dead grip on her legs. She was not going anywhere until he decided otherwise. He increased the frequency of his tongue lashing, starting to feel Jessica was going to be asking for mercy real soon. He could feel she was trying to go up and down, but his powerful arms were keeping her locked in place.

Her vocal expressions of pleasure became louder, moaning in synch with the lashing of his tongue.

The phone rang.

Whathefuck!?

They came to a screeching halt. Jessica breathing rapidly, looking down at him questioningly, her skin glistening with perspiration.

Pierre released the grip on her legs.

The phone rang again.

Who the devil could be calling her room? He decided to answer it. Whoever was calling could be important, but Jessica was in no condition to answer the damned thing, she appeared to be hyperventilating as it was. She slowly shifted off his face, giving him room to move.

Pierre got up, rushing to the phone.

"Yeah?" He barked into the receiver.

A man's voice with a British accent responded at the other end. "My apologies for disturbing you, sir, this is Harvey at the reception. Just checking everyone's okay. We've had a call from the room adjacent to yours, a guest concerned someone may be ill."

Pierre wasn't sure what the devil. "Someone ill? Where, here?"

The reception man sounded hesitant. "Yes, sir. They indicated someone sounded as if they were in pain."

It took Pierre two seconds to understand.

He roared in uncontrollable laughter.

"No, nobody's sick. Thanks for checking old buddy, have a good night." He hung up.

Jessica studied him intensively, a puzzled half-smile on her lips, sitting on the bed cross-legged Indian-style. Her respiration was just starting to slow. "What?"

He told her.

"Aww, my God!"

Pierre laughed again. He could see a flush creeping across her cheeks.

"That's not funny! Seriously, was I being that loud?"

"Guest next door obviously thought so." He laughed again.

Jessica punched him in the shoulder. "Stop it!"

"I'm sorry, I didn't know these damned hotel walls were made of tissue paper."

"You are bad."

"I can call them back and tell them what's going on, if you prefer. You see, Harvey-boy, my partner is just not the silent type."

"Just shut up. Come here." Jessica sprung forward, connecting with his lips.

Pierre mentally cursed the reception guy and whoever next door had called it in. What a bunch of clowns. He'd been on the verge of pleasuring this incredible woman, and that intrusive call could've ruined the night.

Jessica kissed him and he could feel her racing heartbeat against his chest. She was still in the mood.

Thank God.

"Turn around," he requested, pushing her away.

Jessica gazed in his eyes, obediently turning around, reaching for two pillows, placing them under her face. She leaned forward provocatively, her lovely ass vulnerable and inviting.

Pierre just about died from the sight of her. She was laying with her bottom raised high, in total abandon, offering herself to his most intimate desires. She was the stuff dreams were made of, far as Pierre was concerned, with her face hugging the pillow and her delicious love mound up in the air, patiently awaiting his arrival.

And all he'd had to do was ask.

He jumped at the chance. Pierre felt immense relief seeing his cock leading the way at attention as he advanced towards Jessica on his knees. That telephone call could've been the kiss of death for his hard-on, but thank God he was still stiff and ready for action.

Her inviting pussy was positioned exactly where his cock would meet it, no need for Pierre to stretch or scrunch down, Jessica's delicious body was custom-made for him. He had great appreciation for that. If a girl's legs were too long, he would have to push her knees forward to lower the hips. None of that was necessary with Jessica.

He felt her butt cheeks with his two hands, rubbing the skin softly. Jessica was sodden, ready to take him inside. There was enough light in the room to admire her perfect shape. She was all curves. Her sexy buttocks were the right size, round and taunt, and her sensual lips were the personification of a flower painting by a famous southwestern painter whose work he'd admired in New Mexico, but whose name escaped him.

Pierre closed in on her, momentarily aligning his cock with her slippery opening.

He was there.

He slid inside her, agonizingly slowly so she could feel every inch of him. Her muscles tightened, gripping him, urging him deeper.

A soft moan rushed her lips.

Pierre smiled, wondering if the clown next door was sitting there with a water glass to his ear, listening against the wall.

Let him enjoy. Actually, that in itself was somewhat of a turn-on.

Pierre wanted her so bad, his desire was unreal. He looked down at the formidable erotic image of Jessica positioned there on her knees, her ass pushed up against him with his immense hard-on buried deep inside her. Digging his fingernails into her buttocks he slammed in and out of her, loving how she went back and forth with each thrust, her beautiful tits hanging down, swinging softly. She externalized her pleasure with continuous low moans.

He was actually fucking her. Somehow that reality hadn't caught up with him. They'd spent the entire afternoon together and now she had given herself to him. Gawd, what if he hadn't come to her room? Would she have called him later? Somehow he doubted it.

And what the demon was he doing mulling over such bullshit when he had a goddess from Olympus gifting him with her body right here and now? Forget the thinking, concentrate on the pleasure.

Fuck her wild!

He again briefly felt the familiar tingling in his balls, the early warning sign of an impending orgasm in the works.

Oh, shit.

Not yet. He let go of her buttocks, reaching for her upper back. Pierre massaged Jessica's shoulders and neck much like a masseuse would do at a luxury spa. Doing so momentarily defused the progression of his orgasm. He stopped thrusting inside her hot pussy. Massaging her upper back was the activity of the moment. That would delay his orgasm. He needed the distraction. Jessica didn't make much noise, hugging the two pillows with her arms, gently swaying her butt trying to get Pierre to re-start his thrusting.

"Don't stop," she begged.

Pierre continued massaging her shoulders with his hands, at the same time slowly resuming the thrusting of his hips. Jessica was so buttery, well-lubricated, he encountered very little resistance and she moved with him in a sensual ballet that had him gasping for air.

He decided to try something new to delay his climax. Without another thought he spanked Jessica's buttock, hard.

The *whack!* resonated in the room.

"OKAY, WHOA!" she cried out.

Jessica momentarily lurched forward an inch or so, tightening her butt cheeks, but remained as she was.

He quickly rubbed her cheek where he'd hit her, generating heat from the friction. There was no further reaction from her. *God! That was erotic!*

He smacked her again on the same side, equally as hard.

"AWW!" She complained, louder this time.

Pierre once again rubbed the flesh of her buttock, noticing even in the dim light her cheek was turning a deep crimson. "Want me to stop?"

A pause.

"No—don't stop," she begged.

"What? I can't hear you."

"*Don't stop,*" she ordered. Her defiance combined with her pose was electrifying.

Pierre shivered at her acceptance. She liked it! She actually liked the spanking. This was a new experience for him, and he was liking it something wicked. Each time he smacked Jessica's ass he felt a delicious sensation beyond words exploding in his groin.

He wacked her other buttock. This time he clearly felt Jessica's muscles squeeze his cock hard inside her in reaction to the blow.

Wow! That was unexpected and hot as all hell! Did he just imagine that or did it really happen?

Pierre belted her again.

Her inside walls squeezed his shaft one delicious instant again.

Holy Schizophrenia! He had no idea this could happen. Her ass was red, and he was very aroused. In fact, he hadn't noticed his body was now furiously pumping in and out of Jessica in fully autonomous mode, it was once again as if he'd gone on full automatic without realizing it. That's how distracting the spankings were.

He wacked her again, harder.

She yelped.

Yes, there it was, her vaginal walls momentarily squeezing his cock as a result of her reaction to the blow. Welcome to the turn-on of the century!

"Do you want me to stop?" He sure didn't want her getting upset at the spanking, and he had no idea how far was too far.

"You stop and I'll kill you," she whispered, gasping for breath.

Her words made Pierre suddenly go stiff, totally surprised by what came next. A delicious shiver ran through his balls, then another. His legs trembled with unexpected pleasure.

It wasn't possible, but he was coming!

How could that be? He had not authorized it! His orgasm snuck up without any warning, squeezing his balls high into his body, increasing his thrusts inside Jessica, feeling the entire world becoming one big enormous moment of pleasure. Without much warning, his body had reacted to her erotic words and decided it was time to come. That was not possible, words didn't have the power to put him over the threshold, he was a visual animal, images had that power, not words.

He thrust his cock deeply inside Jessica a few more times with uncontrollable passion, feeling his hot fluids filling her, then he stopped, leaning against her, breathing hard, once again, as he seemed to always do, feeling a powerful attraction, gratitude and what he considered love for her. Brief moment of pleasure, but worth all the treasures of the Vatican. This was getting repetitive, he thought, amused. He was just so ready to love the right woman.

You did it, girl. You made me love you in all the ways a man can love a woman.

What in heaven's name had just happened? He'd lost total control of his body, that's what'd happened. And all because of what she said, '*You stop and I'll kill you!*'

Those words of hers had catapulted him into an earth-shattering orgasm. Completely unexpected.

Jessica must've realized he'd come, because she'd jammed her ass back into his shaft with passionate fury while he was coming. Now that he was spent, she remained immobile in the same position, pushing back against him with Pierre deep inside her, but didn't shift or say anything.

He caught his breath, moving away. "Roll over on your back, honey."

Jessica slowly turned, doing as he asked.

"A time for you," he said.

He reached between her legs, finding her clit and rubbing it. He pinched it lightly, tugging on it, then letting go and grazing it in a circular motion with his palm.

Jessica became alive, moaning and breaking into a painful smile.

Pierre wet his finger, slipping it into the puckered entrance to her ass, fucking her with it, while shifting his assault on her clit with his tongue. His tongue was a weapon of pleasure as she gladly spread her legs to accommodate him. The scent, the elixir of her skin was overwhelming. He had no frame of reference to identify the scent, other than maybe coconut milk fragrance, all he knew was he loved the way she smelled and the way she tasted. He was crazy about her flavor.

It occurred to him the clown next door must've heard the spankings. Were they going to get another phone call? If that happened, this time he wasn't going to answer. He'd just rip the damned thing off the wall.

He had to concentrate on pleasing Jessica. Gawd, you don't know how breathtaking you are, girl. Pierre's hands rose up to play with her nipples, tugging them gently with fingers covered in both their juices.

"You are amazing," Jessica whispered, her mouth gasping for air. She had said nothing about his orgasm.

Pierre was still turned on. Licking Jessica was incredibly sexy, and she was becoming more and more aroused as her clit became more sensitive. Her breathing sped up and her heart rate increased.

Her legs started to tremble, she clinched the sheets with her hands, her moaning increasing in volume. Pierre felt Jessica stiffen, his face soaking wet from her gushing fluids.

Then she exploded.

"Oh, Pierre! Ooh, Pierre! Aaawww!"

Jessica wrapped her legs around his back with surprising strength, her hands gripping his hair with uncontrolled passion.

He felt her muscles pulsating around his finger deep inside her ass, her back arching, her hips lifting off the bed. Her body bucked and hopped uncontrollably for a long time. Pierre felt he was riding a wild horse, trying to stay on her clit, trying to contribute to the continuation of her moment of pleasure.

Eight or ten contractions later she collapsed, shaking.

She laid on her back breathing fast, Pierre rested his face on her crotch, loving the wetness. She was wet from perspiration, her female oils and his own sperm. Eventually, a long time later, Jessica revived enough to reach for him. "Come here," she pulled Pierre towards her. He kissed her softly. She was still breathing irregularly, both of them drenched in perspiration.

"You have to go easy on me, my Latin Lover, remember, I'm Anglo, you're going to kill me."

Pierre opened his eyes and focused on the sublime creature beneath him, laughing at her comment. This was one incredible night. The gods of Olympus must've held their annual stockholder meeting and voted to give him the 'Pilot of the Year Award,' or something like that. Jokes aside, he was stunned life had put Jessica in his path. Stunned and eternally grateful.

Time for more.

"You are so damn exciting," he stated, staring into her half-opened eyes.

He then traveled his tongue down to her heaving breasts, tasting her nipples. The flavor was intoxicating, sweet and animal and addictive. Continuing down to her hot lips, he resumed his lashing of her clit with his tongue. She didn't move for a moment, then she jumped.

"*Stop!*" Jessica demanded.

Pierre decided to just ignore her. Of course, she would want him to stop, she was probably over-sensitized from her recent orgasm, but Pierre wanted to give her more of the same. A lot more. She deserved all the pleasure he could give her.

He cupped her delicious buttocks with his hands, licking her clit with a passion. He felt Jessica making a couple of feeble attempts at moving her hips out from under Pierre's tongue, but his broad shoulders prevented her from escaping. In just a few more seconds she'd given up and appeared to be madly enjoying his attention again. Not that she had a choice.

Pierre felt her hips lifting off the bed. Her butt cheeks becoming tighter, and he caught a glimpse of her erect rock-hard nipples pointing towards the ceiling.

"Stop," she blurted, a lot less assertive.

She writhed beneath him.

In your dreams, he thought, smiling. His tongue was getting tired. Her hot, soft flesh was fit for a god.

Jessica lifted her butt completely off the bed, her back arching. She was an erotic sight. Pierre held on to her ass with both hands. Going in her ass was out of the question, since her butt cheeks were so tight together at that very moment, no way he was going to get his finger in there. He'd just have to rely on his tongue. He wondered how long Jessica was going to hold that position. Not very long, he suspected.

Her body was taunt as a bowstring, arching her back like a gymnast, running her fingernails along his shoulders. Pierre persisted, ferociously painting her clit with his tongue as Matisse applying oil to a canvas masterpiece. Jessica was breathing loud, sounding like she was running a race.

He squeezed her buttocks with great force, feeling his fingernails digging into her. She gave no sign of feeling any of it. The pain just didn't register. Pierre kept licking without pausing.

Then in an instant he heard her scream out in pleasure, her body tensing, shuddering with the force of another orgasm. Jessica's climax was so intense

Pierre had to back off and put a little distance between his mouth and her. No way he was going to stay on her clit with such wild bucking. She went on for a long time, trembling, sighing, throwing her hips up. Once she finally settled down and her wild gyrations stopped, he approached her again and licked her one more time.

"No! Please, stop! I can't take any more."

With that, she pushed him away, rolling to the other side of the bed, pulling the comforter over her shoulders, hugging one of the pillows, turning her back on him. Pierre was slightly amused. She was pulling down the curtains on their evening together. Without further ceremony.

He observed her in fascination as she closed her eyes, and in less than a minute appeared to be out cold.

For the love of God.

Pierre was wide awake. It was incredible, this night with Jessica. He took a deep breath, inching closer to the now sleeping goddess. She was incredibly erotic in her innocence. Even more dazzling in her sleep than she had been awake. A seductive sight, if there ever was one.

Pierre wasn't sure what she'd meant when she said she was going to make him love her. He did make love to her, if that's what she was thinking. Otherwise, did she mean love her as in 'love?' that was also thrilling. Yes, he could see himself loving this unbelievable woman.

He was one fortunate sonofabitch. No doubt about that. he snuggled up against her back, spooning with Jessica, reaching with his hand to feel the smooth warm wet curve of her buttock. In the morning, he was going to treat her to the most delicious breakfast the English could provide for them. He'd never visited the hotel restaurant before, but he suspected it was going to be first class. He ran his hand along the apex of her legs, finding her mound still hot and soaking wet. Very beautiful, and very addictive, without the shadow of a doubt.

THE SOUND OF THE shower stopping woke him up.

Pierre tried focusing on the beige curtains and the tan walls for a second, becoming aware that he'd just come out of a deep sleep. In an instant, he knew where he was. He rolled over, looking for Jessica.

The bed was empty. There was enough light in the room to confirm it was morning.

At that moment, the bathroom door swung open, Jessica came out, smiling at him, one white towel wrapped around her body and another one knotted on her hair. She looked fresh and relaxed. Pierre admired her shapely legs, wondering what the odds were of making love to this stunning woman again. And why had he not noticed she had left the bed? Was he that tired?

"Good morning Princess!" He noticed his generous morning hard-on at the same time she did. Oh, great, the *'Pierre curse!'*

"C'mere," he reached for her hand. Might as well be up front about it.

Jessica let go of her towel, allowing Pierre to pull her towards the bed. The white towel around her body fell loose onto the carpet leaving her bare and naked. She climbed on the bed, the other towel still solidly wrapped around her hair.

Pierre was enamored with her body. He had but a couple of seconds to admire her delicious boobs dangling as she approached him on all fours. Her sexy mouth hungrily found his mouth, sucking on his lower lip with great passion.

Pierre didn't get much of a chance to enjoy the kiss as he gasped feeling her strong hand encircling his cock. She firmly wrapped her fingers around his shaft.

"Lean back," she commanded, pushing him backwards. "We're gonna do this my way."

So, his magnificent mahogany-hard-on wasn't going to waste after all.

Pierre stretched on the bed. Jessica was on him in one second, straddling him. He felt her rub the tip of his hard-on between her pussy lips twice, lubricating him. Then she moved her hips forward and down, guiding his wood-hard shaft inside her.

Pierre tightened his abdomen, making sure his erection was at its hardest. This was too good to be true. He hadn't been awake five minutes and he was already inside Jessica. What more could he ask for? This girl was incredible.

She sat on his crotch, rubbing her clit against the base of his shaft, shoving her hips back and forth with great intensity. Her hands resting on his chest allowed Jessica's lusty eyes to fixate on Pierre's.

He had a brief moment wondering how she managed to keep that towel on her head through all the activity.

Her rubbing intensified, the look of concentration on her face suggesting she was getting very turned on. Well, so was he. *Whoa,* if she didn't slow down some, she was going to start a fire down there. Jessica wasn't even blinking, her eyes appeared in a trance, she was breathing harder by the second, increasing the intensity of her hips moving back and forth.

Pierre managed to get a grip on her nipples, being careful not to hurt her. The furious rubbing of her clit against him was really turning him on. He prayed she wasn't gonna make him come before she did. Her breasts were splendid, bouncy and round and perky, and she seemed to be liking the increased pressure he was putting on her nipples. She looked like an exotic Kama Sutra princess, passionately fucking his brains off staring down at him with a towel turban on her head.

He began arching his back off the bed. His legs were young and strong, and he could easily lift her while she pleased herself. That seemed to meet with her approval. Jessica increased the fury of her rubbing. Pierre was honestly surprised she had that much stamina in her. She fucked the length and impressive girth of his shaft with a fury.

Damn, if she didn't climax soon, he was going to shoot off his load inside her. His powerful abdomen muscles lifted Jessica up and down without much effort, while she rubbed her center of pleasure against his groin.

They animal-fucked out of control.

She closed her eyes tightly, raising her face.

"Aaaargh!" She let go.

Pierre grabbed her thighs, keeping her in place, lifting her higher and faster, bucking like a wild horse at a rodeo.

Jessica moaned and made other lusciously sensual sounds while she rode his shaft hard, obviously in the grasp of a delicious orgasm. Pierre kept up the rodeo, feeling himself getting thoroughly soaked from her juices.

Go, go for it!

He abandoned all caution, lifting Jessica even higher with each powerful thrust of his muscular hips. He only had to slam into her a few times when the soul-crushing spasm traveled from his crotch to his chest.

FortheloveofGod!

His respiration stopped. His body concentrating all its strength on squeezing his balls, filling Jessica with his hot life essence, mixing their body fluids high inside her.

"Jessica I'm cuming! Let me cum inside you!"

Was all he could muster, while totally so not in control of his actions. His body lifted Jessica a couple of more times, then he subsided to short, uncontrolled spasms.

That was incredible. Jessica leaned forward resting on his chest, still breathing fast. She was hot and soaking wet.

Pierre was still inside her.

And the damned towel was still firmly knotted on her head.

He laughed.

"What?" She whispered.

"You're funny."

"How so?"

"That towel on your head, Jessica. What'd you do, glue it there?"

"Oh, just be quiet."

She rested her head against his face, allowing her breathing to slow. Pierre was thrilled beyond words. What more could he ask of life than what he had at the moment? Jessica was not just a woman, she was a Muse, a goddess. She was perfect in every way he thought a woman should be. Down to morning sex.

Pierre hadn't really found too many lovers who enjoyed morning sex as much as he did. He wasn't sure why, but few partners had his inclination for morning activities. And since he was blessed, or cursed, with morning hard-ons, a morning lover was—by definition—extremely desirable.

Jessica didn't weigh much, and he loved the sensation of having her passed out on his chest. That was twice he'd lost control while making love to her. He liked to think of this as 'making love,' since he already felt emotionally tied to Jessica. There was some sort of very intense connection between them, that was unquestionable. They hadn't just fucked each other into oblivion. They had made love. At least he felt that way. He'd have to ask her feelings about this. Just not now.

He had to be careful, coming on too strong would have her stampeding out of his life. Even now.

Jessica stirred. "Whew," she expressed, stretching her legs slowly.

"You okay?" Pierre whispered close to her ear.

"Am I okay? No, I'm not okay. You killed me."

"Would you like an encore?" He felt Jessica sitting up.

"You must be insane. No, thank you, Mister. I am sore. I would love some breakfast, though."

He helped her up. "Your wish shall be granted, oh dubious blonde woman."

"Dubious blonde? I thought by now you'd realized I am a natural blonde."

"Hard to tell, since you shaved so beautifully. Not enough hair left for me to judge."

"Trust me; I am a blonde. Let's do breakfast. I need to take another quick shower first."

Pierre smiled. Jessica appeared to be half-asleep. Definitely exhibiting bedroom eyes.

She stood unsteadily, reaching for her turban, pulling it off her head, allowing her wet blond hair to drop on her shoulders.

Pierre stood next to her, placing his arm around her lower back. "C'mon, I'll help you in the shower."

Jessica reached for his waist, steadying herself walking for the bathroom. "I was going to ask you to be careful coming inside me, since I don't have any protection."

Holy cannoli. Again? He must be the dumbest man in the world.

"But then I realized I wanted you to cum inside me. I wanted it very bad."

Pierre's heart had missed a beat. Now it was restarting. She wanted him to come inside her very bad? That was hot. Definitely hot. He was right, there was a flow of something between them, something stronger than mere sex.

"I'm very happy you wanted me to. I wanted the same thing."

Jessica looked at him with great softness in her eyes. She stepped in the shower, running the water. Pierre followed close behind. The water felt hot and refreshing. There wasn't too much room, which was just fine by him. The less room they had, the closer she was to him. He loved standing behind her. Surprisingly, he was hard again. His erection nested directly between her buttocks, right between her legs, ready for action.

"You can't be real," Jessica stated.

Pierre encircled her with his arms, locking his hands just below her full breasts, feeling her rib cage. He felt his crotch pushing against her amazing buttocks, his full shaft wedged between her legs, touching her hot lips.

"Guide me inside you," he whispered against her ear.

Jessica turned her head as much as possible, "Did you really just ask me that?"

"Yes. I want to be inside you." He didn't want to let go of her with either arm.

Jessica reached down between her legs, separating her thighs enough to reach for Pierre's throbbing cock. She directed it back with barely a touch of two fingers, allowing it to slip inside her in an instant, while simultaneously shoving her ass backwards against Pierre.

"Wow!" Pierre exhaled. He had Jessica in a bear hug, no way was she going anywhere. He thrust his powerful hips forward against her derrière, feeling the intoxicating warmth of his hard-on entering her hot pussy.

Jessica reached back, pulling Pierre against her with both arms. She couldn't do much, other than stand there and accept his passion.

Pierre recalled she had complained earlier about being sore. Dammit, how could he forget about that? He slowed his rhythm, concentrating on being gentle. Selfish bastard! He should've thought of that. However, she was going along with his wishes, his inordinate sexual appetite, without any complaints so she must not be that sore.

The feel of her slippery wet body wedged hard against him as he entered her repeatedly from behind was unreal. Could this really be happening to him? He'd dreamed of something like this occurring someday, of making love to this incredibly hot, sensual woman in a shower, after just waking up, but just like many other erotic dreams of his youth, he had doubted they would come to pass. He felt this incredible drive to be inside her constantly.

Jessica was everything he could ever ask for in a woman. Physically, she was delicious and erotic and she could turn him on with a mere glance at her incredible body.

Mentally and emotionally, for what little he knew her, Pierre found her intriguing, interesting, intelligent and sweet. What a winning combination. And he just met her, and now here they were, making love in her shower after a night of lust and passion.

Thank you, St. Peter. Or whomever.

Again.

One millisecond later he was coming inside her, holding on to her for dear life. He thrust his cock as far deep inside her as he could, from the standing position. His ears were ringing, his respiration frantic and very accelerated. The immense pleasure he felt was indescribable. He knew he was emptying himself inside Jessica. Wait! What was it she'd said about being careful? He couldn't think straight. If she'd said something about not coming inside her, it was too late now. Oh, God, he wanted her so bad! Pierre realized he was holding on to Jessica with way too much force. He quickly eased his grip around her chest.

Resting his chin on her shoulder he allowed himself a moment to catch his breath. The sound of the shower pouring hot water on them was all he heard for a moment.

"I can't believe you still had that in you," Jessica voiced, incredulous.

"I can't either. That's the effect you have on me, sweetheart."

Jessica moved away from Pierre, forcing him to slip out from between her legs. She turned in the tight space, facing him. The palms of her hands went up to his face. Her cobalt blue eyes staring into his.

"Pierre, I'm afraid this is the end of a beautiful friendship."

Now what? Crap, did he do something wrong?

"Because I'm falling in love with you."

Pierre felt his ears ringing. Did she just say that? Unexpected, unfuckingbelievable. He didn't know what to make of it, thrilled to death hearing those words, and at a loss on how to respond.

She was falling for him? So soon? How could that be possible? But then again, he had become a firm believer in love at first sight, so maybe this was not so farfetched. And he had to admit he was crazy about her.

He kissed her softly. Jessica's lips felt warm and moist. "Well, then I guess that makes us even, 'cause I've already fallen for you."

Her eyes sparkled, only an inch or so away from his. Jessica kissed him again, then pushed him away. "Are you going to buy me breakfast, or do you intend to keep me here as your concubine the rest of the day?"

"Do I have a choice?"

"Absolutely not!"

"In that case, let's go get some breakfast."

He shut off the water, pushing open the glass door. The bathroom was steamed and the mirror completely fogged up. And the air was cold. Or at least it felt cold to him after basking under the hot water.

He reached for a couple of towels, wrapping Jessica in one and plopping the second one on her head. "You're gonna have to do the turban thing, since I don't have a clue where to begin."

"I'll just blow dry it."

Pierre used a third towel to dry his face, then applied it to Jessica's bottom, drying her like a baby. He was getting a kick out of doing that, her buttocks bouncing gently at his touch. He slid the towel between her legs in an attempt to dry her crotch.

"I don't think that's gonna work too well," she pointed out.

"Why not?"

"Because I'm gonna be wet down there for quite some time today. You, my passionate lover, are gonna keep seeping out of me all day long."

Pierre laughed. "Is that undesirable?"

"No. But I'm going to be the only one in the room knowing why my panties are wet."

Wow!

She was both naughty and eloquent. Pierre was getting turned on again just listening to her.

He sat on the toilet, watching her blow dry her hair, a white hotel towel wrapped around her attractive body. He was hypnotized. Jessica kept looking back at him in the mirror, smiling. She stuck out her tongue at him.

He smiled. "Keep that up, you'll get another spanking."

"Promises, promises."

"I always keep what I promise. Let's go out on the bed. I'll show you."

"Oh, I'm sure you'd like that, but you promised me breakfast."

"I'll spank you first, then I'll take you to breakfast."

"You wish! In another lifetime, maybe."

"Did my spankings bother you last night?" Might as well find out.

"Bother me? Heavens, no. I dreamed of 'em all night long."

Pierre felt his knees go weak, his groin radiating pleasure. Dang! She knew how to get his attention.

Pierre took one brief second to congratulate himself. His decision to return to Jessica's room last night had been so right. One of the absolute best calls of his life, really. Although they had spent the afternoon and part of the evening together, their friendship—as she called it—would never have reached its present level. Before, they had been friends. Now they were friends and lovers. The best possible combination. And all of it at breakneck speed, just the way he preferred it.

He was fascinated with Jessica. Totally infatuated, no question about that. He felt together they could have so much fun. Right off the bat he could have her use his 'Guest Passes,' the stand-by passes Worldwide issued him annually, so they could fly places together. He didn't want to rush into a relationship with her before they had the chance to get to know each other better, but that was going to be a hard one to honor. He was already dying to wrap his arms around her and hold her, kiss her and tell her she was his forever.

Goddamn, he really had a difficult time controlling his emotions. Why was it he would fall head over heels for every girl he met? Naw, that was not true. He thought about it. He only fell head over heels for those girls he ultimately took to bed who were nice to him and had potential.

Did Jessica have potential?

Was sea water salty?

What in heaven's name was he doing rationalizing everything? Of course, Jessica had promise and potential. They had spent hours together during their visit to Harrods's, and all he did then was hold her hand for two minutes. And she captivated his attention then. He was sold back then, he wanted her.

Now, after an unforgettable night with her, the deal was sealed. He wanted Jessica, period. He was going to do everything within his power to earn the love and affection of this most splendid of all women. And from the sound of it, he was already earning her love.

Pierre was going to make her his.

"Thank you," he said.

"For what?"

"For making love with me—in the morning."

"You don't have to thank me. I loved it."

He told her how morning sex had never really been a part of his relationships.

"You don't have that problem with me, Pierre. I just need to go pee and brush my teeth and I'm ready!"

He laughed at the simplicity of her statement. He had definitely found himself a girl made of gold.

Now, however, he had to take care of her other needs, so it was time to go downstairs and find out what sort of delicacies the incredible Brits could provide for breakfast.

COTTON CANDY AND TANGERINES   MR Chevalier

Suzanne

Pierre admired the darkening mauve and red sky ahead of them. It was a spiritual moment for him; from 33,000 feet, the view was majestic. The sun was racing away behind them towards the west at 800 knots, while he flew his wide body Airbus eastbound, in the opposite direction at 600 knots. Doing the math, daytime was moving away from him at 1,400 nautical miles per hour. That meant they were headed into the night at warp speed, twice as fast as people on the ground.

The aviator reached for his coffee cup parked next to his knee, bringing it to his lips. He carefully sipped the hot brew, discreetly glancing sideways at his captain.

They were on the Los Angeles-to-Paris flight, for a total of ten hours and forty minutes. About four hours into the flight, Pierre was still not sure how to behave. A poignantly unusual condition for him.

What was different about this particular flight was that his captain was a female.

That, was a first for him.

And not just any female, Captain Suzanne Brown was a stunningly attractive woman in what he estimated to be her forties. When she'd walked into the flight deck back in Los Angeles while they were still at the gate, Pierre had to catch his breath. He'd never flown with a woman captain before. He knew Worldwide only had four percent of its pilot workforce who were female, so he never really thought about the day when he'd show up in the office to find a female in charge of his flight.

But that day had come.

And she was beautiful. Oh, God, green eyes made in heaven.

And then there was their age difference. That was exciting. She must have ten years on him, although the only sign of age he'd been able to see in her so far were the crow's feet around her eyes.

He'd admired her straw-tone blond hair and ardent green eyes, and ended up speechless.

In all honesty, Pierre had not been mentally prepared for the day when he'd be confronted with a female captain, much less a stunningly beautiful one, hence he'd been broadsided.

Plus, there was the additional and very impressive fact that she was a Check Airman. That got Pierre's attention as much as her good looks. A Check Airman was an airline pilot in charge of checking, training and qualifying other airline pilots. Only the very best were selected for this position.

He wondered momentarily why they didn't call the position Check Airwoman when it came to females.

Pierre's contemporaries mostly didn't have any issues with females in the flight deck, as had been the case with the recently-retired generation of older pilots. He basically considered that if a woman could qualify to sit in that left seat, then she had every right to be there because she had earned it.

Simple as that.

Suzanne had been friendly and efficient, and so far, she'd directed the flight deck like a true professional, in a very relaxed atmosphere. She'd kept their conversation completely professional while they were at the gate, and hadn't really mellowed out until they were climbing out of 10,000 feet on their way to Paris. Pierre did notice—however—a gold wedding band and a good-sized diamond ring on her left hand.

Married.

To be expected. Naturally, that was par for the course. No surprise there. A desirable, intelligent woman such as Suzanne was not going to stay single for very long.

She was polite and friendly, and she'd stayed up front in the flight deck until they reached cruising altitude, at which point she'd excused herself, going back to First Class to have dinner and relax for three hours.

Pierre didn't have much of a chance to visit with her, they merely exchanged the usual pleasantries before she left him in charge of the office. The other pilot on the flight, Brad Caldwell, had then taken over the left seat vacated by the captain.

Not having much in common with the man, Pierre had intentionally kept a silent atmosphere between them. Not a particularly unusual situation, really. Pierre and most of his male contemporaries were perfectly comfortable sitting side-by-side for hours on end without engaging in conversation.

Besides, he needed time to think. The only sounds in the flight deck were those generated by the air rushing past the metal skin of the airplane, and the voices of the air traffic controllers and other pilots breaking the silence between long intervals.

He was captivated by Suzanne, she was obviously intelligent—or she wouldn't be flying this jet—she was so damned attractive, and naturally he wondered how she'd be in bed. Pierre shook his head with a resigned smile, when was he going to stop making sex the central focus of his entire existence?

Never—that's when.

And, the not-so-inconsequential fact that she was married assigned her to the category of 'off-limits, *verboten*, prohibited, not-to-be-messed-with.'

No way under God's blue skies was he ever going to make a move on a married dame. Besides being totally unfair to the woman's husband, it had the potential of generating a veritable shit-storm for everyone involved. There were too many other attractive women out there, willing and available, so why even consider something like this?

And who said he was considering it?

He was merely indulging in some fantasies.

The fact that Suzanne was older than Pierre added an element of excitement to the fantasy that was rapidly developing in his imagination. Without doubt, she'd be more experienced than any woman he'd ever been with. In what ways, though?

That, in itself was enthralling.

He couldn't help wondering with extreme curiosity—again—how she'd be different in bed from other sex partners he'd had in his life.

Intriguing, most definitely. Experience had to count for something, hence he firmly believed she could introduce him to some incredible and yet unknown magic in the bedroom.

Suzanne hadn't given him any signal or reason to believe she was interested in him, her behavior had been exclusively professional, yet Pierre had sensed a certain harmonic flow between the two of them when their eyes first locked back still at the gate. And she exuded femininity.

Could that have been just a product of his overly-sexed out-of-control imagination?

Maybe.

She had a gorgeous and very fit figure, from what little he could tell. He'd caught sight of her cute ass swinging away from her seat when she excused herself to go outside on her break. Even in her uncomplimentary navy blue company uniform he'd been able to admire her sexy butt and her agile body; although the only sign of age he'd been able to see in her—as he'd already determined—were the crow's feet around her eyes.

Those tantalizing emerald-green eyes.

Suzanne without doubt made enough money to pay for the best plastic surgeon in the country to get rid of those crow's feet. The fact that she hadn't done so impressed Pierre and attracted him to her even more. A confident girl, he approved. She liked herself the way she was, without any pretentions.

Self-confidence, a very attractive trait in both men and women.

He knew he was fantasizing, since he'd already come to terms he was never going to make a move on his captain because she was married, but hey, he could still let his imagination play with alternate realities, no?

Come to think of it, Paris would be a lovely city to seduce Suzanne. The most enchanting city of lovers. He imagined himself animal-fucking her blind during the day and then making sweet love to her at night. And in between, they could walk over to some quaint little restaurant on the West Bank and have a candlelight dinner among the Parisians. Wine and cheese and prosciutto and French bread.

He liked his fantasy.

Unrealistic as hell, but also deliciously exciting.

While Suzanne was away from the flight deck Pierre day-dreamed for hours about what he'd do with Suzanne if their bodies and souls connected. As his airplane flew across northeastern Canada in the dark, he wondered what delicious new flavors she could take to their bed because of the ten years she had on him.

Another interesting yet disturbing angle to contemplate in this fantasy of his, what if at the end of a layover of fulfilled desire and passion in Paris Suzanne decided cold-turkey she didn't like him anymore, as had been the case that one time in Denver with Amanda?

That would make for a rather awkward, long, painful and quite interesting flight back to the States.

However, since Pierre was in control of his fantasy, he could fabricate whatever outcome he preferred. Consequently, at least in his imagination, Suzanne adored him blindly all the way back to California. Yeah, that was a much better outcome.

Pierre convinced Caldwell, the other pilot, to take his break next, after Suzanne returned to the flight deck. That way Pierre would have three hours alone with Suzanne during their short night. That would give him some time to feel the waters with her.

Feel the waters? What was he, on crack?

"You didn't want to eat dinner next?" Suzanne asked, having settled herself comfortably back in her seat.

Pierre glanced at her in the darkness of the flight deck, smiling. "Nah, not hungry yet. Brad was starved, so I let him go first."

"That was nice of you."

Pierre was sure her night vision had not returned yet, hence he could see her very clearly, but she probably only saw him as a blur. He glanced at her. She appeared to be about his own height, although he hadn't stood next to her yet, so he was just estimating.

He could see the curvature of her boobs under her white uniform shirt, desperately begging to be let out. He saw himself reaching over to her and ripping her shirt off leaving her there, exposed to his most creative sexual fantasies. Would she make any sound when he caressed her boobs? What about when he sucked on her nipples?

"Where do you live, Pierre?"

Her voice was sexy and clear. Pierre sighed, content. He was confined up there, in the flight deck of a modern airliner, with a striking woman who was his captive audience for the next three hours, or until Brad decided to return, yet he doubted they would get anywhere.

But, regardless, life was good.

"I live in Phoenix, Suzanne."

"Phoenix, eh? Beautiful place. If a little hot."

"Only in the summer. Where are you from?"

"I was raised in North Carolina, but I live in the Bay area."

"San Francisco?"

"Sausalito."

Pierre jumped back into his fantasy. Sausalito. That wasn't a very long flight from Phoenix, really. He could be there in a little under three hours. If she became his lover, he could visit her two or three times a month. So, she lived in the Bay area. Very expensive. As a captain—however—she could certainly afford it.

"You married?" Suzanne asked him.

He gasped. Goodness, she'd plunged right into that pool. They were getting personal now. Wasn't that what'd wished for?

"No, single." Pierre noticed Suzanne turning to look at him in the darkness of the flight deck, as if his body language could confirm his bachelorhood status.

"Really? How old are you?"

"Thirty-three." He resisted the urge to ask her how old she was. Given there was still very little familiarity between them, he felt it may be rude of him to ask.

"You been married before?"

He liked how she was leading the conversation into a personal level.

Was Suzanne just being polite or were her questions indicative of some interest in him?

"No, never been married. Just haven't found the right girl, I guess."

Pierre thought about their arrival in Paris. Once they were parked at the gate in the morning,

Worldwide would send a big bus, the type Greyhound uses, to pick up the crew. The bus would park right next to the airplane, and the entire crew would deplane onto the ramp using the jet bridge stairs. The bus would then just drive out of the airport and transport them to downtown Paris. This procedure allowed the crew to bypass customs and immigration, as well as the busy Charles-de-Gaulle international terminal. Just another way for the crew to avoid unwanted attention. With terrorism rapidly becoming an international sport, crews had to be protected.

Naturally, Worldwide Airlines did this for security reasons, in an attempt to expose its crews as little as possible to any potential terrorist attack.

In his weaved fantasy, Pierre would do his best to sit near Suzanne during the drive into town.

The drive to the Hotel Nikko would take them a little over half an hour. The Nikko was splendid, a deluxe hotel situated on the left bank of the River Seine, and the only hotel in Paris located directly on the river side.

In his imagination, Suzanne was already infatuated with him, and they both knew where things were going to end up. All they had to do was be discrete around the rest of the crew.

Pierre knew the smart thing to do would be sleep three hours as soon as they arrived at the hotel, but in reality, that would be an impossibility with Suzanne. If they ended up in the same hotel room they were going to go hungrily after each other, unable to contain their primal instincts—and forget about sleeping three hours—that was nonsense.

He decided to be direct with her. He'd just ask her in the lobby, what did she want to do?

If Suzanne decided to say good-bye and head for her room to sleep three hours, then their 'thing' would die on arrival. But, if she asked him to join her in her room, then he would know they would be enjoying each other as only lovers can.

"Girlfriend?" Suzanne persisted with her personal questioning.

"Uh, what?" Pierre was jolted out of his alternate reality.

"Do you have a girlfriend?"

"Not one particular girl, no." He wondered if he should elaborate.

"Do you date around?"

He didn't like the way that sounded. It was too much like 'do you fuck around?'

The sky ahead was dark except for momentary flashes of lightning in the distance.

"I meet girls here and there. What about you, you married?"

"Yep, I'm married."

Pierre waited for some additional information. None came. He looked outside, in the direction of the lightning. "Some weather up ahead," he commented.

"I see it." Suzanne glanced down at the computer display in front of her, the one known as the 'Navigation Display.' There, the storms ahead of them were represented by the inflight radar as gradients of red, yellow and green. "We'll be all right. They're moving away from us.

Pierre agreed with her, those storms were still almost one hundred miles ahead, and the winds were blowing them away from their path. Good, their passengers would be able to continue enjoying their sleep without having to deal with uncomfortable turbulence. He liked her, she was sharp.

Pierre returned to his fantasy. In it, Suzanne had naturally asked him to join her in her room.

"Be mine tonight," she had pleaded.

They would wait a prudent length of time for their flight attendants and the other pilot to disappear in the elevators, after which they would ride the high-speed lift to her floor. After so much time on duty they would both have to use the restroom once they got to the room. He'd let her use it first. She'd probably shut the door. Once she exited the bathroom then it'd be his turn to relieve himself. These initial moments would be a little awkward between them but they were inevitable.

As was the case in every layover hotel with room darkening curtains, the only light in the room would come from the bathroom, so the instant he came out in the twilight he'd go straight to Suzanne, her lips parting, expectantly. She'd be standing there wearing only her unbuttoned white uniform shirt and her panties. She had undressed while he was in the blue room.

At that instant, all civility would leave them, and Pierre and Suzanne would go at each other like starved tigers fighting over a prized antelope, casting morality and good judgment aside.

Pierre imagined Suzanne kissing him with hungry desperation, standing tight against him, rubbing her pelvis against his throbbing erection in total abandonment to their lust. He would grab a handful of panties, ripping them off her body with ease. Then his hand would squeeze her butt cheeks with unrestrained desire while simultaneously going deep in her mouth with his tongue.

SUZANNE PRESSED HER HOT lips against his, grabbing a fistful of Pierre's hair, while her other hand plunged inside his pants and shorts, reaching for his cock in all its pumped-up glory. The sensation of having her cold hand on his shaft was fabulous. Pierre anxiously ran his hand down between her buttocks, enjoying the velvet feel of her skin and the heat from her body. They had both repressed their desire for each other way too long. The *crescendo* had been building painfully for hours. It was now mutually understood it was time to indulge in their most primitive fantasies.

"I want you to fuck me! Right now!" She ordered, her green eyes glowing, pulling him down onto the low Japanese-style king-size bed.

Pierre could hardly believe her aggressiveness, but was loving every instant. With his pants and shorts barely off he got on top of Suzanne, shifting his hips to position himself. Her well-toned tanned legs were already wide open, waiting with great anticipation for what was to come.

He barely noticed his increased heartbeat. All his own personal sexual strategies had flown out the window. This delicious creature wanted him to fuck her right here and right now, and that's precisely what he intended to do. He found her hot and wet and willing. He intended to enter her slowly, feeling his cock separating her walls, stretching her, filling her with his solid sword. His erect hard-on tentatively entered her atrium.

Instead, Suzanne thrust her pelvis up unexpectedly and with such passion, Pierre found himself stuffing his huge, erect cock in her as far as he could go, all in a split second.

Whoa!

She pumped her hips with surprising force, taking the lead. She had become the dominant partner. He was incredulous at her sexuality, her intensity. Pierre picked up the cue, synchronizing his thrusts with Suzanne's, both his hands cupping her buttocks, squeezing with all his strength.

She yelped, gasped and squealed under him.

"You are so fucking hot!" He barely managed to blurt out.

Suzanne was grinding her clit against his pelvis with an intensity he found ardently erotic. She obviously knew what she liked and what got her off.

Pierre began wondering if he was going to go the distance or would he spill the beans too early. His entire body was wound tight as a piano wire. And Suzanne had not slowed down one bit since the first moment she impaled herself on his rod. He was directly on top of her, his eyes staring into her mysterious emerald-greens, neither of them blinking.

Eyes are the window to the soul, they say, and the two lover's eyes were locked in a passionate attempt to decipher the other's emotions.

Pierre realized going down on her was not going to be necessary, not at the moment anyhow. Suzanne's experienced relentless rubbing of her clit against the base of his cock seemed to be a familiar way for her to please herself. But that, of course, was only going to work if he stayed hard as a rock. If she made him come inside her too soon, then he'd have to go down on her to pleasure her.

He managed to crack a smile, thinking so, what would he call this? Making love or fucking? Pierre felt a warmth radiating throughout his body, announcing the arrival of a climax. Holy shit, he was still furiously pumping in and out of her, and she was relentless.

"Aww, Pierre!" She cried, tightening her hold on him with her arms and legs.

Pierre felt her slamming her pelvis against his crotch with increasing ferocity.

"I'm cuming, Oh, God, I am cuming, oh, Pierre!"

Suzanne's hungry mouth bit his chin with a fury.

Pierre felt bells going off in the distance, his crotch was on fire, the waves of sweet orgasm reverberated through his cock, his balls, his pelvis. Suzanne buried her face in his neck, holding him tight enough to make breathing difficult.

He exploded inside her, feeling the effect of his juices inside her pussy totally eliminating friction between them. He found her face again, his tongue wrestling in her mouth, exploring her teeth, her lips. The indescribable pleasure he felt was amplified by the knowledge that Suzanne was orgasming under him at the same time. She was breathing in short gasps, panting loudly.

That was a first for Pierre. Never, in his entire life had he ever come at the same time as his mate. That only happened in movies.

Or in his imagination.

"Time for a position report."

"Say what?" Pierre was disoriented, needing a few seconds to mentally return to the flight deck.

Suzanne repeated her command.

"Oh, yeah, for sure!" He took care of her request, still straddling both realities, the one on the flight deck and the other one he'd created in his mind with Suzanne in the hotel room. *Holy Minerva, goddess of wisdom!* He'd mentally transported himself so far into his fantasy he'd practically left the flight deck!

Bad, bad idea.

The power of his imagination was extraordinary; he'd always had that ability since he was a little kid. Pierre could create an alternate reality and immerse himself in it with such intensity, it became difficult for him differentiating between what was real and what was merely a product of his mind.

Only now he was a pilot flying an airliner full of trusting passengers, and he shouldn't separate himself from this reality to such a degree. Totally asinine of him to allow this.

He discreetly looked at Suzanne, wondering how many times she'd attempted to make contact with him while he was in his near trance.

Was his racing heartbeat a result of being startled, or the continuation of his sexual fantasy with Suzanne? He wondered if she had detected what he'd been thinking.

Hard to tell. Better make some conversation to test the waters. Last thing he needed was to piss off a Check Airman.

"Do you have any kids?" He asked, trying to control his breathing. Hopefully, that wasn't too personal a question.

"No, no kids."

"How long you been married?"

Suzanne had loosened her uniform tie, unbuttoning the top button of her shirt. "A long time."

Pierre took that as 'none of your business.' Crap. He didn't know what else to say.

"Sorry, I didn't mean to be rude. My husband and I never had any children. We've been married twenty years and there were just too many things we wanted to do before having children. Then one morning I woke up, and it was too late."

Pierre still didn't know what to say. He nodded his head in understanding.

"Marriage for me didn't turn out exactly as I expected it."

Pierre was frowning. Suzanne had all of a sudden opened up and was confiding in him. That was pleasant and unexpected.

"What do you mean?"

She sighed loudly. "Hard to explain, Pierre. We all have expectations and then time passes and we become part of each other's history."

"You mean, like after you get so used to each other, you just continue the *status quo?*"

"Yeah, sort of like that. You see, we're separated at the moment. My husband suddenly decided he didn't want to be married to a woman who is away so many nights a month. He pretty much told me to quit flying or he'd walk."

"That's pretty cold. Is he a pilot?"

"Heavens, no. he's an electrical engineer."

"So he walked?"

"Yea."

"Where'd he go?"

"Just over to his best friend's place. Couple of miles from our house."

"You don't want to quit flying, do you?"

She looked at Pierre in surprise. "No, would you?"

"Probably not." So, why was Suzanne wearing her wedding band and diamond ring if she was separated and potentially on her way to a divorce?

"I've thought about it," she continued. "But I just can't give it up. I have fifteen years to go before I have to retire, and that's a lot of years to give up."

Fifteen years? Mandatory retirement age for airline pilots was 65, so that meant Suzanne was fifty years old. Wow, that was a surprise. Impressive, really. He'd thought she was in her early to mid-forties maybe. That meant she had seventeen years on Pierre.

"What would you do if you weren't flying?"

She gave him a sad smile. "That's just it, I wouldn't know what to do with myself."

"Financially, could you afford to retire?"

"Yes. I have plenty of money. That's not the issue. I'd be scared to death finding myself with nothing to do."

"What does your husband want you to do, other than flying—that is."

"He wants to buy a cabin in the mountains and a small chalet in the Bahamas, and spend six months at each place."

"Is he still working?"

"He's planning on retiring this year. Paul is ten years older than I."

Pierre understood. The poor guy wanted to retire with his partner, without having to wait fifteen additional years until Suzanne hit sixty-five. Heck, he could be dead by the time she retired.

"So he's planning on retiring and would like to look forward to spending his golden years with you.

You've been his partner all these years. Somehow you flying around the world while he sits in a cabin by himself must scare him half to death."

She didn't respond.

Seventeen years older than he was. His imagination went into overdrive again, wondering what exquisite love-making techniques she could teach him. Dang! Suzanne had been a seventeen-year-old teenager probably having sex in the back seat of her boyfriend's car when Pierre was just a baby. Mind-altering exciting. Also, humbling.

He shook his head in the dark. He had to control the beast. Suzanne needed his listening ear, not his cock.

"You still love the guy?" Perhaps a little too personal. He gritted his teeth, not sure what her reaction would be. He was definitely never going to learn to keep his goddamned mouth shut.

Suzanne's enchanting green eyes appeared black in the dark flight deck. "Of course I do. You don't live with someone for twenty years and not love him."

"How long have you been flying?"

She appeared pensive. "If I could venture a guess, I'd say I've been flying almost as long as you've been alive."

Gee, thanks, Suzanne. He sits there fabricating sexual fantasies about her and she looks at him as just a kid. He decided to ignore the barb.

"So you've had a long and satisfying career."

"You could say that."

"And you're at the point now where you have to choose. Keep flying and maybe lose your partner, or walk away and experience life with him under a different set of rules."

"That's pretty much it."

"Your parents still around?"

"No, they haven't been around for a few years now."

"Do you have any siblings?"

"Nope. Only child."

Pierre was no shrink, but he could detect a certain hesitation in her tone. "You've been flying for a long time, and you think you have enough money put together so retirement wouldn't be a burden. What do you want to do, have you asked yourself that? Continue flying these trips to Europe so you can sleep by yourself in countless hotels night after night? Doesn't that get old? To be honest with you, I've been searching for a girl like you—one not married—obviously, so I can have someone to share my thoughts with, someone I can hold at night. When I find her—and I know I will—I'll never let her go." He stared into her devilish emerald-green eyes.

"Getting to the point, are you saying I should quit flying and retire with Paul?"

"No, I'm saying, that is your partner out there, Suzanne. I'd bet you even money he doesn't want to lose you anymore than you want to lose him. But be realistic, what the demons is he gonna do the next fifteen years without you by his side? That's crazy, that's too much to ask."

He was gonna piss her off, he was sure of that. But what the devil, maybe she needed to hear that.

"I've been flying for a long time," Suzanne agreed.

"I don't presume telling you your business, Suzanne. Please forgive me if I'm being indelicate here, but it seems to me you've been caught up in the inertia of the same activity you've been doing for decades. Maybe it's time to put the brakes on and do something else."

She looked pensive. "Yeah, you may be right."

Pierre decided it was time to shut up. He'd already said too much. In the name of his favorite goddess Minerva, how had he gone from lusting after Suzanne to becoming her spiritual advisor?

"You have any plans in Paris?" He figured it was time to change the topic.

"You mean, other than sleeping by myself in just another hotel room?"

Ouch.

She looked at him with an amused glint in her eye.

Pierre wasn't really sure how to respond. He was experiencing a maelstrom of mixed emotions. He liked her, he wanted her, yet she was off limits because she was married.

But wait a minute! *Technically,* she wasn't married—she was separated. Did that count as off limits? Even more disturbing, Pierre suspected Suzanne could read him like an open book. And he had to admit he was hopelessly in love with her green eyes.

"Yea, other than sleeping by yourself in just another hotel."

"No. not really. Just the usual, sleep a few hours, then drag my butt outta bed and go shopping or catch something to eat."

"Want to have dinner together?" He didn't know why he'd blurted that out.

Suzanne appraised the pilot sitting next to her, with more than just a cursory glance.

"Sure."

Pierre was dumbfounded she accepted, delighted at the prospect and troubled with himself. Why was he violating his own personal rules of life? However, technically, she was married but separated, so that must provide some sort of loophole. Or was he just manipulating the situation so he could pursue Suzanne? And did she even want him?

FIVE HOURS LATER, SUZANNE parked the wide body aircraft at their assigned gate. Another sunny day at Charles de Gaulle airport in Paris. The pilots read through their checklists, shutting everything down after the last of their passengers had left the airplane.

The entire crew descended to the tarmac using the stairs attached to the jet bridge, where a Greyhound-style bus waited with its big diesel engine purring at idle.

Pierre entered the bus ahead of Suzanne. This was intentional on his part. After many hours sitting next to her, he had to give her the option of selecting a seat in the bus. If Suzanne sat next to him again, great, but if she had the need for some solitude and chose to sit somewhere else in the back, that was okay too.

He saw her enter the bus behind him, evaluating her seating options. Suzanne picked a seat across the aisle from Pierre. What kind of message was that, he wondered? For heaven's sake—he was reading too much into this. The woman was married; she was tired after working all night and what the Dickens gave him the idea he had even a hint of a hope of attracting her?

She'd basically told him she planned on taking a nap when they got to the hotel.

So, he had to face the music, that was it—okay—good-bye sexual fantasies. Maybe that was for the best. She did agree to join him for dinner, so at least that could be a pleasant experience.

Suzanne rested her head back, closing her eyes. She didn't say another word during the ride into town.

Pierre wasn't extremely familiar with Paris, but he was sure he'd be able to come up with an interesting place to eat. Taking her to dinner was going to be a consolation price after all. They could take a walk around the Eiffel Tower park after napping and then find some cozy local restaurant to dine under candlelight.

He leaned his head against his own head rest, thinking of Suzanne's serene green eyes, and how they'd left him with an unquenched thirst for her. Those green eyes he now knew he would never kiss.

Paris morning traffic was a bitch. The coach finally arrived at destination. The crewmembers were feeling like fleas sprayed with DDT, tired, jet-lagged, hungry and ornery.

The driver unloaded all the bags onto the sidewalk, accepting the customary tips from the crew.

Pierre and Suzanne brought up the rear, entering the lobby of the luxurious Japanese-style hotel behind the rest of their crew. It took less than five minutes for everyone to get checked in, receive their keys and disappear.

It was only about ten in the morning local time, Pierre considered if they slept three hours and then showered, they'd be able to go out for a walk around one-thirty.

The two pilots headed for the elevator, pulling their overnight bags. Suzanne looked beautiful, the fatigue from their flight making her appear more vulnerable.

"Want to join me in my room?" She asked.

COTTON CANDY AND TANGERINES   MR Chevalier

Monica

Pierre White walked straight to the gate after flying in from Phoenix. The young aviator walked briskly and energetically, pulling his wheelie overnight bag with the flight leather briefcase strapped to it. He noticed, amused, that some traveling businessmen and women in the terminal actually pushed their wheelies in front of them or pulled them alongside as they walked down the concourses. Strange, really. He would never do that. Besides the fact that it looked just plain weird, the entire enchilada would come crashing down if one of the wheelies hit a crevice on the floor.

He was also disturbed by the number of people he saw at LAX traveling with backpacks. For the love of God, he passed two young businessmen wearing elegant dark blue suits and ties, yet in all their Brooks Brothers stylishness, both had yellow nylon hiking backpacks strapped to their backs. A very disturbing sight. Whatever happened to class?

This trip to Buenos Aires was exciting and he'd been anticipating it for weeks. The one-hour commute in from Phoenix to LA had gone relatively smooth and now it was time to go to work. Thirteen hours flying to Argentina capped by a thirty-hour layover there and then back to LA. Not a bad schedule. Plus, there'd be three of them in the crew. These long-haul flights carried the additional pilot, the one known as the 'International Relief Officer,' or IRO. That took the edge off the long duty days.

Pierre had already previously enjoyed flying the South American routes for two months before switching to the London flights. And now that he was back on the Latin American flights he intended to have a blast spending time in Panama, Rio de Janeiro and Buenos Aires. Jet lag was also so much less dramatic flying the north-south routes than it had been flying to London.

Thinking of London brought a sweet and sour memory to mind, remembering the delicate flavor of Jessica. She had been one of the best experiences of his life, and he was sad they'd grown apart. That was one relationship he wished had matured into a lifelong romance. Sadly, after dating for a couple of months Jessica had decided life with an airline pilot was not for her. Someone who was away from home more than half the month was not something she wanted for a husband or a companion.

Jessica was fun and delicious and intriguing and he had come to love her, but when she started her campaign to have him switch careers their relationship came to an abrupt halt. Jessica wanted her man home every evening, in bed with her every night, and that was something Pierre could not provide for her. Not that he didn't love being in bed with her every night, but that just wasn't possible. She reminded him that she quit her job as a corporate jet flight attendant so they could spend more time together, but Pierre repeatedly explained they needed his income to maintain the standard of living they both enjoyed.

The nature of his job had him away from home many days a month. That was one of the reasons why he was paid so well. It was compensation for the time away from home and loved ones. He could not change that. Although he had an aerospace engineering degree, he would never consider leaving flying in exchange for a desk job. He knew if he quit the airlines to get a job with one of the aircraft manufacturers, he would hate his life so bad, it would destroy his relationship with Jessica.

He told her so.

Jessica became upset at this and did not accept the logic. In her mind, she should be primary in his life, and if that meant leaving the flight deck, then be it. Pierre tried to make her understand being an aviator was an integral part of who he was. And besides, if he quit the airlines to pursue an engineering job in the aircraft manufacturing industry, nothing guaranteed he'd find employment. And even if he did, his income potential would be reduced by at least half, which would impact their standard of living. Definitely not something he was willing to contemplate.

Jessica had accused him of not putting her first, of being narcissistic and loving the image of being an airline pilot more than he loved her.

She was wrong.

Pierre really loved her first, flying the machine second, traveling third and all the other perks of being an airline pilot fourth. He wasn't so much into the image of the profession, really. Truth was, he liked what he did, and it made him enough money so they could have options in life.

Ultimately, his reluctance to give up flying poisoned their relationship and they separated. That had been one of the heartbreaks of his life, but there was no fixing it. Jessica needed an accountant, or some other professional who was home every night, and that was just not him.

The aviator arrived at his gate. The shinning new wide body aircraft at the end of the jetway reminded him that his life was flying those magnificent machines. He didn't know if he'd made the right choice letting Jessica go in exchange for continuing to fly these big metal beasts, but wrong or right, it was done.

Jessica would not have been happy married to him flying the line, and he would not have been happy at another job. He sighed. At least they had the memories of their incredible times together. Last time he heard from her, she'd been dating a psychiatrist in San Diego. For all he knew, they were probably already married with kids. The memories of their first encounter in London and their incredible nights together in Cancun were theirs forever. Nobody could ever take those away.

Pierre showed his airline badge to the agent behind the counter. She verified it then walked to the jet bridge door, punching in the combination numbers to unlock it.

He thanked her, proceeding down the jet bridge to his steed for the day. Incredible, he contemplated, a three-hundred-million-dollar airplane awaited his commands at the end of that tunnel.

He was the first one there. Good, he liked it that way. No flight attendants yet and no sign of the other two pilots assigned to the trip. He entered the high-tech flight deck, enjoying the smell of pure oxygen, leather and hot electronics. Pierre secured his overnight bag then proceeded to climb into his seat, securing his flight bag between his seat and the fuselage. He would be needing some water bottles for the trip, but he'd have to wait until the cabin crew arrived to ask for them. The galley food carts were sealed shut and only the flight attendants were allowed to break the seals.

This was a long flight, and he'd have the opportunity to step back into First Class and relax for three or four hours during the trip. He would eat lunch or dinner at that time, depending on which break period he selected. The captain would take the first rest, of course. Then, it was up to Pierre to decide whether he wanted to go next or extend the courtesy to the IRO to go ahead of him. Once they hit Buenos Aires he intended treating himself to a superb cut of Argentinian beef—a *parrillada*. The *Rio de la Plata* delta offered many magnificent places to eat. And oh, yes, he would have the opportunity to listen to some tango. He loved that romantic music. Learning to dance the tango was on his bucket list. He smiled, remembering that magnificent actor, Robert Duvall, who learned how to tango in his later years. That was an example to emulate. Treat a woman like gold, drink wine and learn the tango.

He removed his dark navy blue coat, hanging it in the crew closet. His hat joined the coat. He still continued wearing his airline hat, although the majority of pilots had given it up since the airlines had made wearing it optional. His image of the professional aviator included the hat, and he would stubbornly wear it until the day they dragged his ass off an airplane for the last time on his sixty-fifth birthday.

"Howdy!"

Pierre turned to face his captain for the flight.

"Steve Evers," the captain greeted, offering his hand.

"Pierre White," nice to meet you!"

"You the first one here?"

"Yeah. Flight attendants aren't here yet."

"We're early. And they're here. I just saw them up at the gate."

Pierre instantly liked the man. He had the looks of Cary Grant and a friendly smile. Probably in his late fifties. First impressions were extremely important to him. Pierre's experience in the airlines had taught him that there was no second chance to make a first impression. If the guy he was going to fly with for three or four days was a jerk, he'd be able to tell the moment they met. That made for long trips. Having a horse's ass sitting next to one for days on end encouraged justifiable homicide.

He'd never flown with this Evers guy, heck, it was the first time he'd ever laid eyes on him.

If the flight attendants were at the gate, perhaps it was time for him to take advantage of the situation and step back there to check them out when they first came aboard. Once they scattered to the four corners of the cabin Pierre would be unable to determine if any of his cabin crew merited his attention during the layover. One of his previous dates had pointed out to Pierre his behavior was similar to that of a lion on the prowl in the Serengeti, stalking prey.

He wasn't amused with the analogy. Pierre didn't think of himself as a predator, just an ordinary guy trying to find a girl.

He waited for the captain to strap his overnight bag securely behind him, then climbed out of his eighty-thousand-dollar seat.

"I'm gonna go see if I can get my hands on some water bottles. Want some?"

"Water? Naw, water's for when I'm dirty. I'll grab myself some soda and maybe some coffee later."

Pierre liked the guy already. Nothing like a good sense of humor to turn a trip into a vacation. He walked back to the second exit from the front, just in time to catch the first of his fifteen flight attendants entering the aircraft. Two older ladies, two men, another older gal, a young thing—not his type.

"Good morning!" One of the male flight attendants offered.

"Morning!" Pierre shot back with a smile. He liked some of these more senior professional male flight attendants. They reminded him of the maître d's at fine restaurants in Europe, classy, refined and incredibly pleasant.

Once all the flight attendants arrived, they had to huddle up for the Boss. Steve, their captain, would provide them with a two-minute briefing touching on how long the flight was going to be, the weather, any potential security threats and so on. Worldwide Airlines didn't require the entire cabin crew complement to be present during the cabin briefing, permitting the captain to brief only the top flight attendant known as the 'Purser.' Subsequently, the Purser would brief the rest of his cabin crew.

The arrival of a young bombshell caught his eye like a cat catching a sudden glimpse of a canary.

Wow.

Pierre rapidly admired the girl in her twenties, long silky ash golden blond hair tucked up in a bun, sparkling blue eyes, and a kick-ass figure. Tinker-Bell in a flight attendant uniform. The girl caught him looking at her, but failed to gift him with even the shadow of a smile.

Uh-hum. So, we're as cold as ice this morning, eh?

She held his gaze for a few seconds. Pierre restrained himself, not flashing back what he considered his best movie actor smile. It would put Tinker-Bell on the spot if any of the other crew caught him smiling at her. She seemed shy, escaping towards the rear of the airplane pulling her traveling bags on her wheelies. Undoubtedly, she was going to be working Coach today. No way the senior gals were going to allow a young pristine woman like Tinker-Bell to work First Class or Business Class.

Too much envy and resentment on the part of the old timers towards a pretty young thing? Naturally, they would never admit this to be the case, but Pierre had heard from several young flight attendants he'd dated who had shared with him their impressions of working with the senior gals. The older, more experienced flight attendants—they claimed—had been young and slender and flirted with the male passengers and pilots at one time in their lives, but in their golden years they were no competition for the young new hires, and—like it or not—that generated hostile working environments.

Pierre thought that was pretty silly. Many of the older flight attendants were still quite beautiful and desirable, and he saw the opinion of the younger flight attendants as unfounded.

Tinker-Bell was probably a new hire called out from reserve. That was the only logical justification for her presence there. This was a very senior flight, long legs and a fantastic layover at the other end in Buenos Aires. Only the most senior flight attendants had a hope in hell of flying this route. And yet Tinker-Bell had just made an appearance.

Pierre White uttered a silent 'thank you,' to his favorite gods of ancient Hellas once again, truly grateful for the opportunity to have an attractive woman in his crew. Now it was up to him to catch the gazelle.

Crap, that Serengeti analogy had stuck in his mind after all. Would he be able to get to know her? Hard to tell.

The flight attendants hadn't been onboard long enough to break any of the cart seals yet, so there was no water available. He returned to the flight deck, empty handed.

Steve Evers was already at work, making his nest.

"No luck with the water. The gals haven't broken the seals yet."

He climbed into his seat, pulling out his iPad and headsets. He snapped the iPad on a bracket next to his side window.

"Don't worry about it," Steve smiled. "They'll bring us some once they get organized."

This being the first flight of the trip, airline protocol dictated the captain was going to fly the takeoff and the landing. Pierre would work the radio and actively monitor everything his captain did, watching him like a hawk.

"Gentlemen!"

They both turned to look at the newcomer.

"Gentlemen? "Captain Steve Evers responded, "none of those here present can answer to that description. You sure you got the right airplane?"

The newcomer laughed, offering his hand to Steve. "Michael McDonald."

They shook hands all around.

"You guys going to Argentina?"

"That be us."

"I'm your IRO. Your 'designated eater'?"

Pierre surveyed the newcomer. Young and sharp, late twenties or earthly thirties. Clean cut and self-confident. And as he said, he was the 'designated eater.' That was one of the humorous descriptions going around for the IRO, since they only worked about four hours and spent the rest of the time in First Class being served exquisite Cordon Bleu meals.

"Make yourself at home, Michael," the captain said, invitingly.

"Thank you, Steve, I'll just make myself invisible back here."

Pierre concentrated on preparing the majestic beast for flight. He briefly gave some thought to how he was going to finagle meeting Tinker-Bell back there. It probably wouldn't happen during the flight. Oh, he could go back there to use the restroom about half way to Argentina, and take a stroll to the back of the airplane. Maybe he could catch the girl during a break in the service and connect with her.

Or maybe not.

First thing, he had to find out what her name was. Not sure how to do that either, other than walking back to the rear of the airplane and checking out her name tag on her apron. Yep, that might be worth a stroll to the back. Good, his strategy was starting to take shape. If that marvelous girl was single and unattached, he would do his best to get to know her. Having a companion to enjoy the layover in Argentina would make his time there so much more pleasant. Even if he just took her out on a walk and invited her to have a candle light dinner.

But he absolutely had to find out what her name was. If all else failed and they made the hotel before he had a chance to talk with her, he would be unable to connect with her during the layover.

Pierre was aware many of the new hire flight attendants didn't last long in their relationships with their boyfriends after their first few months flying the line. What usually took place was the crews were so tired after catering to desperate mobs of discount travelers over several days that when they returned home they were 'peopled out' beyond belief.

They wanted nothing more than some personal private time. Sadly, this isolationist behavior transmitted the wrong message to the starving-for-affection boyfriends, who couldn't—for the life of them—comprehend why in God's name their girlfriends didn't have the urge to jump in bed with them and all the other good things which made up a good relationship, the minute they hit home after working a trip.

This situation ultimately resulted in the boyfriend being sent packing. Very common outcome in the airlines.

Pierre selfishly hoped Tinker-Bell in the back was well past that stage with her boyfriend and that she was single and available.

Another potential obstacle in his Serengeti hunt was the IRO. Like Pierre, the IRO was also young enough to represent worthy competition with Tinker-Bell. Pierre had not learned yet if the guy was married or not, but he would investigate this over the next several hours. Michael probably wasn't even aware of

Tinker-Bell's presence among the crew, but that could change anytime during the flight south.

FIVE HOURS LATER, WORLDWIDE Airlines flight 820 was southbound over the Pacific Ocean, slightly southwest of Costa Rica, cruising smoothly at 35,000 feet, on its way to Argentina.

"Beautiful day out here," Michael, the IRO, expressed, content. He'd already been back in First Class for three hours, watching a movie and enjoying the five-star cuisine Worldwide Airlines provided for its premium travelers. Now, stuffed on Chateaubriand with Bérnaise sauce, grilled salmon and Haagen-Dazs rum raising ice cream, he finally began earning his flight pay.

"It sure is a pretty day," Pierre agreed. Their captain had left the flight deck twenty minutes earlier, going back to enjoy four hours of relaxation and pampering. In addition to the Crew Rest area immediately behind the flight deck, the airline blocked a First-Class seat for the crew, and the pilots took full advantage of the perk.

Before departing the flight deck, Captain Steve Evers appointed Pierre as the 'pilot in command.' This meant if anything out of the ordinary occurred, Pierre would be performing the actions and duties of a captain *in absentia* until Evers returned on deck.

Pierre was okay with that. He glanced at the other pilot sitting in the captain's seat. No wedding band.

Crap.

What the heck, he wasn't afraid of a little competition. Never had been. He'd just have to move faster in order to neutralize Michael far as Tinker-Bell was concerned.

With that in mind, Pierre decided it was time to take a stroll back in Coach and investigate what's her name. "Gotta run back there for a second and use the lav."

Michael turned to look at him. "I was wondering when you were gonna have to take a piss, with all that water you've been drinking."

"You okay with that?"

"Sure! Just send one of our attendants up here to join me."

"All right. You got the aircraft and the radio."

"I got the aircraft and the radios," Michael repeated.

Pierre lifted the intercom from the center pedestal, ringing the cabin attendants.

"Hello, Nancy here," a raspy female voice answered.

"Hi Nancy, it's Pierre. I need to use the facilities back there. Is this a good time to interrupt you all back there?"

"Sure. Just give me a second, Hon."

Pierre had absolutely no idea who Nancy was. He hadn't met any of the cabin crew before the flight, so he was in the blind. Flight attendants hated the procedure to exit the flight deck. The flight attendants *really* didn't want to know about the physiological needs of the pilots, but the three-ring-circus put in place with airline crews after the 9-11 attack on New York had forced the issue.

The young pilot unbuckled himself, operating his electric seat in full reverse. He stood, stretching after several hours of being strapped in. "Back in a minute." He reached in the closet for his uniform hat, resting it on his head. He loved acting the part.

Michael, the IRO, was donning his full-face oxygen mask, putting it over his face. Regulations mandated that when one of two pilots left the flight deck inflight above 25,000 feet, the remaining pilot had to go on oxygen. Hypoxia was insidious, and pilots could easily succumb to its effects unaware that their bodies were suffering from lack of oxygen.

A ding announced an incoming call.

Pierre answered it, listening to the Nancy flight attendant informing him that two cabin personnel were waiting outside the flight deck door.

He peeked outside using the peephole installed on the door, confirming there were two women in flight attendant uniforms standing outside. He reached in the center console, pushing a square switch which unlocked the door with a loud 'clack.'

A middle-aged flight attendant with a friendly smile entered the flight deck, stepping aside letting Pierre exit. He closed the door behind him rapidly. Overall, the door had not remained open longer than five seconds. Another security precaution against the mindless idiots out there seeking to attract headlines by attacking pilots.

He surveyed the First Class cabin. Incredible layout really, with individual cubbies enclosing very comfortable recliners. That was the front of the airplane, the section where only the very rich and famous could live. The ones who thought of themselves as the Masters of the Universe.

Or their pilots while enjoying a crew rest.

The wide-body airliner had two aisles running back towards the rear. He chose the right aisle to venture back towards Coach. The other aisle had several serving carts blocking it. As he advanced towards the back of the airplane he concentrated on keeping his gaze looking forward above the seats. He really had no desire to converse with anyone, and he knew passengers would undoubtedly engage him in conversation if he allowed them to catch his eye. His rapid pace kept any of those the flight attendants called 'The Less Fortunate' in Coach from slowing him down.

Dang, this was a long airplane!

He kept up the brisk walk, glancing at several flight attendants taking care of business in the other aisle. No Tinker-Bell.

After what seemed like the longest walk from hell, he approached the very tail of the aircraft. There were four lavatories on each side, and past these, a sizable galley.

Bingo!

There she was. Tinker-Bell in the flesh, busy with some sort of food tray.

"Hi!" He said boldly, giving her his best and most friendly smile.

She appeared surprised, checking out his uniform, then his face. "Hi," she responded, recognition on her face.

"Boy, it sure's a long way back here from the front," he realized that was a very uninspiring pick-up line. The most ridiculous pick up line in the history of flirting, as it was. He must sound like a nerd.

She didn't reply.

"I'm Pierre," he smiled again, offering his hand.

The girl hesitated, then wiped her hand on her dark blue apron, accepting the handshake.

Pierre had taken in her facial features and her figure at lightning speed. He had no words to describe how pretty she was. Even with the dark apron. And lucky for him, she was alone in the galley. No other unwelcome humans to intrude on his action. The stars must be on his side. Or the planets all aligned, or whatever.

"I'm Monica," she finally responded. She still hadn't smiled.

"I'm one of your pilots." As if that wasn't obvious.

"I just had to stretch my legs. I saw you when you first arrived, and I wanted say hello."

"Yeah, I figured you were one of our pilots. I saw you as well," she offered. This time her lips parted in the dawn of a smile. Nothing earth-shattering, but it beat the heck out of the ice-statue she had played thus far.

That pleased Pierre enormously. "They pull you out of reserve?" He asked.

"Yes, I was on reserve."

Aha. He was right.

"Have you flown this trip before?"

"No," shaking her head. "First time."

"It's a fantastic trip. I'm glad you got it. You married?" Might as well cut through the chase.

"No."

"Great! I'm not either. If you're not too tired after we get to Buenos Aires, would you like to join me for a delicious dinner at a little restaurant I know by the water?"

There, he said it. Damn, that was a little too eager, but since they didn't have much time together, he felt obligated to just cut the bullshit and ask her.

Monica hesitated, looking into his brown eyes.

Pierre felt his heartbeat racing, and a hard-on beginning to form.

"You walked all the way back here just to invite me to dinner?"

Ouch, she was direct!

"Yes."

"Okay," she said simply, a smile finally illuminating her face.

"Okay, you'll go?"

"Yes."

"Wonderful! We'll talk again when we get there I guess." He could breathe again.

Something occurred to him. "Hey, have you had much opportunity to come say hello up front in the flight deck?"

"No, we were told to stay away from the flight deck."

"And from the pilots, I assume?"

She smiled. "Yeah, and from the pilots as well."

"Nonsense! You want to come up say hello when you get a chance?"

Monica appeared to think about the idea. "The purser may not like it."

Pierre thought about that. She was right. The purser—one of the older gals—would certainly develop an attitude seeing Monica intruding in her First Class territory. Better he escorts her in. "Are you real busy right now?"

"I was just putting away some of the perishables."

"Would you like to come up now?"

"To the flight deck?"

"Yes."

"I better not." She appeared a little concerned.

Pierre realized, angrily, that some insolent older flight attendant must have intimidated Monica to the point where she didn't feel comfortable going to the flight deck, even when accompanied by one of the pilots.

What the hell was happening to the industry? Since when were the nuts in charge of the insane asylum?

"I understand. I don't wanna cause you any grief with the purser. Let's just wait until we get to Buenos Aires then."

"Thanks anyway," she half smiled.

"Very pleased to meet you, Monica. See you soon,"

He wondered whether he should shake hands with her again. No, probably not the best idea.

He regaled her with his best smile, tipped his hat slightly in salute and left the galley.

Good God, he'd acted like a parody of a pilot in a 1950s movie. Totally ridiculous. The damage was done however, walking back there in an effort to repair his image with Monica would only make it worse.

The return trip to the front of the airplane seemed a heck of a lot shorter, although somewhat uncomfortable. His hard-on had bloomed into its full splendor, and he needed to arrange it inside his shorts, but couldn't do that in public. Lucky his direction of travel was such that none of the passengers could get a good look at his trousers, since he was coming up from behind them. He called the IRO on the interphone and the door swung open, allowing the flight attendant to exit. The door was narrow, so he wasn't able to avoid some unwanted body contact with her. These days of absurd politically correct paranoia one had to become a contortionist in order to avoid any kind of accidental physical contact which could be interpreted as a 'violent rape attempt' by some of the most vitriolic of the flight attendants.

What was the world becoming?

Michael, the IRO, removed his oxygen mask as Pierre parked himself in his seat again.

"No changes since you left," the IRO briefed. "We're still at three-five-zero and talking to the same folks. Airplane is in good shape; weather hasn't changed and nothing new to report."

"Excellent. I got the aircraft now."

"You got the aircraft, boss."

Pierre was still in a trance thinking of Monica. What an absolute doll she was.

Definitely could look at her as an 'orchid.' And she could rapidly become a 'dream' once he got to know her better and their clothes came off.

Was sex all he ever thought about?

What else was there?

He was enamored with women. When an especially cute creature entered his reality, he couldn't help daydreaming about the unimaginable pleasures that could be unraveled. That was his primeval instinct. That was how he was. Other guys were wired different, they collected stamps, or coins, or sports cars. He liked women.

"Goddamn," the IRO began, "you have no idea what happened to me the other day."

Pierre was not really at all interested, yet he feigned he was. "No. I don't know what happened to you. Tell me."

If the IRO detected the sarcasm, he ignored it.

"I got on a plane the other day, went back in the cabin and saw a flight attendant I thought I knew. So, I walked back there and smacked her in the ass, a real nice and friendly open handed spank. And I said 'hi, Monique!' to which she turned around and punched me right on the chin. The bitch cold-cocked me."

Pierre laughed, realizing the guy was an idiot. Even if the girl was his Monique, that sort of physical contact in public was a no-no. He could already imagine what followed. "It wasn't Monique?"

"No, it wasn't. It was some other chick. And she didn't have a goddamned sense of humor at that."

"No, I wouldn't think most women would laugh at you smacking them in the ass while they're on the job. Did she raise a stink?"

"No, no stink. That was all. But she did bruise my chin. Little bitch could punch like a boxer."

"Not a real good move, was it?"

Pierre congratulated himself. One quick trip to the back and he'd secured a dinner date with Tinker-Bell, at the same time protecting her from the IRO, who he knew now, just happened to be an idiot. He had to be careful, though, because at present his connection with her was still only as strong as a silk thread.

A musical double chime brought him back to reality.

A communications device they had up front known as an ACARS had chimed, notifying the crew of the arrival of a text message from Dispatch. The built-in printer on the center console spit out the new message neatly printed on a piece of white paper.

Pierre was closest to the printer, so he read it first.

```
A CREDIBLE BOMB THREAT HAS BEEN
RECEIVED AFFECTING YOUR FLIGHT.
POSSIBLE EXPLOSIVE DEVICE LOCATED IN THE AFT
CARGO HOLD. CONTACT DISPATCH NOTIFY
YOUR INTENTIONS.
```

Holy shit!

Pierre felt as if the floor had dropped out from under him. All thoughts of Monica vaporized. He read the message again.

"Michael, ring the flight attendants. Have the purser ask Steve to get back up here immediately."

"Whassup?"

"Check this out," Pierre handed him the printout.

"Fuck me!" The IRO exclaimed. "This shit for real?"

"It appears to be. Read the top, it says it's a 'credible' threat. That means those pukes in dispatch have reason to believe this threat *might* be real."

The IRO lunged for the intercom set, dinging the flight attendants with the number of chimes indicating an emergency. The flight attendants were trained that upon hearing the designated number of chimes, they should all drop everything, reach for the nearest handset and answer the call; six flight attendants responded to the IRO's call. He gave out instructions to request the immediate presence of the captain up front, and nothing else. That left six terrified flight attendants with butterflies in their tummies, free to imagine the worst possible scenarios.

Lucy Mayer, in her late fifties, was the Purser, the flight attendant in charge of the entire cabin crew. She was one of the six who picked up the call from the flight deck. Being in charge of the First Class cabin she was closest to the captain, who was at that particular moment comfortably stretched out on a First Class luxury seat, enjoying his dinner.

Captain Steve Evers was half way through his smoked salmon with capers when the flight attendant approached him, bending down to whisper close to his ear so the other passengers wouldn't hear.

"Steve, we just got an emergency call from the flight deck. They said you're urgently needed up there." She had an intense look of concern he couldn't possibly miss, and she was squeezing his forearm.

"Get rid of this, please," Captain Evers instructed, pushing away the food tray, scrambling to his feet.

Lucy Mayer helped get the tray out of the way so he could stand. She was terrified, never before in her thirty years with the airline had she received an emergency call from the flight deck. What could possibly be happening that required *immediate* assistance from the captain?

Up front in the flight deck, the IRO was breathing fast, his blood pressure obviously affected by the message he'd just read. Flight attendants were not the only ones with butterflies.

"Now what?"

"We have a checklist in the book for a situation like this. I'm gonna find it." Pierre concentrated on his iPad, bringing up the manual with the instructions he needed to follow. A bomb? On *HIS* airplane? What were the odds, really? He shook his head. Unbelievable. He found the checklist he was looking for.

"Here it is!"

"Where did you find it?" The IRO asked. Michael was thumbing through pages on his own iPad, trying to find the relevant check list. He was too frazzled to do any good.

Pierre gave him the page number.

"We need to do a flight deck lockdown," the IRO pointed out, referring to the procedure of sealing the flight deck against all traffic exiting or entering.

"Yeah, we'll do that as soon as Steve gets back up here." Pierre studied the Navigation Display, or ND in front of him. Using common sense and in view of the situation, he had to consider deviating from their route and high-tailing it for the nearest airport they could use. With a bomb threat hanging over them, their first priority was getting the aircraft on the ground as soon as possible. He was in command as long as Steve was gone, and for all practical purposes, they were under emergency conditions.

Operating under emergency conditions gave Pierre the authority to deviate from any airline or FAA rules if he saw the need.

First things first. He had to get the airplane on the ground somewhere.

There was Guatemala City. No, runway not long enough and lots of high terrain. San Jose in Costa Rica? No, same problems. That left Panama City. Those boys had two very long runways and no real high terrain near the airport. Good, that was it then.

"Michael, we need to divert. We must turn the nose of this here airplane towards a piece of concrete immediately. We're doing better than seven miles a minute, and I wanna cover those miles while we're flying towards a runway."

"Sounds good to me."

Pierre shared his thought process with his IRO, explaining why Panama was the best option.

"So Panama it is. Shouldn't we wait until Steve gets back here before diverting?"

"No. We can't waste any time. If he wants to change the destination for any reason after he gets back up here, then he can do it without too much trouble. Call the controller, declare an emergency and request a vector direct to Panama's Tocumen airport."

The intercom chimed.

"That must be Steve," Michael stated, answering the call. Replacing the handset back in its cradle, the IRO moved his seat back, stepping out of it, going to the door. He used the viewing port to confirm it was the captain out there, then opened the door.

"What's going on?" Steve asked right up. He signaled for the IRO to stay clear of his seat.

Pierre brought him up to speed on the developments of the past few minutes.

After reading the ACARS message the captain agreed with Pierre that diverting to Panama was the best course of action.

"I got the aircraft, you have the radios," Steve ordered, climbing back into his seat.

Pierre contacted the controller on the radio, declaring an emergency and requesting a vector direct to Panama City.

The controller replied that Worldwide was out of radar coverage, so he could not provide a vector, because he had no idea where the big jet was, but he authorized present position direct to Panama by using the aircraft's own navigation system.

Steve was heads down, entering information into the computer. He changed their destination from

Buenos Aires to Panama City, then instructed the airplane to follow the new course. The airplane was equipped with the latest state-of-the-art Global Positioning System, or GPS, perfectly capable of navigating them all the way to the runway in Panama. Or anywhere else, for that matter.

"We need to contact dispatch," the captain stated. "And we'll be descending to ten thousand feet right now. If we do have an explosion, we don't want to be pressurized. If an explosive device goes off while we're still pressurized, we'll pop like a goddam balloon."

Everyone in the flight deck knew that was a fact. However, if a *small* bomb went off in the aft cargo hold, and the airplane was *not* pressurized, they could still have a chance.

The captain reached for a knob on the Flight Control Unit on the glare shield, taking control of the airplane from the computer, dialing 10,000 and pulling on the knob. This action instructed the powerful autopilot computer to reduce engine power immediately and allow the nose to settle below the horizon, initiating a descent to ten thousand feet.

The super-sophisticated autopilot followed instructions to the letter, doing exactly what the captain commanded.

Pierre used the SatCom communications system they had onboard, establishing voice contact with the Dispatch office back in the States. He notified the dispatcher of their intention to proceed to Panama and land there. The company would have to make arrangements to accommodate all their passengers once they arrived in Panama. The dispatcher agreed with the crew's decision and informed Pierre someone had called in a bomb threat together with an accurate physical description of the captain and the tail number on the aircraft. The information had been specific enough to trigger the alarm.

With such accurate details about the flight, the company could not afford to ignore the threat.

Pierre relayed this to his captain.

"Okay, so they don't actually have any solid evidence we have a bomb on this airplane, they're going with assumptions."

"That's what it sounds like," Pierre agreed.

"But we must operate on the assumption that they could be right," Steve stated.

"I'll concur with that, Steve."

Pierre was too busy with the required procedures they needed to accomplish to worry much about the reality of a bomb. Since there was nothing he could do about it anyway, it didn't pay to fret over it. The aft cargo hold was not connected to the passenger cabin by any doors, so going back there in flight was out of the question. And besides, the cargo hold was plum-full of aluminum containers. Not to mention that even if the design of the airplane permitted access to the aft cargo hold, none of them would have the slightest fucking idea how to diffuse a bomb.

Steve picked up the intercom, buzzing the First Class cabin.

"This is Lucy," the Purser answered on the first ring.

"Lucy, Steve here. Listen, we got word from the company about a potential bomb threat which could affect us." He thought he heard her gasp.

"We don't have any solid evidence indicating there actually is any sort of explosive device on our airplane, however, for the sake of safety, we're going to divert into Panama at this time. We're not too far from there and I want you to let the other flight attendants know what's going on, but for right now I don't want the passengers informed about the bomb threat. We don't have any concrete verification about any explosive device, consequently I don't see the need to scare the hell out of our passengers, so please instruct your cabin crew to keep a lid on this. I'm going to come on the PA here shortly and make an announcement about a fictitious mechanical problem which is the reason for us diverting to Panama."

"Okay Steve," Lucy responded. Her voice was not steady. "Where is the explosive supposed to be?"

"In the aft cargo hold," the Captain replied.

Lucy knew her airplanes well enough to realize there was no way to reach the aft cargo hold in flight. She tried remembering if their cabin crew manual had anything for this kind of situation.

Nothing came to mind. Flight attendants were trained to deal with explosives in the passenger cabin, not in the cargo hold.

"How long do we have?"

"I'm still programming the computer here, but I estimate we should be landing in about forty minutes."

"Is this going to be a precautionary landing or an emergency landing?"

Lucy needed to know if they were going to evacuate the airplane right after landing by using the emergency slides, or if they were going to taxi in to the gate and deplane using the jet bridge. A 'precautionary' landing meant the airplane would taxi to the gate under its own power and the emergency slides would not be needed. An 'emergency' landing indicated they would be stopping immediately after landing, possibly on the runway, and conducting an emergency evacuation getting everyone off the airplane in a real hurry.

"It's gonna be a precautionary landing, Lucy. At least for now. So, I don't want you preparing the cabin for an emergency landing for the time being."

"Okay. I'll let everyone know."

"Thank you Lucy, I'll update you in about fifteen minutes."

The captain allowed his Purser five minutes to brief her staff, then picked up the PA handset and made an announcement to the passengers, informing them that a fictitious mechanical problem was forcing a landing in Panama.

No need to scare the devil out of the passengers. It served no purpose telling them about the possibility of an explosive device nesting in the cargo bin. If the bomb was going to go off with catastrophic consequences, what was the point of making everyone's last minutes on this earth filled with sheer panic?

The pilots had a checklist dealing with an inflight bomb threat. It basically instructed them to follow the steps they were already executing.

Once all the items on the checklist were covered, the three pilots discussed the situation.

"After we land," Steve explained, "we're probably not gonna park at the gate. The Panamanians are most likely going to send us to some remote parking area. I'll see if we can get airstairs to deplane our passengers at that point. If those stairs don't appear within three minutes of our arrival, I'm ordering the flight attendants to evacuate the airplane using the slides. I would hate for a bomb to go off after we land safely only to kill a bunch of people because they took too long to get us some stairs."

The two First Officers nodded in agreement.

"I don't know what's going to happen with the flight after we get to Panama. If we ultimately confirm there is no bomb onboard, I don't think we're going to Argentina today either way. I suspect the company's going to fly another airplane down or at least another crew to Panama to pick up our passengers."

"So you reckon they'll just deadhead us back?" Michael, the IRO asked.

"Yes, I believe that's probably what we're gonna end up doing. After this little deviation from our itinerary, I seriously doubt the company's going to send us to Buenos Aires."

Pierre cursed *sottovoce*. There went his plans with Monica.

"Flight availability will be an issue. I have no idea what flights we have departing out of Panama yet today. We may end up spending the night there after all."

"That's provided we don't explode before we get there," Michael put in again.

Steve turned back to look at his IRO. "That's provided we don't explode, yes. How about some positive waves, man?"

Pierre wondered why he was not more afraid. The possibility of becoming fish food in the Pacific Ocean was quite real at that very moment. So, why was he so cool and collected?

There were several reasons. In the first place, the whole bomb thing could be a hoax. Obtaining the captain's physical description and the tail number on an aircraft was really not all that difficult a challenge. Anyone with half a brain could probably obtain that information by simply going to the airport. Second, accepting the possibility of the existence of an explosive device in the aft cargo hold, there were also variations there. The bomb could be small, which would cause minimal damage. Or it could be powerful, knocking out the cargo door. That would not affect the controllability of the aircraft in extreme. Now, if the bomb was huge, then it would blow the tail off and then game over.

So, why worry? In any case, all they could do about it they were already doing, diverting to Panama and flying fast to get there. Also, descending to ten thousand feet and depressurizing the cabin was added insurance. They would burn prodigious quantities of jet fuel at the lower altitude, but what the heck, they had tons of it. They had planned on flying all the way to the end of the world in Argentina, and now they were only going to Panama, which was within spitting distance of their position.

Once again, Pierre frowned, unhappy about the disruption to his dating plans with Monica back there. Well, if they stayed in Panama for the night maybe he could still take her out to dinner.

Godalmighty! How could he think of girls at a moment like this?

He was never going to change.

The enormous wide body aircraft descended smoothly to 10,000, aimed at the Tocumen International Airport in Panama, while the pilots completed their normal and emergency checklists in preparation for landing.

The flight attendants interrupted their cabin service, picking up plates, cups and trash, stowing the carts in the respective galleys. The entire cabin crew had been informed about the situation, and they were frantically preparing the cabin for the early landing. Some of the cabin crew were terrified, some calm and totally under control. They had been instructed not to share any information regarding the potential explosive device with the passengers.

Everyone onboard outside of the cabin crew was now convinced the flight was diverting due to a 'minor' mechanical issue requiring attention on the ground. The passengers were very much under the impression once the 'minor' mechanical issue was taken care of, they would continue on to Argentina. They had not been told otherwise, so they had no reason to think anything different.

Pierre noticed his IRO was perspiring copiously, appearing more nervous as the minutes passed.

"Hey, relax, if we had a barometric bomb in the back intended to go off at a specific altitude, it would've gone off already. Nothing's happened, and I don't think anything will."

"You don't know that," the Nervous Nelly replied.

"You're still alive, aren't you?"

The IRO cast Pierre an unfriendly look. "We still have twenty minutes to go."

"Worldwide 820 contact Panama Approach on 119.7. Good day and good luck!"

Pierre acknowledged the frequency change, then contacted Approach.

"Panama Approach, Worldwide 820's with you at one zero thousand, four-zero DME southwest of Taboga VOR."

"Worldwide 820, Panama Approach. Maintain present heading direct Taboga VOR, expect ILS runway three-right. Altitude at your discretion." The controller sounded friendly, with a heavy Spanish accent.

"Tell him we want to have the emergency equipment standing by," Steve requested. "And also some airstairs to get the folks out."

Pierre did as he was told. He spoke slowly, hoping the controller understood his request for the airstairs. In these foreign airports, quite often the controllers spoke limited aviation English, consequently, deviate a little from the script and *bam!*

They were hopelessly lost.

Captain Steve Evers had not given orders to prepare the cabin for an emergency landing because he felt it was better to keep everyone in the cabin alert and relaxed. If he had to give the order to evacuate once they were on the ground, people would be less frantic and more clear-headed than the case would be if they were terrified at the prospect of an emergency landing.

"Worldwide 820, Panama Approach, maintain altitude your discretion, cleared for the ILS approach to runway three-right. Contact Tocumen tower over Lambi on 118.1."

Pierre repeated the clearance, then Steve repeated it once again. Safety barriers designed to keep the pilots from making mistakes.

"So, everybody good?" Steve asked.

"Let boogie," Pierre put in.

"I'm good," the IRO confirmed.

Pierre smiled, doubting that very much. The guy seemed scared out of his shorts. Aah, a real man.

"Let's start the auxiliary power unit," Steve commanded. The APU was the small turbine engine in the tail which would provide electricity and air conditioning once they shut down the two main engines.

The coast of Panama was visible between the clouds to their left, green and lush in tropical elegance. Pierre could discern the island of Taboga directly ahead. The Pacific Ocean below was deep blue with beautiful aquamarine waters near the beaches.

He wondered, if he planned to sneak a bomb inside an airliner, what kind of detonator would he use? Would he use a barometric one? That would set off the explosive while passing a specified altitude, either climbing or descending. Naw, the better choice would be arming the bomb with a timer, so the explosion could be controlled with some precision.

And when would he want it to go off? Hard to tell. Too many options available. Over a city maybe? Over the ocean? Or how about over the Brazilian rain forest? Pierre realized they had already flown several hours and the bomb—if there was one—had not gone off yet. So, assuming there was one, when could he expect it to detonate?

The possibilities were endless, and all of them unnerving. They were ten minutes from landing, and the suspense increased with each second. Wouldn't it be a bitch if the bomb went off this close to being safe?

He thought of Tinker-Bell back there—Monica, wishing he could reassure her and tell her everything was going to be okay. She could probably call him from wherever she was seated because flight attendants had intercoms located next to their jumpseats, but he had no way of knowing where the devil she was, so he could not call her. Just a fantasy anyway, no way he was going to be calling a flight attendant during the course of an emergency and while under sterile cockpit rules.

He did wonder for a moment if Monica was scared back there. He turned to look at his IRO, strapped in behind them, staring ahead with a terrified look in his face.

Jesssus Christ, man-up, buddy!

The island of Taboga disappeared beneath them, the autopilot directed the airplane to initiate a left turn towards the runway.

Pierre wondered who had called in the bomb threat. If there was no bomb, then that sick sonofabitch had cost the airline a diversion and a bunch of pissed off passengers. It occurred to him the passengers still thought they were going to end up in Argentina sometime after the 'minor' mechanical issue was fixed. Boy, they were going to be upset.   He pondered whether Steve was going to come clean with their passengers after they landed safely, telling them what the real issue had been.

Probably not. Let the station manager deal with that headache.

Well, whoever the sick fuck was who had called in the bomb threat, whether real or not, had totally screwed up his plans to enjoy a lovely evening with Monica along the *Rio de la Plata.*

A few minutes later, finally, the white and baby blue widebody airliner crossed over the runway threshold at Tocumen international Airport. Captain Steve Evers skillfully maneuvered the airplane onto the runway with the soft 'chirp' of his main landing gear wheels kissing the concrete.

Thank God, Pierre thought, feeling an immense sense of relief once the wheels were on solid concrete. They had made it down in one piece without any explosions taking place. If anything went off now, at least they were on the ground.

"Tower," Pierre transmitted, "where do you want Worldwide 820 to go?"

"Worldwide 820, make the next left at the high speed, clear the runway and stop there."

"Confirm you want us to stop on the high-speed taxiway."

"Affirmative. The equipment is alongside you now."

Pierre stared out the window on his right. Yep, the spit-polished parrot-green fire trucks were there, chasing alongside at their same speed, their beacons flashing."

"Airstairs," Pierre called tower, "do you have airstairs ready?"

There was a pause. Then the controller confirmed airstairs were on the way.

"Start timing three minutes," Steve ordered, turning the giant aircraft off the runway at the high-speed taxiway. "If the stairs are not here in three minutes, we're evacuating using the slides."

Pierre reached for the glare shield, pushing a button to start the timer.

"Okay, gentlemen," Steve said, "this is as far as we go. Let's shut her down."

He parked the brakes, flipping off the two engine master switches.

"See any airstairs out there on your side?" Steve asked.

"Nothing. The fire trucks are out there looking at us though. Not doing anything."

The aviators completed their checklists, eating up the three minutes on the timer.

The interphone chime got their attention.

Steve picked up the handset, listening to the flight attendant in First Class.

"The airstairs are here!"

He was immensely relieved. The idea of an emergency evacuation did not give him a warm and fuzzy feeling. Someone was always getting hurt during those.

"Fantastic!" Pierre cheered.

"Yes!" Steve spoke into the handset, "go ahead disarm the slides. Get all the passengers off the airplane and have them walk away as far as possible."

"Michael, go back there, stick your head out of both sides of the airplane and tell me how many airstairs they brought us. Do it as fast as possible."

"Yessir!" The IRO jumped out of his seat, rushing for the door.

Pierre hit the door release mechanism, timing it perfectly. The instant Michael put his hand on the door knob, the door was electrically unlocked.

"Looks like we got everything done. I just wanna make sure they brought us enough airstairs so we don't have to evacuate using the slides."

Pierre understood. He briefly wondered how Tinker-Bell—Monica, was doing back there. She must've been scared out of her pants when learning about the bomb.

"Six airstairs!" Michael yelled back from the cabin. "They brought us six!"

Steve made a rapid mental calculation, deciding that six of those would be enough to get everyone off the airplane without having to deploy the slides.

Five minutes later, the aircraft was deserted. Pierre and Steve walked all the way to the back of the cabin checking every row. Nobody was left. Then they went down the stairs, leaving their possessions behind, Steve holding on to the aircraft maintenance logbook.

"*Capitán!*" a Panamanian man in a green military uniform greeted them on the ramp. The man looked serious with an air of self-importance which was almost comical.

Steve shook the man's hand.

"I am *Comandante* Arosemena, in charge of the airport."

The man looked all business, with his crewcut and military-style hat. His English was flawless.

Steve looked around at the situation. A stream of passengers could be seen walking towards the terminal. Several of his flight attendants were standing around nearby, appearing unsure of what to do next.

"*Comandante,* were you told about the possibility there may be explosives in the aft cargo hold?"

"Yes, we know this. Our bomb experts are on the way."

Pierre wondered what was going to happen next. The logical course of action would be to gather their crew and head for a hotel. But this was another country, and logical courses of action tended to differ significantly from what he was accustomed.

"We're going to be in our airline operations office," Captain Steve Evers pointed towards the terminal. Right then they observed a food truck pulling up next to the rear cargo door of their airplane. The vehicle parked and the back of it was raised a few feet. Then Steve caught a glimpse of a man in shorts and no shirt, wearing a baseball cap, reaching out for the cargo hold handle.

"Bomb squad?" He asked.

"Yes," the *Comandante* replied, a hint of pride in his eye.

Pierre was stunned when he heard the exchange. These guys really took it easy. If there actually were explosives in that aft cargo hold, that unprotected native could very well blow himself to Kingdom come in the next few seconds.

"Get all the flight attendants to move away from the airplane, NOW!"

Pierre and the IRO ran towards a group of four flight attendants hanging around behind one of the wings.

They got their attention and had them all half-jogging towards the terminal in a matter of seconds.

Pierre rounded up a couple of other cabin attendants, directing them towards the terminal as well. Then the three pilots followed suit.

Whatever the devil the Panamanian bomb squad were doing, Pierre wanted no part of it.

Inside the terminal building, another local man introduced himself to them as the station manager for Worldwide. He explained to the pilots also in excellent English that the company had lined up transportation for the passengers and they were being taken care of. They would be driven to a five-star hotel in the elegant neighborhood of Punta Paitilla, right by the water. He further informed Steve the crew would shortly be driven to the same hotel, where they would remain until tomorrow, at which time they would all deadhead back to Los Angeles on another Worldwide flight. The company was going to send a replacement airplane with a fresh crew in the morning to fly the passengers the rest of the way to Buenos Aires.

Hot dog! Outstanding, Pierre mused. The option to have dinner with Tinker-Bell just got put back on the table.

One hour later, the crew of Worldwide flight 820 entered the lobby of a magnificent five-star hotel in Panama City, in the cosmopolitan Punta Paitilla.

Captain Steve Evers notified the crew they would layover at that hotel until noon the following day. Then tomorrow they would head back to Tocumen to board one of their afternoon flights home. For an additional treat, the company had agreed to buy dinner for the entire crew as a 'thank you' for an excellent job.

Pierre hadn't been able to communicate much with Monica, since the entire cabin crew had remained together after deplaning. He'd finally laid eyes on her again prior to boarding the bus to the hotel, and she had looked a little worn at the seams, but not too frazzled.

"You okay?" he'd asked her.

"Yeah," was all she said.

Lining up at the registration desk he let her get in line ahead of him. "You still feel like going out to dinner?"

She stared back. "You don't want to eat dinner here with the rest of the crew?"

"Not really. I've been in Panama before. I know a much nicer place to eat, it's called *Siete Mares*, 'Seven Seas' in Spanish. I think you'd like that better."

Monica didn't reply right away. Pierre speculated she was evaluating the situation wondering what she should do.

"Okay," she replied, simply.

Pierre wet his lips. He felt that fluttery, empty feeling in the stomach.

Yes!

He would've preferred a little more enthusiasm from her, but he really had nothing to complain about. She was going to join him for a private dinner just the two of them. He was once again wearing his uniform coat and hat, looking respectable, although he was perspiring profusely. The humidity in this place was *unfuckingbelievable*. Ten more minutes with his coat on and he would simply die from heatstroke. He'd have to take a shower before anything could happen that night with Monica.

Yeah, right. That was very optimistic thinking. He was delusional, no doubt.

Each crewmember was given a room and individually departed for the elevators.

"What's your room number?" Pierre asked. He and Monica were the last two left at the front desk.

"Nineteen-eleven," she said, showing him her door card.

"Half an hour? Want to meet down here?"

"Sure." She waited for Pierre to sign for his room.

Pierre was very pleased with the gesture. She had enough manners to wait for him. He liked that.

They walked to the elevator together. He noticed the furtive glances other men gave Monica as they crossed the lobby. He and Monica did make quite a pair, he had to admit. And to the rest of you onlookers, go find your own goddamned women.

"Should we tell the others we won't be joining them for dinner?" Monica inquired.

"Yes, don't worry about that. I'll tell Steve—our captain."

Pierre admired her angelic face. She did look fairly young. The sight of her took his breath away.

The glass elevator accelerated smoothly stopping at the nineteenth floor.

Pierre's room was down the hallway from Monica's. "See you in a few minutes."

"Okay."

The young aviator entered his room, admiring the elegant décor. Only one super-king size bed in the middle, but the room was fantastic. Much to his surprise, there was a white ceramic free-standing bathtub at the far end of the room. A door to the side probably hid the toilet. Amazing. Open floor plan, if he ever saw one.

The room was decorated in light blue and green and beige pastels colors. Orange and yellow hibiscus adorning the night tables and the desk. A glass sliding door led to a small balcony outside.

Pierre picked up the house phone. Shit, he had no idea what room Steve was in.

"Good afternoon, front desk, how can I be of service?" The woman's voice at the other end had a cute Spanish accent.

"Hi there. Could you please put me through to the room of Captain Steve Evers? He's with Worldwide Airlines."

"Yes, of course. Have a pleasant afternoon."

He heard an unfamiliar ring tone buzzing twice.

"Hullo?"

"Steve? It's Pierre."

"Oh, hi Pierre!"

"Hey, did you hear back from operations? Did they find a bomb?"

"I did hear back, and no, there was no bomb. The station manager just hung up a second ago."

"No bomb?" Pierre was greatly relieved.

"Nope. They removed all the containers and emptied them. No explosives. It was all a false alarm."

"Those Panamanians are nuts. Did you see their bomb squad guy? He had no protective gear whatsoever."

Steve laughed. "I did."

"I was really looking forward to not exploding. Glad they didn't find a bomb. Incredible what we had to do. Company knows?"

"Yes, of course, our station manager has been in continuous touch with dispatch."

"I'm very happy it was just a hoax."

"Yeah, me too."

"Steve, I'm not gonna join you guys for dinner. I'm taking a pass. I'm bailing out to a small restaurant I know here in town. And I'm taking one of our flight attendants with."

"Oh? You're turning down a free dinner?"

It was generally accepted among airline personnel, pilots were notoriously cheap.

"That, I am. But thanks for procuring it anyway."

"We'll miss you."

"I'm sure. I'll catch you tomorrow downstairs."

"Sounds good, Pierre. Happy hunting."

"Thanks."

Pierre didn't know whether to feel complimented or offended by that remark. Either way, it was none of Steve's business whether his hunting was happy or not. And besides, he wasn't going on a hunt, he was going on a date.

He rapidly stepped out of his clothes, climbing into the free-standing bath tub. It had a hand operated shower head. Not his favorite, but it'd have to do.

Fifteen minutes later Pierre walked out of the elevator in the luxurious lobby. He'd towel-dried his hair, and knew the dampness still present in his hair would never evaporate in this high relative humidity. He wore a white long-sleeved dress shirt rolled up at the sleeves and tan Dockers. It had been his intention to wear them in Buenos Aires. He'd also brought a dark blue blazer on the trip, but wearing it in this humidity was absolutely out of the question. His tan deck shoes with rubber soles complemented his—he hoped—casual tropical attire.

The lobby was gracefully decorated full of banana and palm trees. Lush tropical vegetation. He loved it. The lobby conveyed the impression of strolling through the middle of a tropical rain forest.

They would have to take a cab to the restaurant. It was located in the best neighborhood in Panama—*El Cangrejo*—or 'The Crab,' in English.

He caught a glimpse of Monica's blond hair in the glass elevator.

The lobby was cool and fresh, but very humid. The air conditioners must be working overtime.

She came out of the elevator and Pierre was right there to greet her.

"Hi!"

"Hi Pierre."

She looked radiant and fresh. Her white pants, white halter top and white cotton shirt worn over the halter matched her white shoes.

"You look spectacular."

She smiled, a hint of shyness. "Thank you."

"Hungry?"

"Yes! I haven't had much food today."

"The restaurant is not too far, maybe fifteen minutes from here. We'll need to catch a cab."

Her long golden blond hair was shoulder-length and flowed when she walked. It was much thicker than what he'd estimated when she had it up in a bun.

"Did you excuse us with the rest of the crew?" She took up station right next to Pierre, heading for the front doors.

"Yes, I did. I called Steve and told him we wouldn't be joining them."

"Should I have called the Purser?"

He smiled. She was evidently very new. "No, you never have to call your purser for anything while on a layover. This is your own time. How long you been with the company?"

Monica's enticing voice matched the beauty of the girl. "Four months on the line."

"No kidding! Four months since you finished basic training?"

"Yes."

That explained a lot. "Well, then. Lesson number one. Your layovers are yours to do as you please. The Purser has absolutely no right nor authority to ask you to do a damned thing. You don't ever have to ask their permission for anything."

"Oh? I was under the impression that one had to stay in touch with the purser during a layover."

"No, that's only if you're planning on taking off on your own in some strange city and then yes, it would be a good idea then letting the purser know what your plans are, so in case you go missing, we know where to start looking for you."

"So basically I'm off while we're on a layover?"

"Yes. They didn't tell you this at the Academy?"

"No."

They caught a cab in front of the hotel. Pierre gave the driver the name of the restaurant.

Monica sat very close to him on the bench seat. Pierre could feel her body radiating heat, along with some familiar citric scent, which he found totally enchanting. They were both already perspiring.

"Where are you from?"

"Arizona," she answered.

No shit?

"Really? Where in Arizona?"

She looked at him. "Tempe."

"I live in Phoenix."

"You do? Where?"

"Ahwatukee." Pierre couldn't believe his good luck. Here he was, with a girl straight out of a Walt Disney movie, going to dinner in Panama, and she lived within spitting distance of his house back in the Great American Desert. It was just too good to be true.

"That's awesome!" Her adorable blue eyes sparkled.

"Where did you go to school?"

"Chandler High."

"How old are you?"

"I'm twenty-three."

Whoa! Pierre felt ancient with his thirty-three years. "Have you flown anywhere interesting yet?"

"No, not really. This is the first international trip I've been on. I've been on reserve and all my trips have been domestic short hops. I did go to New York once for a short overnight."

"What do you think of the job so far?"

"I like it. Some of those short flights are really tiring, but I like it very much."

"Planning on going to school eventually, or are you going to stay here forever and make a career out of this?"

She smiled. "I want to become a psychologist. The idea is to do this for two years, then quit and go to school full time."

"Why two years?"

"I always wanted to travel, so I figured two years would give me enough traveling to get it out of my system."

"That's a good plan. What'd you think of our little adventure today?"

She adjusted her shirt, looking at his eyes. "You mean the bomb?"

"Yeah, what did you think of that?"

"I was scared shitless."

Pierre was amused. This one obviously didn't have a problem speaking her mind.

"Turned out we didn't have a bomb on the airplane after all."

"I'm glad. But it still scared me. I almost wet my pants. What made the company think we had a bomb on the airplane?"

Pierre found her additional remark about wetting her pants rather funny. "It was just a false alarm. I'm sorry it screwed up your chance to see Buenos Aires tonight. We get false alarms every so often. Some nut trying to make a name for himself in the news."

"It doesn't matter. I'll see it another time. The other flight attendants were scared."

"We had to think of safety first and that's why we came here."

"Was this a safe place?"

"It was, and a lot closer than Argentina."

"Some of the passengers were asking what the mechanical problem was. Especially when the fire trucks followed us after landing."

"What did you tell them?"

"Nothing. We were told not to say anything about the bomb."

"Little did you know this morning when you woke up you'd end up in Panama having dinner with a stranger, eh?"

She gave him a long look. "So, stranger, wanna tell me how come you're not married?"

Pierre almost laughed out loud. "Actually, I'm between wives. I've been married six times." He said it as serious as he could. Let that one sink in.

Monica frowned, squinting her eyes, studying him. "You have not." Her tone was uncertain, and she did glance at his ring finger again.

He smiled at her. "You're right. Never been married. And in answer to your question, I am not married because I have not met the perfect girl for me yet."

"They told us at the Flight Attendant Academy that all pilots are married."

"They told you wrong. Many are also divorced."

"You know what I mean."

"Yes, I know what you mean. Well, you lucked out, you don't have to play hooky with a married man tonight."

"I would never do that."

Pierre smiled. "I believe you."

The cab parked in front of the restaurant, a three-story concrete building with green awnings across from the Einstein Plaza.

Pierre paid the driver, tipping him generously. Poor guy, having to drive a cab for a living, while he,

Pierre, enjoyed a celebration of life at an exotic restaurant with an angel. Life was definitely not fair.

On the other hand, they could just as easily be dead and feeding the fish at the bottom of the Pacific Ocean off the coast of Panama. Life was nothing but pure luck, nothing else.

He ushered her into the restaurant with his hand at the small of her back. They were helped to a small table in a cozy room with dim lights. Tables were elegantly covered with white and turquoise table cloths and mauve napkins. Only one other table was occupied by a couple. It was too early for dinner in Panama, an international city emulating the great European capitals in their dinner hours.

The host very politely pulled out Monica's chair, adjusting it for her.

"Yikes, this is a really nice place."

Pierre liked her expressions. He hadn't heard 'yikes' since his high school days.

"The food is to die for."

"I take it you've been here before?"

"Yes, once. Months ago."

"And you came here with another flight attendant?"

Pierre laughed. "No, I came here with an old salt captain who wanted to introduce me to this place."

Monica examined his face, as if his body language could tell her if he was lying.

"I am honored to tell you it is your privilege being the first and only woman who's ever accompanied me here." He gave her a wide smile.

"You are a smooth talker."

"Should I take that as a compliment?"

"Maybe," she said slowly.

He liked having her sitting across from him. This way he could admire her dazzling features and delight himself looking at her sexy eyes. She didn't have too much make up on, which he preferred.

"*Buenas noches*, may I offer you drinks to start?"

Pierre looked up at the elegant waiter. The man wore a white dinner jacket, black bow tie and starched white shirt.

"Some wine, or cocktails?"

"We can have a glass of wine or a tropical cocktail, if you'd like," he said to Monica. "Not more than one though, cause we're gonna be deadheading back home tomorrow in uniform."

There he went, violating his own liquor rules all over again. Aw, shucks, one drink wasn't going to hurt. He was getting pretty good at ignoring his own rules.

"I'd love a banana daiquiri," Monica replied.

"Great choice," he complimented. "And I'll have a *piña colada*, please."

The waiter disappeared with the order.

Sitting next to Monica in the taxi, and feeling her warmth had triggered a painful hard-on. Painful because it was caught sideways in his shorts, and he hadn't had the opportunity to stick his hand down his pants to fix it.

He slowly moved his hand along his leg, under the cover of the tablecloth. Feeling his enormous erection, he attempted straightening it out. Not an easy task, with Monica sitting right there in front of him eyeballing him like a cat fixating on a canary.

"Here you go, *señor*," the waiter appeared out of nowhere, placing their drinks in front of them. Pierre just about had a seizure. He immediately pulled his hand out, startled and surprised, trying to control his breathing after the sudden adrenaline rush brought about by the waiter's sudden arrival.

"And are you ready to order some food tonight?"

"Give us a couple of minutes, please."

The waiter nodded agreeably, making himself scarce.

"Are you playing with yourself under the table?" Monica asked, a devilish glare in her eyes.

Holy crap.

"Uh?" He laughed. "No, of course not, why do you say that?"

"Seems to me you were doing some adjusting when the waiter scared the bejeezus out of you."

Pierre was actually embarrassed. And here he thought he was being so slick.

"You're blushing," Monica broke into a big grin. "That's cute."

"No, I'm not! What're you talking about?"

She allowed herself a giggle. "Nothing, nothing. Just my imagination." She reached for one of the two leather-bound menus.

"You clearly possess a hyperactive imagination, girl."

"I don't know what you're talking about," Monica shot back.

Caught with his hand in the cookie jar, so to speak. Pierre decided to ignore the idiotic event and check out the menu. How was it possible a twenty-three-year-old girl had just managed to embarrass him?

"Since you're the resident expert in this here restaurant, what do you recommend, captain?"

"I'm not a captain. I'm a first officer."

"I don't care. You all look the same to me. Only you're younger."

"What do you like?"

Monica scanned the menu. "I like everything."

"Would you like a lobster?"

"Naw, too expensive."

"You're with me and I don't have a wife to support. Regardless of what you may think, I believe I am able to afford a lobster for you."

"Touchy, touchy."

He was finding Monica more interesting as the minutes ticked by. "Not touchy. You are my Princess tonight and I'm here to please you."

"*Oh, really!* Your Princess?"

"A manner of speech."

"What does that mean?"

"Terms of endearment. Nothing else."

"Let's order some food," she immersed herself in the menu, intentionally ignoring him.

Pierre studied his dinner date while she studied her menu. Monica had majestic features, straight out of a modeling magazine. She looked Scandinavian, her darker eyebrows accentuating her perfect eyes. The white skin he could admire above her halter didn't have a single freckle or blemish. And she was only twenty-three, but she had a quick mind and he was enjoying her. The idea of having her under him in bed sent pinball machine butterflies fluttering across his crotch. What were the odds of them ending up in the same bed?

Probably zero.

The waiter returned, notepad and pen in hand.

"Have you had a chance to look at the menu?"

"I'll have the grilled red snapper," Monica ordered.

"Grilled *huachinango* for the Miss," the waiter acknowledged, writing it down. "It comes with fried plantains and black beans."

Monica nodded. "*Huachinango?* That's fine."

"No lobster?" Pierre asked her.

"No, thanks. The *huachi*—whatever—will do."

"Okay. I'll have the shrimp and seafood soup. Do you like shrimp?" Pierre watched her pass the menu to the waiter.

"Yes."

"How about a small shrimp cocktail to stimulate our appetites?"

"I'd love one."

Pierre ordered two cocktails. His erection had not been adjusted yet, so he was rapidly becoming uncomfortable. Hard as a rock and ready for action. He was gonna have to excuse himself and go visit the men's room in a moment. Except she'd know what was happening to him. Her proximity was driving him insane with desire.

"Are you dating anybody?" He was curious how such an incredibly delicious girl wasn't already taken.

"Yes," she looked him in the eye.

"Really? Who?"

"You."

His heartbeat peaked. Pierre could actually feel his heart palpitating. Although he'd initially thought Monica shy, he was getting another view of her. Upon careful reflection, she was as shy as a Bengal tiger.

"We *are* on a date, are we not?" Monica added.

"I suppose we are. I was just wondering if you have a boyfriend back home." He hoped he was no longer blushing.

"Would I be out on a date with you if I had a boyfriend back home?" Her inquisitive stare reflected higher intelligence.

"I don't know, would you?"

"Certainly not!"

"So you're on a date with me because I'm single and unattached?"

"What are you, dense?"

Whoa, she was direct.

She paused. "I'm here with you because I like you."

As simple as that? He was so damned excited being with her he was feeling light-headed.

"And I know you like me. Why else would you travel all the way back to the galley at the back of the airplane to ask me out?"

Pierre laughed. "Nothing shy about you, eh?"

"Not true. I'm very shy when I have to be. I saw you checking me out when I first came on the airplane."

"You don't miss much, do you?"

"Not really."

"I had to invite you out. You captured my imagination from the moment I saw you."

"I'm glad I did," she said, meeting his stare. "I'd be curious to know some of what you imagined."

"Relax, nothing indecent."

"Sure."

Pierre reached over across the table, placing his hand on hers. It was cold. "I'm glad you came out with me."

Monica flashed him her most captivating smile yet.

That sent waves of pleasure down to his groin. Ah, what the hell. "I have to use the restroom for a second to wash my hands, I'll be right back." He left her without another word. His enormous proud erection protruding from the front of his pants, a very obvious bulge, but he was confident Monica hadn't seen it because of the angle when he left the table.

Pierre didn't know exactly where the facilities were, so he hoped the restrooms were by the entrance. Monica was turning out to be more Cajun pepper and less honey, which was extraordinarily exciting.

He walked around the bar, finding a door marked with the silhouette of a man in a tux. Once inside the rest room he checked out the place, rather small at that. Very clean and smelling of disinfectant. Nobody else was there. He rapidly slid his hand down his pants, grabbing his hard-on, repositioning it straight up to rest against his lower abdomen, pointing at his navel. That was it. The relief was instant and wonderful. He washed his hands admiring himself in the enormous mirror. He wondered if his dark hair and dark eyes made him appear mysterious to Monica.

The young flight attendant was looking straight at him, smiling as he approached the table again.

"Wash your hands?" She had a sparkle in her eye.

This girl is nothing but trouble. I love it.

"I did, thank you."

"Straighten yourself out?"

Pierre gasped.

She was smiling at him. "Was that an indelicate question?"

"You are terrible," he scolded.

"A natural human reaction," she replied.

"What?"

"Being aroused when in the presence of the opposite sex."

Holy shit.

"Like I said, you don't miss much, do you?"

"I thought we'd already established that."

"And so, are you aroused as well in the presence of the opposite sex? What is it you call it, *'girlwood'?*"

"That's none of your business," she replied.

The waiter returned with two shrimp cocktails served in soda fountain glasses. They were huge. Two packs of salted crackers accompanied each cocktail.

"Geez! These look magnificent!" Monica unwrapped her silverware from the linen napkin, with great enthusiasm.

Nothing else was said while they devoured the fresh shrimp swimming in tomato sauce, condimented with lime juice, cilantro and chopped raw onion.

"That was so good," Monica finally broke the silence.

"Huge shrimp. Not like the ones back home, where our local seafood franchises advertise *jumbo super mega colossal prawns* and they're thirties or forties."

Monica looked puzzled. "What's that mean?"

"Thirties or forties? That's how one categorizes shrimp, based on how many it takes to make a pound. Say, for example tens, would mean that it takes ten of those to add up to one pound."

"Got it."

"Were you really nervous back there today when we had the bomb scare?"

"You already asked me that. Like terrified. Pissing myself."

Her honesty was refreshing and funny.

"Were you?" She waited for his response, her eyes locked on his.

"No, I must say I wasn't pissing my pants. Honestly, no. I was too damned busy to think about it much. I had so much to do in preparation for our landing I didn't have the luxury to worry about being scared."

She held her eyes on him a moment longer, as if trying to decide whether he was as brave as Captain America or just full of shit.

"Our other pilot was pretty affected by the situation. Michael's his name. He was perspiring heavily and hyperventilating. That's probably because he had nothing to do with the preparations for landing, so that left his mind with plenty of time to consider the different scenarios."

"In other words," Monica put in, "he was scared shitless."

"In other words, yes."

"Why didn't he have anything to do?"

Pierre explained what an IRO did.

"Really? For real? Like he only works four hours out of the thirteen-hour flight? Does he get paid for the entire thirteen hours?"

"That he does."

"That's unfair! We have to work the entire flight all the way down to Buenos Aires, and we don't get paid that much. How much does he get paid?"

"I don't know exactly, it depends on many factors, seniority, the kind of airplane he flies, whether it's a domestic or international trip."

"Just ballpark."

Pierre didn't normally encounter too many flight attendants willing to touch on the financial differences between their salaries and the pilots'. It was a rather delicate subject.

"I don't know how long he's been flying for us. Say he's been here four years, then he'd probably be making around $190,000."

Monica inhaled loudly. "That's a lot of goddam money."

Pierre agreed. He was somewhat uncomfortable talking money with her. With Monica's four months on the line she was probably grossing around $26,000 and change, or thereabouts.

"And he gets paid the same as you guys even though you're doing most of the work?"

Pierre laughed. That was one way to put it. "No, he doesn't get paid as much as we get. He gets paid for the same number of flight hours, but not the same amount."

The waiter reappeared escorted by a second individual helping carry the trays. The trays were carefully placed on a table next to them. The waiter removed the metal lids covering the food, holding the ceramic china plates with linen napkins. He placed an exquisite-looking *huachinango* filet in front of Monica, warning her the plate was very hot.

The aroma was enough to make Pierre's mouth water like a dog presented with a box of sausages. His mind had been on sex so intensively; he'd ignored the painful complaints emanating from his stomach. What a fantastic place the restaurant was. Elegant, relatively small and discrete. And the food was stupendous, second to none. That's one thing—Pierre reflected—in his profession as an airline pilot, he was blessed with the opportunity to visit many varied restaurants in cities the world over. Not even the very rich and famous could do that with the same frequency.

The waiter deposited a very appetizing bowl of fish and shrimp soup for him. The red tomato-based broth was so hot white delicate smoke rose from it.

"*Bon appétit, mademoiselle,*" he offered.

"Thank you," Monica responded.

Pierre was relieved she knew what he meant. Often, he'd dined with men and women having no clue what he was saying. He was generally embarrassed, having to explain the idiom to the less educated. It made him sound fake and pretentious. In reality, it was a just a manner he'd been taught during his growing up years with his family. It was simply polite manners, wishing someone a 'good appetite,' when initiating a meal.

Would she be willing to end up in bed with him at the end of the night? He wasn't really sure. She was turning out way more outspoken than he'd thought her to be, which he liked, but he still could not get a good feel for her mood. And for a twenty-three-year-old, she appeared to be impressively intelligent. In his profession, it was not unusual for Pierre to run into some lovely good-looking women who unfortunately exhibited the mental intellect of Bamm-Bamm, of *The Flintstones.*

They enjoyed their food without much conversation.

"What do pilots get paid?" She finally asked, after dabbing her lips with a white linen napkin.

Pretty direct, eh? "It depends."

"Yeah, I understand all those things you told me. But, annual salary, what's it amount to?"

Pierre somehow liked her directness. "Take Steve, for instance, he probably grosses close to three hundred thousand. I think he's been here about eighteen years."

Monica's eyebrows arched up and her eyes got big. "No shit? Three hundred thousand?"

"Yep."

"Is he one of the highest paid?"

"No, the guys flying the big Boeings make a little more."

"Damn! No wonder then."

"What?"

"At the academy they told us all pilots are like rich."

Pierre smiled. It was all a matter of point of view. To him 'rich' was someone with millions.

"They told us pilots are all married and we'd never be able to marry one, so we should just stay away from you guys. They said all pilots play around on their wives but ultimately never divorce."

"And who told you all this, your instructors at the academy?"

"Yes."

"Were they male or female?"

"Mostly female, why?"

"Monica, the female flight attendant instructors who taught you the basic indoctrination at the academy were basically two kinds of women. One kind, married to the same husband for a long time, would not have an agenda and they would be nice and straight with you. The other kind, the unmarried, divorced or unhappily married flight attendant turned instructor, probably intentionally misguided you. Those old gals weren't able to land themselves a pilot during the years they flew the line, and now that time has passed and they're no longer young—like you—they resent your position. So, they try to sabotage your chances of marrying a pilot someday. The attitude is, if they couldn't do it, neither should you. Some of those gals are bitter and twisted, and they don't have your best interest at heart."

Monica's eyes were attentive, appearing to be listening carefully.

"This is not unusual and don't blame them for it. The same thing takes place in hospitals. Young nurses are continuously hunting for a doctor to marry. Some of the nurses sleep around trying to land themselves the lifestyle only a doctor can provide for them. Many nurses don't succeed at this, and in their older years they resent the opportunities younger nurses encounter."

"That's an on fleek analogy."

"On fleek?"

She stared at Pierre. "What're you, deaf? On fleek, like in 'good.'"

A woman approached their table carrying a wicker basket with a dozen long stem red roses wrapped in cellophane.

"Buy me a rose for the lady?" She asked, in fluent English.

Pierre could not place her. She was middle-aged, but did not look Panamanian. Her outfit was colorful and she smelled of incense. She wore a red and yellow bandana on her head, and huge yellow loop earrings. Hard to tell her age. She had kind eyes.

"Yes, please," he responded, going for his wallet. He didn't bother asking Monica if she'd like a rose, she was so polite she'd probably turn it down, just like she did with the lobster.

The woman held out one stunning deep red rose with a very long stem, offering it to Monica.

"Thank you," Monica said to the woman, accepting the flower, raising it to her nose.

"What do I owe you?" Pierre asked her, holding open his wallet.

"Ten dollars," the woman answered with a tired smile.

Pierre liked her. She had sincere dark eyes, almost black, and a kind smile. He took two twenties out of his wallet, reaching out for her hand. "Here you go. Thank you so very much." A woman making a living under such difficult conditions deserved some help. Who knew what her story was.

The woman looked at the money, taking on a serious look. "You're very generous. Thank you."

Pierre turned to Monica. She was holding the rose to her nose, enjoying the fragrance, her eyes smiling at him.

"You are a good man," the woman added. "I'm gonna do something for you, I'm gonna read your palms."

Read their palms? Aha! That's what she was! A gypsy! That's why she looked familiar. Pierre gave her another long look, yeah, her attire and her self-confidence confirmed it. He'd seen many like her in

Europe. Roma, the gypsies called themselves. Delightful people, mysterious and with a joy for life and a love for dancing and music unequalled in other cultures.

The woman reached for his hand, not asking for his consent, carefully concentrating on the palm, she used her index finger, tracing the lines on his hand. Pierre didn't for one second believe in palm reading, but he wasn't about to be rude to the poor gal. if she wanted to read his palm, he would allow it and produce the right amount of awe.

"You're a strong man, with a big heart, and you will accomplish great things in your life." She paused for emphasis.

Monica looked on, appearing extremely fascinated by the experience.

Your life line is long. You will live a long life and produce many children."

Pierre realized whatever perfume the woman was wearing did smell like incense. Her hands were soft, dark and very strong.

"You cheated death recently," the woman voiced.

Pierre was torn between laughing and saying *'whathefuck!?'* Where'd that come from? That was definitely strange. They had all cheated death—so to speak—with the bomb scare. The more he thought about it, the more he convinced himself it was just a coincidence. These fortune tellers used enough generic arguments that could adapt to any situation. Yeah, that was it.

The woman released his hand, reaching for Monica's without asking for her permission either.

Pierre reached for his drink, sipping the *piña colada.*

"You also have a long life line. And I see more."

Monica glanced at Pierre, smiling nervously, sheepishly allowing the gypsy woman to read her palm.

"I see here the two of you two are going to end up together tonight, and your man should know that you, my dear, have a very hot and tight pussy, and you should also know your man here is dying to fuck you."

Pierre spit out *piña colada* clear across the table.

Monica laughed out loud, taking her hand back.

The gypsy woman smiled playfully at Pierre one last time, winking at the aviator, she picked up her rose basket and departed towards the back of the room.

Monica was still laughing.

"Whatta hell was that?" Pierre reached for his napkin, wiping *piña colada* from his chin.

"Thanks for the rose," she responded, smiling and still trying to contain laughter.

"That was most interesting," he stated. He didn't quite know what to say. He was thrilled and immensely relieved Monica was not offended or insulted by the gypsy woman. The fact that she was amused by it was great. He'd been completely blindsided. No way in a thousand years he could've imagined what was gonna come out of that gypsy's mouth.

"Sorry about that," was all he could say.

"Nothing to be sorry about." Monica had the rose held up to her nose, still enjoying it.

"She was a gypsy," Pierre explained.

"Really? How'd you know?"

"I've seen them in Italy."

"I got my palm read by a gypsy?"

"I think so."

"Awesome!"

"Did you like your fish?" Time to switch topic. He still didn't know what to think. Should he call the manager and complain about what took place? Nah, that was a dumb idea. No need to get the poor woman in trouble. And besides, her words had aroused him on the spot. He wondered what the effect had been on Monica.

"She embarrassed you?" Monica asked.

What? He stared at her dark blue eyes. "No. I was wondering if she embarrassed *you.*"

"No. She surprised me, that's all."

"Well, was she right?" Might as well dive into the pool head first.

Monica laughed again. "Ha! That's none of your business." She sipped her banana daiquiri. "And yes, the fish was delicious!"

Pierre was thrilled. The gypsy woman had injected the element of sexuality into their evening. God bless her. Giving her the cash had been spontaneous, without any ulterior motive, and it had paid back tenfold. He upgraded the odds of ending up spending the night with Monica to maybe thirty percent. Was that overoptimistic? He was a

e

daydreamer, no question about it. Nothing wrong with being optimistic.

"Tell me," Monica placed the red rose on the table. "Have you dated a lot of flight attendants?"

"Inquisition time?" Pierre joked.

"No, just curious. Spill the tea. Do you date flight attendants—other than me, that is?"

"I have on occasion. Yes. I've also dated non-flight attendants."

"Non-flight attendants? That's cute."

"Would you like some desert?" Pierre was at a loss with this puzzling girl. He was dying to lick every inch of her body, pleasure her all night, yet he was uncertain what he was dealing with. At first he'd thought he'd met a very innocent young woman, naïve even, one who would provide him with only limited challenges, mentally and physically. A pleasant dinner companion, if nothing more.

Now, however, he was realizing Monica was way more worldly than he'd expected. And more exciting. The vibes he was receiving from her were intense and very sexual.

"No, thanks. No desert. I'd love some coffee, though. I'd love an espresso."

"If that is what your heart desires." Pierre lucked out, catching the waiter's eye.

"Could you please make that a double espresso?" Monica added, her incredibly sexy eyes blinking at him.

Whoa! A double? She was gonna be bouncing off the walls tonight. He thought about that for a second. Maybe that wasn't such a bad idea. Would coffee enhance her sex drive? He'd absolutely no idea. If nothing else, she'd be wide awake.

Pierre realized his erection had been at attention all through dinner. Good God, if he continued like this, he was going to be the proud owner of the worst case of blue balls in the northern hemisphere. He smiled. Most of the muscles in his body were toned and hard. He fanatically worked out every chance he got, sit-ups, pushups, jogging, weights. He took great pride in his body, and he believed he should stay in top shape if he expected beautiful women to shower him with their gifts.

It was only fair, otherwise, what right did he have to expect gorgeous women in his life, if he wasn't willing to reciprocate with a body they would enjoy. That, and his career depended on his health, he had to pass a physical exam for a medical certificate with an aviation medical examiner every six months; but in all honesty, his primary motivation for keeping in shape was not that certificate. His primary motivation were the girls. His most important muscle had been hard as a rock through dinner. Nothing short of amazing.

He asked the waiter for two double espressos, and two shots of Sambuca.

"What is that?"

"What, the Sambuca?"

"Yes."

"It's an Italian anise-flavored liqueur. It's colorless and you pour it into your espresso. It adds a bit of zing to the coffee. It's actually quite delicious. I'll let you sip mine first, if you don't like it, you don't have to try it."

She seemed pensive for a moment. "No, that's okay, I'll try it. Sounds kinky."

Kinky? That was an interesting choice of words. To him 'kinky' was spanking her or licking Nutella off her nipples, or using butter for lubrication.

"Do you like licorice?"

"I love it."

"Good! Sambuca tastes just like that."

"You're gonna be up all night with a double espresso," Monica opinioned, stating the obvious.

"So are you for that matter, *mademoiselle*."

"So now you speak French?"

"No, just that one word."

"Three words, actually. You said *'bon appetit'* earlier. So, what're we gonna do when we're up all night with our caffeine highs? Wanna go for a walk on the beach?"

What were they gonna do? Pierre visualized the many wonders he could experience with Monica in her bed, all of them incredibly erotic and none of them having a thing to do with a walk on the beach.

"Definitely a bad idea."

"Oh?"

"This is Panama, Monica. You and I go for a romantic walk on the beach at this time of night, we run the risk of not being alive in the morning. Plus, the tide is very dramatic here, I think the ocean goes out half a mile during low tide, which is about this time of night. And when that happens it stinks like a fish market. All sorts of fish and marine life end up trapped among the rocks when the tide recedes. All those organisms die and rot and stink up the beach."

"Eww, sounds awful."

"Not a very romantic place to visit at night."

"Why would we be dead in the morning?" She was perspiring slightly. He was beginning to notice the temperature in the restaurant was a tad too hot and humid to be entirely comfortable.

"Panama can be a dangerous place. You can find yourself with a knife in your back at the bat of an eye. Some folks here would stab you just to steal your watch. We just need to be real careful where we go."

"A lot of criminals?"

"It's a poor country, Monica. A Third World country. And you look American, which makes you a target. A lot of these folks are piss-poor. Remember, you can't make an empty sack stand straight."

"That doesn't sound too good. Let's just go back to the hotel then, and sit by the pool. I saw it when I came down the elevator. It looks like real cool."

"I'll go with that."

"Yas!" she gleed.

The waiter returned with two white demitasse cups on a silver tray. The espressos had arrived. The man carefully gave them each a cup of the delicious-aroma coffee, followed by brandy snifters containing clear liquor.

"I take it this is the Sambuca?" She asked, wide-eyed.

"Yep."

"And are those coffee beans I see at the bottom of the glass?"

Pierre nodded assent. "We're supposed to chew on those after drinking the liqueur to neutralize the flavor of the anise." He poured his Sambuca into the steaming hot coffee. "Here, try this one first. If you don't like it, you don't have to drink it."

"That's okay, I'll just try mine," she poured he liqueur in her coffee, stirring it with a mini-spoon.

Pierre watched her carefully taking a sip of the brew.

"Hmm!"

"Like it?"

Monica smiled. "It's delicious!"

Pierre wondered how the night was going to work out. He didn't have to fly the next day. The company was going to deadhead them—fly them—back to the States on one of Worldwide's flights, which meant they were just going to sit in First Class and sleep and eat and watch movies all the way back to California. Which in turn meant he and Monica could stay up all night without a worry in the world. That's provided she wanted to stay up all night.

How lucky could a man be? He didn't consider himself more worthy than the next guy, yet the stars had aligned for him and he found himself in Panama, finishing dinner with a deity, contemplating the possibility of making love to her all-night long. Or just fucking her silly, depending on what she wanted. That's *if*, things worked out that way. He had a habit of getting too far ahead of the game and then having it fizzle in his face.

A double espresso? He'd never had one of these before. It was going to be an interesting night.

Monica stared at him with steady eye contact over her cup, not saying anything as she sipped the steaming hot coffee.

Pierre decided to hold her gaze. If she was going to eat him up with her eyes, he could play the same game. They boldly stared at each other for over a minute. A bond was established.

She sighed loudly. "That, was so good, it makes me sick."

He wasn't sure he caught her drift. Was she saying she liked it? She didn't add any clarification, and he didn't ask. Pierre finished his brew and signaled for the check. Some of her expressions were flat out new to him. Was he that much older he didn't know what girls were saying any more?

He paid with his American Express card, giving the waiter a generous tip.

"Thank you. That was really good," Monica said.

"You're most welcome. Thank you for the terrific company. Sorry you didn't have a lobster."

She smiled. "Numbnuts!"

The young pilot pulled out her chair, standing behind her. Monica very naturally reached back for his hand, holding on to it.

Pierre inhaled deeply, feeling the old familiar tingling in his crotch. He hadn't expected that. Yes! To say he was delighted would be the understatement of the evening. Holding hands with a girl like her was by far one of his most favorite things in life. It also meant she was interested in him! Didn't it?

He led the way, finding a taxi parked out in front of the restaurant. The air was still hot and muggy.

Pierre had heard pilots talking about how the humidity in Panama was so bad, one had to take three showers a day. Damned weather was so humid, you took a shower, walked one block and bam! You needed another shower.

Inside the taxi Monica sat very close to him again. Pierre decided it was time to lay the cards on the table, his pulse quickened. He had his arm resting on the back of the seat behind her head. He lowered his arm embracing Monica, moving closer to her, searching for her lips.

She accepted his kiss, seemingly shy at first, but a few seconds into it she entered his mouth with her tongue, reaching for his chest with her hand. She worked the top button of his shirt feverishly, desperately trying to get inside. She finally succeeded, inserting her hand inside his shirt, feeling his powerful pecs. She caressed him at first, then squeezed and groped. Her touch sent incredible electro-chemical pleasure signals to his groin. He felt gooseflesh in his arms.

He also tasted butter and garlic on her lips.

Monica shifted, sending one of her legs over his, her other hand reaching behind his head, running her fingers through his hair.

Her hot tongue dueled with his furiously, passionately. Pierre reached for her waist, enjoying the sexual feel of her strong body through her clothes. She was in remarkably good shape. His arousal was pegging. She smelled of clean and hot.

Monica ran her hand down to his crotch, squeezing, trying to get a hold of his solid hard-on from outside his pants.

Pierre's heart missed a couple of beats. *Yao!* He hadn't been expecting that. Having this incredible woman feeling his most private part was an overwhelming erotic experience. Just too hard to believe it was really happening.

He sneaked a peek at the driver, reassuring himself that the Panamanian could not observe them making out from his seat up front.

His hand found Monica's breast, filling the palm of his hand with the sensual feel of it. Her nipple felt hard and rebellious under her halter top. She was just as aroused as he was.

Pierre was incredibly turned on by the action with her tongue. Monica appeared obsessed with exploring every inch of the inside of his mouth with it, and her warm breath hitting his face was electrifying.

"We're here, *señor*," the driver announced, apologetically.

Pierre sat up, looking outside, gasping for air. Monica's head rested on his arm, her ash blond hair ruffled, looking at him with fire in her eyes. She slowly released the hold on his crotch.

They were parked in the driveway in front of the main lobby of their hotel. Pierre was stunned at how fast they'd gotten there.

"*Gracias!*" Pierre voiced to the driver, adjusting his shirt and helping Monica sit up.

Pierre went out the door, helping Monica climb out behind him. He paid the driver, holding her hand and walking towards the entrance.

"What 'ya say we skip the pool?" The outcome of the night would depend entirely on her next answer.

"You got my vote."

Halleluiah! And the earth trembled and the angels sang!

He decided not to ask her whose room they should use. At this point, with the level of arousal they both had, much better not to talk. Don't say anything. He issued a silent prayer to Aphrodite, goddess of beauty, love, desire and pleasure, thanking her and begging her not to let them run into any of their crew while crossing the lobby. He wanted nothing to spoil the mood. He led Monica by the hand to the glass elevator. The car silently arrived within seconds of him pressing the 'up' button.

They were alone in there, no witnesses, so Pierre considered kissing her. No, the glass walls prevented intimacy. They were visible and exposed to everyone in the lobby. And he was so goddamned hot and bothered, he wouldn't be able to stop at just kissing her. He'd rip off her clothes right then and there. Instead, he released her hand, rubbing her back with his palm. Her body was strong, and she was willing and ready, which only made the erotic anticipation even more painful.

She was standing with her back against Pierre, merely inches in front of him, looking down at the lobby's tropical forest as the elevator climbed. Monica reached back with her hand, discretely sliding it between his thighs, gently making contact with his erection. She applied pressure to his bulge, cruelly stimulating him with unbearably delicious sexual pain while the elevator silently took them up to the 19th floor.

Pierre remained in place, easy prey to her charms. The powerful Bengal tiger, immobilized, bitten firmly in the neck by the gazelle.

The elevator stopped seconds later, its doors silently sliding open.

Pierre left the elevator at a fast pace, dragging her behind him by the hand. What the devil was his room number? He fumbled in his shirt pocket for the door card.

Entering his room, he managed to catch a wall switch and a night table lamp, turning those off on their way to his bed. That left one solitary light bulb alight in the room, casting enough soft illumination to provide an atmosphere of romance. He embraced Monica, lifting her off the carpet, rolling around and throwing himself backwards on the bed, landing them both on the mauve 400-thread cotton duvet. She was on top of him.

Monica placed her hands on the sides of his face, kissing him firmly, sinking her teeth into his lower lip—hard.

Whoa! What was it with girls and lip-biting?

She ripped open his shirt with unsuspected strength, sending all his buttons flying in different directions.

Good-bye shirt.

Pierre was so turned on he was breathing like an Olympic athlete in the middle of a competition. He had to slow down or he was going to hyperventilate—or just plain cum in his pants. Monica fumbled with his belt, finally releasing it.

She yanked down his pants and shorts as one, lowering them to his knees, not bothering to unbutton them. Pierre saw her grab his shaft, directing it to her mouth.

Bythegodsofolympus!

How had Monica transformed herself into such a hot insanely passionate lover? Was it the Sambuca? Or the double espresso? She was exceeding his expectations by a magnitude of ten. This incredibly hot, sexually charged woman was definitely not the shy little flight attendant he'd eyeballed entering his airplane earlier that morning.

Pierre watched her bury his entire cock in her mouth. The sensation was superb, out of this world, magical and erotic, not only physically, but visually as well. Although he was staring at this gorgeous woman sucking on his cock, his brain was having difficulty accepting it. Erotic beyond erotic. Monica locked eyes with him as she slowly moved her head up and down, stimulating his shaft. He was amazed how she could suck it all in without gagging. How was she breathing?

The goddess sat up, removing his erection from her mouth, strings of saliva connecting her lips with his cock. She removed her shirt and halter and bra, aggressively pitching them behind her back. Then she stood, rapidly lowering her white pants. She was out of them in an instant. Her panties, if she'd had any, must've gone with her pants, Pierre concluded, for he didn't get a chance to catch even a glimpse of them.

"C'mere!" She ordered, climbing on the bed on all fours, alongside Pierre. She plopped down on her stomach, her arms straight out reaching for a pillow. "Get up here! I want you to fuck me."

Pierre's mind was deliriously aroused from sensory overload. Monica's lean, feminine sexy body had him speechless. Her magnificent breasts put Venus de Milo to shame, they were literally mouth-watering. He was dying to suck on those nipples. Her narrow waist and the bare skin of her pubis had him in awe.

Being strong and athletic, his muscular legs got him up on his knees in an instant with minimum effort. Whatever Monica had in mind, he was going to provide, with *gusto*.

His cock jutting out proudly, he advanced towards her on his knees, shaking the bed. Monica laying on her belly had separated her legs just enough so he could see her lips staring at him from between her buttocks. Her submissive position waiting there for him turned him into an animal.

Pierre straddled Monica, one leg on each side of her provocative hips. The inside of his powerful thighs made contact with the warm flesh of her butt cheeks. He momentarily considered going down on her to get her wet, but the sight of his shinning cock, still soaked and dripping with her saliva cancelled that thought. He'd have no problem going inside her without causing her discomfort.

Placing his hands on the upper part of her buns he used his strong abdominal muscles to direct his hard cock to her opening. Looking down he confirmed he was there, at the entrance to paradise. His strong slim hips thrust forward inexorably with unstoppable force, driving his dick deep inside Monica to the hilt.

Whatever sound of pleasure she gave out when she felt the entrance of his shaft encouraged him to just fuck her blind. He noticed in the dim light Monica held on to the cotton comforter with her fists, clutching it with a fury.

Pierre pumped in and out of her at a medium pace, gradually accelerating the rhythm. The slapping sound of his abdomen hitting her buttocks with each thrust was unimaginably erogenous. He hoped his balls were hitting her clit. Monica moved her hips slowly from side to side, as if attempting to avoid his advances, limited by the iron grip Pierre's legs had on her. Realizing she wasn't going to have much room to wiggle, she switched to a back and forth motion, meeting his thrusting cock in a perfectly harmonized dance.

Pierre looked down, taking in the sensual sight of his significant manhood going in and out of Monica. His shaft was long and thick, gleaming from her juices, and the visual was almost hallucinogenic. He might as well be doing meth, he speculated. It just didn't seem real. The image he was enjoying of Monica's adorable little ass pumping against him was phenomenal. In his most erotic dreams, he could not even begin to imagine such a perfect body, such an enchanting woman pleasing him like this.

The young aviator's powerful arms transmitted the considerable strength of his biceps and triceps to his hands, which held Monica's adorable round buttocks in a powerful, inescapable grip.

He realized he was about to go out of control.

Argh! He couldn't do that to her! His own personal ironclad rule was to always pleasure his partner first.

Always!

He slowed down his frenzied thrusting almost to a halt, trying to decide what to do. Monica had asked him to fuck her like this, in what he thought was called the 'lazy doggy' position; would she be pissed if he rolled her over and drove her nuts with his tongue instead?

"What are you doing? Don't stop!"

Pierre laughed quietly. The tone of her voice dissolved any doubt he may have had about continuing to make love to her like this. Well, that solved it.

He increased the rhythm again, feeling the muscles on his legs tightening from the effort. His six-pack abdomen was hard as a washboard. No question his body was not going to keep up this pace without exploding—soon.

The insane pleasure in his groin was matched by the sight of Monica trapped underneath him, her legs held tightly together flat on the bed, yet his rock-hard erection had found a way to go inside her without any resistance. Even with her legs closed together, Pierre could penetrate her at his whim at the apex of her long legs.

His powerful abdominal muscles maintained a consistent pace sliding in and out of her very tight vagina, slamming into her with unsatisfied lust. And he could feel how hot she was, as hot as the gypsy had promised earlier that evening. And Monica was responding to his continuous sexual stimulation by pumping her booty back and forth with considerable strength. Her frenzied movements made Pierre wonder if she was going to orgasm like this.

The heavenly explosion began in his balls, intense waves of pleasure radiating to his cock, increasing in intensity going from pleasurable to painful, then radiating to his lower abdomen and up to his chest. His respiration slowed dramatically, his hips increased the velocity and the ferocity of his thrusts, trying to go even deeper inside Monica. Then he felt it, his hot sperm shooting out deep inside this marvelous, ardent woman. He wasn't able to think rationally; his autonomous reflexes had taken over his body and mind. He was feeling like he did at the onset of sneezing. Totally out of control.

Monica didn't do anything dramatic, she merely attempted to pump her ass against him while he went into orbit. His weight prevented her from doing too much, trapped as she was under Pierre.

It didn't last very long, never as long as a woman's orgasm, but regardless, Pierre was grateful. Grateful to have been given this opportunity. He released Monica's buttocks, noticing the crimson marks his powerful hands had left on her butt. Once again, he marveled why women never seemed to complain when their buttocks were grabbed with such strength during sex.

He had not stopped sliding his cock inside Monica, only now he was pumping at a very slow pace. He noticed his shaft was glistening and fluids were slowly leaking out from inside her onto the bed.

Monica was still on her stomach, her face buried in a pillow, her arms tightly hugging the feather cushion.

Pierre attempted to control his respiration, taking in the sweet erotic image of Monica's nudity, still locked in place under him. He breathed deeply, mentally checking his legs, making sure he hadn't suffered from a cramp. Then he slowly removed himself from her upper thighs.

Monica turned, reaching for his hand. "Where'd ya think you're going?" She sat up Indian-style, reaching around his neck with both arms. Her lips were hot and moist when she hungrily went for his mouth.

Pierre was ready and more than willing to please her, but he was momentarily at a loss. His usual technique didn't seem to be working here. He decided to give it another try.

"Lay back," he commanded, pushing Monica away. Her big eyes smiled at him. She knew what he wanted.

Monica reclined herself on the bed, unfolding her legs.

Pierre had a splendid view of her hot, tight, pussy, as the gypsy put it. God bless that woman.

He was going to take his time with Monica. No hurrying. He intended to go down on her for an hour, if she could stand it. Pierre was aware from cockpit conversations most of his buddies considered oral sex with a woman a waste of time, an imposition.

What a bunch of idiots, he thought, smiling. Nothing more satisfying than being able to stimulate a woman to the point of insanity with one's tongue. And then again. And again—all night long.

Pierre admired her cleanly shaved pubis, no hair visible anywhere. But the cleft between her vaginal lips was clearly visible, pouting at him. Placing his hands on her sensuous hips he lowered his face between her legs. They had all night, and he intended to drive her looney with pleasure every minute of it.

His hot tongue brushed her inner thighs, making sure he didn't touch her clit or her lips. He wanted to work up to those. Monica didn't reach for his hair, strangely so, instead, he saw her fists clenching the bedcover again. He wasn't terribly displeased with that. Much more enjoyable making love without having to suffer from being scalped.

Monica's breathing accelerated. She shifted her hips with small movements, left and right, forcing Pierre to follow her. He tightened his hold on her hips.

She smelled of soap and the aroma of fresh tangerines. He was intoxicated by her scent. Pierre ran his tongue parallel to her four lips, slowly applying enough pressure so she would feel his tongue. He could feel the muscles of her inner thighs tightening up with each lick from his hot tongue.

Some music or candles would've been a sweet addition to their lovemaking, but he hadn't had a chance to prepare any of that in their frantic frenzy to go after each other. He peeked at her, delighted to see her eyes closed, very much giving him the 'go ahead' to trigger her orgasms any way he saw fit.

Pierre ran his hands along her inner thighs, slowly, caressing her gently while his tongue found her hot lips. He used his tongue, separating those elegant rose petals with a deliberate brush stroke. He pushed his tongue inside her as deep as he could for an instant, then he licked up, finding her super-sensitive clit.

Her loud moan and a shifting of her hips confirmed he was on the right path.

Magnifique!

He was back in control doing what he knew he was good at. She deserved to have her world rocked, and he was gonna be the one to do it. He doubted in her young life she'd ever experienced a more dedicated and considerate lover, so she was in for a treat. Very conceited on his part, some would say, but he believed in giving to Caesar that which belonged to Caesar; he was good at this, why not admit it? He had dedicated himself to learning how to please a woman, and his efforts had to show some fruit. He adored women, if the good Lord ever made anything better than a pretty girl, he kept it for himself.

Pausing momentarily, he enjoyed the close-up of her most delicate parts. Monica was indeed built like a flower, eye-pleasing curves and a magic scent. Pierre decided to get her heart going, slipping his hands under her buttocks, he engaged her clit with his tongue, licking her at a rapid pace, his powerful shoulders keeping Monica's legs apart. Instantly, she was alight with desire, her breath coming in gasps as she clutched him.

Their bodies were hot and slick with perspiration.

She reacted by lifting her hips off the bed, relentlessly driving her sensitive lips against his face. He looked up, enjoying the sight of her very erect nipples, her eyes at half-mast as if in trance, her mouth gasping for air. Good, she was enjoying his attention. Her legs began to apply pressure to his shoulders, her hips now a foot above the bed. Monica was balanced on her toes and shoulders, the rest of her body was now arched off the bed.

"Stop!" She screamed, attempting to push away his shoulders with her very strong hands.

He ignored her, increasing the tempo. Her clit was fully erect and vulnerable to his enthusiastic tongue.

Her butt cheeks cupped in his hands were taunt and solid.

"Oh, God. Stop!" she cried again, less energetically.

Pierre felt the strain on his tongue, he was breathing fast. He concentrated on trying to control his breathing, determined to continue his delicious torture until she lost control. He was amazed at her stamina. Keeping her body arched like that required a lot of strength even with him holding up a lot of her weight cupping her butt cheeks with his hands. He himself was inconceivably aroused again.

"*Aargh, Pierre!*" she deliciously complained, trying to get a good hold on his shoulders, shaking uncontrollably. Pierre increased the brush strokes with his tongue, realizing he'd finally managed to send Monica into a tail spin. He could feel his erection was also back in action. But this was not the moment to bring it into play.

"*Oh, God, Pierre!!*" She shoved her crotch against his face, trembling and shaking. Her young body was in the grip of a most violent, delicious orgasm. The scent of tangerine permeated his nose. Was that wonderful fragrance coming from Monica, or was his brain—once again—associating one of his most favorite smells with this woman he liked so much?

Her butt cheeks were as solid as his biceps. At that moment, Monica didn't need any help from him supporting her hips. He loved hearing her repeatedly calling out his name. What an incredible turn-on. He continued stimulating her until she finally had enough and allowed herself to plop back on the bed, exhausted, breathing like the gazelle after a vigorous run escaping from a lion.

PIERRE WOKE IN A panic. Oh, shit, where was he? Had he missed his report time? He rolled over, searching for a clock on the night table. Monica was there, sleeping face down next to him, hugging a pillow. Her beautiful sensual body uncovered and provocative.

It all came back. They didn't have a trip to fly and he had not missed report time. Plans for the day were focused on a pleasant deadhead back to Los Angeles while enjoying First Class service on one of their flights.

He was enormously relieved.

And there was absolutely nothing as wonderful or pleasant as waking up with a gorgeous creature asleep next to him. He was lucky. No, better than lucky, he was being given a gift by the gods.

He allowed himself to enjoy the visual banquet Monica provided, admiring her body. Her skin was lightly tanned, her blond hair spread across her pillow. He moved closer, planting a very soft kiss in the nape of her neck, as gentle as the touch from the wings of a butterfly.

The smell of tangerines invaded his nose and lungs. That aromatic gift, he reflected, must be a sign destiny had intended for them to end up together on this magic night. He so loved that scent. But was it the perfume she was wearing or was it Monica's natural scent?

She was sharp and funny, and he'd really enjoyed their time together at dinner. He wanted more of her. And he was amazed at her ability to express herself with total blunt honesty.

"What time is it?" She stirred.

"Good morning beautiful. I have no idea."

Monica rolled back, facing Pierre. "Good morning," she planted a soft kiss on his lips.

Pierre really liked that. He was already hard, so maybe they should enjoy each other before breakfast.

"The gypsy was right," he reminded her.

"Oh? How so?"

"She said you were hot and tight."

"*Hush!*" Monica touched her index finger to his lips.

He placed his hand on her hip, pulling her close.

Monica's hand, on her way to his hip brushed past his solid shaft. "*Merci!* You are ready for lovin again?"

Pierre just stared at her, saying nothing.

"What time do we have to meet downstairs?" She asked.

Pierre realized he didn't have a clue. Since they hadn't joined the crew for dinner, whatever instructions crew scheduling had issued, they never got them.

Much as he was dying to enjoy Monica again, he forced himself to sit up and reach for his cell phone. He had to call the skipper and inquire about the plans for the day. Pierre wondered if their cell phones would work in Panama.

"Steve? Pierre. Good morning."

"Hello Pierre! You live!"

"Yea, I realized I didn't connect with you again last night. What's on the agenda?"

"I guess crew scheduling didn't call you?"

"No."

"No sweat. They called everyone else last night, informing us that we had to meet down here in the lobby at eight this morning to head for the airport."

Oh, shit. Pierre glanced at his cell phone. It was 10:05.

"But then when we were all down here at eight they called me again changing the report time to twelve noon. We all took a vote and decided to let you guys sleep in. I assume Monica's with you?"

Pierre laughed.

Caught.

"Yeah, she's with me. So you guys decided to let us sleep in? Very considerate—thank you. I owe you. So now the report time is noon?"

"Yeah, that it is, and I managed to finagle breakfast for the whole crew. The company's paying for it to make up for the early wakeup. We're all down here in the lobby waiting for the brunch buffet to start in a couple of minutes, if you two wanna join us."

"Thanks Steve, ya, we'll be down shortly."

He ended the call, informing Monica of the events.

She didn't bat an eye about being caught. "Yum! Brunch! I'm starved! Let's shower and go down to eat!"

Pierre smiled at her refreshing enthusiasm. She was an extraordinary woman, and he was the luckiest man in the history of the world. However, he would've much rather eat her than some bacon or eggs Benedict, but that was no longer a choice this morning.

Pierre

Pierre rode the elevator down to the Operations office. He was so relieved, being out of the noisy terminal. LAX was pandemonium, just too many people there for his taste.

He was scheduled for a Rio de Janeiro flight, and was excited about the trip. Brazil was one of his favorite destinations. The food there was out of this world delicious, the beaches full of interesting people and the music absolutely enchanting, aah, the *Bosanova!* And with twenty-five hours there, he would be partaking in all of those good things soon enough.

He was also cherishing the possibility of connecting with some hot girl. Rio was not the safest city in the world, but he knew a couple of restaurant bars frequented by international airline crews where he may be able to find an interesting girl. Some of the

European airlines flying to Rio employed stunningly beautiful flight attendants.

He'd been frustrated for weeks, mostly because he hadn't enjoyed the company of a pleasant female for quite some time. He frowned, trying to recall the last time he'd had sex. Heck, that wasn't even part of the equation. He had to do something to break this dry spell away from women, it was killing him.

Maybe he was asking for too much. He wanted a beautiful woman to love. One he could talk to, preferably educated and well-traveled. One who liked him for what he was, and didn't try to change him. The ideal woman had to enjoy sex as much as he did—that was vitally important. She also had to be independent so his career would not be a burden to her. Someone intelligent, capable of entertaining herself those days when he was away from her. And what could he provide such a woman?

He could offer honesty, loyalty, undying love and a dedicated sex partner. He wasn't Casanova, but he felt he could provide some very hot sex.

He thought of himself as a caring man; he made enough money he could treat her like a queen. Pierre was not tight with money—he actually detested stingy people. When he found the woman of his dreams he would spoil her and care for her and entertain her.

THE AIRLINE'S OPERATIONS OFFICE in the lower level of the Los Angeles International airport terminal was crowded. Two thousand Worldwide Airlines pilots were based there, some flying to South America like Pierre, some to Europe and many others to Asia and

Australia. A few hundred of these illustrious aviators were there today preparing their flights to destinations all over the globe.

Pierre had no real desire to fly to Asia, the flights were too damned long over water with nothing to see and he wasn't particularly interested in the big cities on the other side of the Pacific Ocean. He considered most of Worldwide's destinations along the Pacific Rim too dangerous to explore on his own. When he was on a layover or on vacation, the last thing he wanted was to worry about his safety.

Why ask for trouble, when Australia and New Zealand, on the other hand, he considered quite civilized and enchanting. He definitely wanted to fly down there and take a look at those fantastic countries. He liked the people from 'Down Under' a lot, and although he hadn't been there yet, he had plans to eventually bid those routes. Many of his colleagues though he was nuts, but he really wanted to travel there to see the salt water crocs, the Kangaroos and the barrier reef.

He walked to his mailbox, consisting of a hanging folder alphabetically arranged alongside two thousand others.

Pierre retrieved a one-inch-thick pile of papers and envelopes from the folder, wondering how many of them demanded his immediate attention. A quick glance through the stack put his mind at ease. Nothing extremely urgent. He could sort through all these docs in the airplane on his way to Brazil.

The huge room designated as Operations was crowded, dozens of pilots standing around, energetically talking to each other and to a few flight attendants. The international flight attendants had their own Ops center somewhere else nearby under another gate, but some of the cabin crews invariably drifted over to mingle with the aviators.

"Hello Pierre."

He turned to look in the direction of the voice.

He'd recognize that voice anywhere.

No way!

Standing there not three feet from him was Kirsten, in all her glory.

His Kirsten.

And she looked stunning, absolutely incredible, desirable, her bedroom eyes smiling at him in that seductive way of hers, her sexy figure with all her tempting curves discernible under the uniform. If anything, she was even more attractive than the last time he saw her. More than shockingly beautiful, she was a creature between fantasy and magic! An irresistible mythological fairy princess. The stuff his dreams were made of. She also appeared more mature, which added to the attraction.

Sensory recognition sent his body into instant arousal. A delicious feeling in his groin sent waves of pleasure to his brain.

The Kirsten Effect.

He was speechless. He still thought of her often, but their paths hadn't crossed again.

"Hi, Kirsten," he finally responded. Real original, he thought. After all this time and that's the best he could come up with? But what else could he say? He hadn't seen her in over two years.

There was a skinny and not very attractive captain standing next to her, ignoring Pierre, looking at something on the other side of the room. Pierre recognized the guy, the crews had nicknamed this captain 'The Vulture,' for whatever reason. Pierre had never flown with the guy, but he'd heard he was a real nice man and they'd been introduced once before, if his memory didn't fail him.

Pierre had no idea what the captain's name was or what the dude was doing with Kirsten. The captain didn't say anything, he just looked past Pierre, suddenly walking away from both of them. Apparently, he had somewhere else to go.

Thank God for that.

The pair stood there momentarily staring at each other awkwardly, their eyes communicating intimate unspoken words. The powerful attraction he'd felt for her when he first met her long ago at *Viera's* in St. Louis rekindled on the spot. Rekindled? No, it exploded like the goddamn Fourth of July fireworks. He had to take a deep breath. And another.

"How've you been?" She asked, her batting eyelashes highlighting her incredible eyes.

"Not too bad, I guess. You?"

She gifted him with her most captivating smile. "You're the best-kept secret I ever had," Kirsten confessed.

Secret? He wondered. Why would she keep him a secret? "What do you mean?"

Kirsten paused, as if deciding how much to share with him. "I never told anyone about you or how much you meant to me."

He wanted to tell her how much she'd meant to him as well, but that would sound lame. If he cared so much for her, why had he eliminated her from his life? Pierre didn't know what to say. Undoubtedly, he was still terribly attracted to her, the infatuation was still there. How could it not be? And from the vibrations he was sensing emanating from her, the mutual magnetism was still very active between them.

"I've looked up your schedule many times," Kirsten confessed. "Often I thought of just flying out wherever you were on a layover and meeting you."

Pierre was surprised. He'd no idea. He rapidly revisited the events that damaged their relationship. Somehow, those events no longer seemed all that dramatic or consequential. So, she'd slept with another guy who she'd been dating all along anyway. Back then she just didn't know how to get out of it. But she had eventually given the dude his walking papers after all. Her timing had been deplorable, and the situation uncomfortable, but Pierre felt more mature and for some strange reason, those events didn't bother him hardly at all anymore.

"You flying with the Vulture?"

She laughed. "Yep. Going to Paris."

"You look stunning," he told her.

"Thanks."

"You married yet?"

Kirsten gave him the intimate, sensual look he remembered so well, "do I look married to you?"

Pierre took a very deep breath; he was feeling intoxicated with excitement. He'd heard those same words before, a long time ago.

"No," he said, shaking his head, "you're right, you don't look married. You don't have the look of a satisfied woman about you yet."

"Ha!" She continued staring in his eyes. "I don't think I'll ever have that look again."

"You were married already?"

"No, who said anything about being married? I was talking about being satisfied."

"Oh?" He feigned ignorance.

"Don't play innocent. I'm sure you remember."

Pierre laughed. "How could I not remember?"

An Encyclopedia Britannica of unspoken words flowed between them.

He was in awe of her. "So why didn't you fly out to meet me at one of my layovers?"

"Wasn't sure how you'd react. So, I never did it. I left you a few cards in your mailbox though."

Pierre felt guilty. He remembered the cards years before. He'd liked her cards very much, but he'd never responded. What an idiot he was. He should've replied. "I know, I saw them." That did seem like such a long time ago.

"You still angry with me?"

"No, of course not." Angry? What sort of an idiot was he? Being angry at this delicate, thoughtful creature? Looking back, perhaps he'd overreacted to the situation. Yeah, she had lied to him, but should he have judged her so hard? Everyone lied, he just hadn't learned that reality of life back then.

"I was immature," he admitted.

"So was I."

Pierre felt the adrenaline surging. Wow, just talking to Kirsten had him hot and bothered. Absolutely incredible. There was some very potent chemistry there. Unfinished business?

Powerful stuff. Even without any physical contact whatsoever, he was already sporting the mother of all hard-ons.

"What gate are you going out of?" He looked at his watch. He'd better be heading towards his airplane. For the love of Zeus! He didn't want to cut short his time with her, but he absolutely had to get going.

She told him. Her gate for the Paris flight was very close to his Brazilian flight.

"Want to walk with me to my gate, or do you have to wait for the Vulture?"

"No, I'll walk with you.

Yes!"

Pierre felt a surge of excitement. Kirsten, *his* Kirsten was suddenly back in his life again.

They rode the elevator in silence. The terminal was busy, crowded with travelers frantically searching for their gates, others trying to find AC outlets to plug their screens, a dynamic and constantly moving mass of humanity. Pierre looked at it as the super-Greyhound Bus Station of the future.

Only, the future was *now*.

He rapidly oriented himself, heading for his gate, with Kirsten at his side.

They walked past a random beige door with a combination keypad on it. It was marked:

'Restricted Entry
Authorized Personnel Only.'

"Hang on just a sec," he said to her, approaching the keypad. He entered a combination he'd learned from one of the gate agents. Much to his delight, the door clicked open.

"Come with me," he held the door open for her. It let them into a stairwell going downstairs. Pierre had no idea where it led, but he didn't care.

Kirsten hesitated for an instant, then followed him in.

The moment the door closed behind them, they were alone, and the annoying deafening noisy terminal was no more. Pierre turned around, embracing Kirsten without warning, pulling her towards him. His strong arms holding her tight, letting her know that he was strong, and that he still wanted her.

Her delicious body felt wonderful against him—memories of another time—and he knew she was feeling his erection through their clothes.

Kirsten's lips parted, her blue eyes bright and glossy, a look of surprise in them rapidly turning into joy.

He kissed her tenderly, savoring the taste of her delicate lips, taking in her fragrance, recognizing it.

Cotton candy.

Kirsten raised her arms, hugging him, kissing him back, softly at first, then hard and passionately.

Romeo and Juliet, Apollonia and Michael Corleone, two lovers reunited.

Pierre couldn't resist her. He ran his hand down the side of her body, absorbing the exquisite shape of her hip with his hand, reaching under her skirt, feeling for her.

He found an obstacle.

Pantyhose?

Since when did Millennials wear pantyhose? Was that a required uniform item? He was somewhat amused by the find. Well, with that barrier between them, he wasn't going to feel Kirsten's skin under her dress anytime soon.

Her breath was warm and smelled of Kirsten. He was euphoric. All the memories of their times together were triggered back when he kissed her.

Dammit to hell, he had to go fly.

"Sweetheart, I'm so very happy to have bumped into you."

"I love you," she whispered, out of the blue, holding him tight.

Pierre was surprised and delighted to hear those words coming out of her mouth. He couldn't believe his ears. He never expected to hear that.

Her words were music to him.

"I've loved you since the day I met you, Kirsten. I just didn't know it. You are the kindest, sweetest, prettiest, most wonderful woman I ever met in my life."

She didn't say anything. Just held on to him.

"From the first instant I laid eyes on you at *Viera's* so long ago, I just wanted to hold you close and be with you forever. I've thought of you and dreamt of you so much these past two years. I was just too stupid to act on it."

She stared at Pierre, her baby blues penetrating his very soul, trying to decipher his intentions.

"When do you come back from Paris, Kirsten?" He loved holding her in his arms.

"Day after tomorrow."

"I'll wait for you here when you come back from Paris to take you back to Phoenix with me. Would you want to do that?"

Kirsten looked up, gasping, surprise in her eyes.

"*Yes!*"

"I'll be at your gate then, waiting for you when you come back."

"You mean that?" She was still staring into his brown eyes.

"From the bottom of my heart."

He kissed her again, feeling his mouth on hers, forcing her lips apart so that he could plunder her mouth. His head was spinning, feeling terribly protective of her, and rather unhappy at the prospect of having to leave her behind. On the other hand, he was jubilant at a generous destiny that had steered her back into his path.

Kirsten, *his* Kirsten was back in his arms. How lucky could he be? Was this real?

He briefly considered calling in sick for his flight and asking Kirsten to do the same. If they did that, they could just go back to Phoenix together right now and pick up where they left off two years ago. The very thought of having her in his California-King bed made his knees weak with anticipation. He was going to send her to The Magic Kingdom of pleasure. He planned on showering her with love and affection and gifts and joy. He intended to defend her and protect her and make her his Guinevere. And he was going to give her the option to quit working, and they would fly to Paris together and have breakfast in some quaint little restaurant.

Pierre was giddy at the prospect of calling in sick.

Then his sanity returned.

It was way too late in the game for Pierre to call in sick without creating a horrible major ripple in the crew-scheduling world. If he called in sick it was already too late to avoid a significant delay to his flight. Crew scheduling would have to find another First Officer and bring him out to replace Pierre. That could take hours. He definitely was not going to do that to his paying customers.

Besides, there was another small issue. If they both called in sick, then they wouldn't be able to avail themselves of their free flight privileges to return to Phoenix. The company—justifiably so—prohibited the use of passes when employees made use of their sick leave.

They could all the same just rent a car and drive the six hours back to Arizona, but that option still implied screwing his passengers, and he was too much of a professional to ignore them. His customers had paid a lot of money to be flown to Brazil on time, and he was going to deliver.

Besides, there was no need to panic. He could sense Kirsten was feeling equally attracted to him, the bond between them felt strong and reassuring, so he felt pretty confident she'd be there in two days' time, joining him. And then they'd have all the time in the world to be together.

So, for now, they'd both have to go on their respective trips and meet again in two days.

He could wait. A couple of days were nothing. Destiny, or Karma, or whatever had orchestrated this situation, he was not going to blow it again. It was just incredible, Kirsten being there with him.

Too good to be true.

"Be forewarned," he told her, "this time, I'm not letting you go."

"Promise?"

THE END

TERMS OF USE

The author gratefully acknowledges the copyrighted or trademarked status and trademark owners of the following, mentioned in this work of fiction:

Absolute Vodka, Academy Awards, Adidas Stan Smith, Airbus, Amazon, American Airlines, Apollonia, Arizona State University, Bam-Bam, Blue Tooth, Boeing, Bostonian Shoes, Brooks Brothers, Brown Eyed Girl by Van Morrison, Bud Light, Budweiser, Chase Bank, Chewbacca, Jar of Hearts by Christina Perri, Coke, Costco, Crest Toothpaste, Delta Airlines, Dolce & Gabbana, Flintstones, Garmin, Gillette, Google, Greyhound Bus Lines, Haagen-Dazs, Hallmark, Harrods's of London, Heineken, Honda Odyssey, Hotel Nikko, HP, Hyatt Regency, iPad, Jell-O, KFC, Krispy Kreme, Lexington Hotel, Lionel Richie Say You Say Me, Luby's Cafeteria, Luke Skywalker, Michael Corleone, Marriott Hotels, Nutella, Obi-Wan Kenobi, Omega Flightmaster, On the Road Again by Willie Nelson, Otis Elevators, Paco Rabanne, Pascal Jolivet, Pepsi, Ramada Inn, Restaurante Tres Mares, Robert Duvall, Say you Say Me by Lionel Richie, Scenic Cruiser, Scotty of the USS Enterprise, Sleeping Beauty, Southwest Airlines, Sports Illustrated, Star Wars, Steven Spielberg, The Encounter Restaurant, Tinker-Bell, Toshiba, Trader Joe's, United Air Lines, Viagra, Victoria's Secret, Visa, Visine, Walmart, Yelp.

Manuscript line edited, copy edited and prepared for publication by Cyber Rose Design, LLC.

Cover design by OriginalSyn.

464DB3A3221D3873763AF4C9CCCC1F19A70B82702F4724EE5
C674EE7A9740573

COTTON CANDY AND TANGERINES   MR Chevalier

ABOUT THE AUTHOR

Aside from his literary dalliances in a multitude of genres including romance erotica, M.R. Chevalier is an entrepreneur, impresario, and adventurer. His first romance novel, "Cotton Candy and Tangerines," was published in November 2016 and another title is forthcoming.   He savors fine wines and craves intelligent conversation, and Italian cuisine.

It is M.R. Chevalier's sincere hope that you find this romantic novel to be provocative and entertaining in equal measure.

You can find MR Chevalier on Facebook.
https://www.facebook.com/CottonCandyandTangerines

You can also visit his website.
http://www.CottonCandyandTangerines.com

Also available as an eBook on Amazon.